Eli Amir was born in Baghdad in 1950. A prize-winning activist, once saying in Cairo, "How can we without us knowing each other?"

CW00919579

THE DOVE FLYER

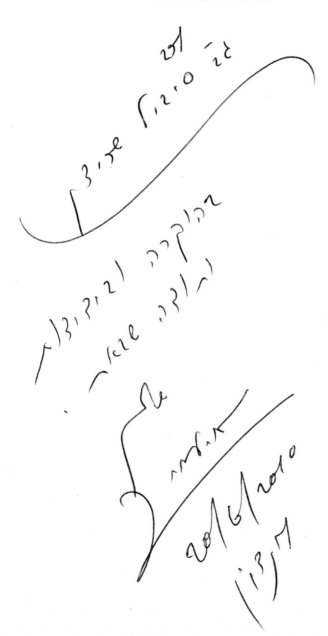

THE DOVE FLYER

ELI AMIR

Translated by
Hillel Halkin

HALBAN
LONDON

First Published in Great Britain by
Halban Publishers Ltd.
22 Golden Square
London W1F 9JW
2010

www.halbanpublishers.com

A CIP catalogue record for this book is available from the
British Library.

ISBN 978 1 905559 18 3
Originally published in Hebrew under the title *Mafriach Hayonim*
by Am Oved Publishers, Tel Aviv, 1992

**This book has been selected to receive financial assistance from
English PEN's Writers in Translation programme supported by
Bloomberg. English PEN exists to promote literature and its
understanding, uphold writers' freedoms around the world,
campaign against the persecution and imprisonment of writers for
stating their views, and promote the friendly
co-operation of writers and free exchange of ideas.**

Typeset by Spectra Titles, Norfolk
Printed in Great Britain by
MPG Books Ltd, Bodmin, Cornwall

To Ophira
and to the memory of
my father, Salim Liahu Khalaschi
and
my mother, Miriam Moshi Moelm

1.

Although we should have been sleeping on the roof as we
always did during the summer in Baghdad, my mother had yet
to bring up the beds, fit them with mosquito netting, and put
the water jug out to cool on the balcony. Perhaps she was loath
to acknowledge the change of the seasons or feared the late
spring sandstorms that turned the city's skies red.

My father saw storm warnings too, which had raged like a
whirling sword since the hanging of the wealthy Jewish
merchant Shafik Addas. Every night the CID, the Iraqi secret
service, visited houses in search of weapons, two-way radios,
and the Hebrew textbooks distributed by "the Movement", as
the Zionist underground was called by us. Hundreds of Jews
were dragged off to torture chambers and forced to confess at
summary trials staged by the military regime.

Shafik Addas was not a native Iraqi. He was a Syrian who had
turned up one day in Basra, the City of Date Palms, and gone
into the car import business from which he made a fortune put
at millions of dinars. Among the regular guests in his mansion
were wazirs, emirs, sheikhs, army officers, even Regent
Abdullah. Addas was to Basra what Big Imari, my father's
cousin, was to Baghdad. It was his overconfidence that proved
his downfall. Instead of taking – like Big Imari – a Moslem from
a prominent family to manage his affairs, deal with government
officials and bribe them when necessary, he ran his business

himself and acted the equal of any Arab. He was envied and made enemies, and neither his aloofness from his fellow Jews nor the life of a dyed-in-the-wool Iraqi that he led were able to save him in the end.

A hot desert wind blew that night. Lying in the *kabishkan,* my little attic room, I couldn't fall asleep. It was asphyxiatingly hot and I was worried. Worse yet, Miss Sylvia had picked the next day to test us on Hamlet's "To be or not to be" and I wanted badly to outperform George. *To be or not to be.* What choice was there? I was too young to dwell on death but the fate of Shafik Addas kept me awake. One spin of fortune's wheel and even a *muhtashem* like him, a potentate at the height of his career, was just another Jew at the end of a rope. Although I hadn't seen it, I could picture the screaming mob in the square. Both old Hiyawi and my Uncle Hizkel had been there and told me about it.

It had happened less than a year before, right after Passover, during the wave of arrests that followed the establishment of Israel. The new defence minister Sadik al-Bassam, or Sadik el-Bassam Damn-His-Soul as we Jews called him, had wanted to teach us a lesson. Shafik Addas was a godsend. The editor of the Basra newspaper *An-Nas* had asked him for a "contribution" of a thousand dinars and Addas had refused to comply. What, he had thought, could a mere journalist do to him when he was friends with everyone in the government and police?

Now, lying in bed, I couldn't help reflecting how the choice of whether to be or not to be was sometimes made without knowing. Two days later the editor published a vicious article accusing Addas of selling arms to "the Zionist gangs" and spying for *ad-dowa al maz'uma,* "the make-believe state", as Israel was called. The newspaper demanded an investigation, and as soon as copies of it reached Baghdad there was a clamour for Addas's head. It was practically a holy war; the whole country talked of nothing else. The only one who seemed unaffected was Addas himself, who – or so it now seemed – had lost his instinct for survival. The night before his arrest he was secretly visited by the provincial governor, Fahri el-Tabakchali, who urged him to flee to Iran in a speedboat that was waiting to take him safely across the Shatt-el-Arab and out of danger in half an hour. Addas wouldn't hear of it. "They have nothing on me," he insisted each time the governor quoted the proverb *El-hazima ranima*, "He who runs for his life takes it with him as his loot."

The next day Addas was arrested. The trial lasted three days. His three lawyers resigned one by one because the judge, Abdallah en-Na'san, a Jew-hating army officer, refused to hear any defence witnesses. Sadik al-Bassam signed the death warrant at once, after which the Regent equivocated for three days. He was Addas's friend and knew better than anyone what a patriot the condemned man had been. Yet when Addas's wife went down on her knees before him, he could only stare at the ground and reply that the matter was no longer in his hands.

"Kabi, my boy," said old Hiyawi, "what can I tell you? The day before the execution I went to Basra with your Uncle Hizkel to fast and pray with the Jews there as Rabbi Bashi told us to do. On the way I wanted to say a prayer at the tomb of the prophet Ezekiel in Kifl. I was afraid your uncle would refuse – you know what a firebrand he is – but he not only agreed, he said he had been thinking of it too. By the time we reached Basra there were mass demonstrations in the streets. Even small children were carrying effigies of Addas and calling for his blood. And the next day – woe to the eyes that saw it! – he was hung in front of his home. Once wasn't enough for them; they actually strung him up twice. I'm an old man and I've never seen or heard the likes of it. The mob went as wild as if the prophet Muhammed had come back to life. There were thousands of Moslems from Basra and the area, and some who had come all the way from Baghdad. Whole families. They waited up all night, dancing and shouting *Allah akbar*. We were afraid to go out and watched through the cracks in the shutters. Kabi, what can I tell you? We live in a country where judges mock justice and rulers know no mercy."

In their hotel that night he and my uncle didn't sleep a wink. Hizkel, from whom I heard the story too, said that Addas's trial reminded him of the Dreyfus Affair, which had inspired Herzl to write his book *The Jewish State*. My uncle was a passionate believer in Zionism and an expert on its history. After Addas's death he wrote an editorial titled "Confessions Of The Hangman's Noose" for which the newspaper he published was shut down. "The trial of Shafik Addas," it said, "was the trial of every Jew. If an Addas can be hung, who will save the rest of us?"

I tossed and turned on my wooden bed until I felt as if I was rocking in a hammock. I dreamed of purple fields and of a great eagle that carried me to the fabled gates of Jerusalem and knocked on them with its beak. And then, all at once, I knew for a terrifying fact that the knocks were on our front gate. It was useless to try to ignore them by pulling the blanket over my head. I got out of bed and stared blindly into the dark. *They're here.* They would find the arms. They would take my father.

I roused myself and went downstairs to my parents' room. The light was on and my mother stood by the double bed with the colour gone from her face. My father lay in bed. He had been running a fever for three days and had dark bags beneath

4

his bloodshot eyes. Strands of thick grey hair stuck out from his woollen cap and his thin moustache had all but vanished in his unshaven face.

"They're here!" whispered my mother in an unsteady voice. "What will we do, Abu Kabi?"

"Kabi, open the gate for them," said my father.

I headed for the courtyard, stopping at the end of the long hallway to grope for the light switch. My breath came in shallow spurts. The banging on the gate made me tremble. "I'm coming, I'm coming," I tried calling in Moslem Arabic, but the words came out in a Jewish dialect. I turned the big key and lifted the heavy wooden latch that my Uncle Hizkel had made not long before. I was immediately pinned against the wall. Four soldiers burst inside, dragging Hizkel who lived nearby. His bloody face was beaten to a pulp. His wife Rashel followed frantically behind them.

"Look what they've done to him!" she wailed.

"He'll swing for it," said a soldier, running a finger over his throat.

"No!" She let out a scream and reached for Hizkel, clutching at his shoulder.

"Out of the way, you!" barked the soldier.

2.

The devastation lasted a good hour-and-a-half. At four in the morning I was back in the courtyard again, accompanying the soldiers to the gate. Hizkel was lying by the cesspit. He seemed to be trying to smile at me with his swollen lips that were mashed out of shape. Rashel sat beside him with a frightened look, stroking his wounds as if drawing the pain from them. One of the soldiers, named Adnan, was in a vile mood because an oil lamp had shattered in his hands while he was searching the cellar. He rammed the *jalala,* the wooden chair-swing, with his rifle butt until it split lengthwise and calmed down only after booting Hizkel in the ribs. Rashel tried desperately to shield him and was driven back with a blow to her chest. Her eyes filled with tears.

Adnan studied the oil stain on his uniform. I wanted to throw a lit match at it. Would I ever carry out any of my fantasies? Not until the day that I could overcome my fear of these soldiers.

An officer appeared in the courtyard and ordered that Hizkel be taken away. Before he could get to his feet he was dragged to a jeep outside, his eyes two white flares in the dark lane.

"*Kus um-el-yahud,* get the hell up!" yelled Adnan.

Hizkel tried raising himself with his handcuffed arms, collapsed, and tried again. In the end he got to his feet with Rashel's help. He stiffened when he saw me, turning his head away from the soldiers to hide a grimace that seemed to say:

Hush not a word you know nothing. Perhaps Rashel, who was not in on the secret, was not meant to see either. She supported him while Adnan eyed her trim body in the glare of the headlights. "Instead of messing around with these Jews, we ought to be fucking their wives," he said.

"Watch it now," said the officer with a wag of his finger as he climbed into the jeep by the driver. "Allah let you off easy this time." Two soldiers pushed Hizkel into the back seat and sat on either side of him.

"Hizkel, Hizkel," wept Rashel. The jeep disappeared around a curve in the lane, leaving behind a stench of exhaust. Rashel threw back her head, buried her face in her hands and burst into sobs. "They'll hang him like Shafik Addas," she said, shaking all over. She bit her lips.

"Don't even think of it," I said, putting my hand on her shoulder. "He'll be back, I'm sure of it. Come on inside."

"I want to go home," she said. Her eyes had an eerie, blank look. "I need to be by myself." She slipped away and left me standing there.

Only now did I feel how exhausted I was from all the tension and anxiety. Who knew what their next move might be or what they would do to Hizkel? They were sure to come back for my father. They always took the heads of families. I locked the gate and ran up the steps to my parents' room. "They're gone!" I shouted, as if to exorcise the stifling fear.

"And Hizkel?" My father sat up in bed.

"They took him."

"God give him strength," murmured my mother with tears in her eyes.

"Did they hurt him? Tell me the truth," demanded my father. I said nothing.

"Did they search the cellar?"

I knew that my mother knew nothing and so I made a face as if to say: *Hardly at all. They didn't find a thing.*

"I should have gone downstairs and tried bribing them."

"They would have taken you too," said my mother.

"If they had wanted me, they would have taken me from my deathbed. He's my own flesh-and-blood, damn it all! I should have tried. Who knows if we'll have another chance? It's the damn fear that keeps a man from thinking straight."

"I'm going to Rashel's," said my mother, belting her house robe.

"You do that, woman. And tell her to get in touch with Menashi Zleiha, the lawyer, and to give him my name. He can send me the bill. Kabi, walk your mother over and come right back."

I went with my mother. "Whatever made us move to this damned place and this damned life," she muttered as we crossed the courtyard. She meant that we should never have left our old house in the Moslem neighbourhood of el-Me'azzam for the Jewish quarter of Taht el-Takya. My mother blamed everything on that decision. If only we had stayed put, my father wouldn't have fallen in with a bunch of shiftless Zionists who played at being heroes. What kind of life was that for a forty-year-old man with a wife and children? "*Waweli*, everyone's gone mad: the Jews, the Moslems, everyone!"

It was beyond her. The Moslems had always been good neighbours. They had looked after us and protected us. We had all drunk from the same well. And then ten years ago, along came the *Farhood*, the anti-Jewish riots, and nothing was quite the same again. But, since daily life had gone back to a semblance of normality, why set up underground groups and run risks for a Jewish country far away? It could only lead to more hangings and persecution. "Allah have mercy," my mother said in a loud voice, kissing the mezuzah on Hizkel's front gate as I followed her through it.

"Why is the house so dark?" she asked Rashel, who was sitting in a trance on the marble bench in the courtyard. She switched on the light and led Rashel indoors. The courtyard looked like a battlefield. The torn quilts and scattered feathers made sense, but even after having seen our own home ransacked I couldn't fathom the broken dishes, pieces of which lay everywhere. I stepped inside and stood aghast in the doorway of my uncle's study at the sight of his torn, trampled books and dumped desk drawers, their contents splattered with smashed ink bottles. Rashel and my mother went into the bedroom and sat on the bed.

"Did they find anything?" asked my mother.

"How should I know? They took all sorts of books and papers." Rashel's eyes betrayed her shock.

"Oh my God, what have we got ourselves into?" murmured my mother.

Rashel wrung her hands. "What am I going to do?"

"Abu Kabi says you should go to Menashi Zleiha, the lawyer."

"Where was he? Why didn't he come downstairs to help his brother?"

"I told him not to. He's sick. He's had a high fever for the past three days. A beating could have killed him."

"Only Hizkel stuck his neck out. Now they'll hang him like Shafik Addas." Rashel spoke the words to herself as if she couldn't stop them.

"You mustn't talk like that," scolded my mother. "The prophet Ezekiel will protect him."

9

Blouses, brassieres, even a pair of purple pants, littered the rug. My mother saw me staring at them.

"Go home to your father, Kabi," she said. I blushed and left. My father was on his way up from the cellar when I returned. "You're just in time," he told me. "I forgot to bring a bulb. Go and get one and come downstairs."

We screwed in the bulb and switched on the light, sending the bats flitting to their holes. There was a strong smell of oil from the broken lamp. "Quick," said my father. "We have to finish before your mother gets back. It's best she does not know."

It took all our strength to move the old iron stove. We lifted the floor tiles beneath it and opened the wooden case that Hizkel had made. My father took out a flat box with the parts of a Thompson submachine gun and some cases of ammunition. I remembered how proud I had felt a few months ago to be taken down to the cellar when my mother and little brothers were away and was shown the hiding place in case I had to get rid of the arms in an emergency.

"I'll take them somewhere," said my father.

"Let me do it," I said. "Tell me where."

"No. I want you to go carefully to the souk and make sure there's no army or police around."

The windows facing the street were all lit. Querying eyes peered out at me. Farha, the cross-eyed widow who slept with the dove flyer and knew and gossiped about everything, was beside herself. "What happened?" she asked, pawing at me nervously. "Why did they come for Hizkel?"

"Mind your own business," I told her.

"Listen to him!" she exclaimed to the neighbours. "Just the other day he was still filling his pants!"

I ignored her and continued up the street. Although I was

supposed to be looking out for soldiers, in the darkness I was more afraid of djinns, those demons who were compared by some to flickering flames and by others to leech-like dwarves, vampire bats, huge, buzzing caterpillars, monsters dancing on the wind. Although there was a special incense used by Indian fakirs that was said to drive them away, the best method of sending them scurrying to their lairs was to stab their weird forms with a knife. Of course, I knew that this was all superstition, and my father worried me more than the djinns. Still, when I stuck my hands in my pockets, I wished that I hadn't left my penknife in my other trousers.

The first grey glow of dawn in the sky was too weak to light the narrow lanes that wound between the crowded, piggybacked houses. I was at the edge of the neighbourhood now, near the street that led to the souk. Although they were generally up by this hour, the bakers, greengrocers, and *chai'ikhana* or teahouse owners had not yet appeared; they too must have heard of Hizkel's arrest and were taking no chances. I thought of Rashel sitting among the debris of her home, her purple pants at her feet. She was half a woman and half still a girl, and she was attractive even when she cried. *You idiot,* I told myself, *what kind of thing is that to think about now?* I ran home. My father was dressed, his hair was combed and a straw shopping basket slung over his arm. "Is the coast clear?" he asked.

"They're gone. I didn't see one soldier or policeman."

"Wait for me here," he said, "I'll be right back."

I heaved a sigh of relief when he returned safely twenty minutes later, without the gun.

"Remember, Kabi," he told me, "if anything should ever happen to me, go to Abu Saleh the baker. He'll be in charge."

By the time my mother returned from Rashel's, he was in his pyjamas and grey dressing gown again.

"She wouldn't even let me help her clean up," grumbled my mother. "She always has to do everything by herself."

3.

As soon as it was light, I went as usual to buy bread and *kemar*.
In the street I met old Hiyawi on his way to synagogue, a bag
with his prayer shawl and phylacteries under his arm.

"Ah, Kabi," he said. "Why don't you come with me? After last
night, we need to pray." He nodded with his chin towards
Hizkel's house. "The poor thing."

"Who?"

"As if you didn't know. She's a fine, a truly fine woman. The
plagues of Pharaoh upon them, damn their souls! It's worse
now than in the days of the Turk." Hiyawi always spoke of
Turkish times with nostalgia. He patted my face with a bony
hand. "Don't you worry, my boy. 'For the Lord will not forsake
His people nor abandon His heritage.'"

"Amen," I murmured, afraid he might spray me with spittle.
"I'm going this morning to see Rabbi Bashi, God preserve him.
I'll see what he can do for Hizkel."

"Allah give you long life," I said.

"Only the rabbi can get us out of this. He's our leader and
prince. None of your rebel upstarts against him is worth the
dust on his feet."

"My Uncle Hizkel is no upstart."

"Don't play innocent, boy. Your uncle doesn't appreciate the
rabbi. I pity his wife, though. Come to synagogue. Prayer does
wonders for the soul. It restores a man to his God."

"So you've told me."

"And your answer is no again, eh? I suppose you have more urgent business."

"As a matter of fact, I do."

"Well, buy me two pittas and the Lord bless your day." Hiyawi took some money from his robe. "And make sure they're soft, boy," he said, pointing to his rotten teeth.

"All right, all right," I said. "You don't have to remind me each time."

I gripped my basket and walked on without looking back. If I was being followed, it was best not to show that I suspected it. In the little paved square in front of the souk I kept an eye out for Ismail, the Moslem street-gang leader who, something told me, worked for the police. Perhaps it was his asking so many questions each time he turned up in our neighbourhood to challenge us to the belt fights that he always won.

I wanted to run and had to force myself to act nonchalant. At the entrance to the souk a dense procession of mourners swept by me. Men in dark cloaks and dotted keffiyehs and women in veils and dark dresses appeared like wraiths from the underworld, engulfing me as if they were a swarm of black crows. Professional mourners dressed in black, their faces rouged and ashes on their heads, could have been ghosts. At a sign from their leader, a chorus of female voices let loose blood-curdling howls of grief and the terror of death. I thought of the wizened old crone who had wailed through the seven days of mourning for my grandfather and who had frightened me so with her shrieks that I ran to hide in the cellar, from which not even the cries of the bats could pry me loose.

Curious onlookers, some of them Jews, lined the rooftops, staring at the black-draped coffin that bobbed precariously upon the hands that held it. *Well, that's one Arab less,* I told myself, guiltily thinking of Miss Sylvia who liked to talk in her English literature class about humanism and the love of mankind. The funeral passed by. A heavy-set, unveiled woman, no doubt the dead man's mother, staggered behind the coffin like a blind dove, striking and scratching her face. The professional mourners beat their breasts lightly, grazing them with their fists while shrieking as if torn limb from limb. I had to force myself not to laugh. I knew it was their job to stir the other mourners, but it amazed me how well they performed it, as if they were grieving for their own sons. Gradually their cries grew distant and the day went back to normal.

Souk Hinuni, the Jewish market place, rarely stopped to catch its breath. Its bustle started well before sunrise and lasted until long after sunset. Only the lack of electric light kept most of its stands from staying open till midnight. There were hundreds of them, each with its colours and smells. The porters beneath their baskets of fruit, shouting at the shoppers to make way; the donkeys braying at the crowds that blocked their carts; the fiercely bargaining customers; the passers-by talking in loud voices; the women shrilling with joy to meet old friends; the cries of the stuck kerosene wagon drivers; the bubble of gas burners in the teashops; the deep roar of the bread ovens – without its symphony of sounds, the souk would have been as dreary and lifeless as it was when it shut down on Sabbaths and Jewish holidays.

"Hot sambusak, hot sambusak!" The smell of cumin and chickpeas in bubbling oil tickled my nostrils. I stood by the sambusak stand as I did every morning, put down my basket, flexed my stiff shoulder muscles, rubbed my hands with outstretched fingers, reached out for a piece of the hot pastry, and bit into it, thinking for the umpteenth time: *Paradise must taste like this.* As I slipped my change into my pocket, I saw a policeman heading towards me. I started to choke, spraying spittle like old Hiyawi and bits of chickpeas in all directions. "*Ala keifak, ibni,* easy does it," said the sambusak vendor, wiping his stand with a dirty rag. "Move over, my boy, give someone else a chance."

The man in uniform took his place beside me. I was too paralyzed to move. Instead of taking my basket and walking on, I stood there feeling as if my burning face had been deep-fried in oil too. Why hadn't I gone straight to the bakery? "*T'fadl azizi* Here you are, my friend," said the sambusak man, offering the policeman a slice. Although clearly intending to take it, the policeman gave it a deliberating look. Even after he bit into the crisp surface, smacked his lips, and flashed me a smile, I felt that he was staring at me suspiciously and my attempt to say knowingly "Good, eh?" ended with a doughy lump in my throat.

It was only when he turned away from me to ask for a second helping that I realized that guilt was not written on my face. I picked up the basket and moved on, throwing away the last of the sambusak with a sick feeling in my stomach. Although I felt like kneeling and throwing up right there, I kept going to the bakery, pushing my way through the crowd of customers at the door. Devilish flames shot from the cast-iron oven, before which stood Abu Saleh el-Hibaz, the baker and local hero, with a white keffiyeh around his head. Abu Saleh was a large, solidly-built man with a furry mat of black hair on his chest, a bullish neck with which he could lift a sack of flour like a feather when he wished to impress his admirers, dark, roguish eyes, and a swarthy, good-natured face that never lost its gleaming smile.

Balls of dough were arranged on a rectangular kneading board at his side. One by one he took them in his big hands and flattened them with loud slaps, then pounded, stretched, and tossed them from palm to palm until they were the shape of thin platters. These he placed on a small cushion singed at the edges and flipped onto the wall of the oven, repeating the process over and over. When there was no room left in the oven, he began to sing in a deep bass voice:

Get your hot pitta,
Step up and eat her,
Come buy her before
I don't have any more!

I knew it was pointless to try talking to him now. Luckily, Mi'tuk the rhymester wasn't there, because once he arrived the two could go on all day inventing verses about the baker's fragrant bread. Abu Saleh winked when he saw me. Did he know? He took hold of some tongs and peeled the pittas, steamy and crisp with the smell of life itself, off the oven wall with quick movements. Spreading them on the counter, he looked at them with fresh wonder and let out a whistle of admiration.

I felt a tap on my shoulder. It was Amira, my friend Edouard's gorgeous sister, wishing me a good morning. Every boy in the neighbourhood was in love with her. So was Abu Saleh, who wanted to marry her. I nodded hello, my eyes on the pomegranates of her breasts.

"Morning, princess," beamed the baker. When Amira had been a little girl and he an apprentice, he had sculpted her tiny clay dolls and statues and baked them in the oven. As she grew older, she received her own private *hununa*, a small, flaky pitta made just for her. Later still he began singing verses to her, inviting his customers to join in.

> By the window sat Amira,
> Doing her embroidery.
> Six curls tumbled on her forehead:
> Three and then another three.

> Up the street came a brave laddie,
> To her window secretly.
> Six whole hairs were in his moustache,
> Three and then another three.

> Through the window looked Amira,
> And his heart burned ardently.
> Six sweet kisses did he give her,
> Three and then another three.

> Soon enough word reached her father,
> And he smouldered wrathfully.
> Six slaps on the cheek he gave him,
> Three and then another three.

> The poor lad with shame was stricken
> And turned red indignantly.
> Six tears down his cheeks did trickle,
> Three and then another three.

Although Abu Saleh el-Hibaz had asked for Amira's hand, her father, Abu Edouard the dove flyer, thought his princess deserved better. The fact was that ever since the two men had competed to buy the bakery, Abu Edouard could not stand Abu Saleh. Amira's father had coveted the bakery for the large open space at its rear, which would have made a perfect place for his junk yard, and Abu Saleh – so Abu Edouard told my father, who tried arbitrating between them – had sabotaged the deal by convincing the Moslem seller that he, Abu Edouard, would not be able to keep up the payments. Yet even though he refused to talk to the baker, on whom he had sworn to take his revenge, he went on relishing his bread, and most of all his barley pittas, there being none better in the neighbourhood.

Abu Saleh plastered the walls of his oven with more dough, told Sami, his assistant, to look after the customers, and beckoned me out to the yard. After looking to make sure there were no eavesdroppers, I said:

"They've taken Hizkel."

"I know," said Abu Saleh, sitting on a stool and wiping his brow. "We'll make them pay for it. And we'll spring Hizkel, too. You don't know how much he means to me. I was just a dumb kid when I first met him. He took me into the new vocational school that he opened and I was in the first class to graduate. You should have seen how thrilled he was to see me, he who never thought I would amount to anything, reading his newspaper to the illiterate shopkeepers around here! After the *Farhood* he and your father asked me to join the Shabbab el-Inkath, the Emergency Youth Brigade set up to defend the Jewish quarter. I was already its commander when we started the Movement. I remember Hizkel saying at our first meeting: 'We'll rebuild the kingdom of Judah – we'll restore our past glory – we'll make history!'

"It was like hearing the wingbeats of the angels. We followed him to a man, my whole class. It was in my cellar that we celebrated the first anniversary of the State of Israel, swearing allegiance to it and reciting the Psalms as if the Messiah had come. I wanted to go there right away, to fight in the Jewish army, but Hizkel was against it. He wanted me to be here in case there were more *Farhoods*. 'We're the captains of this ship,' he said, 'and we won't leave it until we've got all our passengers ashore.'"

Abu Saleh wiped his brow again with a grunt and said: "Lord, who can fill his shoes now? *Waweli*, I left the oven full of bread!" He ran back into the bakery, from which came a scorched smell, scooped the pittas from the oven, threw the burned ones into a rusty can, and laid out the good ones on the counter. When the crowd of customers thinned out, he handed me our daily order, adding two soft pittas for Hiyawi and four for Rashel. "Tell her to keep her chin up," he whispered. "And that I swear by all the bread in the world to free Hizkel. We'll all go to Jerusalem together."

Fat'hiya, the pretty Bedouin *kemar* seller, was sitting on the floor by the right-hand wall of the bakery. In winter she moved to the other wall to be closer to the oven, sitting cross-legged on a thin cushion while listening to the musical crackle of the pittas and Abu Saleh crooning Bedouin love songs:

> Would I were a golden chain
> Worn around thy neck,
> Sometimes falling on thy heart
> Sometimes on thy breast.

Now and then their eyes met, and as soon as the bakery emptied she flashed him a smile, her one gold filling, or so she thought, adding a winsome touch to her rows of white teeth. Then they went down to the cellar to drive the rats from their holes with the groans of their love making.

Fat'hiya was cloaked in black from head to toe, revealing nothing but the cracked soles of her feet. The thin black kerchief on her head offset her desert beauty with her coal-dark eyes that were painted with kohl and her golden nose-ring. "*Ya ayuni, ya Kabi,*" she said to me. "You're late this morning, I've kept some *kemar* for you, though." With a long mattress-maker's needle she sliced a big piece of the jelled butterfat that had been boiled and cooled, transferring it from its shallow wooden bowl to the serving board I had brought with me.

"*Mashallah*, the *kemar* came out extra good today," she said as she did each morning. Her complexion was like the *kemar*, smooth, soft and silky. "Kabi," she asked in her caressing voice, "*ichar bich el-yom ya huya?* You don't look your usual self."

"I didn't sleep so well," I said.

She grinned at me mischievously. "Who's been keeping you awake, Amira?"

"You," I answered. We both burst out laughing. A policeman sidled up and asked flirtatiously:

"What are you selling there, little sister?"

"The cream of your dreams," said Fat'hiya.

"Like you, my sweet. A real beauty, isn't she?" he asked me.

"You bet," I said.

The policeman wagged his head. "Will you look at that! The boy's still a child and he's already got an eye for the ladies. You better watch out when he grows up."

"He's a man already, mashallah," said Fat'hiya, spitting to one side against the Evil Eye.

"What's your name?" asked the policeman.

"Kabi."

"Last name?"

"Imari."

"That rings a bell. Wait a minute … wasn't someone by that name arrested last night?"

I took a deep breath and tried to look calm and unhurried, though all I wanted was to take to my heels.

"A relative?" he asked.

"Not that I know of." I smiled at Fat'hiya and wished her a good day. The most important thing, I remembered my father saying, was always to look natural.

4.

Hiyawi was standing in front of Rashel's house, looking like a
scolded child. I waved his soft pittas in the air. "The Lord bless
you and keep you," he said in the words of the Priestly Blessing,
placing his hand on my head with a mournful smile. "The Lord
make his face to shine upon you and be gracious to you." He
kissed his fingertips, touched them to his eyes, patted my face,
and asked: "What does she have against me? Why won't she let
me help her?"

"How am I supposed to know?" I retorted. As I was heading
for my front door, he stopped me and handed me some bills.
"Here, these are for her."

"She has all the money she needs," I said, returning it.

His bottom lip quivered. "Give it to her. She can use every
dinar she gets."

"All right, all right." I pushed open Rashel's wooden gate.

"Kabi!" she cried with relief when she saw me. The white dress
she had on displayed her trim, full-breasted body. Impaled by
her honey-coloured eyes, whose meaning always eluded me, I
reached into my basket to hide my embarrassment. "These
pittas are from Abu Saleh el-Hibaz," I said, putting them on the
marble bench. "The money is from Hiyawi."

"The first of them will be the death of my husband and the
second of me," she said.

"I thought it was Hizkel who recruited Abu Saleh."

"Hizkel is the mind and Abu Saleh is the body. One needs the other."

"And Hiyawi?"

"That's a long story. I'll tell it to you some other time. Give the old lecher his money back." I could hear a stifled scream in her voice. "You're too young to understand," she added, seeing my curious look.

"Exactly two-and-a-half years younger than you are!"

There was a loud knock on the door. "They're here," Rashel said, stiffening. A shiver ran down me. She couldn't get herself to move and so I put down my basket and went to open the gate. All was lost: they would take my father now too. We should have left this damned place while we could have!

Abed was standing at the gate. "It's you?" I gasped, the air sucked from my lungs all at once.

"The black slave in person." It was his way of referring to himself.

"Why did you have to knock?"

"Walk in on a woman without knocking? Who taught you manners?"

"But you're here all the time."

"For Hizkel, not for her."

Rashel relaxed when she saw him.

"I'm sorry to hear what happened to Hizkel," Abed said. "Abu Kabi told me to take you to the lawyer's. When is a good time for you?"

"I don't need to be taken," Rashel said with an obstinacy I had never seen before.

Abed stepped backwards with a submissive smile. "It's just to escort you through the Moslem neighbourhoods," he apologized. He had spent all morning helping my mother clean up the mess left by the army.

"I'll manage on my own," said Rashel. When he had shut the gate behind him, she said to me:

"What does your father take me for, sending his servant like that?"

"He could have been arrested if he had come here," I told her. Didn't she understand his situation?

"And why didn't he come downstairs last night to see his brother, to talk to the police, to try bribing them?" The question, which clearly haunted her, seemed addressed more to herself than to me. The unwelcome memory passed through my mind of Hizkel being dragged outside like a sack of rice by three soldiers and dumped by the cesspit. "Keep an eye on him!" the officer, who had a chest covered with decorations, had ordered one of his men. "You stay here," he had told Rashel. Glancing at the faint light from our house across the courtyard, he had asked me: "Where is your father?"

"Upstairs," I stammered. "He's sick."

"Move, you son-of-a-bitch!" barked a soldier.

I climbed the stairs ahead of his studded boots. My mother was standing in the doorway. "Good evening," she nodded to the officer.

"It's almost morning," he replied with a look at my father, who had the blanket pulled up to his chin. "You Jews are wearing us down. Every night it's another house. Where are the weapons?" My father didn't bat an eyelid.

"I asked you something," said the officer.

"What's that?" replied my father hoarsely.

"Where are the weapons?"

My father shook his head uncomprehendingly.

"We'll know everything soon enough. Your brother will talk. He's lying out in the yard now. Maybe you'd like to take a look at him. I'm giving you one last chance to avoid an unpleasant interrogation."

There was no need to say more. The allusion to the Iraqi secret service sent a shudder through us. My father kept shaking his head. "No matter what happens to me," I remembered Hizkel telling us, "you don't know a thing."

The officer lit a cigarette with a silver lighter and offered one to my father. My father broke into a hacking cough. The officer made a face, stepped away as though from a consumptive, and turned to my mother. My two little brothers, woken by the noise, held onto her dress and stared at him with frightened eyes.

"With your permission, ma'am," he said with exaggerated courtesy, "I'd like to conduct a little search."

"Please do," said my mother, too scared to notice the mockery in his voice.

Our house was reduced to a shambles. Could my father have managed to bribe them? Certainly, the pointless havoc that they wreaked had seemed like an invitation to him to do so. Even he admitted that it wouldn't have hurt to try. Anyone living in Iraq in those days could have told you as much ...

"He was against our marriage from the start," Rashel now said angrily about my father. "He told Hizkel that my family had no money, that we were nobodies."

"Where did you hear that nonsense?"

There were tears in her eyes. "He's had it in for me ever since I asked him not to pressure Hizkel into leading the Movement."

"Come on, forget it. Why don't I go to the lawyer with you?" I suggested.

"Thank you. I don't need anyone. I'll be fine." I couldn't tell if she was reassuring me or herself, but it seemed a good time to leave. At the gate I turned around. "Don't go without me," I said trying to sound firm. "The law office isn't open yet anyway."

Abed was waiting outside. "What will I tell Abu Kabi?" he asked. "He'll be furious." The perpetual twinkle was gone from his little eyes.

"Leave that to me and go and open the shop. My father wants us to carry on as usual."

"Thank God they let him off." Abed's big hands dropped to his sides and he lowered his head meekly, baring equine teeth. "Kabi, walk me to the shop," he said, putting an arm around me and leading me back towards the souk. "And Allah have pity on your great-grandfather."

Hiyawi was already in his tobacco shop, sitting in his tattered old easy chair and drinking the morning coffee he had bought from a vendor. He was tapping the coffee cup rhythmically. My father's shop, which had been purchased from a cloth merchant who sold up in a hurry and moved to India, was nearby in the middle of the neighbourhood. Three steps above street level, it had a large interior and boasted at its front end, visible through the display window, a superb antique glass chest with a selection of my father's best timepieces, the ones he took special pride in. Two work-tables, his own and Abed's, stood behind it. Towards the rear of the shop was a green safe and a nook for guests with a couch, a coffee table, two chairs, and some planters that my mother had insisted on. Three framed photographs hung on a wall. The middle and most prominent one was of King Faisal. To its right – guaranteed, my mother believed, to bring the business good luck – was a photograph of the late, saintly Rabbi Yosef Hayyim, and to its left, another of my great-grandfather.

The shop had no telephone. There weren't many phones in Taht el-Takya. Although my father had begged the Postal Service for one and paid out bribe money, he had never got anywhere. The only shop with a telephone was Hajj Yahya Abd el-Hak, the metalworker's across from us, which also happened to belong to the neighbourhood's only Moslem. Hajj Yahya was a stooped, sombre old man with clear skin and a tricornered beard. He wore a white robe and turban and had a brown bump on his forehead from bowing to the ground so many times in prayer. I liked to look at him and his snow-white robe, which was always immaculate, though he spent the whole day hunched over his lathe. He had two sons. The eldest, Ghassan, was a colonel in the Iraqi army and hated Jews; he had fought as a volunteer in Palestine in '48 and wanted his father to move to a Moslem area. Twice a week, trailed by his bodyguards, he came to visit the old man in his shop, carefully hitching up his trousers to keep them from getting creased and sitting in the only chair, from which he watched the passers-by in the street with his head flung proudly back. His arrival never failed to excite the neighbourhood. Abu Saleh el-Hibaz would come especially to look at him, standing in front of my father's shop and staring with childlike wonder at Ghassan's gold-buttoned uniform with its insignia. Before returning to the bakery he would swear that in the Land of Israel he would be a high officer too.

Hajj Yahya's second son Karim was younger, plumper, and totally unlike his grim brother. He belonged to various organizations for the protection of minorities and considered himself a friend of the Jews, and before becoming a famous and very busy lawyer he had frequented Taht el-Takya nearly every day and dropped in on my father's shop, which served as a local meeting place, to drink coffee, eat the torpedo-shaped burghul *kubba* made by Baruch the Kurdish *kubba* king, and chat with Hizkel and my father about Middle-East politics, the intrigues of the British, the regional interests of the Americans, and the dangers posed by the Communists. He was on familiar terms with the shop's other visitors and often joined them for a friendly chat over a cup of bitter coffee or sweet tea.

Late in the afternoon I often sat in a corner of the shop, pretending to be reading or doing my homework while listening to the grown-ups talk and wishing that I could be one of them. Hizkel was usually there, stretched out on the couch and napping, or else smoking an aromatic pipe and telling my father the latest news, after which they discussed recent political developments and sought to fathom the motives of Abu Naji, as the English were called, or the byzantine ways of the Anglophile prime minister, Nuri es-Sa'id, whom everyone referred to as "the Pasha". Among my father and Hizkel's visitors were Jews from wealthier areas, too, like Bab-esh-Shargi, Ilwi, and el-Kerada. Some of them knew my father from his teaching days, while others simply enjoyed the company of the watchmaker with the legal education who was a member of the renowned Imari clan.

My father, who knew that nobody bought watches first thing in the morning, was not an early riser, and Abed, his Kurdish Jewish helper, opened the shop for him. He tidied up, polished the shop window, aired out the thin Persian rug in winter, sprinkled water on the black floor tiles in summer, and turned on the overhead fan. Abed loved the shop and its business like my father, who often sent him to fetch merchandise, collect debts, make payments, shop in the souk, and even help my mother and us. Abed came to our house regularly for the noon lunch break, and while my mother was filling the *safartas,* the multi-level food bucket, with cold fruit and slices of watermelon for the afternoon hours, he ate with the rest of us, burping with pleasure and savouring Hiyawi's expensive Zabana cigarettes. My mother treated him like one of the family, inviting him for holidays and celebrations, giving him my father's old shirts and suits, and even trying to find a nice Jewish wife for him. Unable to do enough in return, he ran little errands for her, accompanied her to the souk, carried her baskets, and even went back a second time to buy the fruit or vegetables she had forgotten. He also looked after us boys like an older brother, joking and playing pranks with us, or sometimes scolding us and giving advice. In cold, rainy weather, when I was loath to leave my warm bed for the morning's pittas and *kemar,* he went in my place, dropping my little brothers off at school and even hoisting me onto his shoulders to keep me out of the muddy streets rutted with cart wheels, donkey hooves, and the bare feet of Kurdish porters. Indefatigable, he was also a jack of all trades who could break down a wall, fix a leaky pipe or tap, replace an electric socket, change a cracked floor tile, plaster and whitewash. He worked quickly and surely, and I liked nothing better than watching him.

The one thing Abed did not like to fix was watches. His big, strong hands balked at the precision of the work, which sometimes called for consulting English catalogues, and my father, who was a perfectionist, gave him none but the simplest tasks. Abed worshipped him. He was eternally grateful for having been taken on as a young orphan, and while my father would never have dreamed of dismissing him, his greatest fear was that this might happen. After sixteen years in my father's service he still did not dare look at him directly, and it never occurred to him that my father needed him as much as he needed my father.

My father had paid for Abed to study in Hizkel's vocational school, where he had been in the same class as Abu Saleh el-Hibaz. The two had joined the Movement together too, and Abu Saleh liked and trusted Abed. Like many poor Jews, Abed had no doubt that in Israel he would be treated like a king. He lived in a cheap room in Tatran, in the home of a widow – a mother of six who sometimes stole into his room at night to give him romantic pointers. Actually, he had little to learn from her, since he visited Fauzia, his Arab whore, every Friday night. After the blessing over the wine and the Sabbath meal, he washed and perfumed himself, smeared his head with cheap hair oil, put on an old suit of my father's and a tie that had seen better days, stuck a *rib'i*, a half-pint bottle of arrack, in the inner pocket of his jacket, and went off to drink it with Fauzia and tell her of the week's adventures before tumbling on her mattress until the dawn. Fauzia, who kept her Friday nights free for him and stood fretfully turning down customers in the doorway of the brothel if he sometimes turned up late, was genuinely fond of him. He spent a good part of his earnings on her, which greatly displeased the widow, who had hopes that he would marry her and grant her more than the mere crumbs of his virility.

5

My father was sitting down to breakfast in his favourite corner near the kitchen, by the arched window with the coloured glass. He skimmed the crust off the milk my mother had boiled for him, spread it on his pitta, and sprinkled it with sugar.

"Babba," I said, "I'm going with Rashel to the lawyer's."

"She wants to go by herself," said my mother. "She told me so."

"But why?" asked my father.

"Are you worried she'll be kidnapped? The lawyer is a Jew and his office isn't far from here."

"I don't know why she can't do as she's told," he complained, rising from his chair.

"Where are you going? Stay at home and stop looking for trouble. You're sick." My mother set down a porcelain tray with a soft-boiled egg, *kemar,* quince jam, and some cubes of salty cheese in warm water. "Eat, it will give you strength," she said. My father broke off some pitta, dipped it in the orange-coloured jam, and put it back on the tray.

"I'm not hungry," he told her, watching the bees settle on the jam.

"At least drink something."

"We have to leave this country!"

"That's not for us. Leave that to the young folk."

"Are you telling me I'm too old?"

"Drink some tea. It's good for your throat."

"Lots of families have been smuggled across the border. I wanted to leave after the *Farhood*."

"Who was stopping you?"

"You were."

"I was? You were too busy with your watches and your court case against Big Imari. You talked like a Zionist, but all you wanted to do was make money."

"What kind of thing is that to say!"

"It's the truth. All you've ever thought of is yourself. If you had wanted to leave so badly, you could have have done so."

"Without you and the children?"

"How can you even pretend to care about us when you're ready to take us to a country about which there are so many horror stories?"

"Woman, those stories are spread by our enemies. If things were so bad there, no one would stay. And yet not only does nobody come back from there, dozens more Jews set out every day. You believe in God, in the prophet Ezekiel, in the Bible, in the prayer book ... why don't you want to live in the Holy Land?"

"The Holy Land is a dream for the days of the Messiah."

"Woman, the ground is burning beneath us! Who ever thought it would come to this? As soon as I find out what's happening with my brother, I'm leaving. The sooner, the better."

"And I'm not. Get that into your head."

My mother put no stock in my father's dreams of Israel, which seemed to her an impulsive male fantasy of distant conquests and adventures spawned by a sense of personal discontent. He had never forgiven himself for not joining his friend Abu Yosef, who went to Palestine after the *Farhood*. Instead, he, Hizkel, and Abu Saleh el-Hibaz organized the Youth Brigade, which in turn gave birth to the Movement. They

33

collected funds for Palestine, and when reports reached Baghdad about the slaughter of the Jews in Europe and Rabbi Bashi declared a public fast and day of prayer, my father and Hizkel were the first to speak publicly of the need to study Hebrew and prepare for emigration. And yet, in the end, others went while they stayed. Perhaps my mother was right that it was not only she who held my father back but that he was simply afraid to take the plunge. Something bound him more tightly to Baghdad than he realized, a connection he could never break. He himself couldn't explain it.

"Listen to a story, woman," he said, pausing until he had her attention. "Once upon a time a man found a starving, frozen snake. He took it home and fed it and laid it on the warming pan to thaw out, and then he put it in bed with his only son. The boy and the snake became good friends and played together. One day, though, the boy stepped on the snake's tail and it bit him. When the father heard his only son's screams, he came running with an axe, but the snake wriggled away and only its tail was chopped off. The boy died, and after the week of mourning the snake came out of its hole and said to its master, 'It's time I took my leave.' 'My son is dead,' replied the man, 'and I'm all alone in this house. Stay and keep me company.' 'No, master,' said the snake, 'that would be a mistake. Whenever you see me you'll think of your son, and whenever I see you I'll think of my tail.' That's the story of us and the Moslems. They make us think of the *Farhood,* and we make them think of Palestine."

"You and your stories," scoffed my mother. "Why don't you go and see Big Imari? He'll get your brother out of jail."

"Are you starting on that again? I haven't spoken to him for fourteen years."

"Your brother's life is at stake and all you can think of is your own dignity!"

He rose, went to the *jalala,* and ran his thumb over the widening crack. "May the hands that did this be struck off, son," he said to me. "It's time to go to school."

"Today?"

"Especially today!"

Edouard, the dove flyer's son, was standing at the top of the street, his schoolbag on one shoulder and his roller skates on the other. He was the leader of our gang and did not usually wait for me, but today was not a usual day.

"Who'll make us catapults now?" he greeted me.

"What are you talking about?" I asked.

"You mean you don't know?"

It took me a minute to remember that my Uncle Hizkel had promised to make us boys catapults. "That's all that's on your mind now?"

"Do you think the army will come to our house too?"

"Why," I mocked, "has your father become a Zionist?"

"It's enough that we're your neighbours."

"Now you *are* talking like a Zionist."

The old open-top, double-decker bus was full of students. We climbed the stairs; Edouard sat by the railing and I took the seat next to him. As always my job was to signal to him that the conductor was coming so that he could slip down below without paying.

The students sang marching songs as we slowly made our way past the hundreds of wagons and carriages clogging the road. The narrow streets of Taht el-Takya looked like so many city dumps. Tens of thousands of people lived in them, packed into a crazy quilt of brown and white brick boxes nearly as squalid as those of the nearby Moslem slum of Bab-esh-Sheikh. The same strong smell of urine hung over both.

The further we travelled, the wider the streets grew and the more the view changed. Now we were passing Bab-esh-Shargi, Batawin, Baghdad-el-Jedida, and Ilwi, the fashionable Jewish section of modern Baghdad, with its villas, lawns, flowerbeds, palm trees, cactuses, and long avenues of red and white oleanders. It was a different, peaceful world, the very air of which seemed clearer and smelled better. We passed the mansion of Menashi Dahud Imari, better known as Big Imari, which looked as if it had been lifted from the pages of an English tourist brochure. Behind its high walls, large green gardens could be seen from the top of the bus.

My mother had seen Big Imari's mansion only once in her life, but that had been enough to mark the start of my father's troubles with her, for never again could she understand how his cousin had been allowed to inherit all the family's wealth. What kind of man settled for the life of a watchmaker when he should have been a tycoon? She didn't believe his story that my great-grandfather had sent his sons from Imara to Baghdad for an education, leaving Big Imari behind to steal the rice fields. Who needed an education with all that money? My father, it sometimes seemed to me, was doomed to spend the rest of his life explaining that.

At the Frank Ini School in Ilwi, to which buses pulled up from all over town, everyone poured out. Hawkers were gathered by the gates, where students impatient to spend their pocket money were already buying candy and rolls dipped in *amba*, hot, sour mango chutney, even though they had just had their breakfasts. I myself kept my allowance for the break and sometimes managed to hang onto it until the end of the day when I deposited it in my secret savings account.

I remained sitting for a while on top of the bus, looking down on the grounds. Our high school, which already had a citywide reputation – though its first graduating class was my own – was composed of a series of new, white two-storey buildings arranged in the shape of an L. It had a small synagogue, a gymnasium, tennis courts, and a large parade ground, as well as a library and a study hall, and it was a far cry from the neglect of my old elementary school with its broken tiles, flooded hallways, rickety stairs, poor lighting, congestion, and bad smell.

The blare of a horn jarred me from my reveries. The bus moved to make way for a gleaming black limousine, from which Big Imari's son George stepped out of a door opened by a uniformed chauffeur, looking every bit the English lord in his white suit. Unhurriedly, he walked towards the school gate while the chauffeur followed with his bag. *Dandah*, we called him because of his small size, "the Dwarf", and he stuck out his little chest and held his head high like a peacock. The one-eyed Arab gatekeeper bowed low as he passed, a gesture he acknowledged with a nonchalant wave.

"They own a quarter of Baghdad," my father had said somewhat exaggeratedly about George's family one day when we were out for a walk. I knew that their vast fortune came from the rice fields whose loss my mother mourned and that important people were entertained in their home. It was said that Big Imari's parties were even attended by Regent Abdullah who came to listen to that golden-throated enchantress, the Jewish singer Salima Pasha; to feast his eyes on the unforgettable curves and gyrations of the belly dancer Rahia; to hear the divine strains of the zither player Avraham Siyyon Ba'abul; and to soar on the wings of the unsurpassable poetry recitations of Salim Shibbat and Hizkel Kissab. These fabulous nights in the towered mansion were the talk of all Baghdad.

Though an outstanding student, George was known as a primadonna, a pampered, aloof youngster who was given whatever he wanted, including the editorship of our school newspaper, which I had coveted for myself. A great literary future was predicted for him and even I liked his poems with their light, flowing rhymes and simple, unpretentious verses, so different from what was generally published by students who considered themselves poets. There was something surprisingly fresh about them, a courage to be direct that might have derived from the French and English poetry that he studied with his private tutors.

Although I too tried my hand at writing verse, I kept the results in a drawer; there was no point in competing with George on his own ground. Instead, I filled the submissions box with my short stories and other prose compositions. George published all of them. The paper was our only subject of conversation. Three years previously, when we first met in school and he heard my family name, he had said in his shrill voice: "Who isn't an Imari these days?" The words still bubbled like poison in my blood. Did his having been born with a silver spoon in his mouth make him more of an Imari than I was? I wanted badly to crush his conceit, thus commencing an unspoken but by no means unnoticed rivalry. Even though he had the best tutors in Baghdad, I tried to get higher marks. If I were George Imari, I told myself, I wouldn't behave like George did, although just how I would behave was far from clear to me.

I got off the bus, picked two soft sprigs from a myrtle hedge, rubbed them between my hands, took a deep breath of their pungent odour that I loved, automatically murmured a Hebrew blessing, and hurried inside. My class was already lined up in its place for the morning flag raising. We faced a row of teachers, in the middle of which was our revered rector Stad Nawi. A step in front of him stood our headmaster, Rahamim Salim Imari, known to all as Salim Effendi; a tall, powerful-looking man, a Communist, and a cousin of my father and Big Imari, he needed a mere minute to silence us. There was something remarkable about his ability to hush the unruliest student with a glance of his piercing eyes which were reinforced by his large nose, his prominent chin, and his heavy black brows that met over his nose.

We sang "God Save the King in War and Peace" in honour of King Faisal, and next, its strains rising from hundreds of throats, the national anthem. Then Latif, the school drummer, raised the Iraqi flag to full mast while moving his lips in what looked like a prayer. Once, when I had asked him what he said each time he hoisted it, his answer had been: "The kaddish for the dead."

Salim Effendi now delivered his daily invocation into which he subtly wove, as usual, the Communist gospel. In eloquent phrases he spoke about justice, human dignity, the right to freedom, and the duty to rebel against oppression, none of which were part of our academic curriculum. Although the rector was not pleased with these orations and feared incurring the wrath of the authorities, Salim Effendi was undeterred and continued to incite us every morning. "Human beings are born equal and are entitled to the same opportunities," he declared while I thought of George, standing dwarfishly in the row ahead of me and fawned on by all, including Stad Nawi, who knew exactly how much Menashi Dahud Imari contributed annually to our school.

Even Salim Effendi, his fiery words notwithstanding, gave George private language and literature lessons and helped him to polish his verse. He was one of the best foreign language tutors in the city and George had insisted on him, though he and Big Imari were not on good terms. Along with his mother, Salim Effendi too had been cheated out of the rice paddies belonging to our great-grandfather, and the Marxist doctrines that he slipped into George's tutorials were his revenge. Certainly, he had no qualms about taking money from a capitalist and kept raising his already high fees, which Big Imari paid with much gritting of teeth. After the flag raising I debated telling Salim Effendi about Hizkel's arrest but decided against it since his views on Zionism were far from my uncle's.

Our first class was given by Miss Sylvia Perlman, our English teacher. An assimilated British Jew, she was a strikingly blue-eyed, fair-skinned woman with golden hair as smooth as Fat'hiya's *kemar*. She had nice legs too, and a sensational behind that was usually encased in a pair of tight trousers that no Iraqi woman would dare be seen in. Stad Nawi, it was said, had tried dissuading her from wearing them because they inflamed our adolescent imaginations but Miss Sylvia had refused, as a matter of principle, to let her human rights be curbed. Needless to say, she had our support. Sometimes she came dressed in an expensive tweed skirt with a man's jacket and tie that made us snigger. There was nothing conventional about her, not even her collection of shoes, of which she wore, or so it seemed to us, a different pair each day.

Miss Sylvia did not know, or pretended not to know, a word of Arabic. Two of her five weekly classes were devoted to

Shakespeare's *Hamlet,* which she untiringly insisted we declaim in an Oxford English that she demonstrated in a quietly demanding voice. She disliked our Arab accents, especially the sulky Edouard's, whom she plied with homework and requests to read out loud to the class. Indeed, these ordeals so humiliated him that he skipped English whenever he could.

"You should hear what you sound like," she scolded him.

"Like an Arab Jew," he retorted. God knew where he came up with that.

"There's no reason why Orientals like you can't learn to speak a proper English. Look at Mr Salim Effendi."

"I'm not Stad Salim," scowled Edouard.

"Next year, after the summer vacation," Miss Sylvia informed us, "we're going to start a new play by Shakespeare called *Julius Caesar.* As many of you no doubt know, Julius Caesar was a great Roman. In order to understand the historical background of this play, I want you to learn something about him during your holiday. I highly recommend to you the entry on Caesar, Gaius Julius in the *Encyclopaedia Britannica.* The text of the play can be purchased during the holiday from the school office. I have made sure to order enough copies of it from the MacKenzie Bookstore. Mr Edouard Sourpuss, instead of indulging in idle chatter with Mr. Sasson, I suggest that you concentrate your energies on improving your English accent by reading out loud and correctly. At home, of course."

An injured flush spread over Edouard's face. At a hand signal from him, as if at the dip of a conductor's baton, the class began stamping its legs, the din growing louder and louder until it reached the corridor outside. I felt a wave of pity for the poor Englishwoman who wanted only to make civilized beings out of us; European gentlemen loyal to a fading empire. We did not deserve her devotion, her erudition, her articulateness, her Oxford English that Salim Effendi praised so highly. We should have been whipped on our bare bottoms by one of our tutors, or by Hilfa, their brutal assistant. Although I lacked the courage to call for silence, the indignity was more than I could bear.

As luck would have it, the headmaster was passing through the corridor. Suddenly the classroom door opened to reveal Salim Effendi standing there with pursed lips. His probing glance passed over each one of us. No one dared let out a peep.

"She was making fun of me," burst out Edouard in Arabic.

"*Man alamani harfan, malakani abdan,*" Salim Effendi rebuked him quietly. "Teach me a single letter and I am your slave forever." Order restored, he nodded to Miss Sylvia and left.

"As I was saying, Mr Edouard," Miss Sylvia continued as if she had never been interrupted, "anyone can acquire the proper accent with a bit of effort."

Adnan too, the thug who had helped ransack our house? After the last drawer was emptied and nearly everything of value smashed, the officer had barked: "Adnan, go on down to the cellar!" "*Yallah, ya ibn kalb,*" Adnan turned to me and swore, "where's the cellar?" I was petrified. *We're in for it now,* I thought. And yet if they knew what was down there, why hadn't they gone there straight away? I opened the cellar door. The light switch didn't work and my father had told me not to change the old bulb when it burned out. Adnan stood in the doorway of the dark, mysterious-looking room, trying to make out the dim shadows that belonged to piles of beds, old furniture, broken toys, sacks of rice, and emergency barrels of food and cooking oil.

On the opposite wall was a pipe that ran to the roof. The gun, in the case made by Hizkel, was beneath the floor tiles in the far left corner. We had piled the heaviest things over it, including an old cast-iron stove. "Where's the light?" asked Adnan nervously. "There's no electricity, sir," I said. He yanked me away and tried flicking the switch himself. "Go and get a candle!" he ordered – and then, as I began climbing the stairs: "Make that a lantern!" I went back to my parents' bedroom. "What's happening down there?" my mother whispered. My father was having a coughing fit beneath the blanket. "Pray," I said. I took the lantern that hung by my father's bed and lit it. All the worry in the world seemed concentrated in his eyes. Like a man on the way to the gallows, I slowly descended the stairs again. Adnan snatched the lantern. Moving and smashing furniture while I stood rooted to the floor by my fear, he cleared a path to the stove. *He knows,* I thought. *The son-of-a-bitch knows.* Just then he tripped and fell. The lantern broke and everything went dark. A swarm of bats flew out at us. "Hey, what's going on?" yelled Adnan, a note of panic entering his voice. "I don't know," I said. "It could be a djinn. This basement's full of them." The bats flew from corner to corner with shrill squeaks. "Where the hell are you?" shouted Adnan. "Get me out of here!" "I'm coming," I yelled back and led him outside as if he were a blind man. "Did you find anything?" asked the officer. "A whole lot of bats," Adnan said.

Now, imagining Adnan staring dumbly at Miss Sylvia while trying to declaim "To be or not to be" in the King's English, I let out a strange hiccup of laughter. All the night's terrors that I had sought to drive away were burped up with it. It infected Edouard, who began to laugh too, and soon the whole class was in hysterics.

"Out! Out!" screamed Miss Sylvia. "Neither of you will take the test on *Hamlet!* You'll get nought!"

Edouard and I left hastily to avoid being seen by the rector or headmaster. Out of habit, he stopped for a moment at the bottom of the winding wooden staircase where he regularly waited to peek beneath Miss Sylvia's skirt when she came downstairs during the break. Afterwards he would tell us with much relish about her pink lace pants, but when once I tried to catch a glimpse of them myself, I couldn't make out a thing.

"Come on, let's beat it before Salim Effendi catches us," I urged and he sprinted for the exit with me hot on his heels. He and our Communist headmaster had a special relationship. At first I failed to understand what Salim Effendi saw in Edouard, to whom he could talk for hours about the Soviet Union – the one country in the world, according to him, that enjoyed true freedom and equality and had redeemed mankind from "the dunghill of exploitation" and banned all discrimination against Jews. When Salim Effendi mentioned Lenin and Stalin he beamed like old Hiyawi reading the Book of Isaiah. Edouard's eyes gleamed as he listened, and although we usually travelled home together, he sometimes disappeared after school to run mysterious errands for his favourite teacher.

We roller-skated slowly towards Bab-esh-Shargi. I was hungry. Although what I most craved was the oily lettuce leaves on the vegetable stands, we stopped by an *amba* wagon and bought two rolls dipped in the yellow chutney.

"Let's go and see a film," Edouard proposed.

"The day after my uncle's arrest?" Once again I strove to banish the nausea I had felt at the sight of Hizkel's swollen face as he was dragged handcuffed to our house and flung by the cesspit. Had he told the soldiers kicking and shouting at him where the gun was, it would have been the end of us.

"And if you don't go to the cinema he'll be freed?"

"This isn't our day. Now we'll flunk *Hamlet* too."

"Don't go superstitious on me," said Edouard.

I didn't like morning films with their dirty old men who accosted you, but neither did I want to go home and be scolded by my father, who put my education before everything.

"Come on, my treat," said Edouard, breaking into one of the Egyptian crooner Abd el-Muttalib's love songs. He couldn't keep a tune and my ears winced each time he went flat.

"Stop," I pleaded.

"Listen," he said. "When I was a baby, I was dark and hairy and cried all the time. My mother took me to a fortune teller to ask what would become of me. The fortune teller looked at me, touched my forehead, and said: 'He'll either be a singer or a thief.' He laughed with self-satisfaction. "That's why I have to keep on singing."

"You'll never be a singer," I told him. "And you are already a thief."

He knew what I was referring to. "You don't think I intend to pay those stupid Moslems, do you?"

"For God's sake, not today," I said. "I'll pay for us both."

"You don't have to be afraid. They're too dumb to catch me." Edouard's system was to collect torn ticket stubs from the ground and glue them together. Of course, the glued halves had different numbers, but the ushers never noticed, especially since he distracted them by talking in especially foul language. It was a method that so far had got us in free of charge to *The Zero Sign* with Tyrone Power, *Flash Gordon,* Johnny Weissmuller's *Tarzan,* and Laurel and Hardy.

"Antara Ibn Shaddad is playing today," Edouard said, slipping into the queue ahead of me. "Wow, you should have seen the English woman I saw today in men's trousers!" The ticket collector let us in while listening open-mouthed to Edouard's description of Miss Sylvia's rear end. Inside the packed and deafeningly noisy theatre, we were barely able to find two seats together. While a long series of technicolour advertisements was being shown, vendors walked up and down aisles littered with Coca Cola, sweets, and English chewing gum and the audience spat, fought, and jostled for places. Then the lights were dimmed, the young crown prince appeared on the screen with the Iraqi flag at his back, and we stood and sang the national anthem. The lights went out. The tension peaked. "Antara, Antara," came a wild, rhythmic chant accompanied by ominous gestures. Carried away, Edouard began to shout hypnotically too.

There was something frightening about the mob and its cries. I had never felt so out-of-place before. I thought again of Hizkel and began to yell "Antara" in order also to combat the delayed reaction of the previous night's fear. And indeed I seemed to have supernatural powers for with my first cry Antara Ibn Shaddad rode onto the screen on his white horse, a black keffiyeh fluttering about his neck. He was greeted by jubilant whistles, as if he had appeared with his cavalry to lead the audience in a holy war against the English, the Zionists, the heretic Shi'ites and all other latter-day infidels. Eyes glowed in the dark; hands tightened on imaginary swords; throats sounded the battle-cry as if each spectator were the fabled Antara himself. As though in a bad dream I heard a voice call out: "Get the Jewish dogs!" Or was it just my nerves? If only I could be like Edouard, who was screaming his head off with the rest of them. But it was no dream. A flurry of blows rained down on us.

"I'll handle this!" yelled the usher. But the band of Antarites blocked his way.

"*Behiyyat Muhammed,* we're Moslems!" cried Edouard in the Moslem accent he tried to cultivate.

"Jews!" the mob shouted, spitting at us. "Foreigners!" It suddenly dawned on me that, with our European clothes and light skins, that was exactly what we looked like. Although we ourselves did not feel it, they knew. It had never occurred to me before that I was as conspicuous to them as they were to me, that they could sniff me out as surely as I could smell one of them.

"Let me through!" shouted the usher. Our assailants were trying to seize our schoolbags and roller skates while crowding us towards the corner near the lavatories. *This is it,* I thought. They would strip us and bugger us just like in the stories I had heard. My mind went blank.

"Antara! Antara! Antara! Antara!" Little could I have guessed that the great horseman himself would save us from a cruel fate. Brandishing the sword of Islam he was now cutting down his enemies in a flashing dance of metal and as the spellbound crowd rose to its feet, threatening to make the balcony above us collapse beneath its weight, the usher grabbed us and whispered: "Run for it, you little bastards, before you're slaughtered and I'm blamed." Quickly he hustled us outside, and we kept running through the Christian and Moslem streets until we were out of breath. In the end Edouard stopped in front of a sign that said in flowing script NO URINATING AGAINST THE WALL and proceeded to do just that, a devilish look in his eyes. I stood as far off as I could. The sign could have been the work of Shi'ites, who abhorred all contact with us unclean Jews and gave us a wide berth when they passed us on their way to prayer. They were so obsessed with purity that after urinating they wiped themselves with a piece of chalkstone kept in their pockets for that purpose.

"You maniac, you could have got us both killed!" I yelled at Edouard, who loved danger and was addicted to fights and scrapes, when he caught up with me. Generally, he waited for his chance to flaunt his strength in the streets after school, challenging the other boys and cursing or hitting them because he was afraid to show off in front of Salem Effendi. More than once our friendship had got me into trouble, from which I did not always emerge unscathed. Although I would have thought that I was as used to the fear of Moslems as I was to the colour of my blood, I began to shake in the middle of el-Rashid Street. Perhaps my father was right. We needed guns to defend ourselves. I had a black eye, and Edouard a bloody nose. I could feel his chagrin at not having passed for a Moslem.

"So what do you think of the masses now, comrade?" I asked.

"They're downtrodden and illiterate. They need to be educated."

"About Jews! They didn't attack you for being a Communist."

"The imperialists provoke them."

"And you, comrade, propose to spend the rest of your life among them?"

"This is my country."

"God help you."

I had to get home, wash, and change my clothes. It had taken me until my bar mitzvah to persuade my father to let me come home late after school so that I could spend time in the library or with friends, and I couldn't afford to bump into him now. He preferred having me in his shop where he could see me immersed in some book or listening to him talk with his cronies, and it would be foolish to lose my hard-earned freedom because of a brawl with some Moslems.

Once back in Taht el-Takya, Edouard and I ducked into the community bathhouse, washed each other's backs, combed our hair, and did our best to look presentable. As we neared our street I found myself praying that Hizkel had been freed and was home. I broke into a run and was quickly disabused.

In bed that night I broke out laughing again. My stiff pecker hot in my hand, I exchanged my fears of a fate like Shafik Addas's to consoling fantasies of Miss Sylvia, whom I pictured learning to speak Arabic with the accent of a Baghdadi Moslem.

6.

It was more than a year since Miss Sylvia had received Stad Nawi's telegram informing her of her appointment to a teaching position at the Frank Ini School. She was very excited. The thought of Baghdad, the fabled City of the Caliphs, brought to mind the smell of the oriental spices that her father had carried home with him from Transjordan when she was a child. Although compared to her native London Baghdad was a provincial town of barely half-a-million people, she couldn't wait to see its mosques, bazaars, and minarets that she knew from picture books. Within a month she was packed and ready, and braving her fear of aeroplanes, she boarded a BOAC flight with her two suitcases. Disembarking in Baghdad, she felt the heat strike her like an oven. The same Arabs who had talked all the way in loud voices and caused her to hate every minute of the flight now breathed down her neck and shoved her along the passenger ramp, and the white sun blinded her and made her skin feel like glass. Nor was the heat any less fierce inside the terminal, where the Mr Effendi mentioned in Stad Nawi's telegram was not there to meet her as promised and everyone ogled her. After clearing customs and passport control, she took a taxi to the Hotel Semiramis. The lobby was occupied by men only. One, tall and thin with dark hair, a prominent nose, and a Clark Gable moustache (Miss Sylvia had seen Clark Gable in person when he visited Northampton during the war and she and her fellow students had gone to catch a glimpse of him), came over and said:

"My name is Salim Effendi. You must be Miss Sylvia Perlman."

Miss Sylvia smiled with relief, shook his hand warmly, and said that she was thrilled and would like awfully much to go and see exotic Baghdad at once. Her new acquaintance smiled back at her with a mouth full of white teeth, advised her to rest while the day was cooling off, and promised to return in two hours.

Miss Sylvia went to her room and showered, then lay down and tried unsuccessfully to sleep. In the end she rose, put on her white trousers and a thin, transparent blouse, and went back down to the lobby. Salim Effendi gave her a wondering look when he arrived, an enigmatic smile beneath his moustache. She noticed that he had a rosy scar on his right cheek.

There were hardly any women on el-Rashid Street, Baghdad's main thoroughfare, and those in evidence were cloaked from head to toe in shawls and black dresses such as Miss Sylvia had seen only in films and on the aeroplane. All trailed two paces behind their husbands, who stared smirkingly at her with big eyes that travelled from her face to her bosom and down to her thighs, lingered on her posterior, and continued to her feet. Although she felt naked beneath their X-ray vision, their appreciative attention pleased her and she smiled politely back, causing them to cluster even more closely around her. The men laughed and jostled each other, talking in loud voices and elbowing Salim Effendi aside until she was encircled by an expanding ring that spilled into the traffic and followed her in a grand promenade. Gradually she felt that their stares were stripping her bare. The ring tightened around her, the harsh, repellent smells of sour sweat and cheap tobacco given off by the oddly dressed men in their long robes and heavily buckled belts making her gasp. Some wore turbans. Most were barefoot. "Mr Effendi, please help me," she begged. Only then did he plunge into the circle of men and speak to them in guttural tones, smiling and making calming hand motions. "The people here are not accustomed to women in trousers and thin blouses," he told her when he rejoined her. "They've never seen anyone so blonde and fair-skinned outside a film."

He spirited her away from the crowd on the pavement and into the street while explaining that it was a tautology to say "Mr Effendi". Heat-stricken horses pulled slow wagons, and carriages and cars crawling bumper to bumper honked endlessly, sometimes colliding in a flurry of curses and even blows while their passengers reached out hairy hands to her and blew whistling kisses. One man stuck out his middle finger in an unfamiliar gesture, to which she responded with a courteous nod. Thirsty and breathless from the heat, she asked Salim Effendi to stop at a café. He smiled. "Not many cafés in Baghdad welcome women," he said without halting. The noise was oppressive, the smelly air a repulsive, sticky cloud. Barefoot children in torn clothes ran after a low wagon carrying baskets of apples, from which they were brutally beaten back as they tried to steal some fruit.

Miss Sylvia glanced imploringly at Salim Effendi, who had a faraway look. By now, despite his impeccable English with its astonishing if slightly unreal public-school accent, she was beginning to be afraid of him too. It seemed impossible to believe that he had never been to London or studied at Oxford, and that his entire knowledge of the language, as he confessed, came from the British Institute on Al-Wazariyya Street, popular magazines, and the pages of Shakespeare. And yet while he did not strike her as unenterprising, how could he merely go on smiling without lifting a finger to protect her?

As though finally noticing her distress, he pointed at a bus. "A red double-decker!" she exclaimed, beaming like a child who has just been given a familiar toy. A group of boys ran like daredevils beside it, teasing the driver. They were so close to the vehicle's wheels that Miss Sylvia tensed with fright, but Salim Effendi casually ignored them and steered her towards a market place where two blind beggars held out their hands and a group of girls dressed in rags rummaged through rubbish bins and crammed food slops and rotten fruit into their mouths. Pressed around a kerosene cart harnessed to a donkey, a crowd of people waiting to fill oil cans was holding up the traffic. Miss Sylvia followed Salim Effendi into a warren of narrow alleys where the balconied houses nearly touched overhead and each apparent dead end split into more alleys at the last moment, emerging now and then into little squares in each of which something was being sold: mats, fabrics, rugs, spices, vegetables, fruit, meat, poultry, fish – a cornucopia she had never seen in London. Men bargained at the tops of their voices, followed by women with baskets on their heads and veils that it was impossible for her to see through. All around her, heartrending and repellent, were the poor, the blind, the limbless, and the lame. How would Salim Effendi find his way back to the main street? Somewhere she had read about the palaces of the Caliphs that had entrances but no exits, and she felt a great fatigue. Leaden-legged and dizzy, Miss Sylvia took Salim Effendi's arm and to his amazement leaned on him while half-astonished, half-baleful glances were sent her way. When she told him that she was thirsty, Salim Effendi shouted at someone who approached and filled a tin cup with a brown beverage from a large tank strapped to his back. Miss Sylvia tried to ignore the taste and smell of it and concentrate on its refreshing coolness and, meanwhile, Salim Effendi went over to a stand, bargained for some dates, apples, and bananas, and paid for them. In no time he was besieged by a screaming swarm of boys vying for the privilege of carrying his purchase, which was finally awarded to a runny-eyed youth who flashed a happy, buck-toothed grin at his commission.

They headed out of the souk. As she struggled to orient herself, Miss Sylvia wondered how anyone could find his way in this place that had not a single street sign or house number. A wave of panic swept over her. What on earth was she doing here? She felt a desperate longing for London. In front of her a boy lay writhing on the ground to a wild clatter of drums. "That's nothing compared to Bahia," said Salim Effendi, promising to take her to a performance of the famous belly dancer. It was dark by the time they reached the hotel. In its restaurant they were served mutton and a greasy, hotly spiced red soup the likes of which she had never encountered. While Salim Effendi ate voraciously, smacking his lips, Miss Sylvia touched only the thin, round pitta bread. He wished her a good night and said that he would come in the morning to take her to the Frank lni School.

Her room faced a lawn that ran to the banks of the Tigris. Even the river smelled differently from the Thames. The stars shone so much more brightly than any she had seen before that she felt as if she could look at them forever. On the far bank of the river some dogs, so she thought, were howling mysteriously; she could not tell from their long, coughing wails that they were jackals. Feeling afraid, she decided to keep the lights on and checked the door several times to make sure that it was locked.

At four a.m. she was awakened with a start by the voices of the muezzins crying *Allah akbar* from the minarets of the mosques and could not fall asleep again. She sat by the window until dawn, when strange bird song and the pining of doves filled the air. The only sound she recognized from London was the whistle of a train.

In the days that followed, Salim Effendi did his best to help Miss Sylvia get used to her new home. Stad Nawi, the school's rector, had asked him to look after her. "I don't want her thinking like some British colonialist that we've just come down from the trees," he said. Salim Effendi escorted her to Mackenzie's, the English bookstore, and bought her several English histories of Iraq. He took her to the National Museum to see the archaeological exhibits, went sailing with her on the river, strolled with her in the public gardens that seemed so English, and accompanied her to the best stores – Uruzdi Beg, Hasu Ahwan, and even Spinneys, the British emporium where you could find expensive foods and beverages from London. At night they saw a film, or else went to the tourist shows at the Hotel Semiramis where Iraqi performers appeared. It was there that Miss Sylvia first saw Bahia and sensed at once that Salim Effendi was in love with her. Night after night he took Miss Sylvia to see the famous belly dancer, and although she knew that he enjoyed her company — how many Iraqi men had the opportunity to be seen in public with a blonde Englishwoman? — she had no illusions about why he was doing it. Miss Sylvia had nothing but praise for Salim Effendi's quick intellect. He had a sure grasp of social and economic issues and a deep understanding of Iraq and the Middle East, while she for her part intrigued him with her pro-Communist sympathies and her desire to see Iraq freed from the yoke of British imperialism.

When he wanted to know more about her and what had brought her to the country, she told him about her father's army service in Transjordan. As a child visiting him there with her mother and sister she had been enchanted by the sun, the light, the camels, and the exotic clothes. She had loved the dates and oranges and listened eagerly to her father's stories about Lawrence of Arabia and the Arabs' disappointment when their revolt did not lead to independence. Back in England she began to read up on the area, which she resolved to revisit one day. Miss Sylvia left school at the beginning of World War II, took an intensive, two-year teacher-training course, and taught for a while at a girls' school before going on to university, where she fell in with Communist students. The Soviet Union seemed to her a beacon of light in the war against fascism; it was the time of Stalingrad, high ideals, and the fiery speeches of Emmanuel Shinwell in Trafalgar Square. She liked having the future on her side. Sometimes she and her friends would break stirringly into Russian songs, one of which, about a flower in the snow, she now sang to Salim Effendi. She had kept looking for a way to return to the Orient. Salim Effendi told his Moslem friend Tarik about Miss Sylvia, and the two decided to enlist her in their revolutionary activities. It was only then that Salim Effendi revealed to her that he was a leader of the banned Communist Party. He was careful to avoid all physical intimacy with her so as not to increase the risk he had taken, and in any case, he was too emotionally involved with Bahia. Still, he continued to go out with our English teacher, and he promised to take her to one of the concerts being given in Baghdad by the great Egyptian singer Muhammed Abd el-Muttalib as soon as there was a performance that women were admitted to.

7.

Gripping a shepherd's staff and dressed in a long white robe and a *takiyyeh* or peasant cap, Muhammed Abd el-Muttalib stood in the middle of the stage, his eyes focused on a distant point and his deep voice from the land of the Nile pitched to the longings of the dwellers by the Tigris. *Ya habibt el-'alb, irga'i,* "O thou love of my heart, come back to me," he sang, and when he crooned *Ya levli, ya evni* in his inimitable country style the audience turned its misty eyes towards the doors as if expecting to see his desert sweetheart ride in on a gaily bedecked camel and leap into his arms. The *kamanjati* or violin player struck an electrifying vibrato. One could almost smell the faraway enchantment. The sweat dripped from Abd el-Muttalib's glowing face and neck onto his robe. and with a last flourish of his staff he was gone. There was a moment of silence, followed by rapt sighs. Although Salim Effendi had long awaited the visiting Egyptian's performance, had dreamed of it and tried to picture it, the reality had surpassed all imagining. He had sat through it spellbound, downing glasses of arrack and shouting bravos of *tabarrak allah* in an Egyptian accent with his arm around his friend Tarik, who rocked back and forth in a trance. *Ya habibt el-'alb, irga'i,* murmured Salim Effendi, as though diving to the depths of self-oblivion. For once he had laid aside the critical detachment that listening to Western music had taught him. He was one with the audience, an Arab Jew. The sons of Moses and Muhammed were brothers. They had the same God, they were both the seed of Abraham – what else mattered? The stinging sense of not belonging was gone. Not for the first time, he declaimed for Tarik the words of the Hebrew Andalusian poem:

Yea, we woke stunned by friendship's wine,
Too weak to walk on perfume-scented fields of wildflowers
Beneath a sun that donned its cloak of blue.

How much beauty there was in these simple lines, and how much power to bring hearts together. And how well he had rendered them into Arabic, as if the source and his translation were brother and sister! *Tabarrak allah,* he praised himself.

"Who wrote that?" asked Tarik. For some reason he could never remember.

"Musa ibn Ezra. When will you read his poems with me, *ya* Tarik?" asked Salim Effendi, slapping his friend's back.

"We'll find time, we'll find time," replied Tarik.

The next act was Bahia's. The interval was a long one. While running his tongue over lips parched by the smoke-filled room, Salim Effendi waited anxiously for her, the devourer of his days and nights, to appear. Leaving untouched the black olives that he had asked the waiter to bring he kept crunching ice cubes with his frozen teeth as if to quench an inner flame. Suddenly his glance brightened. Bahia burst onstage with little stamps of her feet that trod into dust the country songs of Abd el-Muttalib, her breasts overflowing their sequined dress, a smouldering presence that set hearts on fire and freed hungry tigers from their cages. Bouquets of flowers landed at her feet. Salim Effendi imbibed the sight of her like a cool draught of springwater; his eyes traced the curves of her legs, of her smooth, swelling thighs, of her firm belly with its rippling arabesques that enticed and eluded one at once. Purple tassels, as soft as the dawn, concealed as they revealed. Ah, to be one of them and die! To be the floor beneath her quick feet! To lick her sweat, plunging into the Moslem pool of her! Only thus could he break the chains that kept him, the Jew, apart.

As he did every night, tall, strapping Sheikh Jassem rose to his feet, removed his gilded headband, wrapped it in a necklace of gold coins, and flung it at Bahia's feet. Then, drawing his sword from its scabbard, he cleared his table with a single stroke, leaped on top of it, pressed the blade to his forehead and began to shout rhythmically, "O Bahia, we are yours!" As though in a frenzy, the audience rose and took up the chant. Salim Effendi stared at the gleaming sword through a fog of alcohol. Allah had saved his life! Had he climbed onstage as he had meant to and so much as touched Bahia, he would be a head shorter now. *No, she is not my pot of honey,* he thought, laying a brother-drunk's head on the shoulder of his friend who was sitting with his eyes shut. "Tarik, why don't we invite Bahia for a cruise on the Tigris?" he asked.

"*We?*" The Moslem roused himself from his stupor.

"Yes, we," said Salim Effendi undaunted. Arm in arm, the two men staggered backstage where they encountered a mob. The musicians had already laid down their instruments and stripped off their ties and jackets, and now they stood stretching themselves while white-coated waiters circulated with full trays. Salim Effendi looked for Bahia, his spirits flagging when he failed to see her. A band of sheikhs, led by the fierce Jassem, had surrounded Abd el-Muttalib who was sitting with his shirt unbuttoned, his heavy robe and felt cap discarded, while sipping strong tea and saying "Thank you" over and over. Salim Effendi tottered helplessly among the crowd and, with a last glance at Tarik, handed the Egyptian the bouquet meant for Bahia. "A gift from your Iraqi brothers," he said. Sheikh Jassem looked at him disdainfully. Never in his life had he seen a man give another man flowers. Abd el-Muttalib glanced up and said in a warm, reassuring voice, *Shukran, shukran, ahlan wa-sahlan.*

"We've come to invite you for a cruise on the Tigris," said Salim Effendi.

"*Willak,* get lost!" snarled the sheikh.

"Sheikh Jassem has already invited me, but with his kind permission you can join us," replied Abd el-Muttalib tactfully.

"As you wish," said the sheikh, his eyes whiplashing the intruder. "You are my guest."

The sheikh's bodyguard whispered in his ear.

"Bahia will be coming with us too," added Sheikh Jassem triumphantly.

"*Ya salaam,*" sighed Abd el-Muttalib.

Salim Effendi's heart leaped. As the party was not ready to leave yet, he slipped off to the lavatory which stank from the badly aimed urine of more than one drunk. There he straightened his tie, reparted his hair, and studied his large nose, which definitely did not belong on his face. Something needed to be done about that damned scar, too! He took a last look in the mirror, and then, as though reconciled to his fate, flashed his Clark Gable smile, combed his Clark Gable moustache, and stepped back out.

A large throng was waiting by the exit for a close-up glimpse of Bahia, who emerged tall, stately, and effortlessly fresh-looking. Her white dress caressed the lines of her body and brought out the contours of her thighs. All bowed slightly and stepped back for her. What power she had! Subdued by it, not one admirer dared fling coins at her low neckline or proclaim his passion for her. Salim Effendi shivered as she passed him. He had never been so near to her. He turned to the right and tried giving his face its mirror-trained smile that made women swoon, but it felt frozen in a tight, spiteful spasm. Bahia shook Abd el-Muttalib's hand warmly and said to him:

"Ah, you desert nightingale! What an inspiration you are to me."

"And you, O princess of the dance, were maddening." The two vanished into the large carriage of the sheikhs. Salim Effendi swallowed hard and climbed into a second one with Tarik and the musicians. From his breast pocket he took a pint of arrack in a silver flask and handed it to Tarik. His friend gulped from it noisily, wiped his mouth with the back of his hand, and returned the flask to Salim, who took two large, throat-burning swallows. *Courage*, he told himself. *You are a revolutionary and they are barbarous desert sheikhs.* He pushed back the carriage roof to let in the cool midnight air while thinking of Bahia in the one ahead of him, squeezed between two sheikhs and wanting only to escape the vice-like grip of their knees, the tobacco-stink of their mouths, the flat edge of their swords in the cinctures of their robes. She knew the kind of men they were and what they were capable of. Salim Effendi was sure that she must loathe Sheikh Jassem, who was sitting on her right, pressed tight against her. What could she feel but revulsion for his wild sensuality, the vengeful poisons that bubbled in his blood, the hot haste with which he had killed a man a year ago when she had performed at this same hotel? Although the sight of the victim's blood had transfixed her like a snake, the sheikh had made her go on dancing before permitting the corpse to be

61

dragged out. Knowing that he was a good friend of the minister of the interior, the police did not dare intervene or arrest him, and Bahia danced on.

While the duties of her profession often obliged Bahia to suffer the whims of rich sheikhs, she refused to accompany them to their tents or to spend a night with any of them. Not even Sheikh Jassem, who waited for her after every performance, had been able to overcome her resistance. "The Virgin", he called her, and indeed, her private life was an impenetrable mystery that made him swallow his pride anew every night.

Bahia, thought Salim Effendi, could not have forgotten Sheikh Jassem's daughter Suham, who had been desperately in love with the Lebanese Christian singer Bashir Sam'an. One night, after a performance of his in Baghdad, Suham managed to slip into his hotel room, where the profligate Christian, who had grown up in freer climes, succumbed to her charms. The blood stains found on the sheets the next morning were a clear sign of the loss of her innocence, and one of her many brothers cut her down as she tried to flee the room. Her corpse was still warm when a band of her fellow tribesmen rushed in, undressed the Lebanese singer, raped him, mutilated his member, and locked him in his room. Eventually, broken in body and spirit, he escaped and returned to Lebanon, where he never sang or appeared publicly again. The Lebanese government lodged an official protest and shut its borders for a month to Iraqi citizens, and even though three years had elapsed since then, Salim Effendi was certain that the mere sight of the brutal sheikh was enough to turn Bahia's stomach.

And so, when they descended at last from their carriages and boarded the white boat, and Salim Effendi saw Bahia run a hand through her hair and smile to Abd el-Muttalib, he was sure she must be composing herself while turning to the Egyptian for comfort. Sheikh Jassem ordered the crew to cast anchor by one of the islands in the Tigris where a fisherman grilled huge river fish over a fire. A sharp smell of curry mingled with the hot, sticky vapours of the fish, from whose soft, fatty belly the sheikh tore and loudly swallowed a strip of flesh before passing around the large tray. Drops of fat gathered in his carefully barbered beard. Sitting off to one side with Abd el-Muttalib, Bahia – or so Salim Effendi thought – curled her lips in disgust. He kept his eyes on her, trying to listen to their conversation, and gave a start when she mentioned the name of the great Egyptian belly dancer Samiyya Jamal. In his imagination he heard her telling the Egyptian of her dream to study in Cairo, where she would be discovered and rescued from this sordid life of sheikhs and hotels. Perhaps she was even asking him to take her there and arrange a performance in the palace of King Farouk, or a starring role in an Egyptian film.

Salim Effendi wreaked his passion on a fish tail, licking its fatty skin and sucking its bones while waiting impatiently for Bahia to dance. He wanted to see her undulate by the fire and sorely wished that her tête-à-tête with the Egyptian would be over. After a while he poured arrack over his hands to get rid of the smell of the fish, took a deep breath of the moist river air, and went over to join them, dropping the names of all the Egyptian performers he could think of and of anyone else the latest gossip confirmed them being seen with. Such talk, however, was not to Sheikh Jassem's liking, and although Bahia and Abd el-Muttalib would have been happy to go on chatting, he insisted that the nightingale of the desert sing again. The Egyptian signalled to the musicians, and as the boat drifted

63

slowly down the Tigris in the light of a full moon, he began.

"Thou askest why I love thee – O strange question I shan't answer," crooned Abd el-Muttalib in his tremolo that was unequalled among all the country singers of the Levant. To Salim Effendi it appeared that he was singing to Bahia alone. The straight arrack in the glasses of the sheikhs was as water to a desert wind, and Sheikh Jassem grunted with pleasure and pinched Bahia's cheek. She shrank from him, and Abd el-Muttalib, fearful of what might happen, asked her to dance while he sang. Bahia jumped to her feet, tied to her waist the keffiyeh spread by the sheikh around her shoulders, and flexed her neck slowly as if it had a life of its own. Bobbing coquettish breasts, she fluttered her fingers in the night-blue air at the sheikh, who moved hungrily towards her like a baby to the nipple, then retreated and dodged his outstretched arms. The Virgin! No woman could withstand him – yet for two whole years she had remained obdurate, toying with him every night from the stage and slipping off. *He'll kill her in the end,* thought Salim Effendi, watching the sheikh's eyes.

The black flute player blew into his wooden reed, sending its husky notes down the Tigris. Then the rhythm changed all at once and Abd el-Muttalib sang amorously: "I bow my head to your beauty and your soul sails through my dreams." Once again Salim Effendi felt that he was singing to Bahia alone, but this time Sheikh Jassem seemed to notice it too. *He'll kill them both,* thought Salim Effendi, glassily murmuring the lyrics while shaking his head to the music. *Ya allah,* how he longed to smell her, to bore into her, to subside in her and be reborn from her body like a babe. He clapped his hands and clicked his fingers to her movements while the flautist winked encouragement, feeling both a great weariness and a great peace.

"This is Paradise," said Salim Effendi out loud. *God of the Tigris,* he prayed, *make this night last forever.* He, Salim Effendi, scorned and dispossessed by Big Imari, was in a pleasure boat with a desert sheikh, a famed Egyptian singer, and Bahia! He was one of them at last. For years he had dreamed of this moment, and now here he was, casting into the river the sins of separateness, of the *Farhood,* of the slaughter of the Jews in a Europe he had never been to, of the new Jewish country that hounded him. These were his people; their songs were his songs and Bahia's rhythms were those of his own blood. This night was proof that the children of Moses and Muhammed could build a new world together. If only those sons-of-whores in Jerusalem had not declared their state and ruined everything! He was with Bahia at last. Perhaps for one day, or at least for one night, she would even be his. Was it only the arrack that made everything seem so simple? Once his body, the flesh of Isaac, joined with hers, the flesh of Ishmael, the reconciliation would be complete. He cast a longing glance at her, and as the Egyptian sang his heart out in *Ya leyli, ya eyni* he found himself mouthing the verse from the Psalms, "I beseech Thee, O Lord, grant salvation." Suddenly the boat rocked. *It's just a rough spot on the river,* he thought, *we'll be out of it in a minute.* But the craft continued to yaw. Glasses and bottles fell to the deck with a thud. Bahia stopped dancing and spread her legs to catch her balance. The flute cracked and went off tune. Abd el Muttalib stopped singing and said:

"*Ma'alesh, ya ihwan.* It's nothing, my brothers. The Nile has its eddies too."

"No doubt," said Salim Effendi, bending to clear away the broken glass before Bahia cut her feet on it.

"And what is my brother's name?" asked Abd el-Muttalib.

"Rahamim," answered Tarik for his friend.

"A Jew? In my boat?" Sheikh Jassem leaped up and drew his sword. "You dog and son of dogs, you!" Both Abd el-Muttalib and Bahia rushed to keep the sheikh from Salim Effendi who cowered at the bottom of the boat, unable even to jump into the dark river.

"Let me at him and I'll slice him to shreds!" cried Sheikh Jassem.

Salim Effendi knew that he was looking at the Angel of Death in a Bedouin cloak. It would have been nothing for the sheikh to strike down his two protectors as well. Bahia laid her hand on Sheikh Jassem's arm. "It would be a pity, O sheikh," she said, "to spoil such a marvellous evening for one miserable Jew. Let's put him ashore and continue."

8.

During the few minutes that it took the boat to return, Salim
Effendi was faint with fear. When they reached the dock he rose
from his crouching position and sprang ashore without looking
back, abased to the depths of his soul. Tarik did not join him.
And why should he? He was a Moslem, a blood brother, not a
cringing Jew. How right Hizkel Imari had been when he wrote
in his long essay Tolerated Minorities and Tolerating Majorities:
"The very fact of toleration is a form of discrimination." And
the very fact that Tarik remained in the boat proved that Hizkel
had been right about the moral toll that this took of the
tolerators. But did Tarik have any idea what he had been made
to look like? Salim Effendi walked to the main road, turned
right, and started across the King Faisal Bridge. Only then did
he stop, lean against the railing, and gaze back at the brightly-lit
boat sailing away down the river. Once again he saw Death
dance before his eyes, his lids pulsing even when he covered
them with his hands. The night, which had started out as one of
the most wonderful in his life, could easily have been his last.
And all because he was a Jew. An outsider. A boat without a
river. It was like an ineradicable birthmark, this Jewishness of
his. He would never be allowed to forget it. Not by any of them
– the illiterate sheikhs, the incitable mob, even his own Party
comrades. Someone would always see to it that he was
reminded of the religion that he had inherited like the colour of

his eyes. Absurdly – for its ceremonies and commandments no longer meant a thing to him – he could even be killed for it. Long ago he had come to the conclusion that kissing a Torah scroll or blowing a ram's horn at New Year were like any other primitive rite – an Indian war dance in a film, for example. Although he still sometimes went to Abu Kabi's for a holiday meal, mainly for the good food, and perhaps also because of the odd feeling of loneliness that enveloped him on such days, he hadn't entered a synagogue, fasted on Yom Kippur, or refrained from smoking on the Sabbath for years. And yet could it be that his new faith was no less of a phantasm, that his belief in equality, in human brotherhood, and in men's capacity to change was a delusion too? Was human nature inherently tribal and indisposed to sharing with others? Right now it seemed to him that the most solid of Communist dogmas were so much chaff in the wind. Perhaps he should chuck it all in and go far away, to Czechoslovakia or Bulgaria; perhaps this East that he lived in would never be as ripe for revolution as that one. If only he could hear the warm, familiar voice of the Red Armenian now, quoting the Chinese sage: "My dear Salim! This too is a voyage of a thousand miles and must begin with a single step." Ah, what a pity the Red Armenian was in prison! How he missed him.

A cab looking for late-night revellers pulled up beside him on the bridge leading to el-Rashid Street, but he waved the coachman off and continued walking, The notes of the *kamanja* and of Abd el-Muttalib's yearning still echoed in his ears. *Ya habibt el-'alb, irga'i:* why had Tarik given them his Jewish name, Rahamim? He himself had all but forgotten that he had been named after his great-grandfather. Was it a slip of the tongue? The arrack? Or perhaps envy of the impression he had made on

Bahia? Maybe it was nothing but a simple eruption of long-buried hatred of Jews. He must ask him. No, he would not. If even Tarik could not be trusted, who could be? They had seemed like brothers. His mother, bless her memory, was right. A goy was always a goy.

Salim Effendi struggled with these heresies, unbefitting a Communist like him. The night was drawing to an end, and he quickened his steps and soon reached the entrance to the Jewish quarter. Sounds of dawn came from the souk: the gas stoves bubbling in the teahouses, the rumble of the ovens heating in the bakeries, the clatter of wagon wheels bearing the fresh produce for the fruit and vegetable sellers. The first early birds, his tobacconist Hiyawi among them, were on their way to synagogue for the morning prayer. If only he were a believer like his father, he would join them and say the *hagomel,* the blessing for being rescued from great danger. It made him smile to think that he still knew the meaning of the Hebrew words, and could recite them with understanding. His talent for languages had served him well as a boy in Hebrew school, and he had even been given special lessons in poetry and philosophy that were not taught to the other pupils. And then both his parents had died when he was young and, angry with God, he had lost his faith.

No, it was certainly not Allah who had saved his life tonight. If he should thank anyone, it was Bahia. The need to possess her was now greater than ever. It would be the best revenge on Sheikh Jassem. And on Tarik too. Salim Effendi turned into Brothel Lane, the street on which he lived, loosened his tie and the top button of his shirt, hurried upstairs to his small apartment, threw his clothing on the bed, and stood for a long while beneath a cold shower. Then he took a hunk of cheese from the white cloth hanging on the inner terrace, soaked it in water, added a teaspoon of salt, crushed and stirred the mixture, and drained it as a remedy for a hangover. Like it or not, he had to go to work. One thing he was not was a slacker. He shaved, put on the light suit that always bettered his mood, descended to the corner teahouse, and drank his usual two cups of hot, sweet tea. Glancing at his watch, he decided that there was still time to clear his head by walking to the school, a considerable distance by any account.

Salim Effendi sat in the Najwa Café, where he and Tarik met most days after work. True, he had sworn not to go today after the night he had been through, yet at the usual time he found himself at his usual table. What made him feel so close to Tarik? Was it the Party, among whose future leaders they were counted? The common dream of a revolutionary Iraq? Their drunken nights on the town and its brothels? Or did he need Tarik as a Moslem on whom his own sense of Iraqiness depended? He was never sure if Tarik felt the same closeness to him or simply found it convenient to have a Jewish friend who liked to treat him and shower him with praise and warmth. And perhaps, too, his being a Jew meant that Tarik needn't consider him a serious rival.

Salim Effendi remembered his first meeting with his friend in the offices of El-Hizb el-Watani el-Dimokrati, the National Democratic Party, whose aim was to free Iraq of British rule and institute a parliamentary system. By dint of long, hard work he had advanced through its ranks, only to discover to his surprise, when turned down for a high position, that Jews were hated in the organization no less than Englishmen. As aware as he was of the dangers of ethnic chauvinism, he had never dreamed that his fellow democrats could despise an entire people, if such indeed the Jews were – and so, when the Zionists went to war to create a state in Palestine and the NDP joined the anti-Jewish agitation of the nationalist right, he felt that its atmosphere had become unbreathable. Only a Moslem could be at home in such an organization, in which not all the Iraqi identity cards in the world could help a Jew, and although the NDP's leader Kamel el-Chadirchi was a genuinely good-hearted liberal, Salim Effendi resigned from the party. It was sheer chance that Tarik also had a quarrel with el-Chadirchi at the same time and developed new political views, which he explained to Salim Effendi while telling him of the October Revolution, the class struggle, the capitalist exploitation of labour, the writings of Marx and Engels, the leadership of Lenin and Stalin, and their solving of the problem of nationalities in the Soviet Union. Although Salim Effendi had read of these things before, he had never seriously thought about them.

One night, after staying up drinking so late at the Hotel el-Jawahiri that the manager had to throw them out, they decided to return home on foot. As they lurched arm-in-arm through the empty streets, Salim Effendi's heart welled with brotherly love and it was then that he first declaimed and translated for Tarik his favourite poem by Ibn Ezra. He was still in the midst of its first stanza when Tarik embraced him and whispered that he had a terrible secret to reveal, which Salim Effendi must swear by Moses, Jesus, and Muhammed never to breathe a word of. Only when the triple vow was besottedly uttered did Tarik disclose, in the loud tones of a drunk who thinks that the whole world is hard-of-hearing, that he had joined the illegal Communist Party and that he wanted Salim Effendi to do the same. Salim Effendi did not say yes or no. Despite all the arrack he had drunk, he was too much of an Imari to buy a pig in a poke. Inasmuch as they were brothers, he replied, he would acquaint himself with the new gospel and its prophets, especially since he was heartily sick of the old ones he had just sworn by. Tarik's response was to break into hysterical laughter and proclaim that Lenin was not only the greatest prophet since Muhammed but the one most beloved of God. In the weeks that followed, Salim Effendi read the Marxist classics and was won over by their vision of redemption. It was, he decided, his patriotic duty to join the Communist Party, a step whereby he would become a true son of Iraq and pay his dues for her water that he drank, her dates that he ate, her home that she provided him with. He felt obliged to help save his country from the colonialism of the British and the evil regime of Pasha Nuri es-Sa'id and his lackeys like Big Imari. He and Tarik celebrated the issuing of his Party card by spending all night on the Tigris, and from the next morning on he devoted himself tirelessly to every task given to him.

One day Tarik introduced him to their leader, the Red Armenian. This meeting changed Salim Effendi's life. He was captivated by the Armenian's warm, fatherly figure and by the charm and authority that he projected. He felt reborn, touched by a divine presence that made him an equal among equals, as important as anyone else. All he had wanted and never received from life until now seemed promised to him by that single audience. For the first time he believed with perfect faith that the country of his ancestor, the land of Abraham, was as much his as any Moslem's and would forever be so in the new world built upon the ruins of the old.

The Armenian proposed to Salim the mission of recruiting young Jewish intellectuals with high potential. "Our future," he said, "depends on such youngsters who have the thirst for justice in their blood and the lust for revolution in their souls." Soon after, a bloody demonstration took place in which the Communists traded blows with both the police and the NDP, and Salim Effendi found himself facing his old friends across a skirmish line. Although he was wounded in his shoulder and his cheek, which still sometimes ached from the injury, he emerged undaunted and more ready than ever to do the Armenian's bidding. Despite the unspoken rivalry between them, both he and Tarik were quickly promoted and became their leader's special protégés. And yet now, when they were hard at work on bringing about the red Messiah, Tarik had nearly cost him his life. Why? Although he had sworn to show restraint and not ask him, it was the first question to burst from his mouth when his friend entered the café.

"I wanted to make you sober up," was Tarik's answer. "I saw that you were being carried away."

"But he could have killed me for it!"

"And not for chasing her ass? You know those sons-of-bitches don't give a damn for human life. I can't get over you being in love with that whore."

"Who told you she's a whore?"

"*Wihyatak*," said Tarik. "A belly dancer like her?"

"Just look how low we've sunk. To a European like Miss Sylvia, whom we're all dying to be like, Bahia is a revered artist, while for you she's a whore! As if looking at Maria Montez and Heddy Lamar doesn't give us hard-ons too! Is Ginger Rogers also a whore because she's a dancer?"

"Your problem," said Tarik, "is that you're an innocent. You're living in the Middle East where singers and dancers sell themselves to the highest bidder."

"How can you call yourself a Communist?"

"What does that have to do with it? A Communist is a Communist and a whore is a whore!"

"Look, I'm from Arab-land just like you. I've crawled out of the same shit, and my Jewish parents, to say nothing of their Moslem neighbours, never let me forget that women were second-class creatures, and that belly dancers were whores, and that virginity was everything, and that family honour came before God's. But I try to fight all that. I fight my own parents deep inside me. I struggle to judge women fairly and not by a double standard. Isn't that what the Armenian taught us, that women are equal in all things?"

"Come off it. Do you really think that everything written in the Communist bible is the gospel truth? Find yourself a nice Jewish girl and forget about Bahia."

"I love her, you idiot," said Salim Effendi. "I want her to have my children."

"You should tell your prick to mind its own business," Tarik shot back. "A belly dancer and an intellectual? A Moslem and a Jew?"

"But listen to what you're saying! It's against everything we believe in, every value that we're trying to teach our young people. Are you telling me that you still believe in religion? In nationalism?"

"No one marries an ideology. We have enough values to teach the young without dragging in all that feminist stuff."

"But it's part of it, you can't just leave it out. Did I ever tell you about Edouard, that kid I wanted to recruit? He has a friend, Kabi, one of my Imari cousins. I once happened to hear a conversation of theirs, just by chance. The whole thing was about who was fucking whom, as if a woman were characterized by nothing but her sexual availability. Is that how you're going to teach equality?"

"So what! Show me a horny adolescent who doesn't talk like that. Take my advice and forget about Bahia. And whatever you do, keep away from the Semiramis. You're better off not being seen by that sheikh. I'll stay away too in a gesture of proletarian solitarity. We'll go to the Hotel el-Rafidain. I've heard they've got a new dancer there who can give a hard-on to a corpse."

"One like you, I suppose," said Salim Effendi.

The next day he took his life in his hands and went to Bab-el-Sheikh, the Moslem neighbourhood where Bahia lived and where a Jew did well to steer clear of. He intended not only to introduce himself and wipe out the memory of his humiliation but also to present Bahia with a large gift, confess his love, and ask her to marry him. He imagined himself married to her and pictured the house they would live in and even the sign hanging outside. "Bahia, Performing Artist & Salim Effendi, Teacher", it would say. Although it had originally been tacked on by his pupils as a joke, he had become used to the honorific "Effendi" and now thought it fitting. She would be free, he would tell her, to pursue her career; she had every right to fulfil her dreams and he could respect them, whatever they were. Moreover, he would dedicate himself body and soul to nourishing her with the fruit of the Tree of Knowledge. Was he not a teacher? What greater satisfaction could there be than having his own Eliza Doolittle to educate? The world would yet tell the tale of how, far away in the City of the Caliphs, there lived a blissful Jewish Romeo and Moslem Juliet. By Allah, what a beautiful thought! He had so much to say to her.

And yet having reached Bab-el-Sheikh, he realized that he was afraid to ask where she lived. He had hoped – quite illogically, he was forced to admit – that he would run into her in the street or spy her sitting on her terrace; a Moslem man, after all, did not simply drop in on a woman even if she was a belly dancer, especially if he did not know her family or the people she lived with. Dispiritedly he roamed the neighbourhood until he felt he was arousing suspicion, and then, mortified, he retraced his steps and went home.

For two whole weeks he did not go to see her dance. In the end, however, his longing overcame his fear, and when Tarik was sent on a secret mission to Prague he returned to the Hotel Semiramis and sat at a far table half-hidden by a supporting column. The hall was more packed than ever, for Bahia and Abd el-Muttalib had started appearing together and were drawing large crowds. Had they thought of it that night on the river when she had danced while he sang? Watching them move on the stage like a pair of love birds, Salim Effendi added some soda and ice to his arrack to dilute the poison of jealousy. It was inconceivable, he tried telling himself, that a married man like the Egyptian would abandon his family and followers for Bahia, who would pale in Egypt beside such world-bewitching greats as Tahya Karioka and Samiya Jammal. The stage had rules of its own, and up there not everything that looked like love really was.

Salim Effendi was overjoyed when Bahia seemed to look at him. He felt sure that she knew that he was there, perhaps even that he would be waiting for her afterwards, and he was convinced that it was only her fear of Sheikh Jassem, who once again did his dance on the table with his sword pressed to his brow, that kept her from acknowledging him. His senses thrilled and languished by turn with a tremulous bliss akin to the act of love. *You'll be mine*, he murmured, draining another glass of arrack, the downing of which was barely distinguishable in his mind from the possession of Bahia. Yet even now the possibility that there might be a CID agent in the audience was a reminder to keep his wits about him. The prospect of another night of raids on the Jewish quarter in a dragnet for Zionists and Communists was a sobering cold shower.

The next evening he returned to the hotel. He realized that he was no longer free to whoop or stamp his feet and carry on like a lovesick dove and that from now on he must keep his grunts of pleasure to himself. Although he wanted desperately to go backstage and bare his impassioned heart, he did not dare, and each time he waited for Bahia by the exit, praying that she would emerge alone, she came out with Abd el-Muttalib and sometimes also with the sheikh. The thought of joining them scared him to death. Why, at heart he was still the same little boy who was afraid of Big Imari! All his revolutionary posturing had failed to oust the timid Jew inside him, the cowed orphan looking for a father to protect him from the bullying cousins in his clan. He had to do something. He had to prove that no force could stand in his way. He had to marry Bahia. And yet he did nothing but sit at home mooning.

On the back page of a newspaper lying in the pile that he made a point of going through each day as a Party duty, he caught sight of a photograph of her with Abd el-Muttalib, a man with a heavy, triangular face and a moustache that seemed proportionately too thin. How could a beautiful young woman fall in love with such a man? Salim Effendi looked in the mirror. There was no doubt that he was handsomer. In fact, if it weren't for the damned scar nibbling at his cheek he could have passed for a matinée idol with his Clark Gable hair that was parted on one side, smooth and unruly at once. What did Bahia see in the portly singer who looked twice her age? Tarik was wrong. His love for her was far from hopeless. He sat back in his armchair and began to read the copy beneath the photograph.

As he did, his blood froze. "The great Iraqi performer Bahia," the story said, "is about to leave for Cairo. Rumour has it that the Egyptian singer Abd el-Muttalib is divorcing his third wife to wed the unmarried belly dancer." The print swam before Salim Effendi's eyes and he threw the paper down. That night it was all he could do to get his legs to carry him to the hotel. Not even the usual glasses of arrack could bolster him. After the performance he went to see the manager.

"Is it true?" he asked, dropping the newspaper on his desk.

"Don't you know what journalists are like, *ya* Ustaz Salim?"

"There's no smoke without fire."

"Perhaps, perhaps, but she'll get over it. That's what these performers are like. One day it's this one, the next day it's someone else."

"If she leaves, your hotel has had it."

"A puff of breath puts out a small fire. Do you think Sheikh Jassem will let her go? He'll kill her first. Surely you know his type, *ya* Ustaz Salim."

"Have you spoken to him?"

"It's not the kind of thing one speaks about, *ya* Ustaz Salim."

"But is she going to Egypt or not?"

"Perhaps for a short visit. In another two or three months, it may be. You know what it's like."

"I have to see her."

"Listen, you're a Jew, aren't you? You must know Big Imari."

"What does he have to do with it?

"She sometimes performs in his home, and the Pasha is always there when she does. A word from the Pasha and she'll forget all about it. You know what it's like, *ya* Ustaz Salim."

9.

My mother sat swinging on the *jalala,* a golden-tipped cigarette in her mouth. A morning smoke, one of her few indulgences, was a sure sign that a hard day was ahead of her.

"Where is Babba?" I asked when I returned from the bakery with the pittas.

"With the dove flyer," she said, nodding towards the roof. "The bird-grower is with the birdbrain."

I went up to the roof. My father was sitting with Abu Edouard by the dovecote, wrapped in his silk robe. "You have regards from Abu Saleh," I told them.

"Um Edouard, let's have three cups of tea," the dove flyer shouted down to his wife, a fat woman with a docile, good-natured face. Glancing over the balcony, I saw Amira doing her exercises. The dovecote, which ran the entire width of the roof, was still shut, and the cooing of the imprisoned birds made a sweet melody. Abu Edouard was a sturdy man with a round, meaty face, a broad mouth full of gold teeth, hairy ears, a Charlie Chaplin moustache, thin eyebrows that looked plucked like a woman's, and an annoying habit of pulling at his nose and snuffling back the constant urge to sneeze. A Christian physician had once told him that he was allergic to feathers and should give up his doves, but Abu Edouard had gone on flying them. "Next to Amira," he had said, "they're the biggest love of my life." He expertly blended some ground sorghum with split lentils, filled a few shallow drinking bowls with water, and asked my father:

"Why did they arrest Hizkel now? There's no smoke without fire."

"Isn't it enough to be a Jew?"

"I'm one too. Have I been touched? It's all the fault of your Movement for ruining the Moslems' faith in us. It's a catastrophe."

My father looked at him, took the *masbaha*, his string of amber worry beads, from his pocket and began to click them off loudly. As soon as he reached the last one, he started from the first again. Amira, as gorgeous as ever, brought a tray with tea and a bowl of sugar cubes, served the three of us, and flashed me her smile that I liked to think was mysterious with promise. Although I would have loved to make a play for her, what chance did I have against Abu Saleh, who was just waiting for her to grow up – not to mention her father, who was looking for a prince on a white horse to marry his Princess of the Tigris? He caressed her hand fondly when he saw me looking at her, reached for two cubes of sugar, laid them on his tongue Persian-style, took a loud swallow of tea, smacked his lips, grunted with pleasure, and said:

"We live like kings here. Why spoil it?"

"Even a golden bowl can be full of scorpions," said my father. "Did I ever tell you about the two mice? One lived in a grocer's and one in a barbershop. One day the grocer's mouse asked his friend what he ate. 'I lick the hair oil off the razors,' said the barbershop mouse. 'And I eat like a king,' said the grocer's mouse. 'Why don't you come and live at my place?' And so the two of them went back to the grocer's. That night they came out of their hole and went straight to the cheese, but just as they were about to take a big bite along came a yowling cat and made them run for their lives. As soon as it grew quiet again they tried a second time, but the cat again came running. It went on like that all night. When morning came the barbershop mouse was hungry and bleary-eyed. 'I'd rather have my peace and quiet and a few drops of dirty oil than all the food in your grocer's,' he told his friend, and back to the barbershop he went."

"Your story's got the wrong moral, Abu Kabi. It's all the fault of that bandit state of yours. It's ruined everything."

"And I suppose the people who arrested my brother were saints!"

"Plant radishes, eat radishes," said Abu Edouard.

"Have you forgotten the *Farhood?*" asked my father. "Hundreds of dead, thousands of injured – is that nothing to you?"

"If a Jew didn't forget, he couldn't live. For heaven's sake, the Christians killed six million! If the Moslems slaughtered a few of us too, that's no more than they do to each other all the time."

My father bit his lip. "They'll be hanging us all soon."

"You think Israel is safer than Baghdad? A new war could break out there any day."

"A Jew has self-respect there. He has a Jewish army, a Jewish government, a Jewish state."

"How can you believe that the Arabs will forget Palestine? Jerusalem is there, the holy mosque, the sacred stone. The Prophet's grandson Hussein was killed thirteen hundred years ago and the Shi'ites still mourn for him."

"That's what makes our situation so dangerous," said my father, turning Abu Edouard's words against him.

"We'll survive this too. We'll bribe whom we have to and let it blow over. Before you know it, the military regime will be gone."

"When the dog dies, the dog's curs take his place," said my father. "We Jews never learn our lesson. We're supposed to be a wise people, but I'm not so sure of it any more. For two thousand years we've dreamed of our own country, and now that we have it— "

"We can't afford to take such risks," Abu Edouard interrupted him. "We're a small people. We're just so much spit in the river."

"You don't believe in the victory of Zionism?"

"What victory? Our whole history is one long day of mourning." Abu Edouard opened the door of the dovecote. Dozens of cackling, cooing doves crowded through it. Some circled above him, vying to perch on his shoulders. Flushed and beaming, he stroked them as if they were his children and scattered their feed about the roof. They swooped down on it, pecking greedily with their beaks and hopping quarrelsomely from pile to pile. Abu Edouard measured them with a single glance that took in every one of them, black, brown, grey, speckled, and white. One of his two black doves strutted regally up to him, clambered on to his shoulder, and jumped from there to his head. He brushed the dove off and held it in his palm, running his finger over its head and long neck while relishing the silky texture of its plumage. "There's nothing more beautiful or noble than a dove," he said to me. "*Wallah,* you should learn to fly them."

I scattered a handful of feed over the roof but no doves settled down on me, although I would have loved one to land on my shoulder. Once, when I was seven and someone asked me what I wanted to be when I grew up, I had answered: a dove flyer. The very thought of such a Moslem occupation was enough to give my mother, who made no bones about loathing Abu Edouard, a fit. But my father had no objection and looked on with me now as Abu Edouard lifted a baby dove, inspected its wings, anointed it with a salve made from crushed seeds, and returned it to its cubby hole. For a few moments the world was forgotten and there was nothing but the cackling, fluttering doves and the songbirds who had joined their ranks. I took a deep breath of the morning's fragrances and decided to skip school. I wanted to take Rashel to the lawyer and then maybe go for a walk by the river, eat roast spleen with hot chutney, come home tired and oblivious of Hizkel's arrest, and sprawl on my bed with *Jean Christophe* until the novel settled slowly over my face and I fell into a sweet sleep.

"We have to leave this country," said my father, slapping his knee.

"What for? You've got the river, dates, bread, a graveyard. What more does anyone need?"

"Better death's cup with honour than life's with disgrace," my father quoted.

"What's wrong with staying here? Is anyone making you build the pyramids for the Pharaoh? The Moslems work the land and the Kurds clean the lavatories. Who's going to do that for us over there?"

"We will."

"We will?"

"Yes, we will. When the land is yours, you take care of it yourself."

"A Jew doesn't need land," declared Abu Edouard.

"A landless people is like a starless sky," said my father.

"That's just it. We're not an ordinary people."

"We're a chosen people that—"

"What kind of chosen people has to run after God for thousands of years? And the more we run after him, the more he runs away from us. We should consider ourselves lucky that the Moslems are willing to put up with us." Abu Edouard pulled at his nose and wiped his fingers on his trousers.

"Haven't you heard of Nuri Sa'id's transfer plan? He wants us swapped for the Palestinians like the Turks and Greeks thirty years ago."

"It's just talk," said Abu Edouard. "Is anyone making you leave?"

"It's only a matter of time," remarked my father, taking out his cigarettes and lighting up.

"What about me?" Abu Edouard smiled and took two cigarettes as was his habit, one to put in his mouth and the other to stick behind his ear. Then grasping a long wooden pole with a net at one end, he let out a great whistle. In an instant the flock of doves took to the sky with a loud flapping of wings for the first flight of the day. In ever higher and wider circles the birds wheeled above the roof, riding the air like sailing boats on the water and mingling with other flocks. Abu Edouard followed them expansively. His flock was the largest in Taht el-Takya and no other dovecote could compare with his. It had taken him years of fighting with the other tenants, starting with our first days in the neighbourhood, to get control of the roof. My father had helped him build his dovecote and even lent him money for it, which was never returned despite my mother's protests. A relaxing glass of tea with his neighbour on the roof each morning was all the repayment my father wanted. It was his way, he said, of cleaning his head before starting the day's work.

Abu Edouard and my father often argued about things like

Palestine and Iraq. It was as if my father, who thought that the Jews should end their long exile and uproot Baghdad from their hearts, believed Abu Edouard's conversion to be his one mission in life. Perhaps deep down he thought that this would put an end to his own doubts. I rarely listened to their disputes and waited only for Amira to bring the tea, which I sipped while feasting my gaze on her eyes which appeared to be sending secret messages. Sometimes she seemed to me like a ripe date tree that was puzzled why it wasn't being picked. Now that she had gone back down to the courtyard, I prodded my father to leave.

"In a minute, son," he said. "I want to see the doves come down."

"Yes, indeed," said Abu Edouard. "We'd better take care of our dovecote because we have no other." He stuck his fingers in his mouth and let out his great whistle, and the flock closed ranks like a colourful carpet on a wall of spotless blue and wheeled back down. Abu Edouard shaded his eyes against the white sun and gazed upwards like a general surveying the deployment of his troops. I often marvelled at the link the birds kept with him despite the heights that they reached, returning each time as though to their native home. His love for them came from his father, who had flown doves as a hobby, whereas he himself made money from fattening them up for the tables of the city's well-to-do, including Big Imari. More often than not they came back from their flights with recruits from other flocks. As soon as they landed Abu Edouard appraised them knowingly to see who was missing and who was new.

"We've gained a bit," he announced, unwittingly adding new fuel to the argument with my father, who replied:

"But not as much as we've lost."

"Because of your Zionists."

"You talk like a Moslem." My father wiped the sweat from his face with a corner of his robe.

"All that Jewish state of yours has given us is trouble," retorted Abu Edouard. "It's not our baby, but its shit is all over us."

"Israel is the greatest miracle that ever happened to us," said my father.

"And we're its greatest victim," said the dove flyer.

"In Israel you can live without Jew-hatred. You can live as a proud Jew."

"We've always been part of Iraq and always will be. This is our country. I'm an Iraqi. Life is good here. It's the homeland of us all. A man's religion is God's business."

"A people without a land is not a people."

Abu Edouard ran his hand over the horizon. "I have a land. It's called Mesopotamia and it was also our Patriarch, Abraham's."

The earth, the river, the sky: Abu Edouard loved them all. Not for him the wanderer's staff or the Jew who had two countries, a temporary asylum that he lived in and a permanent home where he did not. A man was not a migrating bird; where he was born was where he lived, and where he lived was where he died. Abraham's first mistake, Abu Edouard told my father, was setting out for Canaan. It was already then, long before the destruction of the Temple, that the Jews became a tribe of nomads. And worse yet, he chose an accursed country to go to, one that the Bible said devoured its own inhabitants. No sooner had the Jews settled in it than they were driven out, and it would happen again this time too. Better to go on living quietly in Iraq, keeping out of the Arabs' hair.

Abu Edouard tended with loving care to the newcomers who

had joined his flock. He gave them fresh sorghum, put out new bowls of water, and led them slowly to the dovecote that they would learn to regard as their home. When it came to doves, the man was a magician.

10.

Since the lawyer Menashi Zleiha was unable to locate Hizkel, and Rabbi Bashi was afraid to get involved, and since Rashel's situation was going from bad to worse, my mother decided to consult the coffee-grounds reader Ezra A'aa. A'aa was a porter who made the rounds of the bakeries with sacks of flour on his back. His hair and eyelashes were powdered so white that he looked prematurely old, but he liked his work, which kept him busy from morning till night, and was much too fond of going from place to place and chatting with the bakers while ogling the female customers with his one good eye to change jobs even when Abu Saleh el-Hibaz offered to take him on in his bakery. Ezra A'aa's mother had been run over by a wagon one rainy winter day when he was a boy, and only the art of reading coffee grounds that he had learned from her made anyone aware of his existence. So ugly was he that not even the most cunning matchmaker could find him a bride, he was by now ready to settle for anyone – a divorcee, a widow, a cripple, a bald woman – capable of bearing him a daughter he could name for his mother, who appeared to him in his dreams and made him swear to be a good Jewish husband and forsake Badriya, his regular whore. Still, although no one eligible wanted him, no one wished to offend him either, since he circulated among the ladies telling their fortunes and reassuring them with promises of rich husbands and bright futures in the secret hope that one of them would marry him. His fee for these services was a lavish meal that had to last him until his next one, and sometimes a small amount of cash.

My mother prepared an okra *kubba* soup and various fruit and vegetables, for before reading the coffee grounds Ezra A'aa had to recite every possible blessing that could be said over food. He arrived weary and perspiring from his flour sacks, washed his hands and face, ripped a piece from his pitta, wolfed down the sweet-and-sour soup and all that followed, and turned to my mother after saying all his blessings to ask for a cup of bitter coffee. His good eye, the one without the cataract, devoured Rashel, sweeping her from head to toe and back again while stopping each time, snagged like my own vision, on the sharp outline of her breasts beneath her thin summer dress.

"Sit next to me," he ordered.

She sat beside him with a look of fear and loathing.

"Drink the coffee and turn the cup over all at once," he instructed her, seizing her hand to demonstrate and twisting it with his own, which brushed against her breasts. She flushed and glanced beseechingly about her, but he only gripped her more tightly and scolded:

"Are you going to let me do my work?"

"Go on, let him get on with it," urged our cross-eyed neighbour Farha, the one who slept with the dove flyer.

"Drink!" commanded Ezra A'aa. Rashel started to drain the cup in one gulp. "Easy does it," he restrained her. "What's the hurry?" He held onto her hand when she was done, breathing heavily and mumbling incomprehensible phrases with his eyes shut before flipping the cup over with his big palm.

A hush descended on the room. The women neighbours stared with awed eyes.

"Light! I need light."

"Is he alive?" asked Rashel.

"I said light!" said Ezra A'aa, breathing on Rashel's cheek.

My mother brought the night lamp and placed it on a stool next to him, and he turned the cup this way and that to study the grounds clinging to its sides. He gulped, sucked his lips, sidled closer to Rashel, and grunted and groaned as if wrestling with the Devil, all the time keeping her hand tightly in his and poking his elbow in her breasts.

"Get on with it!" prodded cross-eyed Farha.

Ezra A'aa put down the cup and threw her a look that made her cringe. Then, like a sultan about to announce the fate of a kingdom, he surveyed his audience. His blind eye grew almost tender and his good eye glittered as he said:

"Do you see that hill?"

Rashel stared blankly at the cup, in which she saw neither hills nor valleys. "Are you blind?" demanded Ezra A'aa, raising his voice. "What's wrong with your eyes? Don't you see the palm tree on the hill?"

My mother stood on tiptoes to see better. Rashel, pale-faced, murmured something indistinct.

"Next Wednesday," said A'aa, releasing Rashel's hand at last, "a messenger will come with good news."

"May Allah have mercy on your mother and father," said my mother.

"Mazal tov," cried the women with joyful trills.

"May your words go straight to God's ears," said Farha, passing Ezra A'aa her cup. "May Allah give you a fine wife."

"Why not you?"

"Me?" Informed by his eyes, which were resting on her heavy thighs, that he was serious, Farha gave a start. "No, no."

"How can I tell your fortune when you spurn me like this? *Nas takul el-tamar wa'anni el-nuwaya h'siti,* the whole world eats dates and I get only the pits."

"Read mine, read mine," cried the women, holding out their cups.

"I can't, I have to rest," said the coffee-grounds reader. My mother handed him some money and he went off to a corner of the courtyard, took a stone from his jute bag, laid it under his head, and fell asleep at once to horrid snores. He was gone in the morning, and when Wednesday came around there was no messenger and no sign of Ezra A'aa.

The lawyer had not been heard from either, and Farha told my mother about another miracle worker, Sheikh Abu el-Tanag, a Shi'ite who refused to visit Jewish homes. When asked about him, Hiyawi lost his temper and snapped at me in the language of the Passover Hagaddah: "What means this worship to you?" Then, more mildly, he added: "Give Rabbi Bashi a chance. He'll come to the rescue as soon as he can."

But my mother kept badgering my father until, his resistance melted by Rashel's tears, he gave in. Hiyawi, who never missed a chance to be with Rashel, accompanied us and we set out for Bab-el-Sheikh where we had not been since the *Farhood*. The riots had spread from there after an inflammatory sermon in the Abd-el-Kadar el-Gailani Mosque, and my heart pounded as we entered the neighbourhood. It was only thanks to old Hiyawi, who could have passed for a Moslem dignitary with his striped robe and black turban, that we gradually began to feel safe. Barefoot children in crude cotton smocks ran after us, begging with outstretched arms. My mother smiled, patted their close-cropped heads as if we were foreign tourists, and threw them a handful of sweets from the basket she was carrying. They dived and fought for them loudly, and we continued unmolested on our way.

In a small marketplace we passed fabrics and haberdashery stands, and others full of fruit and vegetables. A vendor was singing a hoarse-voiced rhyme about dates that were sweet to eat, keeping it up even when a rival drowned it out with a jingle of his own. We turned into a narrow street of low adobe houses, down which stinking rivulets of sewage flowed and swarms of flies and gnats hovered, and stopped to ask a veiled woman, who was shoeless despite her cracked soles, where the mysterious sheikh lived. With a heavy but sure gait, she led us to a courtyard in which a blind dog nuzzled a man singing a melancholy song that likened the soul to a dove. For a long while we sat there, left to our own devices, until we were ushered into a long, low-ceilinged room. It was warm and dim, with a good smell of herbs picked in the swamps of the Tigris, and there was, or at least so it seemed to my vivid imagination, something magical about it. At its far end, as thin as a reed and his nose hooked like a Jew's, sat the brooding sheikh in regal splendour, wearing a white, collarless cotton shirt and a red bandanna like a pirate's around his head. Even though I was thirsty, I didn't dare pour myself a drink from the water jug on the black table. Next to the holy man stood a hookah and a coal brazier over which, although it was a hot summer day, he held his hands as if to warm them. He rose, went to a corner, lit two large tapers, murmured something that sounded like my mother blessing the Sabbath candles, sat down again, sucked on his hookah and inquired:

"What brings you here?"

"My husband has disappeared," Rashel said.

"Be still, woman!" the sheikh rebuked her. "None but the men speak here."

"He's my only brother," said my father.

"You are of the faith of Moses?"

"Of Moses and of Aaron."

"The *dhimmi* who vanishes is not easily found," declared the sheikh.

"May God bless your every word, O sheikh," old Hiyawi broke in. "Here, in the land between the rivers, the strong devour the weak."

If anyone knew what to say in such circumstances, it was Hiyawi. Indeed, the sheikh's face grew a little less stern. "Was he struck by the arrow of love?" he asked. His high-flown language made me want to laugh, but everyone looked deadly serious.

"You are beholding his beloved," answered my father in the same coin.

"Perhaps he took a man's life?"

"A blameless soul," my father said quickly.

"Then why should he have disappeared?" the sheikh wondered, as if that were not the very question we were asking. He put down his hookah, opened a tobacco cabinet, scattered some shredded leaves, rolled two cigarettes, and offered them to my father and Hiyawi, who stuck one in his mouth with constrained politeness. Then, spreading some more leaves over the brazier, the sheikh leaned back upon his pillows, replaced the hookah in his own mouth, and stared thoughtfully at the glowing coals. The mixture of fragrances nearly made me swoon. Everyone stared at the holy man, whose lips were sealed tight. Hiyawi took a snuff box from his robe, tapped its sides, gently removed the lid, and offered it to the sheikh. "My handiwork," he said.

The sheikh took a pinch and inhaled. "*Tabarrak Allah,*" he praised. "The smell of Paradise."

"Glory to the nostrils that know what they smell," replied Hiyawi, leaving the snuff box with the sheikh, who now took my father's hand and held it for a long while as if seeking to make contact with the missing brother. *Allah akbar, Allah akbar, la illaha illa Allah,* he chanted the words of the *Shahada,* the Moslem creed.

"The police took him and he has not come back," said my father.

"A curse on them," said the sheikh. "They are the plague of Satan."

"They have abandoned God and his religion," Hiyawi declared.

"And religion is the voice of justice and of virtue," added the sheikh, as if continuing the same thought.

"*Sadaka Allahu el-azim,*" mumbled my father and Hiyawi together. "Righteous and great is God."

"I'll summon the djinn," said the sheikh. Cold sweat covered my neck. Dealing with demons was no longer a joke. Unless he was laying a trap for us. Why else would he have cursed the police?

"Just find my husband," pleaded Rashel uncontrollably.

"Hush, woman, or you will have to leave," the sheikh chided her. He threw a handful of leaves from a wide-necked jar on the coals, took a glass of water from a stool, poured a white powder into it, and covered it with a dark rag. Then, rising to his feet, he shut his eyes, raised one arm, and whispered into the darkness in an eerie voice:

"O thou wise one, O thou djinn, come and bring us tidings."

There was a thin crackle in the room. I had no idea where it was coming from. The sheikh lifted his thumb, which bore a large gold ring, and the dark rag flew off the glass as if demons were dancing in the water. He tucked his thumb into the fist of his other hand and the demons quietened down.

"Your most honourable name?" he asked.

My father did not understand the question and Hiyawi had to answer for him.

"O thou wise one, O thou djinn," said the sheikh. "Is Hizkel Moshi Imari among the living?"

The demons in the glass began to dance again and a sound like hoarse birdsong filled the room.

"He breathes the air of the Tigris and Euphrates yet," announced the sheikh, his face brightening.

"May God lengthen your days," my mother blessed him.

"Hush, woman! Females frighten the djinn." The sheikh raised his voice. "O thou wise one, O thou djinn, forgive and tell us what the man looks like." Again the husky chirps broke out. "Of average height and sharp of eye," he declared as if Hizkel were standing in front of him. Rashel looked in a state of shock.

"O thou wise one, O thou djinn, be gone now and come again," the sheikh concluded. No one stirred. Although we wanted to hear more, the sheikh went back to sucking on his hookah, inhaling deeply as if after a great effort. A delicate fragrance spread through the room. Rashel had tears in her eyes.

"*Tabarrak Allah,* His grace is upon you. *Tabarrak Allah,*" the sheikh said.

My father reached for his wallet.

"I seek not lucre but charity for all God's creatures," exclaimed the sheikh as if offended. His son, who was waiting by the door, took the money.

Buoyed by the sheikh's words, my father and Rashel flew straight to the lawyer's office, where Menashi Zleiha brought

95

them back to earth. There was nothing new. Hizkel's whereabouts were still unknown.

The days passed slowly. Rashel vacillated between hope and despair. I found myself seeking all kinds of excuses to be with her, went on errands for her, and tried to entertain her with funny stories, but she had other things on her mind and looked right through me. One day when we were sitting on the stone bench in her courtyard she went to Hizkel's room and came back with an album of photographs. I knew that she had been only ten years old when, hiding behind a curtain, she saw her parents killed by looters in the *Farhood*; now, looking at their pictures, she hugged and rubbed herself as if fighting a physical spasm, and I felt sure that she must be remembering those moments. Although I wanted to hug her myself, I sat as rigid as the stone bench, gripping it tightly and staring at the ground.

Suddenly Rashel roused herself. She gave me a strange look, as if wondering what I was doing there, and all the closeness I had imagined vanished at once. I rose to go, but she took my hand, made me sit down again, went to the kitchen, and returned with a tray on which was a bowl of thick *tehini* mixed with date syrup. "This was one of Hizkel's favourites," she said. The very thought of him made me lose my appetite. There was a hesitant knock on the door. I went to open it and saw Hiyawi. Rashel's honeyed eyes turned to ice. He crossed the courtyard with timid steps and laid an envelope on the bench.

"For the lawyer," he said.

"That's unnecessary," Rashel said drily.

"Then for you."

"I said it was unnecessary." Her voice was steely. Then it grew softer. "Has Rabbi Bashi done anything?"

"It's complicated."

"Then who needs him?" Even though Hiyawi had just arrived, she rose impatiently as if he had overstayed his welcome. As he turned to go, she handed me the envelope and said:

"Give it back to him."

I caught up with Hiyawi at the door and slipped it into his pocket.

"Why are you doing this?" he asked her. I would have liked an answer to that myself.

Rashel glanced at him and smoothed her hair. "He thinks I'm … " She began to say something to me, stopped, looked at me suspiciously, went to her room, came back a few minutes later, and said in an agitated tone:

"God damn them! They took Hiyawi's wedding present, the chain and the bracelets."

On my way home from school the next day, the old man called to me from his store. "What did she say to you after I left?" he asked, pouring out tea in two cups.

"What should she have said?" I countered.

"Tell me!"

"She said that they took the chain and the bracelets that you gave her."

"*Waweli,* they were Tifaha's!" he cried, clapping his hands. "O my dearest, have pity on me! I made a mistake. I should never have given them to her."

The whole neighbourhood knew Hiyawi's story. Many had heard him tell it himself, always in the same version and interspersed with the Turkish words in which he had written love poems to his dead wife in happier days. She had been ten when he first met her on the traditional courting day of the 15th of Av, the same age as Rashel when she came to Taht el-Takya. It was a day when Jews from all over Baghdad went to the city's large park for the young people of both sexes to view each other and perhaps chat a bit, thus aiding the matchmakers and sparing the embarrassment of the *ma'aina* ceremony, in which the marriageable females were paraded before the men like horses at a fair. Despite the age difference between them, Hiyawi was betrothed to Tifaha soon after, and four years later he took her for his wife.

Hiyawi came to his wedding dressed in the uniform of a Turkish cavalry officer. A large contingent of Turkish and Iraqi officers had accepted his invitation and come too, for he was so proud of being a Jew that he wanted to show off his faith's rituals. The wedding was conducted by Rabbi Bashi, already a renowned rabbinical judge, and the brief sermon given by him in Turkish was declared captivating by all. The next day the newlyweds set out on their honeymoon for Mosul, "the city of two springs", and wherever they stopped on the way Hiyawi was taken for a Turkish officer and treated with great honour and deference.

And yet after returning to his regiment near the Russian frontier his longings began to gnaw at him so badly that he almost regretted having let himself be drafted into the Sultan's army instead of buying his way out with a small bribe. He had already spent four years studying in a military college in Constantinople and served in out-of-the-way places at the far ends of the Ottoman Empire, and now he was far again not only from home but also from his beloved wife.

After being parted from Tifaha for ten months, Hiyawi was posted to Baghdad. However, she was unable to get pregnant, though in her desperation there was nothing she failed to try. She went to coffee-grounds readers, tarot card readers, soothsayers, and conjurers; she drank potions, slept with charms and incantations under her pillow, wore amulets, and swallowed mystical inscriptions; she smeared herself with the urine of infants and ate the ground-up afterbirths of multiparous women; she visited rabbis and kabbalists for their blessings, and once she even travelled to another city and spent a week seeking the aid of a famous fertility healer. Nothing helped. In the end, all hope lost, she washed herself with watermelon soap, purified herself in a large basin, donned a white dress, and drowned herself in the river. She was seen jumping off a bridge in the darkness, though her body was never found.

Hiyawi tore his clothes in mourning and sat for long months in the courtyard of his house, inconsolably squatting on his haunches. Rabbi Bashi was the one person allowed to visit him, yet not even the rabbi's penance of fasting twice a week for an entire year to atone for Hiyawi's sins in the army, in which he had not always managed to keep strictly kosher or observe the other commandments, could relieve his suffering. At night he slept outdoors with his head on a stone and during the day he read the Psalms, studied the *Zohar,* and immersed himself in cold ablutions, wrestling with God and His angels and begging the Almighty to take his life and release him from his misery if He could not restore his wife.

God did neither of these things, and since Tifaha's body was never found, Hiyawi fell prey to all kinds of strange fancies. He took to walking by the banks of the Tigris and on its bridges while calling aloud to her, and one day he returned home, collected all her belongings and jewelry except for her bracelets, wedding ring, and gold chain, put them in the *jihaz,* that is, the trousseau chest she had brought from Damascus, and threw it all in the river. "Maybe she's embarrassed to come back with nothing on her," he explained, but she and her body still tarried. Although he spoke of her as "my dear departed one", he never was reconciled to her loss, and consumed by grief he often went to the river to tell her of his sorrows. His hair turned grey, then white, then fell out and was gone. Sometimes, on his walks by the Tigris, he saw her floating face-up in the water, her hair trailing behind her and her eyes beaming like beacons from the depths, or else heard her voice speaking to him, laughing and crying by turn. Back in his tobacco shop in Taht el-Takya, he furrowed his brow and racked his brain in a vain effort to remember her words.

"She's her reincarnation," he now said, awaking from his reverie.

"Who is?" I asked.

"Rashel," he whispered in a frightening tone. "The same eyes, the same thumb, the exact same hair, so thick and smooth – it's her reincarnated." I was sure he was out of his mind.

11.

"Cowards!" shouted Ismail at us.

"Who beat you in Palestine, huh?" yelled Edouard.

"The Ingleez!"

"The Jews!" Edouard boasted.

"The Jews? Palestine? Who are you kidding, Mr Communist Revolutionary?" I whispered, teasingly.

"*Yallah,* who's game?" called Ismail, disdainfully scanning us as if already chalking up his victory. "Where's your champion?" And seeing Edouard, our leader, hesitate, he added: "Say the *Shahada* and I'll stop."

What a fool, I thought. He really believed that we had only to say "I testify that there is no God besides Allah and that Muhammed is the messenger of Allah" for our Jewishness to disappear like a stain that came out in the wash. Rabbi Bashi, or Haham Bashi as he was to us all, had told us in his sermons about the Marranos in Spain who pretended to become Christians but secretly remained Jews for generations – and here this imbecile believed that we could be turned into Moslems in a matter of seconds!

"You want us to say the *Shahada?*" asked Edouard.

"Yes."

"Over your dead body!"

"Clear out, this isn't your country!" Ismail shouted. "You're traitors. You don't belong here!"

"We were here long before you Moslems," Edouard called back. "We were born here and we aren't going anywhere."

Yet my father was for clearing out too, and I felt caught in the middle. Why should I have to leave? protested one part of me. Because this isn't yours, answered another. Which was what Ismail, who turned up in our neighbourhood at least once a week to challenge us to a holy war, kept telling us. Old Hiyawi wouldn't let us forget who we were either. "If you're given the choice between converting and death," he liked to remind us, "the Bible says: choose death!"

I took Ismail's threats seriously. Not long ago I had seen him grab a cat by the tail, twirl it around his head, and send it flying against a wall. The thud still sent a shiver down my spine. There were many stories about his exploits, and he was as much of a tyrant with his own gang as with us. The only Jew he had anything to do with, even though she was Edouard's sister, was Amira, who studied in the girls' wing of the Moslem high school that he attended. According to her, he loved Iraqi history and worshipped its heroes. Once, he told her, he had dreamed that the Babylonian king Nebuchadnezzar was returning victoriously on horseback from a war, accompanied by thousands of his soldiers who followed him through the gate of the goddess Ishtar. He, Ismail, the monarch's trusted adjutant, rode beside him, and Nebuchadnezzar, fresh from routing the Egyptian pharaoh Necho, led him to the triumphal platform, handed him the ceremonial bow, and proclaimed: "Ismail my son, I crown thee King of Iraq. Thou wilt conquer many nations and even reach Jerusalem."

Ismail's dream was actually reassuring, since it left no room for doubt that he was mad. Suppose I had gone around saying that I dreamed of being King of the Jews and re-establishing

David's Kingdom! "He's no older than you are and you can beat him," Hizkel encouraged us. "Where's your Jewish pride?" Yet when my uncle watched the next belt fight, he saw us whipped by Ismail again. It was then that he decided to gather us all and teach us the art of the catapult.

The catapults took Ismail and his gang by surprise, and they scattered before our sudden volley while we whooped and capered like billygoats. Old Hiyawi waved his turban in the air, treated us to baklava, showed us his old Turkish army sword, and said: "They won't be back again, not if I know them."

But they were back the next day in full force, each with a catapult of his own, which they knew how to use. This time it was us, licking our wounds, who beat a shameful retreat. Nonplussed, Hiyawi raised his arms and said with a melancholy nod: "What a world! You can't even trust the goyim any more. God only knows what we're in for at the hands of these Ismails. It's them and their ilk who will be running Iraq some day."

Hizkel refused to back down. "You can beat them," he insisted. A few days later he was arrested. For some reason I felt sure that it was Ismail who had informed on him. One way or another, Ismail was a force to be reckoned with when he appeared in the narrow streets of Taht el-Takya, a Moslem bully with an enigmatically arrogant smile. And I especially had to reckon with the admiration of Amira, who liked to sit reading propped on colourful cushions in her window seat overlooking our battlefield, from which she never missed a single skirmish. "He's braver and stronger than any of you," she taunted us, aiming her sharpest barbs at her brother Edouard until he struck back and hit her, which only made her stick out her tongue and jeer harder. Most of her girlfriends were Moslems and she spoke Arabic just like them. Her dream was to win a government scholarship to study engineering in America, from which she would return to build a super bridge over the Tigris, and she had ceased to view Ismail as an enemy from the day he had rescued her from an Arab boy who tried sticking his hand down her blouse. Our stone and belt fights were a form of gladiatorial combat that she enjoyed watching from her window seat.

I jealously had to admit that Ismail was tall and handsome with large, fiery eyes and a head full of black curls. There was something proud and aloof about him, and he was the only one of his barefoot gang to wear shoes. Sometimes I had the feeling that I had known him all my life, perhaps even in some previous existence. Now, mocking and swearing at us like Goliath, he called to Edouard who, no doubt fearing a new rival, had undemocratically vetoed my proposal to enlist the baker's apprentice Sami in our ranks, "*Ya yahud,* what's your weapon today: belts, catapults, stones, or knives?"

"Knives, knives!" howled Ismail's gang members.

"Belts!" decreed Edouard, slipping his own from his trousers.

"Cowards!" swaggered Ismail. "I told you the Jews were yellow."

As he took the field, Edouard's tongue slid between his lips, a sure sign that he was nervous. The two belts whistled through the air, our eyes on the bright gleam of their ornamented buckles, even before their owners closed. Suddenly the belts met and twined around each other. Had Edouard been a bit quicker, or so I imagined doing in his place, he might have jerked Ismail off his feet. But the belts unwound and the tense ballet resumed.

"Lower, Edouard, go for his belly!" I yelled, smacking my fist in my palm while shouting advice along with everyone. A second later Edouard was on the ground, where he remained lying submissively. As long as you stayed on your feet in a belt fight, it was fair play even to kill you, but the minute you were down the unwritten rules called for mercy. Ismail stood waiting for his next victim.

"Cowards!" screamed Amira.

"He's your own brother, you bitch," I yelled back. "Why don't you go and mop the floor?"

"You shut up, Kabi," she shouted down at me. "All you've got is a big mouth."

Before I knew what had happened, I was facing Ismail myself. He raised his hand and everyone stepped back and formed a ring around us. What was I doing? It was already too late to explain to him that it was all a mistake. As though I was someone else watching through a fog, I was dimly aware of twirling my belt, lunging forward, dodging, and springing back. Yet not even the fear that blurred my senses could keep me from hearing Amira scream "You clown, you!" and from realizing that she meant me. Our belts met and with a quick motion Ismail plucked mine away and left me bare-handed. A second later his own belt shrieked over my head, its buckle dangerously close to me. I was about to be killed. Had he knocked me down I would have been safe, but now I would have to grovel of my own free will. And in front of Amira, too!

Ismail took my measure with his eyes. At first I thought I saw contempt in them, as if I were not even worth a whipping. Yet as he went on staring at me like someone struggling to remember, I again had the feeling of having known him before.

"Beat it," he said at last in a toneless voice.

I would rather have been whiplashed than humiliated like that. In a flash my fear yielded to defiance. I had nothing left to lose. As Hiyawi used to say: Once you're wet, you needn't fear the rain.

"Hey, zombie!" shouted Amira.

"You tart, I hope you marry a cross-eyed cripple!" I shouted back with a resolution born of despair. Once and for all I would show her I was no coward. I picked up my belt and charged blindly. Ismail's buckle hit me just above the temple, leaving me dazed from the explosion in my head.

"I told you to beat it, *ya Id.*" He was standing very close to me.

Despite the flashes of pain running through me, I looked at him in astonishment.

"You Jews are our slaves forever," he cried, as if recovering possession of himself, and signalled to his gang. A moment later they were gone.

I stood there surrounded by my friends, one of whom examined the bruise on my forehead and pressed it to keep down the swelling. It took me a minute to come to my senses. Then I replaced the fingers on my forehead with my own, mumbled that I had to go, and took off after Ismail through the winding streets of the souk.

I knew that he was heading for Razi Street, on the far side of the marketplace, which I reached just in time to see him latch onto the back of a passing carriage and hitch a ride. Although my father had warned me against this form of transportation, no self-respecting boy my age hadn't tried it at least once, and I grabbed hold of the next coach to come along and crouched against its tail end. From both hearsay and a bit of experience I knew that I would be safe if I wasn't noticed by the driver right away. But I was and his whip lashed out at me, once, twice, and yet again, each time missing my head, which was protected by the high overhang of the rear wheel. From time to time I peered out of my shell to check that Ismail was still ahead of me. By now we were in the Moslem quarter of el-Dehidwana, passing shops and coffeehouses and speeding southwards away from Taht el-Takya.

Oddly, I felt no fear despite breaking my father's injunction. He had never allowed me to stray far from home. Since the day I was old enough to walk the streets by myself he had placed strict limits on where I went, while at the same time considering it his duty as a Jewish father to acquaint me, as his own father had done for him, with every back alley down which I might flee if trapped by a Moslem mob on my way to school or in the souk. When I was older he took me to Razi Street, to el-Rashid Street, to el-Dehidwana, and to Bab-el-Sheikh and taught me to talk and act like a Moslem and how to tell one from a Jew. When I was born he gave me the Arab name of Sa'id to go with my Jewish one of Ya'akov Kabi, which greatly pleased me though no one ever used it. Later, when I grew older, he warned me never to go to a Moslem neighbourhood by myself; and – as if doubting my obedience – whispered "God be with you" every time I set out somewhere.

I might have put up a better fight against Ismail without my father's fears, and yet here I was, flouting all his rules. The coach sped on and I kept my eyes on Ismail, who was staring down at the road racing beneath him. Was he thinking about his feud with us? Could Moslems like him really feel threatened by a small minority of us Jews? We looked like them, we were circumcised like them, we spoke their language, we sang their songs and danced their dances – what made us any different? Why were their menacing looks and hawklike eyes always trailing us, the strangers, the tolerated *dhimmi* looked down on by the lords of the land?

Ismail jumped from his carriage and turned right, and I followed him as he progressed by fits and starts, speeding up and slowing down as if his tempestuous nature were unsuited to an even gait. Single-storey clay houses with narrow windows lined streets that smelled of burning dung, boiled sheep ghee, greasy food, and rank vegetation nourished by sewage. Ismail halted by a butcher's shop and sat down beside a paunchy man who was straddling a small stool and had on the red keffiyeh of the *mujaheddin*, the Palestine volunteers, while I crossed the street and hid behind the big mulberry tree, which seemed to have shrunk. The long hours we two had spent beneath it, eating its berries and staining our clothes with their dark juice!

Suddenly it all fitted together: my mother's stories about the little house in el-Me'azzam – the butcher's shop with its meat hooks – fat Hairiyya with her son Ismail. The rush of memories was like a picture abruptly coming into focus. It had been so long ago: before the *Farhood,* before Zionism and the State of Israel, before the Moslems and Jews had gone crazy and stopped living peacefully together. This was where I was born, in the little house that I now stood in front of as if ten years had never passed, with its storey-and-a-half and its cellar and its flat roof and its three steps leading up to a wooden entrance gate whose rusty hinges, irregularly oiled by my father, had creaked to a continually changing tune that grew spine-tinglingly sweet towards evening when every unexpected knock bore the promise of novelty and surprise. Only its colour had changed. The house itself looked dreary, almost dismal, and much smaller than I remembered it, though it still had the same smell of basil mixed with goat dung. I was dying to enter it, walk down the narrow hallway, mount the steps to my room, stand on my little stool, and look out of the window at the street below – or else, to climb to the roof and peer down at Hairiyya and Mihsin's courtyard in defiance of my mother's prohibition.

Ismail and I were both our parents' first sons, born two days apart, I at the end of Sukkot and he in the middle of the holiday. Hairiyya and my mother shared nursing the two of us. *Fidwa, ya ibni, ya Id,* she would sing to me, shortening Sa'id to Id, the Arabic word for holiday. It was Ismail's calling me by that name that had brought it all back to me.

Actually, a moment before placing him, an image of his mother had flashed before me, my face buried in the soft, fat folds of her neck. On her side of the fence was a patch of aubergines, the deep purple of which enthralled me. Once I stole one, and when my mother slapped my wrist and made me return it, Hairiyya laughed with her white teeth and said: "*Fidwa, ya ibni, ya Id.* It's just an aubergine. Take all you want."

Sometimes the two of us, Ismail and I, roamed among the palm trees in the fragrant rose garden near our home, or played hide-and-seek among the oleander bushes while listening to the drawn-out cooing of the doves. Once we lost our way and Hairiyya and Abu Ismail the butcher went to look for us. "*Ya wiladi, ya Ismail, ya Id, weynkum?*" she had cried. "Where are you, my sons?" She sounded a triumphant trill when she found us and gave us basil water to drink as an antidote to the oleander flowers that we had eaten.

My mother loved our house, which she was always cleaning or scrubbing or painting or polishing. On Fridays I was sent off to Hairiyya's garden while my mother prepared for the Sabbath unhindered, after which I was bathed in the large basin, dressed in a *dishdasha,* a white smock like Ismail's, and allowed to watch the lighting of the Sabbath candles that were placed out of my reach on the window sill, their white wicks floating in little pools of oil. Her head covered with an embroidered shawl and her breath causing the yellow flame to flicker, my mother murmured the mysterious blessing in its strange language, gazed heavenwards, and prayed – what for I never knew. But the house was full of a great light when she finished and everyone in it felt at peace.

Saturday mornings, when we were forbidden by the Sabbath laws to light the gas burner, Hairiyya came with Ismail to make us tea, boiling milk fresh from her brown cow. Sometimes Ismail spent the day with us, listening with a white skullcap on his head as my father recited the kiddush and sang Sabbath hymns to the melodies of the Iraqi singer Abd el-Wahab. After dinner we raced to the *jalala,* always quarrelling who had won and could swing first. At the end of our last Passover in el-Me'azzam Hairiyya brought us hot, fragrant bread. It was the first I had seen in eight days, and I fell upon it wolfishly in disregard of the manners taught me by my mother.

Summer nights we slept on the roof, where my parents walked about with a funny slouch, fearful of inadvertently glimpsing our Moslem neighbours in a state of undress beyond the low balcony. It was my first realization that being small had its advantages. I liked sleeping under the sky. Sometimes I was woken at night by the call of the muezzin, from whom I learned that there was a Moslem God as well as a Jewish one. My father enjoyed the Moslem call to prayer. When it ended he would proclaim huskily, as though he too were one of the faithful: "*Sadaka Allah el-azim.* Just is the great God."

And then something – I was not sure what – began to go wrong. My father stopped listening to music on the radio and tuned in to every news bulletin, flitting from station to station. He and Abu Ismail sat talking about distant fighting in countries I knew nothing about. One day we heard on the radio that a great war had broken out. Everyone was afraid. And there were new names that I couldn't pronounce, such as Hitler, Stalin, Churchill, and Mussolini.

Afterwards, Australian soldiers appeared with big, funny hats and there were whispered rumours about Jews being killed in far-off places I hadn't even known they lived in. My father and Abu Ismail took to arguing. Sometimes they shouted at each other. My father was for Churchill and Abu Ismail was for Hitler. I was sure that was because Hitler had an Iraqi moustache. Life was no longer the same. Neither was el-Me'azzam. Outsiders appeared, beating Jews and throwing stones at them. One old woman was stabbed. I could tell how worried my father was by the way he pushed away his dish of saffron rice with the back of his hand and wouldn't eat.

One afternoon a burning torch was tossed into our house. My mother put it out in the nick of time. A few days later a crowd of Moslems gathered outside and yelled: "Jews, get out!" Hairiyya stood by the front gate and screamed: "Have you no shame? The Jews have lived with us forever." For whatever reason, they went away, but though it was the middle of the rainless summer my father, who was white as a sheet, said to my mother: "Woman, there are storm clouds brewing. We have to leave el-Me'azzam." My mother clawed her cheeks with her nails and cried without a sound. The tight arch of her lips frightened me. The next day Hairiyya and Abu Ismail helped load our belongings on a truck. The two women kissed and hugged tearfully. At the last minute Ismail sat on the *jalala* and wouldn't get up. My mother begged me to let him have it. "It's too big and heavy," she said. "And anyway, we'll be back after the war." I balked and screamed. In the end we took it, leaving Ismail other toys of mine.

This opened a new chapter in our lives. At first we moved to

Kahwit el-Kebiri, a Jewish neighbourhood into which thousands of refugees had poured. Its ugly, colourless, shapeless houses were covered with tin sheets and huddled so closely together, roof against roof, that you could see what everyone was doing. All winter the rusty tin rattled scarily, threatening to fly off in the wind. Open sewers ran in the streets, turning to frozen dungheaps in winter and muddy cesspools in summer. Hungry children ran up and down the filthy alleys that teemed with stench, noise, and neglect. My mother hated the place and begged to go back to el-Me'azzam. I prayed that my father would agree. "After the war," was his stock reply. But the war dragged on and then came the *Farhood* with its wounded, raped, and dead. The world had gone mad. "Woman, there's no going back," my father said. "Not a Jew is left in the old neighbourhood." He refused even to visit it, and the two of them fought for a long time.

And now I was the visitor. I thought of saying hello to Hairiyya and giving her a big hug. She had nursed me, I was like a son to her. But I was afraid. Perhaps she too had changed.

Ismail stood up. He did not go home, though. Rather, he started down the street, perhaps on an errand for the *majjahed*. The harsh smell of burning dung was a grim reminder of the Moslem slum I was in. Anything – my face, my shorts, my shirt, my leather sandals could give me away. A donkey brayed loudly as if proclaiming my presence and I decided to head back, trying in vain to keep looking straight ahead of me. All around me – or so I had been taught to believe from childhood, the monstrous fear of them as much a part of me as my native language – was an alien crowd of vengeful killers and loathsome sodomites. What was I doing among them? I could be kidnapped and thrown into the river. "If you're ever alone among Moslems," my father had told me, "don't attract attention, whatever you do. Try to behave as naturally as if you were a born-and-bred Arab." And now, of all times, I needed to pee: all I had to do was pee on someone's wall for him to come at me with a knife!

I tried holding it in. *Oh God, give me strength,* I prayed. The ache in my bladder grew worse. *Oh God.* A hot trickle ran down my shorts all the way to my knee. The pressure eased, but now my pants had an embarrassing stain. It was hopeless to try to hide it. My one consolation was that no one knew me in this place.

I started to run. Although Razi Street was still far away, I now had a new worry. How would I get home without my shorts being seen? Suppose Amira was still in her window seat! And even if I managed to change in time, I would still have to explain the bump on my forehead, which must be turning black-and-blue.

The sun hung low above the horizon on a fiery carpet of scarlet clouds. Like a promised salvation, Razi Street loomed in the distance. With the last of my strength I picked up speed and crossed it; then, my physical confidence suddenly gone, I grabbed at a passing carriage and missed. It had seemed so easy on the way to el-Me'azzam. Only now did I grasp what a crazy thing I had done. To hitch a ride to the heart of Moslem Baghdad! How had I failed to be afraid when now, just thinking of it, made me shudder?

The fact was – to be honest, I had known it all along – that my courage came from Ismail. Deep down I had felt sure that I need only call him to be rescued from any trouble I got into. Even if he had clipped me with his belt buckle on purpose, it was because I had asked for it, and I had followed him to el-

Me'azzam in a kind of ecstasy, which only now yielded to the realization that, though startled to see me, he had no more room for me in his life. He had granted me the most I could have hoped for and then – strong, solitary, implacable, a leader of men – had walked away and left me forever. And still I had run after him, consumed by the need for his protection. Perhaps my father was right. Iraq had made slaves of us. It was time to clear out.

12.

Old Hiyawi bent over his work-table, shredding thin tobacco leaves that crackled beneath his crescent-shaped knife. From time to time he poured a white liquid on them from a dark, dirty bottle, the secret ingredients of which, handed down by his father and grandfather, accounted for his renowned chewing tobacco's success. While he once had said to me that a man without secrets was an open book that one soon lost interest in, he had lately taken to grumbling that there was no one to pass his craft on to now that his strength was failing. And yet he could have had the best tobacconists in Baghdad for his pupils, for his blends were much in demand, and despite his complaints about his health, his long, thin Zabana cigarettes with their hollow mouthpieces were as flavourful as ever. It was from them that he made his living, giving the chewing plugs made from the left-over tobacco to his friends and relations, especially to my father and Abu Edouard – who, miserly though he was, made his wife cook Hiyawi dove broths that gave him strength and cleansed his throat roughened by smoke and tobacco.

I liked watching Hiyawi at his work which he performed with the devotion of an artist. The white glow of Baghdad's morning sun lit his gaze of concentration and black eyebrows that arched upwards as though resisting old age. Chewing on his lips, he kneaded the tobacco with his bonily veined, brown-spotted hands and sampled it on the tip of his tongue, relaxing only when the blend was finished and his brows flattened again as rosy skeins spread through his cheeks. He deftly brushed the mixture over the table to let it air, filled his little gold box with the leavings, swept the remainder into a soft leather pouch, cleaned the table and knife with a dark rag, and wiped his hands on his smock.

His morning's work done, the old man put out a stool and sat in front of his shop, took a pinch of tobacco from his box, stuck it between his upper lip and brown gums, sucked its juices, spat a brown jet, lit a Zabana, and inhaled with relish. Soon Mahmoud, the servant who fetched him tea every hour, brought him his morning hookah. Reaching into the pocket of his robe for his silver mouthpiece, Hiyawi fitted it, wiped it clean with his thumb, and nursed the hookah like a hungry baby. He was addicted to hookahs, cigarettes, chewing tobacco, and snuff, and their aromas preceded him everywhere.

Now, absent-mindedly, he ran a hand over the cluster of tobacco leaves hanging in the doorway of his shop. I stood beside him, waiting for my father to return with Rashel. As soon as Hiyawi saw them emerge from a side-street, he signalled Mahmoud to bring tea and another hookah. Rashel passed by without saying hello, as though he were made of air. My father shook Hiyawi's hand and sat down wearily on a stool beside him.

"Anything new?" asked the old man.

"Not a thing."

"You mean he's simply vanished?"

"As if swallowed by the earth," said my father. "I heard you had no luck with Rabbi Bashi."

"It's complicated," said Hiyawi in the same words he had used with Rashel.

"We're not going to be saved by him," said my father. "His time has passed. There's going to be a demonstration against him tomorrow."

"God protect him and give him life!" Hiyawi jumped to his feet. "Who knows what that will do to him? Abu Kabi, don't let them! Do something. Talk to the baker, to the Movement. He's a holy man. He mustn't be harmed."

He was genuinely alarmed.

"There's nothing I can do," said my father. "Don't you remember him saying that we're Iraqis first and Jews second? What kind of way was that for a Jewish leader to speak?"

"Abu Kabi, be sensible. What was he supposed to say? And what difference would it have made? You know as well as I do that the damned Moslems have hearts of stone. This independence of theirs has gone to their heads. The Turk and the Englishman kept them in check, but now that the horses are holding the reins, they've run wild. Excuse me, Abu Kabi. I'm going to warn Rabbi Bashi."

Hiyawi rose and began to lock up.

The next day he told me about his visit to the rabbi's office in the Jewish community building on el-Samwel Street by the river. While waiting to see Rabbi Bashi he could feel the tension in the air, although the Jews lined up outside the door seemed no different from the usual petitioners: a woman asking for a donation to marry off a fatherless daughter, another seeking a divorce from a missing husband, a man requesting a good word to a cabinet minister who would help his son get into college. When all had had their audience, Hiyawi entered and said:

"Rabbi Bashi, there's going to be a demonstration against you tomorrow."

"Many are the thoughts in the hearts of men, but the counsel of the Lord shall prevail," replied the rabbi with a quote from Psalms.

"Perhaps you should let the police know," Hiyawi said worriedly.

"And inform on my children? Turn them over to the goy? They need to be prayed for!" Rabbi Bashi looked skywards through the window. "O Lord, shelter the dove who sheds for Thee a tear of love," he chanted softly and explained to Hiyawi that the people of Israel were like a dove longing for its Redeemer. All Fate's blows to them were the travails of Redemption, as was every affront and indignity that he himself suffered lovingly. He slapped his desk as was his habit when concluding a conversation, rose, and said:

"Come, let's go to synagogue."

Rabbi Bashi rarely said the afternoon and evening prayers in public, preferring to recite them in his office, and no sooner had he stepped into the street preceded by his mace-bearer and followed by Hiyawi, who kept a disciple's two paces behind him, than the word spread quickly. Jews put aside what they were doing, left their shops and work places, and lined the streets to pay homage to the tall, broad figure whose ample stomach was hidden by a bright blue robe girded by a gold-embroidered white silk sash. Grasping his carved black staff, the rabbi surveyed them like a king reviewing his subjects. Many seized his ceremonially extended right hand to kiss and bring it to their foreheads, and women pushed their children into his path to make sure they were given his blessing.

Christians and Moslems too saluted the holy man, the Haham, who halted at the corner near the Rabbi Ezekiel Synagogue and stood looking at the nearby mosque and church. There were times of the day and of the year when the muezzin sounded his call of *Allah akbar* to the faithful, the cantor and congregation in the synagogue joyfully sang "How goodly are thy tents, O Jacob," and the church bells pealed all at once. Perhaps this was why Rabbi Bashi favoured the Ezekiel Synagogue and made it his own to pray in on Sabbaths, holidays, and weekday mornings, when he attended the early service. It was there that he also received guests like Big Imari, who walked all the way from his home in New Baghdad on holy days when travel was forbidden, just for the honour of sitting beside the rabbi and being called up to the Torah.

Rabbi Bashi gave his sermons in the Ezekiel Synagogue too, and while only a few scholarly souls followed all their recondite allusions, the sanctity of his words could not be doubted. These homilies, which were spiced with popular sayings and proverbs, were great crowd-pleasers. Once even King Faisal came to the synagogue to confer his Passover greetings. Rabbi Bashi met him on the steps of the building, intoned "Blessed be Thou O Lord, our God, King of the universe, who hath bestowed His glory on flesh and blood," translated the Hebrew blessing for the monarch, and declared while pointing to the mosque and church: "You see, Your Majesty, we indeed have one Father. One Lord has created us all."

"Rabbi, pray for me too," replied the King, kissing him in front of everyone.

The synagogue and even the women's gallery were full when Rabbi Bashi arrived. All rose as a mark of respect to kiss his hand, ask his blessing, or simply regard him reverently. The majority of those present were the elderly men who congregated there regularly, spending their days studying and chatting amid the ancient smell of sacred books. Sometimes, sighing nostalgically for the irretrievable days of the English and the Turks, they stretched out on the cushioned pews to snooze, or else sat eating the meals brought to them by charitable souls like my mother. No matter how sound asleep they were, a few always managed to sit up in time to nod deferentially to Rabbi Bashi, who now lowered himself into his velvet chair, glanced at the crowd, and whispered to Hiyawi leaning over him:

"See how my people honour and love me."

"Indeed, Rabbi," said Hiyawi. "Whom greater than you do we have?"

"The young folk may kick and balk," said the rabbi, "but such is the way of the world. Each generation rises up against the one before it."

"They no longer even go to synagogue," protested Hiyawi, sitting beside him.

The cantor bowed and began the service. Rabbi Bashi breathed deeply, shut his eyes, and prayed with great intensity. His face, which had resembled a proud angel's, now bespoke a God-fearing humility. Despite his age, he genuflected with youthful agility, each bending of the knees bespeaking devotion, supplication, and the joy of union with his Creator. Hiyawi, who felt that he was beholding the mystical light of God's Creation, was certain that the rabbi had put aside his body and risen to the rung of pure spirit, from which he was praying for the welfare of his people. When Rabbi Bashi left the synagogue, all rose again to clear a path for him.

"Hiyawi, come dine with me," the rabbi said, as was his custom when he wished his solitude to be eased by the old tobacconist's company.

"It will be my great pleasure," said Hiyawi, walking behind Rabbi Bashi to his home in the Christian quarter with what almost looked like a dance step. As usual several petitioners were waiting outside the rabbi's home, in front of which the police guard, who spoke a perfect Jewish Arabic, bowed deeply to him. Rabbi Bashi received them in his study, and when the last of them had left he stepped out into the immense courtyard, inhaled the night air, and lifted his arms towards the sky as if conducting a debate with it. Then he and Hiyawi washed and sat down to eat, waited on by the rabbi's valet, after which they said the Grace after meals and retired to the study. Rabbi Bashi bent over an open copy of the *Zohar* and chanted aloud from it, explaining the text while smacking his lips as if over a rare dish. The beatific tobacconist forgot all his troubles, and after the two men had tea and coffee, followed by a glass of arrack that the rabbi asked for and drank in small sips, the latter's mood grew so mellow that he began to sing in a sweet voice:

O build the gates with silver and carnelian.
For Thee my soul yearns and great is its yearning.

He sang ecstatically, tapping the floor with a foot, drumming on the table, and clapping his hands in rapture while Hiyawi joined in huskily. When they had finished, the tobacconist produced a fine Zabana, and although Rabbi Bashi rarely smoked, he took it and puffed at it like a boy with his first cigarette.

It was midnight when they went to bed. From his room Hiyawi heard the rabbi get up and go to the toilet every hour. Although lately he had had trouble urinating, he had no time to consult a physician. At three in the morning Rabbi Bashi rose as usual, washed, drank his coffee, and telephoned Mi'tuk, the head of the burial society, to inquire who had died during the night and when the funerals would be. He asked for details of the deceased and their families, jotted down the addresses of the mourners, consulted his calendar, and planned his condolence calls; then he phoned Rabbi Yosef to inquire who was newly wed or betrothed and Rabbi Ya'akov to ascertain what was new in the rabbinical world and its academies. Having brought himself up to date, he set out with Hiyawi for the early prayer. On their way they stopped at Abu Samir's teahouse, which was little more than a long, low burrow next to the synagogue. Abu Samir was waiting for them in the doorway and served the rabbi his first glass of special tea. A second was given to him after the prayer, and then Hiyawi walked Rabbi Bashi to his office and returned to Taht el-Takya.

I met him coming up the Lane of Doves. Patting my face with his big hand, he asked me to wait while he changed and soon he returned in his best clothes. I was hoping that Rashel would appear, but though she had said the day before that she would be at the demonstration, she was nowhere to be seen.

We set out for the community building. I stole a glance at the old man as he walked by my side. The worry had lifted from his face, and he obviously hoped that the protest had been called off and that the day would pass peacefully. Indeed, it was still early, but before long a flow of dozens, even hundreds of silently marching women and girls, many dressed in black, emerged from the houses and lanes: wives of jailed husbands, mothers of abducted sons, fiancées of vanished young men. They filled the little streets and soon they entered the courtyard of the community building and headed for the rabbi's office.

Rabbi Bashi's secretary, who knew Hiyawi, cleared a path for us to the office. I stood on tiptoe, trying to spot Rashel in the crowd, but Hiyawi pulled me into the office after him. Although

I had passed the rabbi many times in the street and had heard his sermons in the Ezekiel Synagogue, I had never been so close to him before, and I caught my breath and stared as if to discern the divine light that my mother said he gave off. Even when invited to sit I remained stiff and tense on the edge of my chair, my eyes on the mole on the rabbi's grey-flecked cheek that was framed by a thick white beard. Now and then he brushed or wiped his nose with a blue silk handkerchief. The heavy black glasses hiding his eyes seemed to create an impassable distance, and his *imama*, the lavish turban that he wore, made him look so tall that his presence filled the room.

"The protesters are women?" he asked Hiyawi sharply, strumming on the desk.

"Times have changed, Rabbi."

The tall secretary entered and stood at the back of the office.

"Have you phoned the ministry of the interior?" the rabbi asked him.

"They said they would call right back, Rabbi."

"What do the demonstrators want?"

"The Messiah," said Hiyawi.

"All is in God's hands," Rabbi Bashi declared.

"And in yours," Hiyawi said reverently.

"Who is the boy?"

"The son of Salman Hoshi Imari."

"Give my regards to your devoted mother," Rabbi Bashi smiled at me. Then his face grew sombre again. "Have you heard from your Uncle Hizkel? It isn't possible to visit him?"

"Yes," I said, confused. "I mean no. We don't know where he is."

"I can't tell you how many times I've spoken to the minister about him. If only they allowed visits! Try the ministry again," he told his secretary just as the telephone rang. The secretary answered.

"Hello … hello … Your Excellency? Yes, Rabbi Bashi … Isn't this Your Excellency? … but there's a big demonstration here." He lowered his voice. "I understand … I understand … Hello?" He replaced the receiver and stood looking at it. "The minister … "

"Won't speak to me?" said Rabbi Bashi.

The secretary stared at the ground. Hiyawi rose and backed to the door as if forbidden to see the rabbi in his distress. I left with him.

"Is there any news?" a woman outside asked us, a gleam of hope in her eyes.

"The salvation of the Lord cometh in a twinkling," said Hiyawi. His face was ashen.

The demonstrators crowded into the rabbi's office, the smell of their sweat mingling with the scent of wood and books. Their leader, a heavy-set woman with a red birthmark on her cheek, stood by the bookcase like a smouldering volcano. Suddenly she threw back her head, thrust forth her bosom, and clawed at the carved wood with her nails. "Allah!" she cried. "They took my only son. Allah, why do you permit this?"

She was joined by cries and wails. I caught a glimpse of Rashel standing outside and tried to get to her, but a new wave of women drove me back into the office and besieged the rabbi on all sides.

"You're against the Movement," the woman with the birthmark accused him. "You don't care what happens to our children."

"How dare you!" exclaimed the secretary, raising his voice.

"No one has touched *your* son," she retorted, pushing him aside. Rabbi Bashi looked on silently.

"Are you a rabbi or a pawn of the Moslems?" cried someone else.

The secretary sought to silence her. "Do something!" shouted the women. Rabbi Bashi rose, rapped the desk with his ring, held out his hands as if to commence a sermon, and announced: "I proclaim this a day of prayer and fasting!" In the ensuing hush he made his way through the ranks of demonstrators, his right hand extended as usual. No one kissed it. The woman with the birthmark followed him and cried:

"We didn't come here to be told to fast. To the palace!"

"To the palace! To the palace!" cried the demonstrators, surrounding Rabbi Bashi.

"Show the rabbi some respect," pleaded Hiyawi in a choked voice. "Show respect for the Torah!"

"Allah has betrayed us," cried the woman with the birthmark, planting herself in front of Rabbi Bashi. "Have you too?" Backing him into a corner with her bulk, she swept the turban off his head with a tumultuous movement. There was a hush. The rabbi eyed the crowd, now turned into a mob, with twitching nostrils. Few returned his stare. Hiyawi bent down, picked up the turban, brushed it off, blew the dust from it, and handed it to the rabbi, who donned it wanly and straightened up without a word. Hiyawi kissed his hand. "Show the rabbi respect," he murmured in a choked voice. "Show the Torah respect!"

"To the palace!" cried the woman with the birthmark, the mob jostling after her. Rashel was in the middle. I called to her, but she didn't hear me. The tall secretary pushed Rabbi Bashi ahead of him, ushering him out of the office while shielding him with his long arms. In the crush to leave, the glass panes of the bookcases were shattered and sacred books and pictures of famous rabbis fell to the floor. Hiyawi held onto my hand and leaned faintly against a wall, looking dazed and confused. When everyone was gone he retrieved a photograph of Rabbi Yosef Hayyim and kissed it. I knew that he would insist on picking up every book, cleaning it, and kissing it too before restoring it to its shelf with a blessing, and I didn't have the patience to wait. "Don't go to the demonstration," I told him, freeing my hand. "You could get hurt. Wait for me here. I want to find Rashel." I left.

The mob outside was getting unruly. The women and girls had been joined by a flood of office workers, labourers, students, shopkeepers, and peddlars from the Jewish neighbourhoods of Kahwit el-Kebiri, Kahwit el-Zghiri, Tatran, Kucht Bahr and Taht el-Takya, turning the rally into a giant octopus. The handful of policemen flailing at its tentacles were swept away and lost their clubs, and the protesters headed for el-Rashid Street.

Sirens began to sound. Trucks drove up and unloaded hundreds of police who encircled the lead protestors in a khaki ring and clubbed them indiscriminately. Shots were fired in the air and men and women shoved into armoured vehicles. The marchers began to panic and lost momentum. Caught in the crowd, I was rammed against a drainpipe. I grabbed it and shinnied halfway up. From my perch I could see the mob swirling like an eddy on the Tigris, its edges breaking off and flowing towards the narrow entrance of our neighbourhood which was blocked by a contingent of police. Not only had I not found Rashel, I was worried about Hiyawi too. Perhaps I shouldn't have left him. In the end, he might have decided to see for himself what was happening.

Just then I caught sight of Amira waving and yelling something. Could her family have joined the rally too? I clambered the rest of the way up the pipe and ran along the rooftops until I came to a cluster of men looking down from above. In the middle of them stood Abu Saleh el-Hibaz. "We did it, Kabi!" he exulted when he saw me. "We brought out all the Jews in the city. Hurrah for the Movement!" The men around him cheered.

"Just watch them stampede to Israel now," he said, observing the scene like a general. "Run to your father, Kabi. He's at the top of the lane. Tell him to scatter his men and lie low because the police may be looking for him. Quick!"

I dashed from roof to roof but couldn't find my father. Near his shuttered shop I descended to the street, but he was not there either. Fat'hiya, the Bedouin *kemar* seller, stood worriedly scanning the mob. "Have you seen Abu Saleh, Kabi?" she asked. "For God's sake, say something."

"Don't worry," I told her. "I saw him a minute ago and he's fine."

"You swear by the Prophet?"

"I swear to God. Where's my father?"

"He shut the shop and went that way," she said, pointing towards Razi Street.

The shops were all shut. Here and there a food stall had been overturned and yellow *amba* dripped by a sambusak stand. I saw Rashel running towards me in a crowd. Her hair was a mess and she held her shoes in her hands.

"Rashel!" I yelled, fighting to get to her.

"I was nearly trampled," she said with a look of horror.

"Have you seen Hiyawi?"

"No."

"I'm going to look for him."

"Are you crazy? They'll arrest you too. Isn't one person in the family enough?" She grabbed my hand and pulled me after her. "Come to my house." On the way I spied my father shouting at people to open their houses and let in the fleeing demonstrators. I called out Abu Saleh's instructions to him and followed Rashel. She shut the gate behind her and went inside. When she returned from the kitchen with a tray of tea, I saw that she had changed her dress and fixed her hair. The cardamom-flavoured smell of the tea revived me.

"We were lucky this time," she said. "Hizkel isn't going to be freed by either Rabbi Bashi or demonstrations. The only thing that can help is a good Moslem lawyer with connections."

"I'm going to look for Hiyawi," I told her.

"Don't be a fool," she said. "He can take care of himself."

But I was already back in the street. Jews were still running in all directions. Hiyawi was standing in front of his shop with his turban awry and his robe torn, struggling to raise the metal shutter.

"Everyone's closed and you're opening?" I shouted to still the guilt I felt. "Go on home. Why look for trouble?"

He didn't answer. I lent a hand and helped him raise the shutter.

"The world's upside down," said Hiyawi. "God's grace has abandoned us. Allah, where are You? What kind of old age is this for me?"

He entered his shop, still mumbling, and washed his hands with water from a jug. Then he opened a cabinet, took out an ancient-looking Book of Psalms, wiped its binding with his sleeve, and kissed it as if it too had fallen on Rabbi Bashi's floor. Sinking into his armchair, he put on his reading glasses, opened the book, and began to read in a soothing singsong in his hoarse but clear voice:

"Happy is the man who has not followed the counsel of the wicked nor stood in the pathway of sin … "

His face grew soft and fresh as though rejuvenated. I stood marvelling at what a battered old book could do to a Jew.

13.

Each time she pictured his interrogators torturing Hizkel – pulling out his nails, ripping out his hair, hanging him on meat hooks, plunging white-hot pokers into his flesh – Rashel was too sickened to sleep. All night she paced along the wall of her courtyard, skirted the stone bench, turned around, and paced back. The darker and quieter it grew, the louder her clogs clacked against the flagstones, vengefully keeping us awake and reminding my father of his suffering sister-in-law whose husband he had not found. As if he hadn't done all that was humanly possible, going from office to office, police station to police station, prison to prison! As if he hadn't explored every lead, hired the best lawyers, turned for help to Rabbi Bashi, to every prominent member of the community, to whomever he could think of! He was too worried to sleep well himself, but Rashel's protest vigil outside his window – there was no other way to construe it – robbed him of what rest he might have had. Night after night he tossed and turned in bed, only to rise in the end, tiptoe downstairs on bare feet to keep from waking us, and pace parallel to Rashel on our side of the courtyard wall. All the cigarettes he smoked there could not still his fears or silence the persecuting clogs. You bitch, he longed to have it out with her, do you think that you have such a monopoly on pain that no one else deserves to sleep if vou can't?

He repented, however, stricken with compassion, when he

heard that Rashel had dreamed of Hizkel lying on the ground beneath a fisherman's net filled with large rocks, which his police investigators threatened to cast down on him if he did not reveal the weapons and his accomplices. Afraid to fall asleep, she had dozed off towards morning on the courtyard bench, gripping it tightly, only to awake with a start and cry out, "Help, help, they've buried him!" My mother ran to her.

"You were just dreaming, child, relax," she said, stroking Rashel's head.

"Why doesn't Abu Kabi go to Big Imari?" wailed Rashel.

"Big Imari hates Abu Kabi and Hizkel. He won't do a thing for them." It was hard to convince Rashel when my mother didn't believe it herself. Neither said a word while she went to make Rashel sweet tea in a gold-rimmed little cup. My father was sitting, unkempt and unshaven, in the bamboo chair outside the kitchen when she returned, his pyjama top buttoned to his neck. My mother took a cigarette from the pack on the divan and tried working the silver lighter.

"It's out of fuel," said my father, lighting a match for her.

"When will you go to Big Imari?"

"Can't you understand that he only cares about his own neck? The last thing he wants is to be identified with the Movement. He won't help any more than Rabbi Bashi, so why make a fool of myself?"

"Rabbi Bashi isn't your cousin. You and Big Imari have the same blood. Go to him. Can't you see what that poor woman is going through?" She nodded towards Rashel's house.

"You think I don't want to save Hizkel? 'Husbands are found and children are born, but a brother lost is gone forever' – I know the proverb too. How many more brothers do I have?"

"Then why not go? Why this foolish pride of yours?"

"You know what?" my father said sarcastically. "You're right. It's foolish pride. We Imaris like to die on our feet."

"There's more to life than pride. Sometimes one has to swallow it. Maybe your cousin will even return some of what he stole from you."

"Aha, the cat's out of the bag! It's the money that you're after. He can go to hell with all his millions!"

"As if money didn't matter. Better rich than poor when the wolf's at the door."

"Woman, get it out of your mind," my father said in a low voice. "You know I'm followed everywhere."

"*Waweli!* You are?"

"Why do you think they haven't arrested me?"

My mother clapped her hands in distress. "What will we do?"

"We'll sit it out. It's a game of nerves. Sometimes the best thing to do is nothing at all."

She went to the kitchen and came back with two trays laden with pittas, quince jam, fresh *kemar,* salty cheese, and coffee. Putting the bigger tray in front of my father, she stood holding the other, which was for Rashel.

"Now you're feeding her too?" my father said. "Leave her something to keep her busy."

"Never mind. She needs all the help she can get."

My mother felt responsible for Rashel. The match with Hizkel had been her doing. He had liked to join us for Sabbath lunches, at which she always served *chamin,* a stew that simmered overnight until the shells of its hard-boiled eggs turned brown, and that year she suggested that he have a look at the attractive young lady who lived with the old woman in the house next door. At first he begged off. Someone active in the Zionist underground, he told my mother, had no business getting married; no one knew what the future would bring and it was best to put such things off until he reached Israel. In the end, though, he decided to humour her, and one wintry Saturday he went up to take the sun on our roof and get a glimpse of Rashel in her courtyard. He stayed there for rather a long while, and though his face betrayed no emotion when he descended, the next Sabbath the two women were our guests.

The meal was a long one. So was the conversation. I myself was embarrassed to talk in Rashel's presence, because my voice was breaking and I never knew what sound – a masculine baritone or a childish alto – would be produced next. Hizkel left the following day for Basra, where he often travelled on business, and was away for a month. While Rashel made no inquiries about him, she began to spend long hours in our house conversing with my mother and getting to know our friends.

When Hizkel returned, my mother arranged another meeting. Since Rashel was an orphan with no one to give her away except for a distant uncle, Hizkel proposed to her himself, Hollywood-style. My father was cool about the match, while Hiyawi, whose fawning attentions to Rashel had made everyone ask what an old widower wanted with a girl young enough to be his great-granddaughter, was crushed. Nevertheless, he agreed to ask Rabbi Bashi to officiate at the wedding. My mother was thrilled when the chief rabbi consented to give his blessing to the match and considered this a good omen.

It was only after the wedding that we discovered that Rashel was cold and aloof, to say nothing of pampered and lazy. She resented the closeness between Hizkel and my father and wanted to move to the wealthier neighbourhood of Ilwi. Yet Hizkel refused, bought the house she lived in and another small unit next to it, and turned them into a big, beautiful home. An amateur carpenter, he made all the furnishings himself: the large double bed, the carved chests, the little end-tables, the library, his study with its long, many-drawered desk in which he kept all his manuscripts and outlines for the books he planned to write. Although he had married Rashel, as the saying went, with her wedding dress as her only dowry, he now indulged her every wish and even cooked for her.

My mother professed that it was beyond her how the same womb could have borne two men as different as Hizkel and my father, who never did a thing around the house and wouldn't even make himself a cup of tea. It was a lucky thing for Rashel, she said, that the two brothers weren't alike. And yet not only did Rashel fail to appreciate my mother, who had expected to be looked up to like an older sister, she stopped coming to us for Sabbath meals, spent as little time in our house as she could manage, and disregarded my mother's advice to give birth to her first child as close as possible to nine months from her wedding night, like a good Jewish wife. Only respect for Hizkel made my mother conceal her annoyance, yet now that he had vanished, pity made her give total support to Rashel. Why, the child was barely married two years and already abandoned! If only she had had the sense to get pregnant, there would at least have been a baby to hug and comfort her. More than once my mother had wanted to talk to Hizkel about the matter, but had kept from doing so by her reluctance to seem nosy. Now, arriving with the tray of food, she found Rashel, her hair uncombed, staring into space on the stone bench.

"Here, my sister. Wash and have a bite to eat," she said, laying the food on the bench and departing.

Rashel picked up the tray, took it to the kitchen, opened the glass-panelled cupboard, and took out the mixture of sesame paste and honey that had been Hizkel's specialty. With a sinking feeling she noticed that the jar was almost empty. Despite the morning sunlight, the kitchen was in shadow. She had always liked its dimness, which let her wake at her leisure and sit silently listening to time's cogs turning slowly while sipping tea and cardamom with Hizkel, whose plans to open a window in the wall she had opposed. Now, however, the darkness heightened her sense of loneliness. She finished the food on the tray with an appetite she had not had since the day of Hizkel's arrest, took her coffee back out to the courtyard, and sat wondering how to spend the day. It was a question that she asked herself each morning and was never able to answer. Sometimes she simply dozed on the bench, abandoning herself to the sun's rays until they stung.

But today she felt the need to do something. The question was what? She rose, stretched her arms and legs, and as though by instinct, began to do warm-up exercises. From there she passed to the calisthenics that Hizkel had made her perform with him each morning, working on her legs, her arms, her hips, and her neck while careful not to pull a muscle because she hadn't exercised for a long time. She skipped until her hands tingled from the rope and her cheeks had a rosy flush, grinning at the delicious flow in her limbs as the sweat poured from the roots of her hair and her face and body relaxed. Then, alarmed by the pleasure she had allowed herself, she reverted to her stern look.

Yes, she would go today to see Karim Abd el-Hak, the Moslem lawyer recently hired by her brother-in-law. He was the son of Hajj Yahya Abd el-Hak, the owner of the metalwork shop facing Abu Kabi's watch shop. She did not need an escort and would tell no one where she was going. This would be her chance to find out the truth and discover whether Abu Kabi and his wife were keeping it from her. She was tired of sitting at home like a prisoner and staring at the walls all day long. Since Hizkel's arrest she had not known what to do with herself. She lacked the concentration to read the translated novels and detective stories that she once had devoured, and on the rare occasions that she felt like going out, she was so closely watched that she nearly choked on everyone's concern. What would people say if she were seen about town while her husband was being tortured by the police? You couldn't take a step in Baghdad without worrying what someone thought. She and Hizkel had often talked about this. "You just have to say the hell with it," he had told her. And yet flying in the face of her whole upbringing was easier said than done.

Now, however, a sudden burst of energy made her feel that she was ripe for Hizkel's message of freedom. She took a cold shower, dressed, and looked with satisfaction in the mirror at her young, feminine body. For weeks she hadn't allowed herself such self-scrutiny, making do with the quickest of glances. Although the weight she had lost brought out her prominent cheekbones, she did not like the colour in her cheeks or the anxious look in her eyes, and for the first time since Hizkel's arrest she took her lipstick and applied a thin stroke. Um Kabi and everyone else could make all the faces they wanted! The Moslem lawyer needn't see her looking wretched. She did not want his pity. What she wanted was his respect which alone could persuade him to use his connections on her behalf. She should make him want to do his best for her. Everyone knew that Moslem men preferred Jewish women. They were freer, bolder, and better educated than their Moslem counterparts who hid behind long robes and veils and never went out with their husbands or even shared in male conversation, an act that was deemed brazen and rude. A Jewish woman's company could be enjoyed, especially if you liked Jews anyway. When he was a law student, so Rashel had heard, Karim Abd el-Hak had spent long hours in her brother-in-law's shop, chatting about all kinds of things.

Although it was still early, she decided to set out before there was time to change her mind, quickening her steps as she passed Hiyawi's tobacco shop. When she turned to look, however, he was not at the window. Abu Kabi, too, was not yet in his shop, where his servant Abed was bent over a table. Nearing Abu el-Izingula's lotions shop, Rashel was piqued by the scent of rosewater and bubbling oil and made a note to drop in on her way back. She hailed a horse-drawn cab on el-Rashid Street, took it to the lawyer's office, found him alone there, and introduced herself.

Karim Abd el-Hak rose to greet her with a look of surprise, inviting her to sit down only after ascertaining that no male escort was following. He thumbed through some papers to hide his discomfort, smiled awkwardly, and offered her a cigarette from a golden box. He was a man of about thirty-five, a bit older than Hizkel, with a large, heavy body, a high forehead, black curls that glistened with hair oil, and a carefully groomed moustache. There was something about his warm brown eyes that inspired confidence and Rashel quickly overcame her fear of being alone with him. And yet though she needed to know if he too believed that her husband was a traitor, she didn't dare put the question to him.

"I'm glad you came," said Karim Abd el-Hak, lightly tapping his left hand with a ruler held in his right. "There are some things I'd like to ask you."

He rang a bell on his desk. A black servant in a white tunic appeared and said: "Yes, Excellency?"

"What will you have to drink, Madame Imari?"

"Anything."

"Tea?"

Rashel nodded and the lawyer told his servant: "Tea for madame and coffee for me, please."

The servant bowed and left, and the lawyer asked Rashel about the Imaris, about Hizkel, about her and her husband's social circle, and about herself, although he must already have known some of the answers from his long acquaintance with Abu Kabi and Hizkel. Rashel told him about Hizkel's date business; about the night school Hizkel had established for working men; about *The Daily Mail,* his newspaper that was shut down after the trial of Shafik Addas; and about his love of poetry and literature to which he was more devoted than to his friends and family. She was sure that the police had made a foolish mistake and felt as if she were protesting Hizkel's innocence not just to the lawyer, but to her husband's interrogators and judges as well.

And yet suddenly, wondering whether Karim really cared about the case or was simply curious about the life of a Jewish couple, she faltered and regretted having come. The lawyer took a firmer tack.

"Madame Imari, you know that I often saw your husband in your brother-in-law's shop and I must say that I was greatly impressed by him. Now, after all that you've told me, I'm even more so. But are you quite sure that he wasn't dealing in weapons?"

"Weapons? I never heard of that," Rashel said. The lawyer's level gaze made her squirm. Did he know more than she did? As he saw her out, he said:

"Please forgive me if I put you through an ordeal. There are certain things that I need to be certain of in order to construct a solid defence."

"Abu Kabi says that all this is just a way of putting pressure on the Jewish community."

"Perhaps. Perhaps. The secret police are as cunning as they are cruel. They're like that everywhere. They'll balk at nothing. You must stand firm. I believe that your husband is alive."

His voice was warm and reassuring, and on her way home Rashel clutched at the hope that everything would be all right. *He's alive, he's alive,* she kept telling herself. Soon he would come home and they would go back to their old life. Once again Hizkel would rise early, take her hand, and lead her to the courtyard for their morning exercises, after which they would breakfast in the kitchen on foamy milk fresh from the cow, two-minute eggs, Hizkel's sesame paste with date syrup, and *gaurag*, the hard, dry pitta that Abu Saleh baked for him especially. At first she hadn't liked this bread, much less her husband's loud munching of it, but his love of food was so infectious that soon she was eating just as noisily, with her mouth wide open like his.

Once Hizkel had left for work and the house had quietened down, Rashel would return to bed for a delicious hour of morning sleep, after which she read, drank coffee, and went out to smell the scents of the souk, see the people there, and eat *zingula* or some sweet bought at a stand. Then, coming home, she lay down to rest until Hizkel returned in the late afternoon and it was time to help him, the head chef, with dinner by preparing such side dishes as stuffed spleen and garlicky aubergine. After eating he showered and shaved, and then they spent the evening out. Sometimes they took a carriage to the King Faisal Bridge on the banks of el-Kark, stopped to gaze at the twinkling enchantment of the lights in the river, made a circuit of Baghdad's wealthy neighbourhoods, returned by a second bridge to the city centre at el-Risafa, and proceeded to the Casino for Dutch beer, ice cream, cream cakes, and bowls of pistachio nuts before walking slowly back to Taht el-Takya. In the darkness of the narrow, unlit streets Hizkel hugged her and covered her with sweet, furtive kisses of electrifying impropriety. They took her breath away, setting her so on fire that she tore herself from his arms and begged him to hurry home and fling himself with her on their large wooden bed for a night of unending love.

Her memories were so real that she could actually smell the sharp odour of his armpits and feel the pain of her longing for him, her carnal desire. Allah! Only now did she realize how happy she had been, what blissful nights she had had. The damned Movement! It was to blame for everything, for her loss of Hizkel after all she had been through. She had sensed from the start that it would end badly, especially on the nights he had left her to go to Basra or God knew where. Not that his underground work was not romantic or did not add adventure to their lives; yet Israel itself had seemed little more than a distant and dangerous place to her. Despite Hizkel's attempts to convey his enthusiasm to her, it was only grudgingly that she promised to go and live there with him one day. She would have preferred to visit first, and no matter how often he told her that he had to set a personal example as a leader, she knew how difficult it would be to give up her life in this Land of the Two Rivers in which her parents and ancestors had lived and died. Her whole world was here! And something told her, too, that it would be easier to maintain the ardour of her marriage in Baghdad. If even Hizkel's trips to Basra left such a hole in her existence, what would happen in his dreamland, which would – all she had heard and read made her sure of it – rob her of him even more than the Movement did in Iraq?

Like most Baghdadi Jews, Rashel had hoped that a Jewish state in Palestine would be created peacefully by means of the compromise of the UN partition plan; she had never dreamed that the whole Arab world, Iraq too, would go to war because of it. Yet not only had this war failed to cool Hizkel's zeal, it had made him as fanatical a devotee of the Movement as the dove flyer was of his doves, so that his work became her rival for his love. Her feminine instincts told her that his dreams were fundamental to his being in a way she was not. Although in their double bed at night he devoured her with passion and promised her the sky, the next day his mind was somewhere else. A man so special would have to be fought for tooth-and-nail.

And then, in one night, everything had collapsed. The hopes and dreams had turned into nightmares that made her stomach churn constantly. She regretted letting Hizkel convince her not to become pregnant. She should have listened to Um Kabi's advice that no man's will could withstand a woman's wiles.

She was close to tears by the time she reached Taht el-Takya. The joyful confidence inspired by the lawyer was gone and once more she felt like a small, unprotected orphan. She was sorry now that she had gone to see Karim Abd el-Hak by herself. Perhaps she had talked too much. She wondered whether she should go straight to Abu Kabi and tell him about the meeting. He would hear about it from the lawyer anyway.

She stood at the top of her street, debating. She did not feel like going home, where everything reminded her of Hizkel, and for a while she wandered about the souk as if trying to vanish in the throng. There was something comforting in the lusty cries of the vendors as they bargained with the women out shopping. A thin young man looked at her dreamily and sighed: "Ai, those breasts should be carved in marble!" Despite her fiercely reproachful glance she was inwardly pleased and tossed back an unthinking head like a proud swan.

She considered stepping into Abu Saleh's bakery but hesitated.

Since Hizkel's arrest, the baker hadn't been to see her. Perhaps he had a guilty conscience, or thought that she was under surveillance like Abu Kabi. Or possibly he feared what people might say if he, once a constant visitor in their home, dropped in on her in Hizkel's absence. She wanted badly to find out from him if Hizkel really had dealt in arms. The pittas he sent her via Kabi were not enough.

And why hadn't Hizkel told her the truth himself? Was it because he didn't trust her enough to make her an exception to the rules of undercover work, even though no one loved him and worshipped him more than she? She would give her life for him, he would yet see! Could it be that at heart he had the same low opinion of women as other men? And yet he was so different from them, even from his own brother. Perhaps he was guilty and had kept her in the dark for her own good. In recent months he had sometimes gone out at night with his work tools and carpenter's overalls. Making furniture for their home was one thing, but why, she had asked, was he returning to his old trade and even taking on night work when his business was doing so well? His only answer had been that he was preparing for their new life in Israel, where a knowledge of carpentry might come in handy, and she had felt it best not to press him. She knew from her own and her sister-in-law's experience how stubborn the Imaris could be and hoped that this latest caprice of Hizkel's would pass more quickly if unopposed. Had he been running weapons all along? Mentally and emotionally exhausted, she followed her feet home. Yet after standing for a while in front of the gate with her key in the lock, she took it out and went to see my mother.

"I was looking for you," said my mother. "Where have you been?"

"To see Karim Abd el-Hak." The words were out of her mouth before she knew it.

"Alone? Without Abu Kabi?"

"Yes."

"You shouldn't have. A woman like you with a Moslem? What will everyone say?"

"He's my husband's lawyer."

"A Moslem is a Moslem, and men are men. What did he say to you?"

"Nothing new." She took off her wedding ring, breathed on it, and polished it on her dress.

"You have to trust in God."

"Maybe you'll tell me where to find Him."

"Hush, His name be praised," my mother scolded. "We must have faith in the Holy One, Blessed be He in Heaven, and in Rabbi Bashi on earth. You're pale. Have you eaten?" Without waiting for an answer she went to the kitchen and brought back a plate of Rashel's favourite meatballs stuffed with rice.

My mother could not even prevail upon Rashel to visit the shrine of Ezekiel. "Hizkel el-Nabi will protect us," she declared of the prophet my uncle was named for, who was said to be buried in Kifl, a little town on the Euphrates. Every year she made a pilgrimage to his tomb that my great-grandfather had rescued from destruction by bribing the Turkish officials not to raze it and the nearby inn.

The Imaris had been the shrine's patrons ever since. My mother's visits there were generally in the company of Hizkel if he had time. These trips created a closeness between them, for on the way they would talk about God, the prophets, and religion, things that did not interest my father. When Hizkel came down with a bad case of jaundice before his marriage and lay so ill in our house for a month that both the doctors and my father feared for his life, my mother gave him fresh watermelon juice, nursed him day and night, and trusted in the holy prophet. It was at the shrine in Kifl, too, that my uncle had been circumcised, after which my grandmother bathed him in holy spring water, laid him on the blue velvet drape of the tomb, and prayed out loud to the prophet Ezekiel: "This is your son. Now take good care of him and give him a long life!"

When Hizkel was little, my grandmother made the pilgrimage with him twice a year. Although the smoky smell of the wax candles in the chapel full of petitioners made him feel faint, he imagined as he stared at the velvet drape that he could see the white-bearded, glowing-eyed prophet, looking exactly as his mother described him. So faithfully was he raised to pray to him for health and success that even afterwards he lived his life as if sure that the prophet was watching over him. Even after the *Farhood*, which shook the religious convictions of many, he often stopped off to light candles in the shrine on his way to Basra.

My mother, who never doubted faith's rewards but had despaired of getting Rashel to go with her to synagogue even for the weekday Torah reading, convinced me to accompany her instead, in the hope of finding the old kabbalist Shimeil Yosef

Darzi. Her eyes glowed reverently as we entered the house of worship, in which she sat as usual in the front row of the women's gallery, a thin white kerchief hooding her eyes that she kept on the prayer book while waiting for the Holy Ark to open like the gates of Heaven. So great was her love of hearing the Torah read that one might have thought she was standing at Mount Sinai itself. Each time the scroll was taken from the Ark she instinctively reached out a hand and brought it to her mouth as if she had kissed the holy letters, a tear of happiness welling in her eye for the bounty of the Creator in saving her family and her people from all trials and tribulations.

My mother had inherited her religious belief from her own pious mother and from her father, my grandfather Rabbi Moshi, who had studied with Rabbi Bashi in the talmudic academy at Beit-Zilha and died young of a mysterious illness before I was born. Her reverence for Rabbi Bashi went back to her childhood when she had been told by her father of his great learning, encyclopaedic memory, and secret mystical powers.

As the kabbalist Shimeil Yosef Darzi was not there, a woman advised my mother to leave a message with S'hak Limnashir. S'hak Limnashir was known as a "blesser", a man whose good wishes for health, wealth, happiness, and success in studies, business and marital life were of great value and available for a pittance, or sometimes for nothing at all. Often my mother visited him in his run-down hovel near the synagogue, sometimes taking us with her. Since he lived by himself, she brought him food in the *safartas,* which he wolfed down so hungrily that grains of rice flew into his beard and over his dirty robe. Although he honoured my mother greatly and never minded taking time to talk to her, I tried to avoid him. As if the Devil in person were to blame, I kept losing the amulets that he wrote for me, which only worsened the fears that they were supposed to quieten.

My mother conferred with S'hak Limnashir in private. He gave her a written blessing for Rashel and promised to tell her when the kabbalist returned from Basra, where he had gone on a mission for a wealthy Jew.

14.

"You'll drive Rashel crazy with your soothsayers!" exclaimed my father when informed of my mother's intention of inviting Shimeil Yosef Darzi to our house.

"He reads the *Zohar*. He knows secrets."

"I don't believe in them," my father said.

"You won't go to Big Imari, you won't let me see the kabbalist ... the only person you're willing to turn to is a Moslem sheikh!"

"The kabbalist will do as much good as the sheikh did," muttered my father, who had no choice but to agree.

Shimeil Yosef Darzi did not arrive unaccompanied. With him came an entourage of elderly disciples in white robes who sat in our courtyard eating, drinking, and singing psalms while he inquired about Hizkel and his physical appearance, his interests, and his arrest. Shimeil Yosef Darzi's grey robe and red fez with its ornamental coil marked him as a man who took pains with his looks. His beard was carefully trimmed and his forehead had a polished gleam. For his disciples, who hovered over him and catered to his beck and call, he seemed to have little use.

"Bring me your children," he told my mother.

"All of them?" Wonderingly she assembled us. The first to be disqualified was me. Next my younger brother Nuri was asked a single question and dismissed with a wave of the hand. That left eight-year-old Moshi. The kabbalist drew him close, peered into his eyes, and announced: "This is the unblemished young soul that I seek."

That evening he took Moshi to the synagogue. My mother's eyes were bright with joy and Moshi's with tears. Out of curiosity, I also went along. Shimeil Yosef Darzi seemed none too happy about this, but he could hardly forbid me to attend prayers. As soon as we arrived one of his ancient helpers began to go over the letters of the Hebrew alphabet with Moshi. Although I was too bored to return a second time, Moshi was taken back every day for an additional dollop of learning.

"They'll drive the boy out of his mind," my father fumed.

"What has he done to deserve this?"

"He's studying Torah," replied my mother blissfully. "I'll have a son who's a scholar."

Hiyawi was angry too. Shimeil Yosef Darzi, he told my mother, was neither a rabbi nor a kabbalist but a greedy charlatan whom he knew from the days when he had studied with him and my grandfather in Rabbi Bashi's academy. "How can you compare the two?" he cried furiously when my mother retorted that the man was a disciple of the saintly kabbalist Rabbi Yihudah Moshi Ftaya. "He doesn't come up to Rabbi Ftaya's shoelaces!" Rabbi Ftaya, said Hiyawi, possessed the powers of healing, divination, reading a man's former lives, and conversing with the angels and the devils. On Saturday, when the kabbalist was invited back to our house for the Sabbath lunch, he, Hiyawi, intended to make himself scarce.

My mother spent the whole week preparing Shimeil Yosef Darzi's banquet. She made my father and Abed bring the large Passover table from the cellar, spread it with a white cloth, and set out her best china and silver as if the Pasha himself were coming to dine. When the kabbalist and his followers arrived after the Sabbath morning service, they found the table covered with a glorious array of appetizers. There was a vegetable salad diced into tiny cubes and seasoned with parsley, mint, and thin slivers of lemon; bowls of pickled gherkins, baby eggplants, and green plums; salted okra and black-eyed beans; cloves of Persian garlic marinated in curry; hot-and-sour mango chutney, the very smell of which made your jaws ache with hunger; chopped onion in lemon juice and sour red fish sauce; and bowls of spring onions, parsley, pepper-grass, mint, basil, hot peppers, and mild peppers in vinegar and salt. Ranged among these the length of the table were platters of fried fish strips and fish roe, steamy hard-boiled eggs and browned potatoes from the Sabbath *chamin*, and fried slices of aubergine and courgette – all of which, needless to say, was merely to work up an appetite.

After washing his hands, Shimeil Yosef Darzi lifted the large silver goblet and said the blessing over the wine, to which the gathering responded with thunderous amens. He then blessed Abu Saleh el-Hibaz's special Sabbath pitta, stuffed it with fish roe, Persian garlic and pepper-grass, and took a bite. A smile of pleasure creased his face and he nodded to his followers. At once hungry hands launched a noisy assault on the food, punctuated only by premature burps. When the kabbalist finally stopped to rest, he poured himself a glass of choice arrack, mixed it with cold water, and proposed a toast to the life and health of Hizkel Imari, bringing a tear to Rashel's eye. He then belched, wiped his lips with a linen napkin, and broke into a prayer that began:

> I keep the Lord's Sabbath
> And the Lord keeps me,
> And thus we are bound
> For eternity.

It was now the turn of the *tbit*, a stew of chickens stuffed with meat, rice, and slices of tomato spiced with fragrant ground cardamom. With it was served the *facha*, the stomach and intestines of a sheep stuffed with the same mixture and flavoured with *numi basra*, the delicate, paradisical-scented lemon of Basra. "The dish that cooks the slowest is for the Sultan," said the proverb, and so both the stew and the *facha* had simmered for twenty-four hours. Their vaporous aromas invoked cries of approbation from the kabbalist and his band which, grunting, dug in with hands and teeth, shovelling into their gullets and maws far more than these could conceivably have accommodated.

The next-to-last course was one of my favourites: a cold okra *kubba* soup made with balls of ground rice and meat spiced with onion and Basra lemon and cooked in a thick reddish broth. Already stupefied by so much food, the kabbalist revived at the sight of it as if he had been fasting all day. He ate more slowly now, smacking his lips after every bite. "Bless your hands, Um Kabi," he murmured, grinning and bobbing his head with delight. The fact of the matter was that my mother hadn't tasted her own cooking yet, since she, my father, Abed, and I were too busy serving the kabbalist's guests and making sure that everything was to his liking – the precise requisites of which had been explained to us by his advance staff. We brought dessert and strong tea with mint and cardamom, and after reciting the Grace, Shimeil Yosef Darzi delivered a sermon on the importance of the Sabbath as if he were Rabbi Bashi himself.

By now our large courtyard was full of neighbours and curious onlookers, all waiting to see what the kabbalist, who had been the talk of the neighbourhood all week long, had to say. Even Hiyawi had broken his vow not to come. Shimeil Yosef

Darzi asked for a glass bowl that my mother had been told to prepare, filled it with clear water boiled and cooled at his request the day before, and demanded a bit of oil. Pouring a few drops of it on the water, he raised his right hand and called to my brother Moshi – who, dressed in his holiday best with new shoes and a golden skullcap, had been dancing and singing apprehensively amid the kabbalist's band.

"Come forth, O blameless soul, O pure of heart!"

Like Isaac about to be sacrificed, my brother was brought forward. You could hear a pin drop as the kabbalist gripped his shoulder and stared at him with dark, burning eyes. "What do you see, my son?" he asked.

Moshi looked at the bowl. "Hebrew letters," he said.

"The holy tongue, the holy tongue," ran a whisper around the courtyard.

"Hush!" cried an elder.

"Read what it says," commanded the kabbalist. "Alef, Lamed, Kuf, Zayin, Het," said my brother.

"The letters that spell Hizkel!" said the kabbalist. "Read on."

"Resh, Alef, Yod, Het, Samakh," read my brother painstakingly. The kabbalist and his band consulted in whispers.

"*Asir! Hai!* Hebrew words!" exclaimed Shimeil Yosef Darzi triumphantly. "A prisoner! Alive!"

"Hallelujah!" came joyful cries from the crowd. "A saint! A great saint!" The kabbalist silenced them with a raised hand, turned to Moshi, and asked:

"What else do you see?"

Moshi stared at the floating drops of oil and said nothing. "What else, my son?" The question was repeated more insistently.

Moshi went on staring without a word.

The kabbalist crimsoned. Bending over, he whispered something in Moshi's ear, then asked in his hoarse voice:

"Where is Hizkel?"

Moshi stared blankly at the bowl of water, looked back up at the kabbalist like a forgetful pupil, and broke into a sweat. All eyes were on his face, which looked on the verge of tears.

"Why don't you leave the boy alone," cried Hiyawi.

"Shame on you for raising your voice at the holy kabbalist!" he was rebuked.

"Can't you see that he's a swindler?" exclaimed Hiyawi. "He's making fools of you all."

"Heretic! Unbeliever!" scolded one of the kabbalist's band.

"How can you talk like that to a saint?"

"For our sins we have been punished with exile," grieved the kabbalist. "There is no faith in our camp. Therefore Heaven spurns us."

"It's a sad day when the Kabbalah has come to this!" Hiyawi shouted.

"We no longer keep the Sabbath. Our doors have no mezuzahs. The commandments are not observed. We are miserable sinners!" mourned Shimeil Yosef Darzi in defence of his honour.

"You're just out to make a fast dinar!" Hiyawi accused him, his face red.

"Throw him out of here!" shouted a disciple, approaching Hiyawi with clenched fists. Three more of the band shoved the tobacconist until he nearly fell.

"Take your hands off him!" cried my father. "He's my guest." There was a sudden hush.

Rashel was biting her lips and nervously fingering her dress.

She had sat there wanly, disappointed in God and in man, and now she rose with a sigh and left. Moshi fled weeping from the band of old men and buried his head in my mother's lap.

In the melancholy mood that descended on the courtyard, the kabbalist and his band made their shamefaced getaway like a troop of unsuccessful acrobats. I peered into the bowl of water. There was nothing remotely resembling a letter there, only drops of floating oil. My father put his hand on my shoulder and signalled to me to follow him. We left without a word of goodbye. My father walked slowly, his neck hunched between his shoulders. After a while, he took out a packet of cigarettes from his pocket.

"Babba, it's the Sabbath!"

"To hell with the Sabbath!"

"Babba, Jews will see you."

"To hell with the Jews!"

"Babba, at least wait until we get to a Moslem neighbourhood."

"To hell with the Moslems too!" He lit a cigarette, inhaled deeply, and slowly exhaled for the benefit of the Jews sitting on their terraces.

"God doesn't keep accounts," he said to me. "Little people whittle Him down to their own size. Religion is something in the heart." He rarely talked about God, and now I wasn't sure whether or not he believed in Him. Although sometimes he said things like "I swear to God" or "I wish to God", I never knew if he meant them. I knew that the *Farhood* had changed him, and that he had gone back to eating non-kosher food and smoking on the Sabbath as he had done before marrying my mother, the daughter of Rabbi Moshi. Once, during a bitter argument years earlier, I had heard her accuse him of having done and eaten every possible abomination before their marriage, when he had "lived with that singer". I didn't know then what "living with" someone meant, or that my mother was referring to Salima Pasha. In my imagination I pictured my father living next door to a woman who sang all the time and brought him disgusting food.

We left Taht el-Takya, crossed el-Rashid Street, and passed the el-Rafidain Bank, heading north towards the el-Watani Cinema and turning right at the square onto the bridge across the Tigris. The low, depleted river flowed sluggishly between banks of thick red clay that resembled swollen lips. Little islands spotted the rivers, their shores licked by the brown waters that swirled around them like weary lovers. How different it was from the raging winter torrent that pounded at the bridge as if about to sweep it away! In cold weather my father and I sometimes stopped on our walks at the nearby Farhat el-Mazlum Café to drink a cup of piping hot tea and thaw out before the coal fire. When I was a small boy he used to spread his legs and hold me between his knees, the heat from his body warming mine while he nursed a hookah and watched the mighty river through the window. Later, I was given a chair of my own. It was a regular Saturday custom, sometimes preceding a long hike in the city park and sometimes following it.

Since Hizkel's arrest, however, my father had stuck close to home, wanting to be there if news should arrive. He had even given up his beloved morning dip in the river, and now he seemed utterly despondent. We descended to the river bank, hired a white boat, and sailed to an island past bright green papyrus reeds. The river was teeming with fish, *shibut* and *sluk* and *ktan* and *abu-sweif*, and a fisherman already had a fire going. The twigs crackled and sent up a flare to the islands all around, which soon answered with bright signals of their own. In no time the river was a lyrical blaze of spitted fish beneath a canopy of blue smoke dotted with red sparks. The smell made my mouth water.

My father took some "white soul milk", arrack mixed with water, and poured it on his hands like a Jew washing before a meal. He muttered something under his breath and emptied the rest of the glass – and then, for the first time in my life, he poured me one too. I sipped it warily, this elixir of the Caliphs, feeling its sharp, bitter flame scorch my throat. The smell of the mastic it was scented with, so liked by him, repelled me. Although I had drunk arrack on the sly with my friends, I had never developed a taste for it. Not wanting to disappoint him, however, I pretended that it was heavenly and murmured my appreciation.

A musician tuned his lute while another tightened the skin of his drum by heating it over the fire. Gyrating like the tongues of flame, a bosomy, generously proportioned young singer, heavily made up with rouge and mascara, started in on Muhammed Abd el-Wahab's bucolic *Mahlaha Isht el-Falah*, "How Sweet Is The Farmer's Life". I had never been so close to a half-dressed woman before, except for once when my mother had sent me on an errand to Rashel, who – perhaps absent-mindedly and perhaps thinking that it was my mother – opened the door in a sheer chiffon slip. She quickly shut it again and went to put on a house robe, but the fleeting glimpse of her bare breasts and thighs was enough to get a rise out of my member, which was like the biblical pillar of fire by the time I could back out of the door. Now too, as the steamy fish was laid on our table in its incense of curry and cumin, my eyes were riveted to the female form in front of me. My father ripped off the fish's head and tail, dipped them in amba, and began to eat with his hands, first devouring the meat and brown, crackly skin and then gnawing at the fins. Popping a filmy eye into his mouth, he said to me with a smile:

"Eat up, son. She's not about to run away." I did, feasting with mouth and eyes at once.

"Watch out for the bones," my father warned me. "They're tricky." He picked the spine clean, sucked the bones of the head, licked his fingers, and washed them with pungent arrack; then, burping with ceremonial vigour, he loosened his tie, leaned back in his chair, stretched out his legs, and grunted with pleasure. A fragrant hookah was brought with our cardamom-flavoured coffee, and he inhaled its blue smoke while staring dreamily ahead with half-shut eyes. Leaving the coffee untouched, he kept downing more glasses of arrack.

"Babba," I said, pointing to the emptying bottle.

"Son," said my father, "some men drink to get drunk but I drink to stay sobre." The singer returned to the makeshift stage, her curvaceous figure now sheathed in a long black dress, and began a sad, quiet number.

O lullaby my brother
For the smell of my mother is upon him,
O gladden him with song
For the smell of my mother is upon him,
O make his life long,
For the smell of my mother is upon him.

My father stifled a sigh. His eyes clouded and I saw them glisten brightly before he turned his head away. The last, soft light of evening departed slowly as the black robe of night dropped over us, leaving the golden fires to glint in the still water. A lone shepherd's flute sounded mournfully on the bank. The first stars shone in the sky. The river took on the silver sheen of the moon. From somewhere in el-Kark came the voice of the muezzin chanting the praises of God. *Allah akbar. Allah akbar.* There is none beside Him.

"Allah," sighed my father. "What have you done with my brother?"

15.

On a night of the new moon my mother dreamed that her father Rabbi Moshi pulled Hizkel out of the waters of the Tigris, brought him back to life, dried his wet body, sat him on a mat, and gave him a handful of dates. Waking my father and me early in the morning, she announced that we were going to Grandfather Moshi's grave.

"What about my exam?" I asked.

"Your grandfather, may he rest in Paradise, will see to it that you get a good mark."

"I have some important business this morning," said my father, trying to beg off even though he knew that it was hopeless.

"Just look at him! Is Hizkel my brother or yours? Come on, hurry up." Apart from its intrinsic virtue, the visit to the grave, my mother thought, had been endowed by her dream with great powers. My father gave me a lugubrious look, threw up his hands resignedly, and said:

"Come, son. It's time we said our goodbyes to the dead anyway."

I looked at him.

"Yes. We'll be leaving for Jerusalem soon, and they'll be staying behind until the Messiah comes. Go and get Hiyawi." It was a standing request of the tobacconist that we take him with us whenever we visited the cemetery.

"Rashel too?"

"She won't come," my mother said. By now Abed had arrived to take my brothers to school. We ate and drank our morning tea hurriedly, and my mother donned her long-sleeved blue dress and her light blue kerchief. Although her eyes looked tired, the rest of her brimmed with energy. I had an aversion to these forced treks to the cemetery, which I joined only under duress. My mother herself visited the graves of her family every new moon and holiday eve to light candles and put pebbles on the tombstones. "The dead protect us," she liked to say.

We boarded a horse-drawn cab on Razi Street and I sat up front on the high seat by the coachman, feeling like the captain of a ship. On the side streets I was even allowed to hold the reins. We passed white houses with doors painted blue against the Evil Eye and huddled masses of indistinct hovels from which trickled streams of malodorous sewage, and entered a grove of palms that reminded me of my childhood enchantment at the sight of the endless miles of sylvan date groves on the way to the Prophet Ezekiel's shrine in Kifl. The gaunt, bony horses plodded ahead of the carriage and turned off onto a side road where carpets of brightly coloured flowers surrounded us. Peasants in crude cotton smocks stood with watering cans amid the rows of blossoms that stretched wave after wave in an infinite plain of crowded tombstones. I both liked and feared this route, which I had refused to travel on to my grandfather's funeral, even though I had loved him dearly.

My father roused himself from his reveries. As though divining the thickening lump in my throat, he said to me:

"Death is part of life, son."

The thought did not comfort me. Death was death and no less frightening if the road to it led through fields of flowers.

The old cemetery had convolutedly spread in every direction over the years and was now a veritable city of the dead – an eerily quiet one, out of earshot of the tumult of Baghdad. Here and there a gap-toothed fence flanked the graves, as if discouraging their occupants from escaping. Near the entrance a large, vaulted brick structure housed the victims of the *Farhood*. My mother took two skullcaps from her bag.

"Is there ever anything you don't think of?" asked my father.

"Who would if I didn't. You?"

"I can't even say a good word about you," he protested sullenly, like a scolded child. Hiyawi had already gone off to give instructions to some Kurdish workers who knew and respected him. "Someone has to look after these graves," he would say to us. "The souls of our ancestors hover over them. If we all leave Iraq, they'll be left here by themselves."

"God give you long life," my mother would bless him with a grateful glance while my father hid a cynical smile beneath his moustache. Now he watched Hiyawi moving off into the distance with the workers and grumbled:

"Old age makes some people wise and others imbeciles. In the end nothing will be left standing here. The Moslems won't leave a stone untouched."

Having finished with the workers, Hiyawi began to cut across the cemetery, every tombstone of which was familiar to him, in the direction of the impressive tomb of Rabbi Yosef Hayyim. There were many legends about this saint. According to one, he made the rounds of the graveyard at night, making sure that no one harmed it. Once, it was said, when a Moslem had sought to pass urine on a grave, the pious rabbi had frozen it into an icicle from which the man died an agonizing death.

My mother, who was handing out alms to beggars, all crying

"Charity saveth from death," gave me a few coins to disperse and earn a good deed. Her unguided feet led us among old tombstones and mouldering graves to the tomb of my grandfather, which was so overgrown with moss that I could barely make out his name. The "sh" of Moshi was erased and the Hebrew dates of his birth and death were indecipherable. I stood there feeling absurd. Could he see us, hear us? Did he know that we were here? Was his soul really circling above us protectively as my mother said? And would it come with us if we went to Israel or stay behind with its bones, forever haunting the rows of graves? And perhaps it would do nothing because there was nothing – no soul, no afterlife, no nothing except the worms that ate our remains, as Salim Effendi told Edouard in his tirades against religion.

Hiyawi returned, handed us prayer books, and began to chant verses of Psalms. I tried reading along with him, but the muttered words made no sense. When it was time to say the kaddish, I noticed that a minyan of ten men, no doubt prearranged by him, had gathered around us. Although I knew the prayer and had heard it many times, I was so muddled that I said "amen" in the wrong places. The Aramaic words had a portentous ring of death and mourning. I prayed to God that I should never have to say them for my parents.

My mother lit a candle and murmured something with an upward glance. The words of the *El Malei Rahamim,* the "O Lord Full of Mercy", with its prayer for the eternal peace of the departed, unclogged the fount of her tears. When Hiyawi finished, she placed some small stones on the grave and burst out crying, sobbing so hard when she exclaimed, "How could you go and leave me an orphan?" that I too had tears in my eyes.

I headed back for the front gate. Women were wailing by the

mass grave of the victims of the *Farhood,* whose names were being chanted by a cantor:

Chahla daughter of Rachel Mash'al.
Abraham son of Hatun Chiflawi.
Tifaha daughter of Maryam Me'allem.
Abraham son of Maryam Me'allem.
Farha daughter of Zbeida ...

Farha, the daughter of Zbeida? Although the name sounded familiar, I couldn't place it. I stood looking at the brick vault.

Hiyawi joined me and bent over a grave to adjust its crumbling stones. I stared at the old man, the unsolicited guardian of the graveyard who had no grave to visit here, since his parents were buried in the city of Hilla, not far from Kifl, and his wife's body had never been found. He stepped up to me, laid a hand on my shoulder, and said:

"Kabi, would you like to see my burial plot?"

"We're not leaving you here," I told him. "You'll come with us."

The old man shook his head. "I was born here and I'll die here."

He gave me the creeps. "I don't want to hear about it," I said. I walked to the gate and stood there waiting, wondering what gave me such a feeling of foreboding.

"Did you wash your hands?" my mother asked when she caught up with me.

"No."

"Then do. Three times, without drying them."

"All right, all right."

"May your grandfather's great virtue stand you in good

stead," she said when I returned from washing my hands. Quietly we boarded one of the cabs waiting outside the gate. I huddled in a corner, hardly noticing the carpets of flowers that we passed again. The name Farha kept running through my head. For some reason I pictured a wooden gate and felt that I was close to remembering ... but what?

And then, passing Abu Ya'akub's café, it came to me. I was seven at the time. My father and Abu Yosef were playing backgammon in the café. I was licking an ice-cream cone and watching the boys hitching rides on the carriages as they went by. How I wanted to be like them! Suddenly a square-faced man with a keffiyeh burst inside and yelled:

"God damn the Jews!"

"Let's get out of here," said my father to Abu Yosef.

"Just because of one nut?" Abu Yosef got to his feet, grabbed the Moslem by the collar, and butted him in the head. The man staggered, then regained his balance, drew a gleaming dagger from his belt, and shouted: "*Allah akbar!* We'll kill every last son-of-a-bitch infidel!" My father seized my hand and pulled me quickly out of the café. The other customers hurriedly followed and we all headed for the Jewish neighbourhood of Abu Sifin, to which we had moved after leaving el-Me'azzam. The street was full of carriages packed with Moslems, all waving their arms and screaming anti-Jewish slogans. "*Allah akbar, Allah akbar!* Down with the unbelievers! Lift the sword for Muhammed!"

I didn't understand why they were calling us unbelievers.

Didn't my mother go to synagogue every Sabbath, and my father sometimes too? The short route to our neighbourhood seemed endless. The gates of the Jewish houses along the way had been freshly smeared by the rioters with the blood-red symbol of a hand. We would feel safer once we reached Kahwit el-Kebiri, like an animal in its own territory.

My father panted as he ran, leaning now and then against a wall to catch his breath.

"Babba, we left Abu Yosef all alone there," I said. I could still picture him butting the man and felt proud of him.

"I did it for your sake," answered my father, ducking into Abu Mrad's grocery with me.

"What's the matter?" asked the grocer when he saw us. My father told him.

"Ah, it's nothing," said Abu Mrad.

"I want five kilos of rice, three kilos of sugar, and two cans of oil," said my father.

"You're cleaning out my store," said Abu Mrad. "I'm happy to do business, but I'm telling you, Abu Kabi, nothing will happen. They won't dare move in on the neighbourhood, and if they do, the British army will crack down on them. Don't you worry, it's Shavuot tomorrow."

"I don't like the look of it," said my father. "I have a bad feeling. Something tells me it won't be a happy holiday."

"Then we'd better start making it one right now," said Abu Mrad, reaching under the counter for a bottle and two glasses. He filled them and said:

"Here's to your health! And to Kabi!"

"I hope I'm wrong," said my father, draining his glass. Abu Mrad switched on an old radio sitting on a shelf. The rich voice of Salima Pasha filled the store, but my father's face didn't move a muscle as he shouldered the sack of groceries. When we opened the door we heard shouts and he cried:

"Lock up quick and go home, Abu Mrad. They're coming!"

We took off with a swarm of black locusts in white keffiyehs on our heels. The streets emptied of their Jews, who dived into courtyards and houses like a flock of frightened birds. We ran to the clatter of metal shutters being pulled down in store after store.

"Babba, they're right behind us!" I yelled in terror. Although my father tried running faster, the sack slowed him down. We turned into our own street and he kicked at the gate of our house as if it were the last shelter on earth. Once safely inside, he dropped the sack and rammed home the bolt. "Is Nuri home?" he shouted at my mother.

"Yes. What's the matter?"

"There's a riot."

"A riot?"

"They're killing Jews."

"What are you talking about?"

"Stop asking so many questions and help me bring the locking bar."

He dragged the wooden bar by himself to the gate, wedged it firmly in place, and went back for more things to pile behind it.

"Don't ruin our holiday table," said my mother.

He glanced at the table in the courtyard, which was already set, and said: "Woman, there's not going to be any holiday."

"Where's Hizkel?" asked my mother.

"In Basra."

"Just when we need him, he isn't here."

"I suppose he should have known there would be a riot."

"*Waweli* for our lives!" cried my mother, standing there as stiff as a board. I helped my father drag the sofa to the gate.

"The red slip covers!"

"Is that all you can think of?"

She removed the expensive silk covers and ran to the cellar with them.

"It's either our property or our lives," my father called after her. "Make up your mind, woman!" But while he went on piling furniture against the gate, she returned and started gathering up her good silver and china. Guessing my father's intention of adding the stripped table to the barricade, she was about to protest when she saw him stare at the steps leading up to the roof.

"What are you looking at?"

"They can come from there too."

"What will we do? Maybe we should go to el-Me'azzam. Hairiyya and Abu Ismail will protect us. They're good Moslems."

"And who'll protect them?"

"Then what will we *do*?" My mother burst into tears.

"Stop your wailing! I want you to boil all the oil in the house. There are two cans in the sack, too."

"What for?"

"To pour on their heads."

Between one plea to God and the next, she began heaping curses on the Moslems.

"Woman, save your breath and take Nuri down to the cellar," said my father. He had already forgotten about the oil and now went to the kitchen, came back with a sharp meat knife, and laid it on the table. My mother took Nuri to the cellar. Half drowned out by the cries of *Allah akbar,* the wails of women and the screams of children could be heard everywhere.

"Go up to the roof and tell me if you see them coming," my father said to me.

I stretched out on the low roof and looked below. From the next courtyard little Farid glanced up at me, his eyes glittering with fear. His father stood by the gate with a wooden club. A young Arab ran out of Abu Mrad's looted store carrying a large case of something. Another Arab tried grabbing it and the two began to fight. More and more black robes were pouring into the neighbourhood and spilling down its streets. Hands waved swords, daggers, pistols, clubs dipped in tar. A pot-bellied man with an axe slipped and fell in a puddle, sending the knot of men behind him sprawling on top of each other. He struggled to his feet, a column of muck, wiped his face on his sleeve, and started hacking at the gate of the house across from us, which belonged to a widow named Farha. As he smashed his way in, she ran zigzagging around the yard and finally took refuge in a corner. Although I no longer had a view of her, I could see the man closing in. He looked as if he were hunting down a chicken. Then he kneeled and disappeared from sight.

I didn't want to know that I knew why Farha suddenly stopped screaming. The Arab rose, arranged his clothes, and walked away.

Now, returning from the cemetery, it struck me that I had forgotten her right away. I might never have thought of her again had I not heard her name recited among the victims of the *Farhood*. And with her, in scattered fragments, the rest of that day came back to me too. On the rooftops around me I could see our Jewish neighbours, armed with whatever they had been able to grab – a stick, a stone, a knife, an axe. Some had fled from courtyards overrun by the rioters. A cluster of men on one roof inspired me with confidence, and for a moment I became a general in my childish imagination, sending my forces here and there.

Evening came and it grew dark. Beside the rioters, there were now djinns to fear too. While the shouts of the mob had died down, bonfires burned in the courtyards of the pillaged houses and Moslems danced around them wildly. From the rooftops came groans and laments. My mother lit the oil candles on the holiday table, her voice choking as she said the blessing. Or perhaps she had lit them earlier, before going down to the cellar; everything was jumbled in my memory. One thing I was sure of: my father had not covered his head. Neither had I. I heard him say in a voice charged with hate: "Pour out Thy wrath upon the Gentiles that know Thee not." I knew that the words came from the Passover Hagaddah. Once he had explained at the Seder that we said them because that was our only answer to being killed by the goyim.

"We have to eat something," said my mother.

"You can eat if you want to," my father said. "I'm going up to the roof. It's quiet now, but I'll be able to see from there if more of them start coming."

I couldn't remember eating the Shavuot dinner, but I did recall standing with my father on the roof until nearly daylight, looking silently at the sparks still rising from the smouldering courtyards. We heard bullets and explosions and my father said:

"Those may be troops loyal to the Pasha. Maybe they'll rescue us." He didn't sound very hopeful. Now and then he ran in a crouch to the toilet at one end of the roof.

"Are you afraid?" I asked.

"Yes."

"I'm thirsty."

"Can you wait?" Before I answered he had gone down to the courtyard and come back with the water jug.

"Babba, will they come again tomorrow?"

"I don't know. I hope not."

"Why are they doing this?"

"Because we're Jews." He murmured something else that I couldn't make out.

"What did you say?"

"A prayer in God's language." He hugged me so hard that I could feel his heart beat. Time seemed to have stopped.

It was as the new day dawned and my mother had just said "Thank God, that's the last of them", when we heard them coming again.

"Pack a few necessities," said my father.

"What for?" my mother asked.

"I have a plan. You'll leave now, via the roof, for Rabbi Sasson Kiraba's house."

"I'm not going anywhere without you," said my mother, sitting down on the ground. "Allah will protect us right here."

"Maybe you can tell me where this Allah of yours is. Sleeping off his holiday dinner, I'll bet."

"May He forgive you in His great mercy! How can you talk like that?" My mother struck her hands. "Because of you, He'll punish us all now."

"I suppose that what happened in the neighbourhood last night was because of me too."

"He'll punish those responsible also!"

"Yes, and we'll watch from the graves where we'll lie slaughtered. Woman, both Allah and I will manage without you. Take the children and get out of here. Don't you hear them coming? There's no time!"

Nuri grabbed hold of my mother's dress and began to cry. My father sent me back up to the roof to see what was happening. Down below I saw a big, hefty woman lumbering with a club towards our house. She looked like Ismail's mother Hairiyya.

Even their women are out to kill us, I thought. I looked again. It was Hairiyya.

"Hairiyya's here!" I shouted.

"We're saved," exclaimed my mother.

"Some saviour," said my father. "They'll cut her throat too." And he yelled: "Hairiyya, go away! They'll kill you."

"Let them try!" answered Hairiyya, positioning herself before our gate. She lifted her club and yelled: "We've lived with the Jews longer than anyone can remember. Let no one touch them!"

Strangely enough, the rioters skipped our gate and even fled from it. A minute later the army arrived. Quiet was restored at once. My father opened the gate for Hairiyya. She hugged me in her fat arms and threw them around my mother, embracing her for a long while. Then she sat down by the desolate table. I could see that she wanted to say something but didn't.

"I'm going," my father said.

"Where?" asked my mother.

"There are wounded to take care of and dead to be buried." He came back towards evening with Abu Yosef, who had a bandage on his shoulder. Their clothes were smeared with blood and they looked grey. Without a word they sat on two stools. My mother was still with Hairiyya in the kitchen. After a while Abu Yosef said loudly:

"I'm leaving for Palestine."

"What's your hurry?" called my mother from the kitchen.

"I don't feel like waiting for the Messiah."

"Not every Moslem is a murderer," said Hairiyya.

"That's so. But we're not safe here."

"He's right," my father said.

"They've polluted the soil of Iraq for us," said Abu Yosef.

"They weren't in their right minds," Hairiyya said. "Someone's twisted them."

"If it's happened once," Abu Yosef rejoined, "it can happen again."

My father went down to the cellar, came back with a bunch of keys, and handed them to Hairiyya. "These are to our house in el-Me'azzam. Keep them. It's hard to believe we'll ever need them again."

16.

My memories of the *Farhood* made my father's fears of a recurrence seem terrifyingly real. Every Moslem I looked at had the square face of the man who had tried knifing him and Abu Yosef in Abu Ya'akub's café. Ismail too. One day he would also lead riots against Jews, perhaps even rape and axe to death old Jewish women like Farha.

I skipped school one day and took a long walk to the house in Kahwit el-Kebiri that we were living in at the time of the *Farhood*. My mother, who never talked about those days, was not nostalgic for it as she was for our old home in el-Me'azzam. Although I had never been back there, I now wanted to see the place where the *Farhood* had started. After wandering all day through the errant maze of memory, I dropped in on Hiyawi in his tobacco shop.

"Hiyawi, where were you during the *Farhood?*"

"Kabi, my boy," he replied with a sigh, "why pick at old wounds?" For a while he was silent. Then, finishing his tea and rubbing his face, he said: "What can I tell you? It wasn't God's work, it was His creatures'. You know Hajj Yahya. My shop has been opposite his for forty years, and we're two old men who aren't long for this world. I want you to know that the afternoon before the *Farhood,* when I could already smell trouble, I went up to my roof to take a look. One thought I had was asking Hajj Yahya to take me in; we had known each other since he moved into the neighbourhood, and he had always shown me the respect due to a God-fearing Jew. Hearing voices up the street, I made my way along the rooftops until I spotted a large crowd of Moslems gathered outside his shop. Would you like to know what I saw? Hajj Yahya was standing on the steps and egging on the crowd, which kept shouting *Allah akbar*. At first he spoke too quietly for me to make out his words, but gradually he raised his voice until he was ranting like a preacher in a mosque. I had never heard him say such things. I didn't know if I was dreaming or awake."

"What did he say?"

"Kabi, my boy, what can I tell you? It was your usual anti-Jewish diatribe: 'The Jews are meant to be miserable slaves! Allah has commanded us to kill and destroy them! They're infidels, unbelievers, the worst enemies of Islam! Their own prophet Moses called them a stiff-necked people! The Holy Koran says they're no better than pagans! They should be dealt with by a holy war! It's a virtue to kill them, and whoever does will have a place in Paradise!' Those were his words, and each time he stopped for breath the crowd yelled *Allah akbar*. There was no place for me to run. Kabi, my boy, I just went limp. I prayed to God to shut the man up, but he went on foaming at the mouth:

"'What Islam thinks of the Jews is recorded in Sa'ad bin Ma'ad's verdict on the tribe of the Beni Kurayza: Death to every Jewish fighting man! Death to every Jewish male child! Captivity to every Jewish woman and girl! The entire tribe to be wiped from the earth! Such is the holy judgement of Islam. There can be no peace with the Jews. There can be no reconciliation with the infidels. There can be nothing but war until the last of their corpses have rotted beneath the sun! O ye

Faithful, search the Jew out: in the street, in the alleyways, in the markets, in their houses, in their cellars, in their cupboards, beneath their beds, behind each tree – everywhere! Ferret out the last of them as did Mohammed in his war against them, when the very trees and stones called to the Moslem warriors: Come, a Jew is hiding behind us. Kill him! Slaughter him! And may Allah be with you!'

"That," said Hiyawi, "is what he said. The whole crowd kept shouting *Allah akbar. Allah akbar!* And he –"

"Stop!" I interrupted with a shudder. "I don't want to hear any more."

"Kabi, my boy, listen to me. I myself have one foot in the grave, but you and your children will have to live with these people. You have to realize that they've always felt this way. Let me explain what Hajj Yahya was talking about. In the seventh century, during the lifetime of Muhammed, there were two Jewish tribes, the Beni Nadir and the Beni Kurayza, living near Medina in the Arabian Peninsula. They were Arabs from the desert with the same blood and traditions as the other tribes, the only difference being that they believed in the God of Israel. The Beni Nadir gave in and submitted to Islam, but the Beni Kurayza, who were very strong and had powerful allies, stuck to their Jewish faith. No matter how Muhammed tried converting them, they refused. He wanted them to accept him as the last of the prophets, but they told him that prophecy had ceased with the destruction of the Temple. In the end, he decided to destroy them and surrounded them with his army. On the eve of the crucial battle, their head men agreed to let Sa'ad bin Ma'ad arbitrate the dispute. This Sa'ad was a tribal leader once allied with the Beni Kurayza – and he ruled that they all must die. That was the verdict Hajj Yahya was alluding to. As for

Muhammed, the great saint told his followers, 'Sa'ad bin Ma'ad has given us the judgement of the Most High God in Heaven,' and proceeded to take the beautiful Jewess, Rihana bint Imar, for his concubine, and a fifth part of the loot from the annihilation of the Beni Kurayza.

"Kabi, my boy, just so you don't think that I'm a babbling old man, take the same books that Hajj Yahya did and see for yourself what's written in them. It's beyond me why your father wanted Karim Abd-el-Hak, Hajj Yahya's son, to be Hizkel's lawyer. And don't forget, he was our neighbour for dozens of years! If someone like him who knew us, who ate our bread and drank our water, helped start the *Farhood,* whom can we trust? Lord, the things that happen because people are not what they seem! And don't let your Arab-lovers like Abu Edouard, or that Communist Salim Effendi, tell you that it was only the work of an inflamed rabble. Is Hajj Yahya, who knows Moslem scripture and has been to Mecca and who has a senior army officer and a famous lawyer for his sons, is he rabble? In that case, they all are."

"Didn't you ever ask him why he did it?"

"Of course I did. But all I got out of that pathetic conversation was a lot of verses from the Koran. 'There is no strength or succour but from Allah.' 'We are from God and to God we return.' 'Allah is great and victory will go to the Believers.' 'May Allah pardon all sinners.' It was the last conversation we ever had, and there wasn't a word of sorrow or regret, nothing but pious slogans. From there I went straight to the cemetery to help bury the dead. On my way I hummed the Psalm 'Thou hast placed me above my foes and I rejoice,' because I knew that it was we who would triumph in the end. And we did. The *Farhood* came and the *Farhood* went, but we Jews are still here."

"But what makes them like that?"

"Oof," Hiyawi grunted. "We've been asking that question since the day the first Jew was hated, and God alone knows the answer. All that an ordinary man like myself can tell you is that they've never forgiven us for not becoming Moslems and accepting Muhammed as the greatest prophet. They envy us for being God's chosen people when they are the descendants of Hagar, the handmaiden of our Matriarch, Sarah, and they can't get over their Koran having been stolen from our Bible, from which they took even their belief in one God. In everything we came first. We were even here in Iraq before them. And the most unpardonable thing of all is that, as hard as they've tried, they haven't been able to keep us from surviving. It's envy, my boy, pure envy – and now that your Uncle Hizkel's friends have gone and got themselves a Jewish state, God help us!"

"But what is there to envy?" I exclaimed. "They treat us like dirt!"

"My boy, the Bible tells us that envy is harsher than death. When a man has two eyes, one is jealous of the other. It's no easy matter to understand."

"But if you believe all you say, Hiyawi, what are you doing in Baghdad?"

"Baghdad is as much ours as theirs. Don't they themselves have a proverb that says, 'Heaven is the One God's and the earth is all men's?' Besides, our Patriarch, Abraham, came from here, and there's no other place in the world I'd rather be while waiting for the Messiah to redeem us in Zion. You can live with Moslems if you accept their way of doing things and make your peace with their being top dog. That's what we've done for generations, and in better times than this one, too. Back before the war, when there was still no Zionism and no rabble-rousing Mufti of Jerusalem and his Palestine, we felt safe here. Old King

Faisal, may God have mercy on his soul, and the Pasha, whom I've known since Turkish times, and the Pasha's brother-in-law Ja'afar el-Askari, and many others, were our friends. Why, I used to go on tobacco-buying trips to the most remote villages, where no Jew had ever been before! It was only when Faisal died and his son Ghazi took over the throne that our troubles began. And now that we Jews have a state with its own army and flag and anthem, and right here in Baghdad there is a Zionist underground with young men who know how to defend themselves, is it any wonder that the Moslems are furious? They can't fathom a contemptible creature like a Jew suddenly standing up tall. How can *dhimmis,* underlings like us, behave like masters and claim an equal place among the nations?"

"Hiyawi," I said, "you're making my head spin. One minute you're on our side and the next you're on theirs." I mentioned Ismail's mother Hairiyya, who had walked on her stout legs all the way from el-Me'azzam, club in hand, to help protect us during the *Farhood.*

"That's human nature, son. There are good people and there are bad people. It's all a matter of who you happen to have in mind."

17

Shortly after the demonstration, Rabbi Bashi was rushed to Meir Elias Hospital. Some said that his heart had given out, others that it was a nervous reaction to being betrayed by his own people. That same day, Abu Saleh el-Hibaz called for a general strike in the Jewish neighbourhoods. Schools were closed, stores and businesses were shut down, and the souk was empty. Even Jewish civil servants took the risk of staying at home. Hiyawi sat on a stool by the door of Rabbi Bashi's hospital room, reciting Psalms and refusing admission to everyone. It was only after much soul-searching that he decided to tell the rabbi about the strike and the police cordon around the Jewish quarters.

"They've lost their senses! I must see the wazir," said Rabbi Bashi, unable to remain a moment longer in his sick bed. It was all Hiyawi could do to convince him to wait while he himself went home and dressed for the occasion, putting on his golden robe that smelled of mothballs, his elegant turban, and a silk sash around his waist.

Together the two men went to the offices of the minister of the interior, where Hiyawi waited at length in a hallway while Rabbi Bashi conferred with the wazir. From there they drove to the royal palace. Rabbi Bashi was flushed and upset when he returned to the Chevrolet, in which he sat breathing heavily after settling into the back seat. As they drove through the

Jewish streets of the city, Hiyawi leaned forward to hide the slogans on the wall calling for the rabbi's resignation.

Back in his study, Rabbi Bashi took off his dark glasses. His large brown eyes were muddied with sorrow. "They are a rebellious house, hard of forehead and stubborn of heart," he said, quoting Ezekiel. "Do they really believe that if I resign they will run this community better than I did? Well, let them try! What do they know about the corridors of power? A leader has to have common sense. I suppose they think that we're living in a democracy like Great Britain. Can't they see that Pharaoh's heart must not be hardened? They want me to come out with an open declaration of support for Israel. Don't they know I would like nothing better? If I could I would dance in the streets for having lived to see a Jewish state. But what would I say to the king and the Pasha – that they should please be so kind as to put up with our dual loyalty? Our rabbis of blessed memory said it long ago, right here in Babylon: *Dina de-malkhuta dina,* the law of the land must be obeyed. You should have heard the tongue-lashing the wazir gave me. 'You're aiding and abetting traitors! Is this how you reward our support for you? If the smuggling of Jews to Palestine doesn't stop, and the illegal weapons and their stockpilers aren't handed over, we'll have to see to it ourselves. One way or another, the serpent's head will be chopped off!' Those were his exact words to me.

"Look here, Hiyawi. If the members of the Movement want to throw dice for their own lives, let them – although even then it's my duty to warn them as my sons. But why should every Jew in this country have to suffer for it? In what way has my people sinned? Let them go ahead and play at politics if they want to. Did I stop them from establishing the Movement? Did I forbid them to train youngsters to use weapons, to hide arms in homes

179

and synagogues, to endanger the lives of women, children, and old men, to take advantage of innocent Jewish girls by using them as gun runners? Great God above! Do you know what the Moslems will do to them? They'll rape them and trample their honour on every rooftop. And it's the women who are demonstrating against me! Did anyone let me know? Did anyone consult with me? My sons and daughters, the youth of this community, have been snatched from me, corrupted and imperilled and exploited to turn the Moslems against us. Yet when it ends in arrests and police terror, whom do they all come running to? To me!

"They want to leave this country? I wish them bon voyage. But just because they're in such a hurry, must all the Jews of Babylon, the mother of our exiles, be condemned? Let them go, I say! Have I tried to keep them here? Have I informed on them to the authorities? I've watched over them as if they were the apple of my eye. Every one of them is a dear child to me. Master of the Universe, what have I done to deserve this? Is this my just reward?

"I could go on. I admit that when the State of Israel was declared, I rushed to pledge the community's allegiance to the crown and the country. What was I expected to do, invite the King and the Pasha to a Purim party? Celebrate in a Baghdad that was burying those who had died fighting in Palestine while oceans of black-cloaked Moslems rampaged in the streets with cries of vengeance? The Tigris would have turned red with Jewish blood! If they want to fight the Moslems, they're welcome to be heroes, but let them realize that we've only stayed alive until now because we've been too weak to fight. Don't they know that peoples stronger than ourselves have taken on the Moslem world and been exterminated? The fools! The perfect simpletons! How could I intervene for my people, how could I extract a single concession, if I antagonized the government? They think they can teach *me* love of Zion – a man who has been waiting longingly for the Messiah's white donkey since before they were born! And what do I see instead? Donkeys and sons of donkeys! They accuse me of condemning Zionism in 1936. And indeed I did, as God is my witness. But they forget that those were the days of that accursed rebel Bakr Sidki; that the Nazis, a plague on their memory, were already in power; and that the Mufti, may God shorten his days, was knocking at the gates of Baghdad. The skies were cloudy with dark omens. Who but a total nincompoop would have come out for Zionism at such a time? The Englishman was weak. Had the Moslems decided to slaughter us all, who would have stopped them? Tell me, Hiyawi: do I need to beg forgiveness from the fools who endangered our very existence? Master of the Universe, what have I done to deserve all this? Is this my just reward?

"I could go on. In the midst of the war, shortly before reports, so frightful that they made my heart bleed, began to reach us about our European brothers, I was summoned by the pro-Nazi minister of the interior, Yunis Sab'awi, a leading supporter of Prime Minister Rashid Ali el-Kailani and an ally of the Mufti, may his name and seed be blotted out. He sat there surrounded by his lackeys, gave me a sugary smile, and said: 'Rabbi Bashi, the mob is clamouring for Jewish blood. Tell your Jews to prepare clothing and provisions and be ready to leave Baghdad for a secret location in the desert, where I will protect them until the hysteria dies down.' He looked so angelic that I almost believed him, and I told him that I had to consult with the leaders of the community. But on my way back from the meeting, I suddenly felt faint. The world went black before my eyes. Each step I took rose up against me, and when I returned to the office my secretary informed me what the promptings of my heart had already told me – that Yunis Sab'awi with his honeyed tongue was preparing a concentration camp, a kind of ghetto, where the Moslems could do what they wanted with us.

"I burst into tears, and they were still on my cheeks when I went to see Regent Abdullah. You, Hiyawi, are the first person to be told about the details of that meeting. I removed my turban, flung it on his desk, and said: 'Your Highness, I will not don the Chief Rabbi's garb again until you revoke the decree.' He was astounded by my tears and exclaimed: 'The Lord protect you, my esteemed Rabbi Bashi! I've known you for years, and I've never seen you this upset.' I sat down as he requested and said: 'Your Highness, you Moslems and we Jews are cousins. We have the same father, the same God created us both – why then are my people being sold into exile and the Devil knows what else? Have we not been loyal? Have we not fulfilled our obligations? Do we not pay our taxes? Do you wish to go down in history as a wicked reviler of the Jews?' 'My dear Rabbi Bashi,' the Regent interrupted me, 'in the name of Allah, what is the matter with you? What are you talking about?' I told him about Sab'awi's plot. He reached for the telephone, spoke to someone, and said: 'Rabbi Bashi, calm yourself. Sab'awi's plan will never be put into action.' When I put the turban back on my head he smiled and said: 'I never realized that you had such thick, dark hair.'

"Since then, Hiyawi, it has turned white. And from what? From our Jews! That conversation took place early in 1941. On the 3rd of April Rashid Ali el-Kailani seized power, Regent Abdullah fled Iraq, and the *Farhood* broke out, presided over by the Mufti of Jerusalem, a curse on his name. Who knows what might have happened had we already been rounded up in camps? And yet now the women demonstrate against me! What did I not do to save my people from the stone hearts of the Moslems? Did I not fawn, did I not cajole, did I not threaten, did I not plead for protection until the danger had passed? More than once I was mocked for it. Me, a butt of their mockery! But as badly hurt as I was, I put up with it all rather than let a single hair fall from a Jewish head. And when the *Farhood* broke out, I risked my life by venturing out to care for the wounded and to comfort the bereaved. I took care of the orphans, I arranged marriages for Jewish girls who had been raped – and who am I now attacked by? The very same women! Master of the Universe, how can You keep silent? Do I deserve all this? Is this my reward?

"I could go on. May my Father in Heaven forgive me, and all dwellers on earth too yes, I have every right to their forgiveness. For thirty years I have ministered in office, and there has been only one *Farhood*. One! And that too was during the war, when the Regent and the Pasha had just regained power from Nazi sympathizers. The government was still not in control, and the rabble took over the streets and slaughtered us. But there were massacres of Assyrians too, and of Armenians and Christians and Turcomans, and of Shi'ites and Sunnis who slaughtered each other. Who knows how to hate like an Arab? Who is more berserk than an Arab fighting a holy war against the infidel? And whom do they blame for it? Me! Master of the Universe, where are You?

"I could go on. I even helped our Jewish Communists, those idolaters of Lenin and Stalin. Right here, in the cellar of this house, which could have easily been burned down in retaliation, they hid their underground newspaper *al-Sharara*.

Did you know that, Hiyawi? A young rascal named Yosef Cohen was caught with a batch of illegal papers, which could have landed him in jail for life, or even at the end of a hangman's rope. Who interceded on his behalf with the police and secret service? I did! And who is now accused of not protecting Jewish youth? I am! And who is demonstrating against me? Women, mothers! Master of the Universe, is this what my ministry deserves?

"I could go on. I did all I could to stay on the best of terms with King Faisal, and when Faisal died I spared no effort to woo his fickle son Ghazi, and when Ghazi was killed I knocked on the gates of the Regent, a weakling and a homosexual. Day and night I laboured to make them respect the Jewish religion and believe that I was guided by Divine Providence – yes, to convince them that I was a saint, though no one knew better than me how unsaintly I was. Oh, I know, Hiyawi. Many Jews in Baghdad, you too, think I really am one, and I never spoke out against it. But was that for my own sake? For years I fought to have the Jews taken seriously. I tried to put the fear of God in the Moslems' hearts, to persuade them that the slightest harm to my people would bring down the wrath of the Almighty. What didn't I do, what pagan rites didn't I nearly sin with, in order to awe them? Amulets, and crystal balls, and gifts, and gratuities – and for whose sake? And it is now me who is called a traitor! Why, I so instilled in their uncircumcised hearts the belief that God granted my every request that King Faisal himself asked me to pray for his health, and the chief-of-staff, damn his soul, begged me to intercede for the army! I did everything to be liked, to be consulted, to be confided in, to be invited to arbitrate their disputes – and for whose sake? Slowly the Moslems learned to respect me and to avoid harming the least Jew. And now I stand accused by these women of abandoning Jewish prisoners in jail! Do they think that I command the heavenly hosts? Do they take me for Samson or for Gideon? Deprive me of my title, of my robe, and I am an ordinary man. Master of the Universe, wherefore do the Gentiles say, 'Where is their God?'

"I could go on. They say I've kept aloof and not mixed enough. But is it possible to lead a stiff-necked people for thirty years while being on close terms with everyone? They say I covet honour. Maybe so. But the rabbi who is not honoured is soon dishonoured: Was it *my* honour that I sought? The honour of my ministry was the honour of this community and everyone in it, large and small. And whom, pray, was I honoured by – my own people? No, by the Moslems. The Moslems! King Faisal came to my house in person, riding his white mare, and on holidays he visited the Rabbi Ezekiel Synagogue to bless me and my congregation. Moslem dignitaries in mourning asked me to address them with words of consolation. It was they, not the Jews, who honoured and loved me. Yes, loved! What Moslem would have dared knock the turban from my head? But a Jewish woman did it with my whole congregation looking on, and not one of them so much as rebuked her. Yes, I know, Hiyawi, no one but you. That is why you are with me today and I'm unburdening myself in your presence. Master of the Universe, have compassion on Your people! Is this any way to treat their leader?

"I could go on. My fellow rabbis, whom you and I studied with long ago, have never ceased plotting against me. Do you remember, Hiyawi – why, who could forget! how they deposed me from the Chief Rabbinate and then turned the knife in me by annulling my ordination? And for what sin? For declaring kosher a chicken brought to me by a penniless, hard-working woman with eleven hungry mouths to feed – a properly slaughtered chicken ruled inedible by her local rabbi because a needle was found in its gizzard! I looked at that wretched, weeping soul who couldn't afford to buy meat for her Sabbath *chamin* more than once a month, and I felt such pity that I told her she could eat it and banned only the gizzard. Who would have made a fuss over such a thing anywhere else in the world besides this envy-ridden Babylon? Jealousy and ambition – that's what drove them despite all their learning to make me a pariah and shed my blood. They weren't satisfied until they had gone to the authorities and asked them to remove me from office! Nuri Pasha, who was better disposed to us in those days than he is now, came personally to my home in the middle of the night and asked me – not even he could wield the power of compulsion – to resign until tempers calmed down. And I did. And without saying a harsh word about my enemies either. I cast no aspersion on them or their views, and eventually they came to their senses and begged me on bended knees, right here in this room, to resume my ministry. And afterwards I made no attempt to settle scores with a single one of them. Yet what do the women demonstrating say? That I'm hungry for power! Master of the Universe, how long will you let Your Jews abuse me?

"I could go on. Is it any wonder that none of my sons wished to follow in my path? The long line of rabbis in my family has come to an end. My son Sha'ul is an agronomist. Meir is a doctor. Salman is an engineer. My daughter Victoria, my pride and joy, studied psychology. Gentile sciences! And who is to blame for this? I am, naturally. As if I did not have enough infernal problems! At least I can say that, unlike other children, mine still observe the Sabbath. And do you know why? Because I forbade them to travel abroad, knowing that they would never dare desecrate the holy day in front of me. For their sake I made my peace with the younger generation, I overlooked its youthful sins in the hope that it would cleave to the holy flock and not be lost to our people. On the contrary, I told myself: if we are fated to study Gentile wisdom, we might as well excel at it too. Even the young souls who, I'm sorry to say, have been lost to the worship of Stalin are stray sheep who will return to their Father in heaven. Just take a look at what has befallen the children of the Moslems! Generations come and generations go, but the Jews of Babylon, God's name be blessed, remain forever. Master of the Universe, return us to Your bosom and we shall return!

"I could go on. Who knows better than you that from the moment I rise in the morning until the moment I go to bed at night I have only my people's needs and concerns in mind. Do they think I have power over them? The power of a slave, that's what I have! When have I ever put myself first? Since the day I assumed this ministry, I have not done a page of my own work. I had started to write two books, one in rabbinics and one on the Redemption, the completion of which, as you know my dear Hiyawi, is my life's dream. Both now lie like moss-covered stones. It breaks my heart that I have no time for Torah. Am I fated to depart this world without leaving behind a single work?

"It's twenty years since I became a widower. The years have come and gone, season has followed season and feast has followed feast, and I have remained alone and celibate. Twenty years without a wife! Ask our holy Torah and it will tell you how bad that is. My meals are not meals. My bed is not a bed. Never once have I taken a day off like our wealthy Jews, and even on our holidays I run from place to place and funeral to funeral.

Am I made of iron? Believe me, I am flesh and blood, I have the same needs as everyone. And yet I have sworn off the pleasures of life and avoided the courtyards of the rich. Never once have I left this country or even much travelled in it. The only trips taken by me have been when my presence was demanded by some tragedy.

"Like Moses I have looked upon the Holy Land from afar, seeing it only with the mind's eye. How I have longed to prostrate myself on the tomb of our Matriarch, Rachel, to pray in the Cave of Machpela, to breathe the sacred air of Safed, the city of kabbalists, to rest my head on the stones of the Wailing Wall and cover them with tear-stained kisses while slipping a note between them with a Jew's desires. Ah, Master of the Universe, I feel that for thousands of years I have been making my way towards the Holy Land and still I have not arrived! Do you think it is only your Movement that longs for Jerusalem? But it is my duty to remain here with my congregation. What have I devoted my life to if not the art of survival, that most Jewish of arts that is the holy task imposed on us by our Father in Heaven until our Messiah comes? Every day I pray for him. Why, Master of the Universe, do you shut Your ears? The six million in Europe waited for You in vain, and now we wait too while You keep silent. Forgive me if by my words I have sinned.

"Yes, indeed, Hiyawi. I know we mustn't speculate on God's hidden ways. But I am only flesh and blood, and sin though it be, a man cannot refrain from speculation. It was here in Babylon that our people's history began. It was in this Land of the Two Rivers that God told Abraham to go forth to the place that He would show him. And I, Chief Rabbi Bashi, the Haham of Babylon, I say to you – this is what my great work on the Redemption will prove – that it is from here too that the

Messiah will go forth and bring us back to our holy land. Here the Redemption will begin and here I will await it! Your Movement does not begin to understand me. Daily I sit weeping by the waters of Babylon as I remember Zion.

"I've grown old, Hiyawi. I'm not the man I used to be. My daughter Victoria asked my permission to leave Baghdad for Israel. Night after night I stood staring at the stars above and could not find it in me to say no. She's gone. Ten days ago my son Meir, my last support, came to see me. He joked and made small talk, and the more he did so, the more I knew that he had something to tell me. 'Babba,' he finally said, 'I've decided to leave. There's no future for me here. The community is dwindling. My Moslem patients don't trust me any more. Not long ago, when one developed a rash from some penicillin that I prescribed for him, his family wanted to kill me. If his wife hadn't protected me with her body, I would have had a dagger in me. And now the ministry of health wants to send me to the provinces to be a country doctor who hands out aspirins. Babba, you should leave too.' That's what he said, and I couldn't bring myself to utter a word. If I hadn't been sitting down in this chair, Hiyawi, I would have collapsed. Whom do I have left besides Meir? Who but my grandsons can still make these tired eyes light up? And do you know what I said to him? 'Go,' I said. 'Go, my son, and God be with you. Just don't renounce your Iraqi citizenship, so that the Moslems can't say, 'Rabbi Bashi's son has also spat into the well that he drank from.' Go to Israel via a third country, and when you get there, kiss the ground for me but don't try getting in touch. There may be repercussions if anyone knows that you're there.

"Yes, Hiyawi, those are tears you see in my eyes. My sons have left me and are gone. But I am the captain of this ship, and I will not abandon it as long as a single Jew is left here. They can have my head on a platter if they wish. I've handed in my resignation to the government."

Rabbi Bashi fell back in his chair and said no more.

Hiyawi rose, threw himself at the rabbi's feet, and burst out crying.

From that day on, Rabbi Bashi rarely left the confines of his home. His driver disappeared, the synagogue beadles deserted him, and other rabbis ceased paying calls. One by one his servants and attendants slipped away. Only a few last loyalists, led by Hiyawi, still visited him, and they too received a cheerless welcome.

18.

A demon of cleanliness had got into Rashel. It was as if she were atoning for some great sin. She washed and scrubbed the kitchen, the cupboards, and the floors, and then continued with the courtyard and even the roof until everything gleamed. She might sit for a while on the stone bench to rest and let her thoughts wander, but soon she would rouse herself with a shake of her head and return to her buckets and mops. And yet no matter where she carried them, her anxieties persisted. Sometimes she lay barefoot in her thin dress, her loose hair on the courtyard stones that were still wet from the sudsy water that had collected in their cracks, staring at the green wooden gate through which she dreamed Hizkel would appear, seize her passionately in his arms, and quench her body's flames. But the gate remained shut and she bit her lips until they bled and rolled on the ground until the nearest wall brought her up short.

She lay gazing up at the sky and thought of her childhood. She liked to remember being taken in her nicest clothes to synagogue by her mother, on whose knees she sat in the women's gallery while looking down at her father, the cantor Moshi Habusha, as he rocked back and forth in his blue-and-white prayer shawl and spurred the men to heartfelt amens with his prayers. Best of all she liked the dark-red wooden Torah cases with the little silver bells on top. Pomegranates the bells were called, and when the cases were opened her father read what was inside them in a strange language. Later they were carried around and the men touched them and kissed the tips of their fingers while her mother held out her hand and murmured something devotedly. The synagogue, her father told her, was the house of God, and he was the king of the world and the father of the Jews. Then came the *Farhood* and the Moslems slaughtered her parents before her eyes.

Although she had never been in a synagogue since then, not even with Hizkel on Sabbaths and holidays, Rashel – incessantly harangued by my mother about prophets, kabbalists, and God – had striven to regain her faith after Hizkel's arrest and even made the pilgrimage to Kifl. Now, however, after the debacle of Shimeil Yosef Darzi, she had given up hope and all but ceased going out. Although this made Hiyawi, who was exquisitely attuned to her anguish, more concerned for her than ever, his efforts to bring her solace continued to be rebuffed, which only increased his desperation to help. Baffled by her passion for solitude, he took to going up to his roof during the hot afternoon hours and peeking into her courtyard like a jealous lover. One day, as he watched her sprawl on the ground and stare up at the sky in her fashion, there was a knock on the gate. Rashel did not rise to answer it. She remained on her back until the gate was opened by cross-eyed Farha, who informed her that a lawyer had come to see her. To Hiyawi's astonishment, it was Karim Abd el-Hak, who said: "Please forgive me for coming unannounced, Madame Imari." What had the world come to when a Moslem man could walk in like that on a Jewish woman?

Rashel jumped to her feet and straightened out her dress. "Is there any news?" she asked.

"Yes. I've found him! He's in the Central Prison."

"I don't believe it! I don't believe it!" She jumped up and down like a little girl, then shut her eyes, stood on tiptoe, and held out her arms as if to embrace the lawyer. For a moment Hiyawi thought she had gone mad. "You mustn't!" he nearly shouted, biting his hand to restrain himself. Just then, though, Rashel opened her eyes and said:

"There is a God in heaven."

"As long as there's money on earth," laughed the lawyer.

"I'll sell the house."

"You won't have to."

"Did you see him? Is he all right?"

"Yes. He asked me to come straight here and tell you."

"I don't believe it! I don't believe it!" As if exhausted by the tidings, she sank onto the bench and curled her legs beneath her. "Can I visit him?"

"*Allah karim,* God is magnanimous," Abd el-Hak replied enigmatically. He put down his briefcase, straightened the handkerchief in his jacket pocket, ran a hand over his slicked-back hair, and looked at her.

"When is the trial?"

"It hasn't been set yet."

"What is he accused of? What will they do to him?"

"It's too early to say. But at least we've found him."

"*Allah yihafdak,* God look after you."

"If you'll be so kind as to come to my office in two or three days, I'll know more," said the lawyer, picking up his briefcase. "Forgive me for barging in like this. I would never have done it if I didn't know your family and realize how worried you were. Honour comes first with us."

"God bless your coming!"

"Tell Abu Kabi I was here," Abd el-Hak said as he left. "He wasn't in his shop."

Hiyawi told me the news when I stopped by his shop on my way home from school. Spraying my face with spittle, he seized my hand and asked me to ascertain Rashel's plans. As soon as I stepped into her yard she ran to me, covered me with moist kisses, put her hand on my waist, and began to waltz with me as though we were in a film. "Hizkel's alive, they found him!" she cried, spinning me around while I capered like a goat to keep up with her, my schoolbag jogging on my back. I was so embarrassed that I stepped all over her feet, but she paid no attention. Suddenly she let go of me, flew off to the columned arcade, and whirled around and around beneath it until she collapsed on the wet floor with her hands and legs outstretched.

"He's coming back to me! I won't need your father any more. And I'll be rid of that old fool Hiyawi. No more pitying looks, no more gossip, nothing but Hizkel! We'll walk in the streets, we'll go to hotels, we'll waltz in the dance clubs. I'll be free, free!"

The gleam in her eyes, the silky waves of her hair in which the sunlight glinted off the drops of water, the wet dress that clung to her body, revealing the thrusting nipples on the rounded knolls of her breasts, the purple pants outlining her pubes, the golden wheatfields of her thighs: all carried me away in a wild whirlwind. I wanted to bend down and touch her, to spread myself over her, to gather her in my arms and kiss her madly. My God, what was happening to me? As if what I did to her in my fantasies – in which I treated her, the wife of my uncle in prison, like a painted whore in one of the fleshpots of Baghdad – wasn't bad enough! I removed my schoolbag and held it in front of me with both hands to hide the swelling tent in my trousers. Her eyes smiled at me and I wondered for a moment if she wasn't reading my thoughts. Rising and gripping my shoulder, which sent a shiver of delight down my back, she said:

"Come back this afternoon and we'll go together to the prison."

I sped home and found no one there. It was pointless to go to my father's shop. No doubt he had gone off to look for some new clue to Hizkel's whereabouts. And if he was there, he would have already heard everything from Hiyawi.

When I returned to Rashel's, I noticed that the brows of her almond-shaped eyes had been shaped. She must have gone to the *hafafa,* the woman who threaded away the unwanted hair of brides before their weddings. Did she actually think that she and Hizkel would be allowed to spend the night together? Even her dress resembled a bridal gown, white and tight-fitting with a high collar and cloth buttons. Over it she had tossed a flowery silk scarf, and she had on low-heeled, black, patent-leather shoes and carried a white leather clutch bag. While I stood wondering whether to go with her – as if I could possibly refuse! – she brushed her hair and put on lipstick and perfume, and suddenly transformed herself into a mature, determined woman. I felt relieved that my father still knew nothing and could not endanger our plans.

"Where to?" whispered Hiyawi as we passed his shop.

"The Central Prison," I answered in low tones.

"Are you out of your minds? There's a hanging there today."

"Whose?" I asked. He went on staring fixedly as if he hadn't heard me. "Tell my father and Abu Saleh that Hizkel's been found," I said quite unnecessarily.

"Take good care of her and Allah look after you both," Hiyawi called after me as I hastened my steps to catch up with Rashel's quick stride. When we reached el-Rashid Street I started to hail a cab.

"I'd rather walk," Rashel said. "I want to breathe the fresh air, to see people."

"We have to go through Moslem neighbourhoods."

"Nothing will happen to me," she said, radiating a new confidence. It was almost as if she thought that she need only go to the prison, explain that everything was a mistake, and receive her husband back on the spot.

We passed the Jewish shops near Taht el-Takya. Most were closed for the afternoon siesta, their owners snoozing in the cool cellars beneath them. Only fat Abu Na'im's clothing store was open and he too was asleep on a wicker mat, drowsing in his white suit and eternal red tie while his young helper stood over him and lazily waved a bamboo fan. Although my father had been urging me to buy fabric for a summer suit, I was afraid of being laughed at, especially by Edouard who dressed with a bohemian disregard for fashion. Now, though, at Rashel's side, there was nothing I wanted more than a white suit and a red tie like Abu Na'im's.

The smells, faces, and costumes changed around us as we walked and the light suits yielded to striped cloaks and dark robes. A stooped old man was pouring buckets of water on the pavement in front of a coffeehouse, sending up vapours from the burning asphalt. The street corner in front of the coppersmiths' market was teeming with shoppers. Without thinking we headed down a narrow street into the souk, where large bellows breathed sparks into fiery ovens and mallets pounded away noisily. I liked this market, whose copper trays and pots were lovely to look at. So was Rashel. Men ran their eyes over every curve of her body. A thin young Moslem sang in a high-pitched voice that struggled to rise above the smiths' din:

O my sister, lift thy dress.
Show me thine ankles, O my sister.

I took her hand and pulled her back to el-Rashid Street. The pavement was crowded with men. From everywhere came the thick, heavy smells, half-tantalizing and half-repellent, of the greasy foods eaten by the city's Moslems. Waiters stood in the doorways of cheap restaurants, calling out the dishes served inside and offering a free taste of each. I had never eaten in these places, which mysteriously frightened me and attracted me like a moth to a flame. In my dreams I entered them as a black-cloaked Moslem with a sheikh's headband and a long chain of amber worry beads. Why, I knew and loved their history, their culture, their poetry, their music better than they did! How tempting it would be to no longer feel threatened by them, their shadows always at my back; to be one of them like Ismail; to walk safely and surely in their midst, free to do what I wanted; to be the salt of the earth – its jobs, its leaders, its government, its God, all mine!

At that moment, though, I would have been ready to settle for less. All I really wanted was to step into Azzam Abu el-Facha's eating place, order a plate of greasy mutton, and sit like a king while I burped noisily, spat on the floor, smoked a hubble-bubble, cracked jokes about the English, made fun of the Christians, insulted the Kurds, and saved my loudest curses for the Jews and Zionists. When I once mentioned this ambition to Hiyawi, he was so appalled that the only sound he could utter was: "Ugh!" My father, on the other hand, surprised me by saying that, although he too had had such thoughts when he was young, they were the fantasies of a persecuted minority. A man had to be what he was. Only in a country of our own would we cease to be abject. If a Jew in Iraq stood up for his rights, his fellow Jews regarded him as a black sheep, the Moslems considered him a freak, and no one showed the least appreciation.

I was roused from my reveries by wolf whistles. Rashel tugged at her sleeves to cover her bare arms and ignored the remarks directed at her, her head held defiantly high. A young dandy blocked our way, stared hard at her, and sighed:

"*Ya* Allah, what a pair!"

She gave him an admonishing smile and said fearlessly in a Jewish dialect:

"Would an Arab like you like to hear his sister talked about like that?"

"No, ma'am," he said abashed, stepping aside to let us pass. I clung to her side, amazed at the grit with which she plunged on into the vortex. The human throng swarmed unhurriedly over the pavements and filled the streets. Coachmen shouted at their horses, cars honked. The swelling din seemed to portend approaching festivities, a summer night of whoring drunkenness in the sin-swamped city. As though from a distant rally, a tide of muffled voices reached us from afar. I had never seen an execution. All at once I was overcome by fear. The street opened out onto a huge square fronted by an imperious stone building, well-known to me from photographs, bearing the large, ornately-written words: "Government of Iraq, Department of Defence." In no time we were in the midst of a screaming mob.

"*Idbahu es-Saha'ina!* Kill the Zionists!"

"*Idbahu esh-Shi'u'iya!* Kill the Communists!"

"*Idbahu el-kufar!* Kill the infidels!"

All eyes were on a scaffold in the centre of the square, which had served as Baghdad's traditional site for executions since the age of the Caliphs. In this land of rulers who came and went, only the hangman was immortal. In front of a gallows stood a prisoner in the clothes of the condemned, his head in a sack and his hands tied behind him. Further back was a row of armed soldiers. Mindlessly swept along by the crowd, we were by now quite near to them. The hangman, a squat, solid-looking individual in a black keffiyeh, tied a rope around the condemned man's neck, circled him ceremoniously like a slaughterer inspecting a hen, raised his hands high, and bowed to the cheering crowd.

"Long live the King! Long live the Regent!" he cried.

"Long live!" the crowd echoed.

"Long live Iraq!"

"Long live! Long live!"

"Long live the Arab nation!"

"Long live, long live, long live!"

He flexed his arms in preparation and the crowd fell still. In the apocalyptic silence nothing was heard but the screams of a woman standing close to the scaffold. With each scream she wrapped her hair around her arm and pulled at it. My vision dimmed. I looked away. Rashel clutched my hand hard.

"It's just like Hizkel told me about the execution of Shafik Addas," she whispered in a frightened voice. The silence was broken by thousands of cries of *Allah akbar* as the crowd stamped its feet and waved brutish arms. Feeling we were being looked at, I began to shout too and elbowed Rashel, who was mesmerized by the gallows, to get her to join me. I had to scream *Allah akbar* into her ear before she understood and added her voice to the death chant. There were tears in her eyes. The hangman stepped up to the condemned man and made a practised, ritual motion. A trapdoor opened beneath the plummeting body, which jerked and squirmed in midair. Everything happened quickly. The screaming woman fainted and fell. The stillness of death that descended on the square roared in my ears. In my blank mind I heard Hiyawi saying: "When a Moslem shouts 'God is great,' run for your life, boy." I held Rashel's hands and pulled her back out of the crowd. An eternity passed before we were clear of it.

"I have to see him," she said, pale as a sheet. "I have to."

"Now?" I croaked. "I'm scared."

"They'll hang him like Shafik Addas." Her frozen eyes were like slivers of glass. I dragged her to the kerb and pushed her into the first cab that stopped.

"To esh-Shorja," I said, naming the Moslem neighbourhood nearest Taht el-Takya.

"Yes, sir."

"As fast as you can," I urged. I pulled down the leather awning and settled back, putting my foot up on the back of the driver's seat like my father. Rashel leaned her head on my shoulder. I felt every bit the grown man. The street lamps were already lit on el-Rashid Street, which seemed subdued after the din of the square. The horse's hoofbeats sounded very near.

19.

All night the hanged man's corpse swung back and forth above my head, about to crash down on me. At last I rose from a nightmarish sleep, tiptoed to the railing of the roof past my father who was tossing and turning and my mother who was sleeping on the wooden cot in her greenhouse, and strained to catch a glimpse of Rashel. She was not on her roof. I descended to the courtyard, groped my way in the dark to the light switch, flicked it on, and walked up and down by our joint wall, running a finger along it. Ah, if only I could step into Rashel's dark house and find her still warm from sleep, her arms reaching out to me! The more I let my imagination run wild, the sweeter were its torments.

In the morning I rapped on her gate with its dove-shaped iron knocker.

"My father wants to go to the lawyer with you," I told her when she appeared. She had a house robe on and her warm morning smell could have come straight from my night's fantasies.

"I was planning to visit Hizkel in prison," she said.

She invited me in and disappeared into the kitchen. The courtyard smelled of coffee, and she soon returned with a tray loaded with steaming cups and accompanied by some date biscuits. She set it on the stump of the palm tree that Hizkel had placed by the stone bench to serve as a table. "Help yourself," she said. I took a sip of the strong, bitter brew, picturing Hizkel, for whom coffee was a sacred ritual, inhaling its life-restoring aroma and murmuring the praises of Allah for giving the world such a gift. Rashel went back to the kitchen, came out again with a lit gas burner, and placed on it a copper pot with double spouts that resembled a pair of twisted, featherless wings. When the water boiled she opened a dark jar, releasing a springlike scent of flowers. Adding dried petals to the bubbling pot, she sealed its lid that was domed like a mosque with strips of mosquito netting dipped in a porridge of clay and sprinkled it with cold water. Fragrant drops of rose water began to drip from the spouts into the bottles that she placed underneath them. So this was how all those odours of rose, basil, cloves, and geranium became hers, clinging to her hair and making her smell as sweet as incense! "Hizkel likes rose water in his tea," she said vivaciously when she had filled four bottles. She handed me one. "This is for your mother."

When I returned with my father, Rashel was in a long black dress buttoned to her throat. She looked pale, almost grim. I noticed that she had no make-up on and was not even wearing her earrings.

We set out. Although he generally preferred horse-drawn cabs, my father hailed a taxi on el-Rashid Street. A slender clerk typing with two fingers in the waiting room of Karim Abd el-Hak's office asked us to sit and knocked deferentially on the lawyer's door.

Karim Abd el-Hak emerged, shook my father's hand and then my own, gave Rashel a smile that made her blush, and cordially ushered us into his elegant office. I stood there taking in its oriental finery: the Persian rug, the Damascene vase, the red velvet curtains, and the oil painting of the palace of Haroun el-

Rashid. A portrait of King Faisal, father of modern Iraq and benefactor of the Jews, looked down in regal splendour from behind the carved wooden desk. No pictures of the country's current rulers hung beside it. Various sizes and colours of fountain pens lay on the desk, but although I had a special weakness for these, filching one was out of the question.

"Have a seat," said Karim Abd el-Hak, pointing to some roomy leather armchairs.

"Have you seen him?" asked my father before he had quite sat down.

"Very briefly, but he's all right," said Karim Abd el-Hak in an assured tone. He rang a bell and a red-fezzed servant brought in a tray with glasses of tea and empty coffee cups. My father put a sugar cube in his mouth and sipped his tea daintily through it. Rashel stirred sugar into hers and let it stand untouched.

"There was a hanging yesterday," she said, the muscles above her mouth trembling.

"*Wilad el kalb* the sons of dogs!" the lawyer exclaimed angrily. "They talk of democracy and hang men like the Caliphs."

"Where are they holding Hizkel?" asked my father.

"What does it matter? As long as we've found him alive."

"But why are they doing this?"

"*Wilad el kalb!* They have no honour and no shame. They disgrace the nobility of the Arabs by violating our obligations to the People of the Holy Book who live under our protection."

"I have to see him," Rashel said.

"The secret service won't let you. It says that the investigation isn't finished. We'll arrange a visit as soon as it's possible. I'm dreadfully sorry that this is happening to a man I like and respect as much as I do Hizkel."

"Even murderers are allowed family visits," said Rashel with tears in her eyes.

"It is indeed inhuman. Unfortunately, this is the government we have. I agreed to take this case because I consider it part of the struggle in this country for democracy and equality before the law. Our treatment of minorities is a crucial test." Karim spoke with an oratorical pathos that was never in short supply in Iraq.

"We thank you," said my father. "We're proud of men like you who help us to believe that Moslems and Jews can live together."

"These are difficult times for us all," said Karim. "I only hope we can get through them. I regret seeing so many Jews flee the country. It's Iraq's loss. She won't be the same again."

"It's good to hear such words in times like these," my father responded.

"You yourself, I trust, are not planning to go to Israel?"

The question took my father by surprise.

"Not before I've seen my brother with my own eyes."

"Your brother supports Jewish emigration. I had many talks with him on the subject prior to his arrest."

"Things aren't what they used to be. We Jews are being harassed. Thousands of us have lost our jobs. It isn't easy, Ustad Karim."

"This is your country. You should be fighting shoulder to shoulder with the forces of progress to change it."

"We're between a rock and a hard place," said my father. "Your Moslem nationalists have made us their whipping boys."

"Running away is no solution. A homeland isn't a hotel that you leave because it's uncomfortable."

"You can't expect anyone to live in constant danger and be afraid all the time. It's too much to be an eternal scapegoat."

"You exaggerate, Abu Kabi. There have been good times too. Even after the *Farhood* there was an upswing."

"That's so. But what about today?"

"Today above all! There are new winds blowing and underground currents at work. Political changes are on the way. There will be a democratic Iraq and you Jews will have a major role to play in it."

"How can we live with you Moslems when you want to destroy Israel and call anyone supporting it a traitor?"

"The government is corrupt and under pressure, and it tries to blame the Jews for everything. It's an old story ... "

" ... that always ends with the same victim." My father finished the sentence.

"We have to do our best to survive the hard times ahead," said Karim Abd el-Hak, offering us cigarettes from a fancy leather case. Rashel shook her head. My father took one. Out of respect for him I was passed over like a small boy. The lawyer ran a cigarette back and forth beneath his nose, avidly sniffing the Virginia tobacco, and lit it with a gold lighter while keeping his eyes on Rashel.

"What is my husband accused of?" she asked.

"A number of things. The most worrisome is smuggling arms in shipments of dates."

"You must be joking," chuckled my father.

It suddenly struck me that whenever Hizkel had received one of his big bundles of dates from Basra, which were tied with spliced strips of bamboo, he had taken it down to the cellar and opened it there by himself.

The monotonous whir of the ceiling fan was the only sound in the room. "What do you intend to do now, Ustad Karim?" my father asked.

"I'll demand evidence. I'll use all my connections and influence to free him, and with God's help I'll succeed."

"*Inshallah,* God willing," said my father, rising to go even though the coffee had not yet arrived, a sign that Karim still wanted us to stay. I got to my feet too. Rashel alone remained seated and made the lawyer promise her that she would be able to see Hizkel. He spread his hands with an enticing smile, then fingered his moustache awkwardly and said to her: "I've learned a lot from this talk, but there are a few more questions that I would like to ask. Please drop by when you have a chance."

"*Taht amrak,*" said Rashel. "As you wish."

As we were standing in the doorway, the lawyer added:

"I'll let you know if there are any new developments. Keep your hopes up." And seeing Rashel's expression change, he added gently: "Your husband is alive. Other men have disappeared without a trace."

"God keep you." She took a bottle from the wicker basket on her arm and gave it to him. "Rose water," she said.

My father, who was stroking his chin in the doorway while waiting for Rashel, glanced back and forth between them. He stumbled as he followed her to the stairs and gave the lawyer an embarrassed grin. Outside on the pavement he said firmly:

"Don't you ever come back here by yourself."

"Why not?"

He looked around. "No goy can be trusted," he said softly.

"But he's a friend of yours and Hizkel's! His father Hajj Yahya is your neighbour."

"They don't come any better. But he's still a goy."

"I don't understand. He's honest, he doesn't make false promises, he's on the side of justice ... "

"And a goy."

"I want to see the prison."

My father deliberated. Although it stood to reason that nothing could be gained from a glimpse of the prison walls, he understood Rashel's need. "All right," he said. "You go with her, Kabi."

20.

The carriage soon brought us to the Ministry of Defence. Unlike the previous day, the square was nearly empty. The few passers-by glanced with fascinated horror at the still suspended body and the puddle of urine beneath it. Rashel's eyelids fluttered as she stared at the dead man, her fingers tightening on me. I leaned forward and signalled the coach-driver to give the scene a wide berth, but he ignored me and drove around the square to get a better view.

I told him to stop and we got out.

Hurriedly we crossed the square, putting the corpse behind us, and headed towards the front gate of the ministry. Iron lions with yawning mouths flanked the entrance and looked more intimidating than ever. Although we were near the prison, we chose to linger behind a broad stone column that shaded us and hid us from the guards. A high fence surrounding the multi-storey building overlooked a large garden with a green lawn and cloyingly sweet, blood-red roses. Motorcycles came and went with a roar. Brakes squealed. Officials with briefcases entered and left on the run. There was enough commotion to think that a war was about to break out.

Ranged closely like children's toys, along one side of the ministry's yard were rows of shiny jeeps and army trucks. As each officer passed through the gate in his freshly-pressed uniform, a swagger stick flamboyantly beneath his arm, the immaculate guards snapped to attention and saluted. *Chocolate soldiers,* I thought contemptuously. *We've seen how well you did against Israel.* It was a good thing they couldn't read my mind. We looked like any couple out for a stroll in the ceremonial world of the Iraqi army.

There was a deafening wail of sirens. An escort of motorcycles circled the square, followed by a gleaming black limousine with two flags on its bonnet, the government's and the army's. The convoy stopped by the gate, where the officer of the guard barked an order and the sentries sprang to attention, heads up and chests out. So inflated that he seemed about to explode, the officer half-waddled to the limousine, opened its rear door, and raised his hand in a salute with an upward toss of his chin. A portly man in his forties whose face I recognized from the newspapers, splendidly dressed in a blue suit with a red tie and a rose in the lapel, stepped out of the car. The Iraqi defence minister surveyed the square with a princely air, wrinkled his nose at the sight of the hanged man, and motioned with his hand. From out of nowhere a polished adjutant appeared at his side.

The minister said something, and the adjutant saluted and departed. The officer of the guard whipped his hand back down from his forehead and bellowed an order with such ferocity that the minister gave a start. The guard presented arms.

"I have to talk to him," murmured Rashel, taking a step as if to run to the minister. But just then the gate slammed shut behind him and he walked off flanked by two officers. I studied his fat neck. What was it like to be him with everyone bowing and scraping? He could seal men's fates by lifting a finger, hanging one and saving another's life. If I were him, I thought, I would pardon Hizkel just to see the gratitude in Rashel's eyes.

I would be merciful … but I would also be a Jew, which meant that I could not be a minister in the first place. You had to be dumb like Edouard, or his hero Salim Effendi, to believe that such a thing were possible.

Some soldiers in khaki fatigues removed the corpse and began to dismantle the gallows. The guard of honour marched back into the courtyard in formation, leaving the two sentries at the gate.

"Let's go," I said, taking Rashel's arm.

"I'll wait for him to come out," she said with a mulish obstinacy.

"Who do you think he is?" I asked. "Haroun el-Rashid, who judged his subjects in the marketplace?" But nothing I said could make her move. She really thought that she need only throw herself at the minister's feet and kiss his hand to have her wish granted as in a fairy tale. In the end a swarthy sentry came to the rescue and told us to clear off.

We walked to the prison. Although I had passed it often enough, now that I had a personal interest I felt that I was seeing the place for the first time. The approach to the huge building was blocked by a concrete barrier draped in an Iraqi flag and flanked by an "in" and an "out" gate. Even without a boundary fence, its grim facade kept pedestrians away. Everyone in Iraq had heard of its notorious torture chambers.

Rashel walked straight to the sentry box by the "in" gate and said without preliminaries:

"I want to visit my husband."

The guard waved his hand as if chasing away a fly.

"Go away!"

"Why? My husband is in that building. Let me in and Allah will grant you a long life."

"There are no Jews in there," said the guard, making a movement with his right hand in which he held a rifle with a bayonet.

"My lawyer told me that he's there."

"I said go away. *Yallah, yallah!*" He rose from his wooden bench, taller than I had thought he would be.

"Please," Rashel begged. "I haven't seen him for two months."

"You fucking Jew whore!" He stepped out of the sentry box and spat at her. "I'll have you locked up yourself!"

We walked away. Rashel was pale-faced. "I told you I should have talked to the minister," she said angrily, as if it were all my fault. "Why did he say Hizkel wasn't there?"

"If you had slipped him a little money, he would have changed his mind."

"Why didn't you say so?"

"You didn't ask. And since when does anyone talk Jewish Arabic to a Moslem?" She was too close to tears for me to say more. She took out a handkerchief and wiped her eyes.

A hot east wind had begun to blow, breathing on my neck and face. Although I knew that this was only the onset, like the first crackle of a fire, its full blast yet to come, the thin shirt that I was wearing felt so heavy that I would gladly have removed it then and there. Instinctively we headed for a café down the street, the dim entrance to which, seen through the afternoon glare, was like a promise of coolness. A plump, genial-looking woman was sitting inside with legs spread and bare thighs. She was wearing golden anklets and the polish on her toes was the same bright red as her lipstick. *Ya Allah!* Was she waiting for customers so early in the day? Her doeish, kohl-rimmed eyes sent me an open invitation, to which she added what I took to be murmured words of encouragement as I stepped through the door. But this only caused me to back out again, bumping into Rashel who was staring at the two of us. "Let's go somewhere else," she said. I turned and glanced up the street, wondering where else we might find shelter. All I had wanted, I reminded myself, was to be with Rashel and now that I was, I shouldn't let a little hot weather fluster me. What was it about women that so attracted and bewildered me? We left and walked slowly like two lost children until we came to a sidestreet with a large mosque and a food-and-drink stand in front of it.

"Where are you going?" asked Rashel.

"Don't speak in a Jewish dialect," I told her, though there was no chance of her passing for a Moslem. We sat on stools beneath a large canvas awning and I ordered a tart glass of tamarind juice and a Coca-Cola for Rashel. Men kept entering the wooden gate of the mosque, beyond which others were washing their feet and wetting their faces at a fountain. From within, where a crowd had gathered for the afternoon service, came cries of *Allah akbar*. The crowd knelt as one man when the prayers started, bending with ease and touching foreheads to the floor.

Once again, in this city of endless mosques, I had to listen to the *Shahada,* the Moslem confession of faith. The hundreds of raised buttocks moving in unison frightened me. What a gifted rabble-rouser could do with such a mass of humanity! I thought of the stories passed down by generations of Jews of wild carnage that had started with such scenes. "When they put on the imam's turban, watch out for the sheikh's sword," was my father's way of putting it. Yet how could the same act of prayer that Hiyawi said purified the soul make men go berserk?

Rashel hugged her knees and stared apprehensively. *Ash'hadu alla illaha illa Allah, wa'ash'hadu anna Muhammed-ur-Rasul-Allah,* came the mighty cry. In the name of Allah and his messenger Muhammed they were ready to slit Jewish throats. What kind of a God did they have? And what kind of a God did we have who let us be slaughtered in His name? Were the two one? Or was Salim Effendi right about there being no God at all, just wars fought over Him?

"I'm afraid," Rashel whispered.

I was too, but her confession made me feel more of a man.

"Let's get out of here," I said. We walked slowly back to the main street. The sight of the prison and its guards actually came as a relief.

"Why don't we go home?"

"No," Rashel said, heading back for the ministry. "I'll wait."

It was all I could do to get her to keep to the far side of the street. I prayed that the minister wouldn't appear. In the state of mind she was in, who knew what she might do?

There was a leather goods shop on the corner that looked like a good vantage point and we stepped into its chill, dark interior. Dozens of belts hung from the ceiling. I decided to buy one and chose a white belt with a big buckle. Rashel made a face. "Aren't you too old for street fights?" she asked. I hadn't realized that, more by way of emulation than of challenge, I had picked a belt like Ismail's. I paid the asking price like a sport, without trying to bargain.

Rashel sighed. "It's so hot out. Isn't there somewhere respectable we can sit?"

"Who knows what's respectable these days, my sister?" said the shopkeeper in nasal tones. "And what's wrong with my shop? Here, have a seat, *ahlan wasahlan.* I'll send out for some coffee in a minute. He ran cunning eyes over Rashel's body.

There was something the matter with his face and voice. Suddenly I realized that he didn't have a nose.

"Who, if I may ask, are you waiting for?"

"My husband —" Feeling my kick, Rashel left the sentence unfinished.

"For a friend of ours, an army officer," I said.

"I know them all," said the man, running a hand over his wares. "They all come to buy from me. Belts, wallets, sandals, everything."

"He's from Imara," I declared unnecessarily.

"From Imara? I can't think of anyone from there." He looked at me suspiciously. "What do you want with him?"

"We have business. Our fathers were students together."

"Sit down, my sister," he said to Rashel, who had her nose in her handkerchief. "Sit down, let the heat break. Does the smell of the leather bother you?" He moved the fan nearer to her, reached for a dirty jug, and offered her a glass of cold water.

She shook her head. "*Tislam ideyk*. May your hands be blessed."

"Is Arab water not good enough for Jews?" he asked indignantly.

The damned Moslem had guessed at once. I had to take the revolting jug to appease him, carefully aim the spout at my mouth while avoiding all contact with my lips, and gulp a jet of cool water. It brought me back to life just enough to make me feel how tired I was. All I wanted to do was to spread a mat on the floor, lie down next to the fan, and sleep forever.

I moved my stool closer to Rashel's. Chin in hand, she sat eyeing the ministry gate. I kept my own eyes on the prison. Although this made our surveillance complete, nothing happened. The afternoon cast a slumberous pall. The belt maker sat with his legs tucked beneath him in an armchair covered with patches from an old rug. From time to time he sucked on his hookah with a soothing burble of water. Despite his efforts to stay awake, which made him sit up now and then with a start, his eyelids drooped and he lapsed into horrible snores. I glanced at Rashel. We both had to cover our mouths to keep from bursting into rude laughter. Now that our host was asleep, I slipped down onto the floor, stretched out my legs, and leaned my back against a stack of hides. Their smell only made me sleepier.

When I opened my eyes again, Rashel was still staring determinedly at the locked gate of the ministry. The belt maker awoke and looked at us as though in a dream. He belched, yawned loudly, took a few swigs from the jug, poured water over his face, and said: "*Ya fatah, ya razak*, may Allah sustain us." He went out, came back with a coffee vendor, and treated us each to a cup of the strong, reinvigorating brew.

"Is your husband a Communist?" he asked.

"God forbid."

"A Zionist?"

"No."

"Did he kill someone? Steal from the government?"

"Of course not." Rashel tried to laugh but only managed to twist her face into a half-comical, half-painful grimace.

"Eat no garlic, have no smell," said the man with a wink. "You don't get arrested for doing nothing, my sister."

"Who said anything about being arrested?" I asked.

He preferred to ignore my question. If only the Arabs' morality matched their manners, I thought, they would be the perfect gentlemen.

"What are you Jews lacking here, my sister? Everything is in your hands: our businesses, our money, our property. What do you need your own country for?"

"We don't," Rashel said defensively.

"Isn't that the truth, my sister?"

He relit his hookah, sucked on it a few times, crossed his legs, and mused: "It's not your fault. It's the shits in the government. They should chop the Communists' heads off and hang all the Zionists. Then we'd have some peace and quiet."

I moved closer to the fan and opened the top buttons of my shirt to dry the sweat on my chest. Though I knew he was looking at me, I nodded to Rashel that it was time to go.

"Where are you rushing off to in this heat? The day shift doesn't end until four o'clock, when the food truck arrives."

I sat down again.

"When does the minister leave?" Rashel asked.

"His Excellency? What do you want with him?" The shopkeeper looked at her doubtfully. "He's a hard, cruel man, my sister." He rubbed his thumb against his forefinger and whispered: "That's the one thing that might work. He'd sell his own wife for money … There's the food truck." He glanced at his watch. "What did I tell you? Four on the dot! It's always on time."

A truck with a canvas top pulled up in front of the prison. The guard boarded and inspected it at length before letting it enter.

"Now they'll all go home: the officers, the soldiers, the office workers – everyone except the prisoners and the jailers. This is the time, my sister, when with the help of a little … " He made the rubbing motion again.

Rashel and I exchanged looks. We seemed to have reached an unspoken understanding that – for a suitable remuneration, of course – the man could be of use.

We thanked him profusely for taking us in from the heat. "Allah bless you," Rashel repeated several times before we left.

21.

She was sitting in the same chair with the same inviting look when my father and I walked in the next day. It was three p.m., an hour when the cafés were generally empty. She told a waiter to bring us coffee, went to open a blue curtain, stepped out into the courtyard, and returned before long having re-applied her make-up. Her perfume was stronger too. She minced across the room like a buxom harem princess in her gauzy dress with its flower print that outlined the round bounce of her behind and revealed her shapely ankles in their wooden clogs, halted in front of us with her hands on her hips, smiled seductively, and cocked her head slightly to one side. She was so close that I could feel her breath on me. Pretending to clean our spotless table, she bent over it with a rag until her breasts spilled from her dress and their dark nipples all but grazed my mouth. My pecker stood up so fast in my trousers that I had to wriggle to make room for it, turning red as I noticed her amused look.

Some two years previously, when my friends and I first developed an interest in the fleshpots of Baghdad, I found myself borne one day by my legs, which were several steps ahead of my thoughts, to a highly recommended address situated off a lane near el-Rashid Street. It was the start of the summer holidays and I ambled along until I came to a huge Ottoman gate beyond which – so I had heard whispered – was a large khan. I stopped a little way off from it, frightened to go any further, though I was no less eager to enter than the other boys of my age whom I saw glancing around them and walking in.

I returned the next day, and the day after that too, until at last I gathered the courage to approach. A policeman standing there like a cherub at the gates of Paradise went through my pockets, searched my body, frisked my legs, patted my rear end as though I were some little queer, and asked if I was a Jew. Only then did he open the gate and hustle me through. Once safely inside, I inquired what he had been looking for.

"A pistol or a dagger," he said. "There are blood feuds settled here all the time. Even with all these searches, there isn't a week without a murder."

The khan turned out to be a passageway to an entire quarter. Beyond it were shops, cafés, roving bands of children. A bent old man was wetting down some dirt paths. In the doorways of the houses dolled-up girls sprawled in chairs, lips rouged, eyes painted, feet rimmed with silver and gold anklets above red-polished toenails.

"A quarter of a dinar!" called out a slim whore with nice eyes. I passed her, blinking rapidly. The further I walked, the more the price dropped. 200 fils. 180. 150. Soon I was swept by the throng into a busy square in which stood a group of Bedouin sheikhs and in the middle, on a tall chair that suggested a lighthouse, sat a thin girl of eleven or twelve with crimson lips and powdered cheeks. Her ankles showed beneath her dress.

"A virgin! Who'll give me one dinar?" cried an auctioneer.

"Two!" came a bid.

"Three!"

"Five dinars!" called a tall sheikh. A stir ran through the crowd.

"Five dinars! Going once … twice … sold for five dinars!" the auctioneer cried. "Congratulations," he said to the winner, whose hand was being pumped by the other sheikhs as if he had been awarded not a child's body but her everlasting love. She was helped down from the chair and the sheikh took her in his arms and carried her like a bride up some stairs to a room, followed by two young men with trays laden with fruit, rice, and roast chicken. The door was locked and the crowd waited below.

Soon the sheikh reappeared to the strains of a band of musicians in the courtyard. A middle-aged woman emerged from the room with a sheet that she spread on a wooden balcony, and the crowd broke into cheers at the sight of the blood. Such proofs of virginity, standard fare after Jewish weddings too, made me feel sick to the stomach. My own meagre knowledge of the facts of life came cloaked in an aura of romantic mystery picked up from the novels I had read.

I left the square and took cover beneath a low palm tree. Behind me was strung a washing line hung with dresses and brightly coloured pants. A tamarind juice vendor stopped to sell me a glass of his sweet-and-sour beverage, which revived me. I continued as though in a trance down the narrow lanes which grew more and more crowded with women of all ages the further I went. "A hundred fils, a hundred fils," sang one in a cracked voice. Another, stout and long-haired, sat with parted legs, her vulva covered by a glimmering silver star. I could have had her for 50 fils. But though hot with desire, I didn't dare act.

Now, sitting with my father, I stared at the temptress, who looked back at me with alluringly parted lips. She must have thought he had brought me for my sexual initiation, perhaps with the intention of joining me, as in some of the stories I had heard.

My father settled back in his chair and glanced back and forth between us with a mischievous trace of a smile. Although shamed by his presence into looking away each time my eyes met the whore's, I quickly sought them out again. I didn't know if I wanted to flee or to bury myself in her flesh. Confident that I was hooked, she walked to the window with a waggle of buttocks and breasts, opened the blue curtain wider, and stood there like a ripe fruit. *She's yours for the asking,* said my father's devilish grin. *Yes, father,* I wanted to say, *I want her. I want to go to bed with her like a real man – like Edouard, who told me all about his night with Lutfiya. But I want to do it myself, at my own speed, and I'll know where to go when I'm ready.*

Those were my thoughts. I would never have dared say them aloud to him. I cleared my throat in embarrassment and forced myself to look at a shelf of hookahs, their red water-pipes coiled like snakes.

By now the whore appeared to have lost hope and had gone back to running a café. She said something that I didn't catch, closed the blue curtain, and switched on the radio to a programme of verses from the Koran. When she began to look for another station, my father asked her not to.

"Are you Jews or Moslems?" she inquired.

"We're all the sons of Allah and of Abraham," replied my father. "Listen, Kabi. That's Sheikh Tewfik el-Mahdawi, the greatest of all Koran chanters." He crossed his legs in his favourite posture, leaned back in his chair, shut his eyes, and was carried off by the sheikh's chant as devoutly as if it were the weekly Torah reading. Now and then he sighed with pleasure or murmured his approval, and at the end he declared: "*Sadaka Allahu el-azim.* Just is the mighty God."

The whore's face softened and she had the waiter bring us tea on the house. My father swivelled his chair to face the prison, which we were there to stake out.

We came back three days in a row. The whore grew accustomed to us and treated us like regular customers. She soon learned that my father liked to drink two cups of coffee and took sugar in his tea at all hours, and she sat chatting with him about this and that despite our baffling indifference to her charms. As if she didn't know how Jewish men felt about Moslem women! True, her frequent glances our way were not without suspicion, but suspicion was a staple of her world. Of ours too. More worrisome was the waiter, a broomstick of a man who arrived every day at noon and viewed us with open dislike. I was afraid he might be a CID agent and my father said nothing to ease my apprehension.

On the fourth day we took a walk around the prison and the ministry, inspecting the grounds between them and every path and sidestreet. The benefit of this, which lay in pushing back the frightening frontiers of the unknown, was mainly psychological. Thirsty and exhausted, we returned to the café where we were succoured with cool water from a jug and bitter Bedouin coffee that my father said was just what was needed. At exactly four the supply truck arrived as usual. My father chose to remain until the muezzin called the faithful for the evening prayer, then rose and placed a 50 fils coin on the table.

"I don't have change," said the proprietress. "Go with Allah's blessing and let the coffee be on me." When my father wouldn't hear of it, she said, "Then pay me tomorrow, brother." He left her the coin and told her to forget about the change.

On our way home we stopped off at Karim Abd el-Hak's office, and my father asked me to wait downstairs. The two spent a long time together. When he returned he put his arm around me and told me that I would be smuggled into the prison to see Hizkel. "Someone will take care of it," he said. I didn't know whether he meant the belt maker, whom Rashel and I had told him about, or whether he had found a more ordinary way of conveying the necessary bribes. The plan, he confessed, was not totally safe but it was the best one possible; he would tell me the details at home. And yet although I asked him not to let my mother know, he did so as soon as he saw her.

"Son," he said in whimsical self-justification, "she is your mother and half of you belongs to her."

My mother didn't think it was funny. "Do you want them to arrest Kabi too?"

"Do you think I would risk my firstborn son? There's nothing to worry about. Everything has been taken care of. I went over it with the lawyer and – "

"You believe Karim Abd el-Hak? Didn't Hiyawi tell you what his father did in the *Farhood?* Don't you know that his brother hates Jews and fought against Israel? How can you trust a man like that?"

"Karim is a friend. There are things I can't tell you. We've looked into every angle."

"And chosen the worst! If he's caught, he'll be arrested." Her voice trembled.

"Do you have a better suggestion?"

"Go and see Big Imari." She lit a cigarette with shaky hands. "That's better than endangering your son."

"Woman, that's enough. Take my word for it, I know what I'm doing."

I heard them arguing late into the night. I couldn't help thinking that my mother might be right.

22.

Although Rashel had spent all night preparing, she didn't finish
until noon. In the morning I found her still mixing and tasting
silan wa-rashi, Hizkel' s favourite date syrup and sesame paste.
Even after adding a handful of ground walnuts and some
powdered cardamom, she wasn't satisfied. I dipped in my
finger, gave it a lick, and said "Fabulous" in the hope of speeding
her up, although my taste buds told me that it was a far cry from
the delicacy that only Hizkel knew how to make. After lunch she
packed a wicker basket with all that Hizkel had been deprived
of these past months: meat balls with saffron rice, fried fish, a
jar of amba, fruit, dried figs, two bottles of rose water, Hiyawi's
Zabana cigarettes, and more. When it was full, she hugged it as
though it were Hizkel and went to get dressed.

This time, in a long, black, pleated dress with shoulder pads,
she managed to look like a Moslem. Although she put on no
make-up, she was her usual stunning self. Only the involuntary
flutter of her eyelids betrayed her nervousness.

My father had on his grey suit, the one he thought brought
him good luck, with a red rose stuck in the lapel, while I wore
the unbecoming costume of an Arab tea vendor. What abstruse
calculations went into the choosing of it I didn't know, but the
general idea was to provide a disguise that would fool not only
the prison guards but also their superiors, who – though they
left the building at four – had to be taken into account.

The taxi dropped us off not far from the prison. "You're on your own now," my father said. "God be with you. We'll wait for you behind the ministry." Though he tried to sound calm, his voice shook.

"God bless your day," said Rashel, squeezing my arm. I tried to ignore the sinking feeling of being alone and at 4:20 sharp appeared right on schedule in front of the large yard with its semi-circle of buildings. Not until the previous night, when I went with my father to see Abu Saleh el-Hibaz, had I realized how professionally everything had been planned. Abu Saleh showed me a detailed map of the prison, pointed out its different wings and cell blocks, and made me learn them by heart.

Fortunately, I had a good memory. "You have to know where you are every minute and where Hizkel is in relation to you," he said. Accustomed as I was to his joking and horseplay, his seriousness gave me confidence.

Now, however, in front of the prison with Rashel's basket on my arm, I shuffled my feet nervously as if I were standing unshod on the burning pavement. I was wondering whether the time had come to take out my tray and little tea cups when I felt a heavy clap and spun around. It took a second to realize that the fat man standing behind me, his hand on my shoulder, was the contact I had been waiting for. I had assumed all along that he would approach me from inside the gate.

"Looking for something, boy?" he asked in a reassuring tone.

"I've brought tea, *ya sidi*," I answered as instructed.

"Come with me." He nodded to the guard at the gate and I followed him through the yard to a building. *Number 3*, I told myself, remembering the map – and sure enough, a moment later I saw a 3 over the entrance.

We entered a corridor. "You have your permit?" my guide asked with a sly look.

"Yes ... I mean ... here it is ... " I answered shrilly, slipping him a 100 fils coin.

"Let me see the basket." He rummaged through it, picked out a black date, popped it in his mouth, and spat the pit on the floor.

"Show me the permit again."

"Here." I handed him another 100 fils. He stood fingering the two coins, stuck them in his pocket, and said:

"Come along."

He walked casually ahead of me, stopping only to ask for more dates by pointing at the basket. "Who are you here to see?" he inquired. His not knowing puzzled me until I remembered Abu Saleh saying: "Each time he asks a question, give him another coin." Or as my father put it: "You can't see the duke without a ducat."

"Hizkel Imari," I whispered, handing over another 100 fils.

"Who's that, a Jew? Now the cat's out of the bag! So that's why you dressed up as a teaboy," he intoned disingenuously, pinching my ear until it burned. "A Jew! But not smart enough to know that Arab teaboys go barefoot and don't wear sandals. Thought you'd put one over on me, eh?"

I gave him another coin. It was just so much small change for a small fry. The big cheese, whoever he was, had already been given his share.

The man left me and disappeared into a room. The bare corridor was deserted. *He'll turn me in*, I thought. *He'll arrest me and I'll be a hero at school. Everyone will talk about me, even Amira and Ismail.* A muffled howl – a tortured prisoner's? – resounded in the empty space. Then another. My hair stood on end. I didn't want to be a hero. I only wanted to go home. The sweat stung my adolescent pimples. Did I have to have my hair torn out, my fingernails extracted one by one, and be assfucked to shreds just to prove to Rashel what a man I was?

It was too late to turn tail and run. I squatted on my haunches like an Arab and clutched the basket, my eye on the door of the room. What was my guide doing in there? Suppose Karim Abd el-Hak had lied and Hizkel wasn't even here? How could a big-time lawyer not have been able to arrange a legal visit? He was after Rashel, that's what. He would string her along until she gave into him. I had heard of such stories before. Hizkel would rot in jail while Karim rolled in the hay with Rashel. That was why he hadn't even asked for a retainer. "Not now," "Not yet", that was all he had said whenever my father suggested it.

The clack of a typewriter, a sign that the door had opened, broke into my thoughts. My guide came out all smiles and signalled that he was ready for more dates. "Sweet as honey," he declared.

"*T'fadel*," I said. "Enjoy them."

"The prisoner is your father?"

"My uncle."

"A Communist, a Zionist, an arms runner, a subversive, a traitor – and a Jew too. *Allah yistur! Allah yistur!*" he exclaimed. "All right, Mr Tea Vendor, let's go to the cell block. You wouldn't happen to have a little tea for me first, would you?"

He chuckled and scratched his head, and I gave him another coin and walked beside him. We passed some offices and barracks and came to a tall, square wall topped with loops of barbed wire and sentry boxes. I knew from the map that this was the maximum security wing. My guide rapped out a rhythm like Morse code on an iron door and a pockmarked jailer peered through a peephole.

"There's a visitor for Imari."

"For that son-of-a-bitch? He should be strung up by the balls."

My guide winked at me. I took out a coin. He winked again. I took out another. He gave one to the jailer and stuck the other in his pocket.

"What about the cigarettes?" asked the jailer.

I took out a pack and gave it to him.

"What about me?" said my guide.

I handed him a pack too.

The jailer shut the peephole. "Watch out for him, he's a real bastard," my guide whispered. "And next time, don't wear sandals." He turned and was gone.

The jailer yanked me inside, stood me against the wall, rammed his fist into my chest, and said:

"Get this, Jewboy: try smuggling one fucking thing in here and I'll kill you!"

I uncovered the basket and said in the snivelling tone in which the weak communicate their subservience to the strong, "There's nothing but food here *ya sidi.*"

"*Yallah,* move!" he said, giving me a kick.

After some fifty metres we came to long barracks with small, heavily-barred windows and entered a corridor flanked by barred cells set in concrete walls that I made out as I grew used to the dim light. The pockmarked man stopped by a cell door and shouted: "Hizkel Imari!"

The greyish cigarette smoke drifting out of the dark interior failed to hide the stink of mould and urine. Out of the haze emerged a barely recognizable face.

"Kabi! Kabi!" His voice was a fractured croak. He looked terribly thin in his oversized striped pyjamas and one puffy eye was shut. Although his head was shaven, his cheeks had a thick stubble.

"How are you all?"

"Fine."

"Rashel?"

"Fine."

"Say one wrong word and you've had it!" said the jailer, raising a menacing hand.

I could see the cell more clearly now. It was narrow and very long. About twenty prisoners sprawled on the floor, their feet pointing towards the centre of the room. One with blubbery lips lay curled by the bars in his filthy underwear, his folded pyjamas beneath his head; black-and-blue marks covered one arm and dark flies that he seemed not even to notice swarmed over a pus-filled wound on his knee. For a second, he opened his eyes and gave me a dismal look. He stank of decay and near him in a corner stood a bucket. A lanky man with a head that jerked like a proud pigeon's stepped up to it, took out his thick, black member, and urinated.

"You son-of-a-bitch, where's your respect?" asked the jailer. "You could have waited until I was gone."

"Here, have some prick juice," mocked the lanky prisoner.

"If you don't watch it, I'll cut your prick off," the jailer said.

"Just tell me if you want it in your mouth or your ass. I'll bet you've never had anything so good."

"Go stick it up your mother!"

"I'll stick it up yours. What do you take me for, a Jew?"

The lanky man stroked his penis, shook the last drops from it, bent over the groaning man on the floor, shooed the flies from his knee, and wiped his sweaty face.

"Allah bless you," the man on the floor murmured weakly.

"He needs a doctor," the lanky prisoner told the jailer. "How many times do we have to tell you?"

"The Angel of Death is what he'll get," the jailer said, spitting close to my foot. He snatched my basket and shoved me away.

"Leave the boy alone," said Hizkel.

"Shut up, you filth," the jailer told him in Jewish Arabic. "You should thank me that I let him in without a permit."

"You asshole!" said the lanky prisoner. "When it comes to bossing Jews you're a big hero."

"Since when are you such a Jew-lover?" asked the jailer. "You should be ashamed of yourself, and so should the dry cunt that gave birth to you."

"You know how to talk like a Jew," taunted Hizkel. "How would you like to become one? I'll fix you up with Rabbi Bashi."

"Watch your filthy tongue! *Allah akbar, Allah akbar.* I testify that there is no God but Allah and that Muhammed is His prophet." The jailer mumbled the confession of faith quickly, this time in the accent of a Moslem. "What do you take me for, a fucking atheist like that Communist?"

He pointed to the lanky man, who spat at him and said: "Come the revolution, you'll hang from a butcher's hook!"

"I'll piss on your grave first!"

"Fat chance of that, you shit-faced lackey of the ruling class!"

The jailer pointed at me. "One more word and I'll throw him out of here."

Hizkel smiled and shook his head to let me know he didn't mean it.

229

"Anyone for cigarettes? Jew-food?" The jailer waved the basket in the air.

Few of the prisoners stirred. Only two approached the bars. The jailer opened the gate and tossed the basket inside, where it was caught by someone in mid-air.

"Give it to Imari!" shouted the lanky prisoner.

"All right, don't shout," said the basket catcher. Hizkel opened the basket, spread its contents on the floor, and said: "Help yourselves, boys. Dig in!"

No one took anything. A single pack of cigarettes was passed from hand to hand. Soon the cell was full of the aroma of Hiyawi's Zabanas.

"Hey, arrack!" cried a prisoner, holding up a bottle. "Booze!"

The jailer slapped me so hard that I saw stars. My face stung all over.

"I told you not to touch him!" cried Hizkel.

"You brought liquor?" screamed the jailer. "That's against the rules. Let's have it!" He uncorked the bottle, held it to his nose, and sniffed. "*Rose water?*" He poured some on his hands and wet his face with it, as happy as a child who has been given a piece of candy.

"It's yours," said Hizkel.

"Trying to bribe me, eh?" said the jailer.

The prisoners burst into catcalls. "We're too good to you, you bastard!" one said. Hizkel smelled the other bottle of rose water. His eyes lit up and he handed it to the tall Communist, who sprinkled a bit on his face. A ripple like an eddy in the Tigris ran through the prisoners, many of whom sat up as they passed the bottle around, each taking a few drops. For a brief moment something stronger had overcome the stench of the cell. It was, I realized, the smell of a woman in a place without hope of ever seeing one.

There was a loud knock on the door of the cell block. The jailer hurried and began arguing loudly with someone while Hizkel motioned me to the corner where the bars met the concrete wall. My cheek was still burning from the blow.

"How did you get in here?"

"It was all arranged." I handed him an envelope with money. "We're working on a plan to get you out of here and give you false papers."

"Is everything out of the cellar?"

"It's all been taken care of."

"I need to see Rashel."

"They won't let you. That's what Karim Abd el-Hak says."

"It's great to see you." He smiled and stroked my face through the bars, then pulled away embarrassed when I tried touching his. "Kabi, I'm full of lice," he said. We both laughed. The man on the floor let out a scream, lifted his head, and let it fall back on the folded pyjamas.

"Did they torture you?"

Hizkel's only answer was a characteristic toss of his head. "When's the trial?" he asked drily.

"No one knows."

"Find a way to get to Israel and take Rashel."

I nodded. On his chest, beneath the pyjama top, I noticed a dark blue mark.

"Tell Abu Saleh to go ahead as planned. I don't want him or anyone in the Movement taking unnecessary risks for me. Tell him that I have complete faith in him and that I know he'll do a good job. Tell him that all our years of working together were a preparation for this."

It was easy to see what had made him a leader. "Kabi, boy, in my study, at the back of my desk, there's a secret panel behind the bottom left-hand drawer. You'll find some of my poems there, and beneath them, a thick blue notebook. If it's still there, take it and keep it for me."

"I'll do that," I said proudly.

"What's happening with my vocational school?"

"The police shut it down."

"That's too bad."

There was a rattle of chains behind me. A towering prisoner with curly red hair and shackles on his ankles and wrists was led into the cell block.

"That's the Communists' leader," said Hizkel with a note of admiration.

"The Red Armenian?" I asked. I remembered hearing about him from Edouard and Salim Effendi.

"In person."

The Armenian walked erect, smiling and lifting a shackled hand in greeting as he passed each cell.

"Long live the Communist revolution! Long live the Soviet Union!" cried the lanky prisoner.

"Down with the government of whores! Down with injustice!" came other cries.

With the last of his strength the wounded man, supported by Hizkel and the tall Communist, struggled to his feet to catch a glimpse of his leader. His torments forgotten, he joined in the slogans in a barely audible voice.

"Hey, you, Armenian!" The pockmarked jailer brandished his gun. "We're going to hang you soon."

The Armenian brushed him and his two armed guards aside as if they were so many sparrows.

"Long live the great Armenian! Down with the regime of Satan!" called the lanky prisoner. The words were taken up by the other cells in a rhythmic chant that seemed to shake the walls of the prison.

"Quiet!" shouted the jailer, his voice drowned out by the din. Retreating, he punched an alarm button and at once a riot squad burst into the cell block with fixed bayonets. The guards pointed their guns but ignored the jailer's orders to seize the Armenian, who merely smiled paternally. The prisoners shouted even louder.

"Long live the Red Armenian! Down with the regime of Satan!" shouted the lanky prisoner. All the men pounded on their iron bars.

Just as a second riot squad entered the block the pockmarked jailer panicked and fired two shots in the air.

"Get down!" yelled Hizkel.

I hit the floor. A guard stumbled over me and kicked me hard. "What the hell are you doing here?" he yelled while aiming his gun at the Armenian. Gasping for breath, I crawled to the bars and huddled against them, clutching the hand that Hizkel held out to me.

"Are they going to kill him?" I asked.

"They wouldn't dare." Seeing the mayhem in the guards' eyes though, he added: "You never know."

The Armenian looked at the two riot squads, glanced at the frenzied prisoners, and signalled to them to quieten down. A deadly hush descended as he was led to his solitary cell at the end of the block. Before entering it he turned and waved like the Pope greeting the faithful in St Peter's Square.

"Long live Lenin! Long live Stalin! Down with the Regent! Down with Nuri es-Sa'id!" shouted the lanky prisoner. The others broke into stormy applause as their leader regained his cell unharmed. The pockmarked jailer quickly locked and bolted its door. The two riot squads were spat and whistled at as they passed back up the corridor.

Although he tried strutting like a peacock, the jailer went off with his tail between his legs. For a while, as if by a command passed from cell to cell, there wasn't a sound. Then, from the block's far end, came the deep voice of the Armenian singing a song full of yearning in a language I did not know. Only years later did I realize it must have been Russian. Or maybe Armenian. What language does a man sing in on the night before his execution? A few prisoners hummed the refrain. A deep melancholy descended on the cell block.

Hizkel smiled at me and said: "On your feet, boy! You'll be all right."

I brushed off the dust and tried to think of something encouraging to say, but my mind was a blank.

"Damn you, are you still here?" yelled the jailer, scrambling out of his guard box.

"I'm going," I said.

He planted a kick in my rear.

"You're a big hero when it comes to Jewish kids!" shouted the tall Communist.

A moment later I was thrown out by the seat of my pants.

I had done it! I was ecstatic. The one problem now was getting past the sentry at the main gate. If only my fat guide were there, another 100 fils would take care of it. And indeed he was, standing in front of Building 3. I handed him a coin and he saw me through the gate.

I went straight to our rendezvous. My father was waiting with his shoulders oddly hunched, his fingers drumming on his thigh. He took a quick step towards me when he saw me, then thought better of it. Holding Rashel's hand, he turned and walked stolidly ahead of me until we reached a deserted alley near the river.

"I found him!" I cried. "I found him!"

"He's all right?" Rashel asked.

"Yes."

We hugged and kissed while she showered me with questions. I talked on and on and she hung on every word and kept asking for more like a child listening to a bedtime story.

"What happened to your face?" asked my father. "Did anyone hit you?"

"I was slapped and kicked around a bit."

"Why?"

"Because they're bastards."

He patted me on the head. "May the hands that did it be struck off."

"He wants you to come to Israel with us," I told Rashel. "He doesn't want you waiting for him here."

"What did I tell you?" said my father.

"I'm not leaving without him."

"We'll talk about that some other time. Let's go home and tell your mother you're all right, Kabi. On the way you can pop into Abu Saleh's for some pittas." I didn't need his knee poking mine to be reminded that neither Rashel nor the lawyer knew of Abu Saleh's involvement in the matter. "And tonight you're all invited to a fish dinner on the river."

In the carriage Rashel sat in a world of her own, her eyes bright with joy.

"Babba, I saw the Armenian," I said.

My father paled. "Is he in the same cell block?"

I tried remembering the sad melody. It was on the tip of my tongue but I couldn't sing a single bar of it.

"They're going to hang him," I said.

"What?" Rashel snapped out of her reverie.

"Tomorrow."

"Hizkel?" she screamed.

"No. The Armenian!"

After Hizkel's study was ransacked on the night of his arrest, Rashel had rearranged it. The scattered books were picked up and replaced on their shelves and the magazines from Egypt, Syria, and Lebanon, which I had read my way through eagerly with his permission, were neatly stacked. (He had also lent me the latest novels of Taha Hussein and Tewfik el-Hakim, as well as translations from other languages). The desk too looked the same, although for some reason it was missing its framed motto that said: "Live for today as if there were no tomorrow and plan for tomorrow as if there were no today."

I found the notebook where Hizkel said it would be, in a secret panel that was a tribute to his carpenter's skills.

23

" … Until the *Farhood* in 1941," wrote Hizkel in his notebook, "I laughed at Jews who dreamed of a state in Palestine. I thought they were eccentrics, like so many before them in our history. Their outlook was foreign to me, for I did not believe in the appeal to power or the resort to physical force. If the Jews, I thought, had managed to preserve their moral superiority and innate sense of justice inherited from the Prophets, this was by being a People of the Book, a small people that had no state, no flag, no anthem, no army, no control over others. This alone made it special.

"Then came the war and the *Farhood* and everything changed. I sat up during long nights talking with my cousin Salim Effendi, and for a while I even considered joining 'The progressive forces of justice, equality, and human brotherhood'. In the new society, Salim Effendi promised me, a *Farhood* would be impossible. Yet beguiled though I was by the idea, which seemed so close to the vision of our Prophets, something kept me from embracing it. It was at this time that the first reports began arriving of the mass murder of the Jews in Europe. The Germans, the greatest enemies our people ever had, were highly popular in Iraq. The government of Rashid Ali el-Kailani sought to model itself on them and planned to deport us to detention camps in the desert where we would be liquidated. More than ever it became clear how dangerous being a Jew in

Iraq was … far more than being an Assyrian Christian, Kurd, or Armenian. I was forced to realize that we had no choice but to have our own homeland like other nations, even if this meant taking up arms and killing and being killed. If we had to die, let it be sword in hand.

"My brother Abu Kabi became a Zionist at this time too. We began to look for a connection to Palestine, for some way of acting, but we didn't know where to begin. And then, one warm evening in early May 1942, I was introduced to a field worker from Palestine, Enzo Sereni, an aristocratic Italian Jew and doctor of philosophy whose father had been a physician to kings. He was a man in his forties, a free and almost insanely brave soul who refused to yield to any obstacle – in a word, a person to be looked up to. Although he knew less than nothing about the Arab mentality and talked about Zionism to everyone, from the most dimwitted Arab coachman to Big Imari in his office and Ustad Nawi in his living room, he felt at home with everyone; his eyes glowed when he spoke of the rehabilitation of the Jewish people, the worker's movement in the Land of Israel, Communism in the Soviet Union, socialism in Europe, literature and philosophy, Marx and Engels.

"To one of our meetings, I invited Salim Effendi. Enzo took an immediate liking to him and was impressed by his Oxford English. He told him about his brother, Emilio Sereni, a Communist and partisan in Italy, and afterwards, when asking me about Salim Effendi, always referred to him as 'my brother's colleague'. And yet in that same first meeting with Salim Effendi he said to him at the end of a long argument: 'Both you and Emilio will realize one day that you have been worshipping a false god whose kingdom will collapse like a house of cards.'

"This bespectacled man, who never went anywhere without a

few books in several languages, lit a fire in my heart. When he told me about the murdered Jews in Europe, I felt that I was flesh of their flesh. The next day I was due to lecture at my school about the blind Egyptian author Taha Hussein, but instead I talked about the Nazi massacres. My students burst into tears. That same night I began to study Hebrew. By the sheer force of his personality, Enzo convinced me that people like me could build a new country. We, the scions of rabbis and Talmudists, would fulfil our share of the great dream of humanity. Everything about Enzo was a revelation: the way he talked, the way he thought, the long conversations we had about reviving the Hebrew language, bringing Jewish immigrants to Palestine, creating a Jewish defence force in Iraq. Next to the new, free world that he opened up for me, my old life seemed poor and pointless. Even the long legal battle with Big Imari began to appear trivial. My date business, my dreams of marrying into money, my plans for recouping the family fortune: all now struck me as beside the point.

"I felt that my life was about to change completely, that I was faced with a new challenge that had the power to compensate for everything. Although I had never been to Palestine, I knew that that's where I belonged. I wanted to be part of the creation of a Jewish state, to put my shoulder to the wheel of independence. The more I threw myself into the Zionist pioneering movement in Iraq, the more I felt that I was involved in something so glorious that it was more precious than life itself. It was a dream that gave me wings and endowed every minute with meaning. Here, in the streets of Baghdad, I no longer jealously watched the Arabs fighting to drive out the British, and the Communists confronting the bullets of the exploiters. We too were an ancient people with our own God and great book, we too had a country and a language waiting to be redeemed! The Bible suddenly seemed to me a realistic, contemporary document. It was from this land of Mesopotamia that Abraham went forth to claim our country, from the Egypt of Taha Hussein that Moses brought us forth from slavery. Not that I imagined myself the equal of such men. Yet I felt that the inner strength that drove me derived from them. Each time I stood facing a new group of volunteers for the Movement and saw the excitement in their eyes, I felt the whole Jewish past behind me and the whole Jewish future ahead of me.

"I had found myself and the purpose of my life. The hidden seed had germinated. I was a different man, with a self-confidence and self-esteem I had never had before. The time had come for me to be a teacher, a father, a leader. For years I had been brought up by my mother to believe that I, who was named after the prophet of the resurrection of the dry bones, was destined for greatness. Now I felt that I was living it. It was as if I had been touched by the seer's hand and heard him say: 'Fear not, son of man! Go thou to the House of Israel and speak my word unto them.'

"I longed for the land of our fathers. I wanted to leave for that place at once. And yet I knew that I had a mission to perform here. Enzo told me that too. 'You have to stay a while longer,' he said. 'Strengthen the foundations, organize more people, give them faith and hope.' I knew that an Italian Jew like him couldn't possibly do what I could. It had to come from us, from within. If we didn't light the torch and pass it on, no one would. There could be no Movement unless we ourselves heard the footsteps of the Messiah. No emissary from Jerusalem could bring Babylon back with him. It was up to us ... "

24

Although a month had gone by since our Ustad Nawi or Stad Nawi, as we called him in our Jewish Arabic, had asked me to write an essay on Patriotism for a competition sponsored by the ministry of education, I hadn't even prepared an outline. The notes I had taken still lay on a table in the library. Lately, I had had trouble concentrating, had neglected my studies, and had taken whole days – some spent with my father on Hizkel's case – off school. I had misbehaved in class too, even in Miss Sylvia's, which was my favourite. Although I knew I should mend my ways, I was summoned to Stad Nawi before I could.

I tucked my shirt into my trousers, combed my hair, squared my shoulders that slumped when I was nervous, and strode anxiously to the rector's office. It was never clear to me what made me so in awe of him and of Salim Effendi, towards both of whom I behaved like a humble disciple. It was time to grow out of it … Yet now too, instead of knocking on the rector's open door and walking in, I stood silently waiting for permission to enter. As if I hadn't been one of his school's best pupils for years! Perhaps I felt guilty for skipping classes and thought this was why he wanted to see me. It was all my father's fault. Although he had always attached great importance to my studies, he no longer took them seriously now that we already had one foot in Israel. And Hizkel came before everything.

At last Stad Nawi sensed my presence and invited me in by

crooking his finger without looking up from the book on his desk. I sat with my schoolbag in my lap, pulling at my knuckles while he went on reading. A highly cultured man and a polyglot who had written many textbooks and translated into Arabic parts of the Bible and *The Travels of Benjamin of Tudela* (a book I had never managed to get through), he was best known as a prominent Iraqi author in his own right. His reputation rested most solidly on his *From A Scrivener's Pen,* a collection of stories that belonged, according to Salim Effendi, "to the genre of realism". This work was taught in Iraqi schools and served as a model for many young writers, who sought to imitate the sophisticated irony of its dry, concise style.

Although Stad Nawi, who for a while had edited the literary supplement of my Uncle Hizkel's *Daily Mail,* was slimly built and looked like an accountant with his round little eyeglasses and briefcase full of books and folders that he carried under one arm, he inspired respect. Despite his quiet exterior, his quick temper had led him to box the ear of more than one pupil. Nothing pleased him more than being introduced as "Ustad Nawi, the celebrated author", a compliment he dismissed with a modest wave of his hand while beaming with delight. He was also fond of hosting literary soirées attended by such well-known Jewish authors as Anwar Sha'ul, Shalom Darwish, and Ya'akub Bilbul, as well as by younger poets and writers, many of them former students; always present, too, was an inevitable guest of honour, one or another noted Moslem literary figure who was needed to make the evening a truly Iraqi one. Recently, my classmate George Imari had been honoured at one of these occasions by being asked to read two of his poems. Green with envy, I had imagined myself standing in his place and declaiming "The *Kemar* Seller", a short story in my drawer that was based on the liaison between Fat'hiya and Abu Saleh el-Hibaz. Invitations were much in demand to these gatherings, which Stad Nawi conducted imperiously, enjoying most his own appearances on the dais – where, deliberately removing and replacing his spectacles while quoting by heart whole stanzas of Hebrew poetry translated by him into Arabic, he basked in the audience's admiration.

He was an unparalleled master of persuasion, equally good at extracting funds for his school and its needier pupils from well-heeled members of the Jewish community and at pulling the wool over the eyes of the ministry of education, which he bombarded with compositions and term papers written by his students on the glories of Iraq, the greatness of her leaders, the splendours of her heritage, the centrality of her position, and the enormity of her contribution to world culture. As part of this campaign he organized trips to Nineveh, Babylon, and the Museum of Antiquities in Baghdad, and lectured us each year on Hammurabi's Code. "No school in the kingdom educates for patriotism like ours does," he boasted proudly in his declarations to visiting pedagogues, some from as far as Egypt, Lebanon, and even Great Britain, who were made to sit through a syrupy series of obeisance's to the King, the Regent, the Pasha, and the ministers of education who came and went with each new government. Each visitor received a modest gift, "a token of appreciation from our students", and an eloquently obsequious speech from our rector that gave every sign of having been spontaneous.

Meanwhile, under the noses of these same ministers, Stad Nawi had doubled the amount of class hours devoted to "religion", the school's official term for Jewish history and Hebrew, and secretly encouraged Zionist activity. Although he was careful to hide any connection with the Movement, it was said that his greatest dream was to be minister of education in Israel one day, and recent rumours spoke of a falling-out between him and Salim Effendi, who was for strengthening the Iraqi component in the curriculum. The students, thought Salim Effendi, should be encouraged to be politically active and even to take to the streets, an idea Stad Nawi was unalterably opposed to. Still, despite tales of bitter backroom fights, the two men continued to appear in public as harmoniously as a pair of love birds.

Stad Nawi's room was carpeted with a Persian rug and had an impressively ornamented heavy black desk piled high with books, some open. On it was also a blue inkwell that reflected back a rosy prism of light at the wide, silvery shade of the reading lamp hanging from an overhead chain. Bookshelves lined the walls and in one corner of the room stood three leather armchairs and a small stool with a glass ashtray.

The telephone rang, breaking the silence. Stad Nawi picked it up with a measured movement and said "Hello ... Yes, Your Excellency," then shut his eyes, leaned back, and listened in silence to the voice at the other end of the line. Suddenly he frowned and thick lines furrowed his brow. He passed a hand over his bald head, then covered his eyes with it. Finally, he declared:

"Your Excellency knows that our school is loyal to the crown. I know of nothing subversive. I'm sorry to have to say that our students have been harassed. Some have been taken out of class by the CID for investigation ... Permit me, sir ... No, no, no, I promise you, there are no Communist or Zionist activities ... "

He fell silent again, dipped a nibbed pen in the inkwell, and jotted down some names. When he finally hung up, he drew a white handkerchief from the breast pocket of his jacket, wiped the sweat from his forehead, blew his nose, looked down at the floor, sighed, and then – remembering me – glanced back up, replaced the handkerchief, and said: "Well, my boy, where were we?" And without waiting for an answer, he asked:

"How is your Uncle Hizkel?"

"He's fine. I've seen him in prison."

"I know." His nod made me realize with relief that I wasn't on the carpet. He knew what my family was going through.

"When is the trial?"

"The date hasn't been set."

"Give Hizkel my best wishes. And try to keep his spirits up. You mustn't forget what a golden pen he wields." He paused, then continued: "I want you to know that it has been decided to appoint you editor of the school newspaper, a position for which you've been highly recommended by Salim Effendi and other teachers. The administration is confident that you will acquit yourself well. This year the ministry of education is sponsoring a contest for the best school newspaper, which we would very much like to win. And incidentally, we're still waiting for your composition on Patriotism."

"Yes, sir," I answered hoarsely. "I've already finished the research. I just have to sit down and write it."

"That's splendid, my boy. I knew we could count on you. You Imaris have never let us down. If there are any problems, Salim Effendi and the rest of the staff are at your disposal. This year especially it's important to win first prize. I needn't explain why."

His eyes fell on the list of students he had just drawn up.

"No, sir," I murmured.

"You'll wait for George Imari in the library," said Stad Nawi, rising to let me know that our meeting was over. "He'll hand over the keys of office to you and any material he may have."

I could have jumped for joy. George Imari out, Kabi Imari in: what sweet revenge! I had been sure that George would keep the job for another year. His father gave so much money to the school that George could have had anything for the asking. Not that he didn't deserve it. He wrote so well that Stad Nawi was not exaggerating when he said that few adults could match his style, and he had given the paper new dash and content. I suddenly had cold feet. Did I have any chance of coming out ahead in the undeclared competition between us?

The library was brightly lit and very quiet. I couldn't resist going to the editor's desk and running a hand over its leather blotter. Tomorrow it would be mine.

A year ago, as assistant editor, I had already planned my first issue: it would be dedicated to the royal house, with both flattering pictures and caricatures of the crown prince, who would soon come of age and assume the throne as King Faisal II. The idea still seemed to me a good one. Salim Effendi would not be thrilled by it, but Stad Nawi would be more than happy and would even send me to the palace with a letter of introduction and a request for an interview. I tried imagining my signature featured prominently beneath the piece.

I waited impatiently for George. But he did not appear and I thought of the proverb of Hiyawi's: "Don't celebrate the wedding before the bride arrives." Well, it was his look-out. What was I worried about? Stad Nawi and Salim Effendi would not have chosen me unless they had confidence in me. And it was me, not George, whom they had asked to represent our school in the national contest. I had never before gathered so much material for a single composition. But though I had pages full of notes, the essay refused to write itself. What country was I a patriot of: the one I had never been to though my father said it was my real home, or the one I was born and raised in that he called a temporary asylum? The one Ismail wanted to drive me from, or the one Abu Edouard refused to be driven to? According to Salim Effendi, Ismail and I would one day share Iraq together, but I did not know whether to believe him.

I had to have a talk with my father. Sometimes I still wasn't sure that I understood what Zionism was all about. Was Hiyawi right in saying that a person could have two countries, one physical and one spiritual? And what was patriotism anyway? The people, the earth, the flowers, the rivers, the smells of Iraq – there were times when I felt them surrounding me like a womb, when all I wanted was to yield to them mindlessly, completely, with a simple, uncalculating love. The most illiterate peasant who ploughed and sowed and lived close to the land, rooted in it like a tree, knew more about patriotism than I did. My great-grandfather had been like that, growing rice and reaping wheat and barley by the waters of the Tigris. He may have visited the Land of Israel, kissed its soil, made the pilgrimage to the tombs of the Patriarchs, prayed at the Wailing Wall, even bought a few hectares of land there – but it was to Iraq that he returned.

I didn't know what to write. George would have been a better choice. Israel was not a problem for him and, living in a house that entertained wazirs and emirs, he knew a lot more than I did. Yet how could I say that to Stad Nawi? He might take the editor's job away from me.

I dipped my pen in an inkwell and tried composing the first paragraph. Everything, I knew, depended on striking the right note at the outset. And yet all I managed to produce was a few doodles and a botched profile of Rashel. By now I was tired of waiting for George, who must have decided to stand me up. What an innocent I was to have thought that he would step down without a fight and surrender the prestige, the honour of having his photograph in the paper, the traditional ceremony with the minister of education, the right to publish any of his poems! And perhaps I had only wanted the job in the first place so that I could strut in front of Rashel and Amira and tell my father that I had ousted George Imari.

The longer I waited, the more face I stood to lose.

As it was, the last schoolbus had left for Taht el-Takya and I would have to walk to Bab-esh-Shargi and take public transport from there. Without a phone at home I couldn't even call my mother to tell her not to worry. I was already getting to my feet when in walked a grinning George.

"Sorry I'm late," he said. "How about coming home with me?"

"To your house?"

"Would you rather we went to yours?"

"What for? All I need from you is the material."

"I have it at home. Come on, the driver is waiting."

"I can't," I said. "It's late."

"My chauffeur will take you home afterwards."

His Lordship turned and headed for the exit as if he would brook no alternative. By the time I reached the schoolgates he was sitting in the back of his black limousine that resembled the minister of defence's. It took me a second or two to realize that the driver was holding the door open for me. I sank into the black leather upholstery and settled in the right-hand corner like the Regent on a tour of Baghdad. Since I had no choice, I might as well enjoy it.

I stretched out my legs and leaned back royally. If only Edouard could see me now! He was not enough of a Communist to restrain his admiration, even his envy. We too could have had a car like this if Big Imari hadn't swindled us. The thought of him made my heart pound. What was I doing? My father had always said that I should keep my distance from him and George – and look at me now!

The limousine was as smooth as Fat'hiya's *kemar*, the smell of its leather mingling with the scent of George's hair oil. At last we turned into the driveway of the mysterious and vaunted Imari home. Although many stories were told of this mansion in Baghdad, most of all by my own family, none of us had ever set foot in it, not even Salim Effendi who gave George his private lessons in school.

We drove past a hedgerow of myrtle bushes, through a big iron gateway set in the high brick wall, and into a large, fragrant garden. Two huge dogs bounded towards me with loud barks as I stepped out of the car. Too scared to move, I threw up an automatic hand in self-defence. George pointed to his feet and said: "Down!"

The two dogs dropped to the ground and fell still, eyeing me balefully with their tongues hanging out. George bent to stroke them. "I'm sorry, I forgot to warn you," he said.

"I'm sure their bark is worse than their bite," I answered, trying to sound nonchalant.

"To tell the truth, their bite is worse than their bark. That's why my father had them brought from London."

The house surpassed my wildest dreams. The polished, carved wooden entrance opened into a wide hallway that led to a huge salon, the black marble floor of which was spread with dark red Persian rugs. The deep sofas and armchairs were upholstered in red velvet. There were crystal chandeliers hanging from the ceiling, vases of flowers on the dark tables, inlaid cabinets in the corners, all kinds of unfamiliar bric-a-brac, and a gigantic pink alabaster sculpture of a finely beaked dove. The walls were hung with paintings and tapestries and in one corner stood an intricately wrought ebony grandfather clock. The room was so large and had such a high ceiling that at first I hardly noticed the hectic activity of the servants who were busy moving furniture and setting up an enormous table such as I had seen only at fancy weddings.

"Is this all for me?" I joked.

"It's for the Pasha."

"Nuri es-Sa'id?"

"None other. He and Regent Abdullah are our guests tonight."

"What's the occasion?"

"Nothing special."

"Will you be there?"

"Yes. I'm sorry to say that I have a role to play."

"What's that?"

"Don't ask."

Although I saw no fans, the room was pleasantly cool. Perhaps George's father had brought air-conditioning from America. My glance fell on a familiar-looking picture on the wall, an oil painting copied from the same photograph of Grandfather Imari that hung in our house. He was, so it seemed, the one member of the family to whom George's father had not given the cold shoulder.

George steered me down another corridor, opened a door, and said: "Do come in, this is my study." In it was a grand piano, a phonograph, a record cabinet, a bookcase, a glass chest with a collection of riding hats, a delicate round table with a vase of flowers, and a desk with a typewriter. The far wall was a glass pane that looked out on a lush tropical garden. A curtain flapped in an open window. "Have a seat," said George, pointing to a corner where some leather armchairs were arranged around a white coffee table. "Music?"

I nodded.

He put a record on the phonograph. For a moment I had an eerie feeling. When I was ten, my teacher once took our class to see *The Phantom of The Opera*. As its hero fled, disfigured by the acid thrown at him, into the sewers beneath the city, a piano played the same dramatic chords I heard now.

"Know it?" George asked.

I nodded again, pretending to be concentrating. "There's nothing like Chopin." He settled back in his chair and shut his eyes while his fingers roamed in space as if playing an ethereal melody. So he was a pianist too, god damn him! When the piece was over, he opened his eyes and asked:

"Do you play an instrument?"

I nodded once more. "Uh-huh."

"Which?"

"The zither," I lied.

"It would be fun to play a duet."

"There aren't any for piano and zither," I said knowingly. "Will you play at the party tonight?"

"What do those jackasses know about music? Power, women, boys, and money, that's all they ever think about."

A brightly-uniformed waiter, looking as if he had stepped straight out of a Hollywood set, knocked and entered. George glanced at me and cocked an eyebrow.

"Tea," I ventured.

"It's awfully hot. Won't you allow me to order for you?" And before I could answer he told the waiter: "Some mango juice and the usual for me."

I was embarrassed to ask what mango juice was. "What does one talk about to the Regent?" I inquired, fingering the back of my chair.

"Politics. Gossip."

"It sounds like fun. Maybe you'd like to write the evening up for the paper."

"No chance of that. That's all my father needs."

"I'd run it in a box at the top of a special issue on the royal house. You'd have an extra-large byline."

"You're doing an issue on the royal family?"

"Isn't it the one thing that everyone, rich and poor, cares about? Who doesn't dream of being a king?"

"Me," said George. I mastered the urge to point out that this was only because he was one already.

The waiter arrived bearing a tray with baklava and two glass pitchers, one with a white liquid and one with an orange one, and poured me a glass from the second. I tasted it warily. It was strange but good, like a cross between peach and apricot juice, and I took care to drink it in little sips like George instead of slurping it in one gulp. When I finished, George poured me some of his coconut milk. This I had drunk before, though never any that smelled and tasted so sweet.

"Perhaps you'll write about tonight's dinner party after all," I urged him.

"On two conditions."

"I accept."

"You're a rotten businessman."

"Like my father."

"You're supposed to listen to my offer first and turn it down, or at least pretend you aren't interested. Then you're supposed to bargain. Accepting comes last – provided, of course, that I've met your terms."

He was clearly enjoying himself.

"All right," I grinned.

"My first condition is that the story be published with fictitious names, my own too, as if it happened in a foreign country."

"And your second?"

"What's the rush?"

"My parents are expecting me."

"Why don't you give them a ring?" He handed me a telephone.

"Our phone has been out of order for the past three days."

He took two red folders from a drawer of his desk. "There are enough essays, poems, and articles here for the next two issues."

I sat back and leafed through a folder. The servant knocked, bowed, and said to George:

"The master wishes to see you."

"My father is at home?"

"He just arrived," said the servant and left.

"He wants to see to the dinner preparations," George said half to himself. He rose from his chair. "He doesn't trust anyone. Come."

"Who, me? No, I'll wait for you here." I gripped the back of my chair.

"Oh, do come on, old man. He likes meeting my guests."

"Another time. Not now. Please."

"You don't know my father," said George. "If we don't go to him, he'll come to us." He stood waiting for me in the doorway. Although I had always been curious about Big Imari, whose name hung over our house like a cloud, the prospect of meeting him frightened me.

"Come. He's not a cannibal." George smiled mysteriously.

I tucked my shirt into my shorts as if summoned to Stad Nawi, combed my hair with the help of the little mirror that I had carried around in my shirt pocket ever since becoming interested in girls, and reached for my schoolbag.

"You can leave your bag here. And try not to look as if you were about to meet Winston Churchill."

"That's how I feel," I said to my surprise. "You have no idea."

"Oh, but I do. Much more than you think."

He led me up the wide hallway like a sheep. Big Imari was standing in the middle of the salon with his hands clasped over his stomach, delivering orders to the servants. He was a tall, slim man in a grey suit and red tie, and as I approached him I made out a head of thick, silvery hair, a pair of darkly intense, commanding eyes, and a broad, strong nose. On his right hand he wore a gold ring inset with a large brown stone that looked like a sultan's signet. His small wife was standing next to him, tightly encased in a turquoise dress like a mummy. She was broad-hipped and snub-nosed with carefully manicured hands, and she wore a pearl necklace and a large amount of make-up. George waited for the servants to leave the room and said formally:

"Father, mother, I would like you to meet Kabi Imari, the new editor of our school newspaper."

Big Imari lifted an eyebrow in his otherwise expressionless face and measured me from head to toe with a glance that seemed to undress me. At a loss, I crossed the room hesitantly, held out my hand, and was given several passive fingers to press, which I did while feeling a fool. George's father shifted his look of studied annoyance to his son. He had, I noticed, the same cleft chin as my father, Salim Effendi, George and me. Inherited from my great-grandfather it was, my father liked to say, the trademark of the Imaris.

"Imari?" asked George's mother.

I nodded.

She observed me with curious grey eyes. "I thought we were the only ones," she said to her husband.

"It's time we drew up a family tree," George said.

"There's no need for that," said his father, his face tightening into a mask.

"What's your father's name?" asked George's mother.

"Salman."

"What does he do?"

"Why must you give the boy the third degree?" complained Big Imari.

"He sells watches," I murmured, feeling myself become small. "Actually, he's a teacher and a lawyer."

"Those don't sound like Imari professions." George's mother turned away from me.

"Oh, yes," I stammered. "And rice." She turned back to face me.

"What was your grandfather's name?" George inquired.

"Moshi."

"I wished you'd stop badgering your guest," Big Imari said.

"Why, father," said George, "my grandfather had the same name!"

Big Imari lit a cigarette from a golden box that he took from his pocket. A servant entered, bowed, and said with a smile:

"Sir, I just took a phone call with the news that your horse has finished first, ahead of the Regent's. My congratulations."

"Congratulations, my eye!" Big Imari grumbled, dismissing

the man with a wave of his hand. "What did I tell you, George! I should have fired that prima donna of a jockey. The jackass doesn't have the brains to realize that winning horses are for the King!"

"Well, he is one: king of the jockeys," observed George.

"He's an employee of mine who should be thrashed. I told him not to beat the Regent's horse. He's had it! I'm surrounded by jackasses."

"Calm down, Abu George," said George's mother. "It's bad for your blood pressure."

"How will I face the Regent tonight?"

"There'll be another race tomorrow."

"Is your poem for the Pasha ready?" George's father asked impatiently.

"It is," said George.

"Add another stanza for the Regent."

"I already did."

"Put it first."

"That won't go with the rhyme scheme."

"Do you think this is one of Stad Nawi's competitions? You poets!"

"Do you write too?" George's mother asked me.

"He writes excellent stories," said George.

"It must be genetic," said George's mother.

"Father's immune," George said softly.

Big Imari pulled out a pocket watch, glanced at it, and returned it to its place. I hugged myself and looked at him, the man whose name was like a red cape waved in front of my father. What had made him so powerful? The two were chips off the same block, yet totally different. I hadn't seen him smile once.

"What are you staring at?" George asked me.

"I've seen that picture before," I said, throwing caution to the wind. "We have a copy of the original photograph in our house."

"How come?" George kept his eyes on his father.

"I'll tell you some other time," I said.

"No, now!"

I stole a look at Big Imari. "It's a photograph of my great-grandfather."

"Father, that makes Kabi and me second cousins."

"George, if only you knew how many people have told me they're my relatives!"

What tact! It was all I could do to keep from hurling the stories of his treachery in his face. My father was right. I should have stayed away from this house.

"I didn't come to ask for anything. George brought me," I said, feeling immediately chagrined. I could have answered him angrily, ironically, sarcastically, innocently. Why did I have to sound so defensive?

"Father," asked George, "how come we both have the same picture?"

"I have no time for an explanation and I don't owe one to anyone," snapped Big Imari with a stamp of his foot. I stared down at my sandals. They were dusty. Why had I let myself be talked into this? If only I had been wearing trousers and a decent pair of shoes! I had often fantasized about meeting George's father one day when I would be richer and more important than he was – and now I didn't even look presentable!

"Lunch is served, sir," announced a servant.

George's mother glanced quickly from husband to son. "Why don't you ask your friend to join us," she suggested.

"But of course."

"Some other time," I said. "I have to get home."

"I've already heard that one," George said. And while I stood there shaking my head, he touched me and whispered: "Roast dove à la Abu Edouard!"

His father blinked at me. "Don't pressure him," he said, turning his back on me.

Back in his room, George gave me the folders with the articles. As I was strapping on my schoolbag, he asked:

"Would you still like a piece on the Pasha and the Regent?"

"Of course."

"Don't you want to hear my second condition?"

"I suppose I do."

"I want a column of my own in the newspaper."

"It's yours, Mr Big Imari Junior," I said.

"You too?" asked George.

"That's what everyone calls your father."

"You must have realized by now that I had my reasons for wanting you to meet him, although this wasn't exactly the encounter I had in mind. My father has never mentioned your family. I only found out about it from Salim Effendi."

"You mean all this was planned?" I suddenly wondered if getting the editor's job wasn't part of it too.

He ran a hand over the piano keys. "Where do you live?"

"In the old Jewish quarter."

"I've never been there."

"You're welcome to visit."

"My father would disapprove."

"What are you, his little boy? We are a generation of rebels!" We both laughed at Salim Effendi's favourite line.

The evening took flight like a flock of doves and with the light breeze of its wings that played in the palm fronds and skipped through the oleander bushes came the scents of the freshly watered garden. I raised my head like a bird released from its cage. Although I had intended to walk home, I didn't protest when George insisted that I be driven.

This time I sat by the driver, who travelled slowly as if to prolong my pleasure. How I would have liked Rashel, or Amira, or even cross-eyed Farha – no, our whole neighbourhood! – to see me in the limousine. The further behind we left the wealthy parts of New Baghdad, the fewer private vehicles were to be seen. By the time we reached the Moslem slum of Bab-esh-Sheikh, we were the only limousine on Razi Street. I hugged my heavy schoolbag and withdrew into myself. Perhaps I should have refused the ride after all. I didn't want George's driver telling him what a poor neighbourhood we lived in, and I was afraid to be seen by my father or to have him hear from some neighbour how I had arrived home. And yet though I wasn't sure whether to confess my visit, I knew that it was pointless to hide it.

With the pretence of having to buy something I told the driver to let me out before we reached Taht el-Takya and politely declined his offer to wait for me. For a long while I wandered through the Jewish souk, imbibing the smells, taking in the sights, and rubbing elbows with the shoppers. I was home.

25.

After sending up the doves into the turquoise evening sky, Edouard swept out the dovecote and the roof. A fiend for cleanliness who loathed the birds' droppings and smell, he ignored his father's orders and hosed down the dovecote as well. In only his underpants, long-legged and trimly built with powerful arms and thighs, a tapering back, a slim waist, a muscular rippling stomach, and a broad, bronzed chest with dark, freckled nipples, he could have modelled for a bodybuilding ad. His secret dream indeed, besides beating Ismail some day, was to look like Mr Iraq, a Christian named Antoine. Every morning and evening he descended to the cellar, where he locked horns with barbells, spring weights, and other instruments of torture according to the instructions in the English manuals that were his sacred texts. I both envied his physique and coppery skin and was embarrassed and perhaps even scared by my urge to reach out and touch it, to run my hand over him as if he were a splendid statue, feeling the muscles of his chest, his wide shoulders, his narrow hips. Living in a city of rampant homosexuality that was the frequent topic of gossip and jokes, I was afraid of catching the contagion. What else could be the meaning of the sweat that formed behind my ears and ran down my neck each time I saw Edouard's gorgeous body? As if it weren't enough to be haunted by women – Rashel, Miss Sylvia, Amira, the whore in the café by the prison, the starlets of the movies I saw, every other female in the street!

Once, Salim Effendi had given us a talk about "the problems of adolescence" with its sexual feelings that could overwhelm you. Although the class was spellbound, he soon returned to his political lectures and to our great disappointment raised the subject no more. I wished I could have talked to my father about such things, but the very thought made me recoil. True, since Hizkel's arrest my father had tried befriending me. I could feel how he wanted to be close. He consulted and confided in me about subjects that were not generally for boys of my age and relied on me as on a grown-up, sending me on sensitive missions and treating me like the brother and companion he had lost in Hizkel. Yet when it came to love, sex, or the plain torments of being a teenager, he was not a man I could bare my heart to. Had Hizkel not been in prison, or so I told myself, I might have approached him, even though I had never done this when I could have; while as for Edouard, I didn't trust him. He was too thick-skinned, too much of a show-off and a scoffer. The one person who might have understood me was George Imari; but I doubted that we would ever become good enough friends for me to open up to him.

There was no choice but to wrestle with my demons by myself. I tried to reassure myself that my mysterious attraction to Edouard was simply my admiration for a physical strength and grace that I lacked and I resolved to build up my own skinny body. For a while I even worked out with Edouard in his cellar and tried aping his exercises. But although I started out energetically each time, I soon tired of his bruising equipment and retired shamefaced to a stool, from which I watched him complete his daily quota of calisthenics. Why couldn't I, a harder worker than he was in school, keep up with him? The answer, I supposed, was that I had the brains, and he the brawn, and that each should stick to what he was best at. Languages, for instance, were something I had a knack for, whereas Edouard was equally baffled by the complexities of literary Arabic and the simpler rules of English, two tongues that every educated Iraqi was proud to know. Even his English manuals had to be translated by me, which was a source of sweet revenge. His dependence on me, that of brute strength on quick wits, made me feel a nasty pleasure as he sat by the cellar table, the mocking look gone from his face, watching me pore over the English-Arabic dictionary of Antoine Elias Antoine, who at such moments outranked Antoine the bodybuilder.

For some reason Edouard felt the need to unburden himself during these sessions and to berate his sad fate at not being loved by his father, who preferred his sister Amira. Although this rarely happened with daughters in Baghdad, Amira had been Abu Edouard's favourite from the day she was born with her silky black hair and beautiful big eyes. The name he chose for her meant "princess" and she alone was served the baby doves that were a delicacy reserved for the tables of brides and grooms or of potentates like Big Imari. Abu Edouard spent what little money he had on buying Amira the most expensive clothes in the fanciest British stores; sent her to Miss Fat'hiya's exclusive nursery school; saved his pennies for her dowry; and did all he could for her while neglecting Edouard. As a boy her brother had retaliated by hitting her or locking her in the cellar, which was full of bats, for which he had been severely punished when his father came home. Even now he sometimes slapped Amira hard when her teasing became too much for him.

Perhaps it was to prove to his father that he could be good at something that Edouard had taken up body-building. As luck would have it though, his father, a tough, oversized Jew who spent his days enjoyably doing nothing when he wasn't flying his doves, valued brains more than brawn – and Amira was brainier than any of us. Fourteen months younger than her brother and eight months younger than me she had already skipped two grades in school and was a year ahead of the two of us. Edouard's father had never believed that Edouard could even get into high school, and his admission to the prestigious Frank Ini School, largely through the efforts of my own father, made Abu Edouard think better of his son and stop thrashing him and picking on him. And yet since Abu Edouard hated Communists as much as Zionists, he was annoyed by his son's friendship with Salim Effendi who had taken Edouard under his wing. It was from Salim Effendi that Edouard had acquired his knowledge of politics and economics – two subjects, to my surprise, that he displayed a talent for and could even speak intelligently about, if from his own limited point of view. In languages and maths, on the other hand, he needed me to coach him and to copy from. Asking Amira for help was beneath his dignity.

Now, standing on the roof with the hose, he reminded me that we had an English test the next day and sprayed me with water when I doubted out loud whether I would have time to study with him.

"Now I'm sure I won't," I yelled.

"Why not?"

"Because. And besides, I have to go to the prison with Rashel."

"Why, what's happened there now? Something tells me you have the hots for her."

"Are you out of your mind?" I asked, aghast. "She's my uncle's wife. They've put him in a cell with some Communists," I added, changing the subject in the first way I could think of. Then, afraid of having said too much, I changed it again by asking:

"Just what do you do at those Party meetings of yours?"

"We study Marxist dialectics," Edouard said. "That's about destroying the old world and building a new one in which everyone will be equal – rich, poor, Jews, Moslems, Christians, Armenians, everyone!"

"In short, you want to play God."

"And you Zionists? What could be weirder than thinking about nothing but the problems of one little people who are no more than a drop in the ocean? What you don't understand is that we Communists are fighting for minorities everywhere, for all peoples." When he got going he sounded like Salim Effendi.

"Are there any good-looking girls there?" I asked to stop his sermonizing.

"Come off it! Do you think we use cock-bait like you Zionists? A Communist only knows the two or three people in his cell. *That's* an underground. But listen!" he suddenly remembered. "There's this one girl I met, the sister of one of my cell members, who's not to be believed. Her name is Gloria and she's a Christian. What an ass she has! Like two watermelons." Edouard sucked his lips as if licking honey from them. "I meet her on the side, and she dances with me and even lets me feel her up. I mean, it's like I do it by accident. You should see the little bitch wriggle in my hands! God, she drives me crazy."

"Would you marry a non-Jewish girl?" I asked.

"You bet! And stick it up every hole she has." I could see his pecker bulging in his underpants. "Down, boy, wait for tonight," he said to it, and when it refused to obey him, he stripped off his underpants and stood stark naked with his member erect in a triangular patch of black moss. He wet it, washed it slowly with a bar of green soap, and hosed the suds from it, making it dance beneath the jets of water while he grunted, groaned, yelled, and calmed down only after jetting his own jissom. Then he put the hose to his mouth and drank in long gulps.

I felt on fire. Although I would have liked to strip too and follow suit, I was too embarrassed to do anything but gape at such bold freedom. Was this what Communism did for you?

"Why don't you join us?" Edouard asked. It was as though he had read my thoughts. "You'll discover a whole new world."

"I don't know. I come from a Zionist family."

"You think we accept every piece of shit that comes along like you Zionists do?"

"Did you ever meet the Red Armenian?" I asked.

"The leader?" His eyes widened. "Not many people have."

"I saw him."

"Bullshit!"

"Would you like me to describe him for you?" I told him what I had seen. Edouard looked at me so seriously that I suddenly wondered if I really knew him.

"Then the Armenian and Hizkel are in the same wing?" he marvelled as if talking to himself.

"You've got it, you pinhead!"

"I have to tell Salim Effendi."

"What I told you was for your ears only," I protested. "And anyway, it can't be that the Party doesn't know where he is. The prison is swarming with Communists. Someone must have got word out."

"I suppose. But I was thinking of something else. Maybe the

Zionists and the Communists can collaborate in springing them both. Why don't you talk to your father and I'll talk to Salim Effendi." He had more imagination than I had given him credit for.

"Are you crazy? Tell Salim Effendi and I'll never speak to you again."

"You should have thought of that before," said Edouard, his old taunting self again. He burst out laughing. "Don't you know you're dealing with the son of the dove flyer?"

"Don't tell anyone," I begged. "My father will hang me if you do."

By way of reply he went to the balcony and called down to the yard for his own father.

"He's not home," Amira answered from below. "Do you want me to bring down the doves?"

"You mean you're a dove flyer too now, you twit?"

Edouard let out a whistle remarkably like his father's and the first birds began settling onto the roof. "Come," he said to me after shooing the last of them into the dovecote. "Walk me to Abu Ednan's. My father's probably there, and maybe yours is too. I have to tell him I'll be home late tonight."

Edouard was right. My father was at Abu Ednan's as usual, relaxing over a glass of arrack while listening to a record of Salima Pasha's. Next to him sat Abu Edouard in an enormous pair of striped pyjamas that were much too big even on him.

Edouard told his father of his plans and went off. I joined the two of them. It was beyond me how two men who had spent so many years quarrelling could be such good friends. Over the radio came the mesmerizing voice of Um Kultoum singing a verse from Omar Khayyam's Rubbaiyat:

I was clothed in life's garments
Without being asked,
And till I'm dressed in death's shrouds
I'll never know why.

The dove flyer sat back in his chair, inflated his chest, pulled at his perpetually runny nose, put one hand on an outspread knee, opened a shiny tin box with the other, tore a leaf from what looked like a little, thin-paged notebook, held it between his thumb and forefinger, sprinkled tobacco on it, rolled it, licked the edge of the paper, glued it tight, and offered it gallantly to my father. My father, who did not like smoking other men's saliva, politely fended off the proferring hand and produced a pack of Craven As from his pocket. This was precisely what Abu Edouard had been waiting for. Taking two of my father's cigarettes, he stuck one in his mouth and the other behind his ear, lit the first, and inhaled the sweet, fragrant smoke while shutting his eyes with pleasure. Then, lifting the glass of arrack, he raised it to his nostrils for a sniff, took a careful sip as if afraid of finishing it too soon, smacked his lips, reached for a garlic clove on a dish of appetizers, and munched it noisily.

"Arrack and garlic!" My father made a face. "You might as well add fire to fire."

"Death alone can change a man's habits," observed Abu Edouard.

My father ordered another bottle of the best Lebanese arrack and signalled the waiter not to pour any for me. Abu Edouard drained his glass in one gulp, popped another garlic clove into his mouth, and downed a second glass as if the bottle were his. The way he took advantage of my father – towards whom he now leaned to tell a joke whose punch line I missed – annoyed me. The two men burst out laughing, though a few minutes earlier they had no doubt been on the verge of tearing each other's hair out. Often I had felt sure that their friendship was over, only to see them forgive and forget a moment later.

My father grimaced as Abu Edouard let out several garlicky burps and took a pinch from his friend's snuff box to counteract the smell. Both men sneezed violently a few times. Abu Edouard poured himself another glass of arrack and declared with a wink in my direction:

"Here's to your Kabi and my Amira! That girl's my pride and joy, first in her class. Not like Edouard, Kabi, eh?"

"Edouard's a good boy," said my father. "God look after them both."

"If only I could afford it," sighed Abu Edouard, "I'd send her to engineering school in America." After a pause he went on: "Abu Kabi, I want to get rich and this time I know how to do it. I'll collect old tyres, cut them into soles for shoes, and make a killing." He spread his arms wide to illustrate the enormity of the idea.

"Wonderful," said my father, who had listened to plenty of the dove flyer's money-making schemes in the past. "You'll hit the jackpot this time for sure."

"Khat's wrong with it?" asked Abu Edouard, noticing the note of sarcasm.

"It's a fine idea," said my father in the same tone.

"Everyone made a fortune after the *Farhood* but me. My luck is black as coal. If I started selling shrouds, people would stop dying."

My father laughed.

"Do you have any better ideas?" asked Abu Edouard.

"Only one," said my father, turning up his palms. "Jerusalem!"

"Spare me!" bellowed Abu Edouard. "My little store is worth a thousand of your Jerusalems." He turned to the Moslem proprietor. "By God, Abu Ednan, you be the judge!"

"Have you gone mad, man?" scolded my father. "Why are you dragging him into this?"

"Shoes from tyres or Jerusalem, which will it be?" cried Abu Edouard like a street vendor.

"Be quiet, you lunatic!" my father hushed him. "Someone will steal your idea."

"You're right. God, how I'd like to be rich! How long must a man wait his turn? *A-na ado-o-nai, ho-shiya na ...*" The chanted supplication from the prayer book was a sure sign that the arrack was having an effect.

Abu Edouard had always dreamed of wealth. His store, which stood opposite my father's and next to Hajj Yahya's, was a dark junk shop in which dozens of locks hung on nails alongside all sizes and shapes of keys, rusty, coal-heated irons with charred wooden handles, metal rods, bits of chain link, a wobbly-needled compass in a glass case, and various other piles of useless things that he rummaged through ceaselessly, taking them apart, filing them down, and soldering them together again. Over the years this bizarre collection had grown to the point that there was barely room for Abu Edouard to sit. It was here he had his brainstorms, as he called the ideas that would make him a wealthy man. One of the most recent of these had been a project to manufacture drinking glasses from old bottles. Gripping a bottle between two wooden boards, Abu Edouard would spit on his palms, wrap a thin chain around the bottleneck, work it back and forth to create heat from friction, douse the bottle with cold water, and slice off its top like a magician to the cheers of the children standing outside his shop. Then he would smooth it with a pumice stone, wetting it from time to time with his spittle, and run his hand over the crude glass as if it were a fancy piece of china.

Apart from the children, people with nothing better to do stopped to watch too. Sometimes, when Abu Edouard was not tinkering with his junk or his inventions, he stood in the doorway of his shop and gave speeches. These were highly popular with the public. Obsessed with the illegal emigration to Israel, he would declare:

"Now hear this, you Jews! Exile is the only place for us. It's no accident that our first and second Temples were destroyed. It suits us, exile does, because Allah would have brought us back to our land long ago if it didn't. Why else would He have waited two thousand years? The Zionist heretics, the Zionist pagans, are perpetrating a dangerous hoax. Israel is not our homeland. It is the homeland of Allah, meant to be lived in only in our dreams. Watch it, you Jews! Watch out for the wrath of Allah and of those who do His work."

Out of the corner of his eye Abu Edouard would glance in the direction of Hajj Yahya, who paid no heed to these sermons. Others, more attentive, whistled and applauded the free performance. Sometimes there would be a catcall, which made Abu Edouard thunder like a preacher in a mosque until the heckler gave up and moved on. Puffing himself up like a proud dove, Abu Edouard would thump his chest and gaze at the mirror on his wall, from which he stared back in his surplus, grease-stained British army overalls that made him look even bigger than he was, his blue beret pulled down eccentrically over his head.

The food vendors who plied the neighbourhood were familiar with his weakness for all things edible. Early in the day, before his first public address, he would consume a red tongue-of-lamb soup. Next would come a dish of black-eyed beans and onions supplied by Ibrahim Maslawi and a burghul *kubba* sold to him by Baruch the Kurd, followed by a lunch sent by his wife. By now, though he still had big eyes, his stomach was full and he had to content himself with large slurps of water from the *ibrik,* the copper pitcher with the long, curved spout, gargling and jetting them in an arc into a nearby alley over the heads of his audience. Thus the day passed until closing time, when he counted the coins in his cash register and went home to wash and change into his striped pyjamas before dropping by Abu Ednan's. There, while waiting for the arrack to go to his head, he would scold himself:

"What a fool I am! When will my lucky number come up? Tell me, Abu Kabi, how will I send my daughter to America?"

My father would observe him pensively, as if thinking the matter over, and murmur half to himself:

"Israel, not America."

On his way home, under the cover of darkness, Abu Edouard would visit Farha the cross-eyed widow, first looking up and down the lane to make sure that no one saw him. He surveyed it again upon leaving and was certain his trysts went unnoticed, although there was no one in the neighbourhood who did not know about them.

26.

Edouard was lying in wait for me by the school gate. Taking me by the arm, he steered me to the tennis courts. Salim Effendi was there, pale and thin-looking, an extinguished pipe in one hand.

"I hear you saw our Armenian comrade," he said straight away.

"I thought he was your leader," I replied.

"He is. But in the new world we're creating there will be a revolution in human relations too. Our leaders will be our friends. How is he? How does he look? Tell me about him."

"He's a redhead," I tried joking. But seeing Salim Effendi's eagerness for details, I told him what I could. He hung on every word. "I heard the jailor say they were going to hang him the next day, but they must have postponed it," I said.

"They wouldn't dare. The entire civilized world would protest. The Soviet Union would never allow it." It sounded like an incantation.

"He's wearing the clothes of a condemned man."

"That doesn't mean a thing. How did you get into the prison?" He laid a hand on my shoulder.

"I'm sorry," I said. "I can't tell you."

"A boy like you belongs with us."

"I've already told him that," put in Edouard.

"I'll have to ask my father," I said firmly. "And please, Staz Salim, this is to remain between the three of us."

"Of course. We underground fighters have to stick together."

The bell rang. We ran to the morning assembly, which was presided over by Salim Effendi himself.

Our first class was with Rabbi Shuwa, who struggled to teach us a chapter from the Psalms. I had no patience for Holy Scripture. All I could think of was having blabbed about my visit to the prison. My father had sworn me to silence and now I had broken my vow.

At home after school, I didn't dare ask him about working with the Communists. He had made it clear that, apart from our family and Abu Saleh, no one was to know I had seen Hizkel. And especially not Salim Effendi, who hadn't got along with my father since the days of the legal case. According to old Hiyawi, the two had agreed to sue Big Imari together, but Salim Effendi had backed off at the last minute and tried settling out of court. Despite the intercession of my mother, who thought my father's cousin had acted quite sensibly, my father took this as a stab in the back. "Big Imari needs to be treated carefully," my mother had said. "He wants to be a senator and he can't afford to lose to you in court. Besides, you're blood relations; today you fight, tomorrow you make up. Family quarrels don't belong in a court. Certainly not in a Moslem one."

My father and Hizkel, however, refused to yield. In the end Big Imari drove a wedge between the three of them and left them all out in the cold. My father and Salim Effendi never forgave each other and soon found themselves on politically opposite sides as the Zionists and Communists vied for the hearts of the city's Jewish youth. My mother alone tried keeping in touch and urged my father to continue inviting his cousin to Sabbath meals and family celebrations. "He's a poor orphan in need of a family," she said. "Besides, someone has to keep the Imaris together."

And so Salim Effendi still came to our house now and then, especially for Passover seders. Although my mother disagreed with him on most things, especially God and religion, I could see that she enjoyed his company and the big words he used in arguing that she, with her soft spot for erudition, admired without understanding. Best of all, she liked listening to him debate with Hizkel.

It was my mother who had presided over the week of mourning for Salim Effendi's parents, who died when he was young. She had cooked for the condolence visitors, served them food, cleaned up after them, and made all the necessary arrangements for prayers and study. It was also she who had convinced Salim Effendi to say the mourner's prayer in synagogue during the next year and who bought him a memorial lamp in his mother's name in the Ezekiel Synagogue; yet, despite all her efforts, his parents' death robbed him of the last of his faith and after the failed case he drifted away from religion completely. Now and then he ran into Hizkel and my father in Hiyawi's tobacco shop, to which he came for a special pipe mixture that the old man prepared for him. My father was angry that Salim had not shown much interest in Hizkel's imprisonment, a fact attributed by my mother to his fear of being the victim of arrest and torture himself.

Salim Effendi waited thirty-six hours for me to ask my father, and then, the following evening, came unexpectedly to our house. My father, who sat silently with him in the guest room, his eyes cold as ice, took his watch from the pocket of his smoking jacket and wiped it with a corner of his blue silk shirt. Salim Effendi chatted with my mother who tried to make him feel at home. Before sitting down she had whispered to me: "Bring some arrack and a few snacks. I'll stay to make sure they don't fight."

Returning with the food and drinks, I furtively drank a little arrack to fortify myself. I knew the talk would come around to me. The two men sat sipping their drinks in silence. Salim Effendi's pipe was clenched between his teeth. At last he said:

"I've asked Kabi for something, and he told me it was up to you."

"Babba," I blurted out, my eyes on the floor, "I told Salim Effendi that I saw Hizkel. He wants to know if I can give a message to the Red Armenian."

"Why did you tell him?" asked my father furiously, "I told you it was dangerous!"

"Do you think I'd put your family in danger?" asked Salim Effendi defensively.

"But that's exactly what you would do to my son for your Armenian!"

"Helping the Armenian is good for us all. It's good for Iraq."

"I neither believe in him nor in the good he does. When will you have the sense to realize that our only hope lies in Israel?"

"Abu Kabi, this isn't the place for another argument. Time is of the essence. The hangman's rope is already around the neck of a great leader. You can help save him."

"Go and see him in prison yourself," said my father.

"Abu Kabi, you know that if they're not on my trail yet, they will be after such a visit, if I can manage it at all. I'll be arrested in no time. That's why I'm asking this of you. I'm sure that neither Kabi nor anyone else could have got into the prison without the help of Karim Abd el-Hak and his brother the colonel."

Although my father said nothing, he gave Salim a worried look upon hearing the names of Hajj Yahya's sons.

"Kabi only has to give the message to Hizkel and he'll find a way to pass it on to the Armenian. Half the prisoners are Communists."

"You know they'll hang Hizkel if they find out he's in contact with the Armenian. He's already accused of being a Zionist and an arms smuggler – and you want him to be a Communist agent too? Where are your brains, man?"

"It's time we Communists and you Zionists worked together. We can rescue them both."

"It could be the end not only of Hizkel but of other leaders in the Movement too. That's a lot to ask for one bird in the bush. The Armenian is already a condemned man. Allah Himself can't save him any more."

"The Armenian is a great man. He's for the Jews, for Israel. He organized demonstrations against anti-Jewish violence."

"I'm sorry." My father's voice was softer now. "My brother and son come first."

"Abu Kabi, I've come to you as family."

"It's not up to me," said my father. "I can't give you an answer one way or another."

"Of course. Go ahead and ask whomever you have to," Salim Effendi hurried to say, grasping at the hint of acquiescence. Although my father clearly was unhappy with this turn of events, my mother intervened to keep the conversation on an even keel.

"Salim Effendi, when will we hear the good news that you're getting married and that your parents' name will not die out?"

"Who has time for that, Um Kabi? I can't even think of marriage. I could be arrested and killed any day. Who needs more orphans and widows?"

My father rose.

"Please, stay for dinner," said my mother. "I have a delicious *selowna*."

"Some other time, thank you, Um-Kabi," said Salim Effendi, aware that my father wanted him to leave.

When he was gone I took my father's hand and said; "I'm sorry, Babba. I shouldn't have done it. It won't happen again. But you know," I remembered, "I also told Stad Nawi that I saw Hizkel and he said he already knew."

"How?" wondered my father, lapsing into pensive silence. After a while he shrugged and said: "You shouldn't have told Stad Nawi either, even if he is pro-Zionist and tries to help. But Salim Effendi is a confused and dangerous man. I knew him back when he was in nappies. You have to sup with him with a long spoon. As a boy he wanted to be a rabbi; then he discovered the Koran and decided to become a Moslem; then he said that he was something called a Jewish Arab; and now he's a Communist. And don't think that's the end of it, either. If he ever gets into real trouble, he'll come running to us for help." My father had forgotten that he was talking about my esteemed teacher and headmaster, whom he had always tried to show respect for in my presence.

"What kind of family are you?" scolded my mother. "Is that any way to treat a cousin and a guest? I wouldn't act that way towards a stranger. Why, you drove him out of the house … Tell me," she asked after a pause. "Was it really Hajj Yahya's son, the colonel, who got Kabi into the prison?"

"You can't believe a word Salim Effendi says," parried my father. "And now he'll get Hizkel into worse trouble because of the Armenian! You don't know what a fool he is."

"That makes it even more crucial for you to go to Big Imari right now."

"I'm not so sure of that," I said.

"You keep out of this!" exclaimed my mother. "Do you even know who Big Imari is?"

"Of course I do. I've been in his house and I've met him." The words were out of my mouth before I knew it.

"How many times have I told you never to go there?" barked my father.

"Do all your quarrels have to be handed down to your children?" asked my mother. "What are we, Moslems who have blood feuds?"

"I'm sorry, Babba. I couldn't say no. George practically dragged me there."

"I can't even trust my own son any more," my father mourned, his voice full of despair.

"I've taken over the editorship of the school newspaper from George."

"We're about to leave Iraq. This is no time for new responsibilities."

"Don't you even want to congratulate me?" I couldn't keep my voice steady. "Do you know how many years I've been dreaming of this?"

"*Mabruk*, son, I wish you success," said my mother. "What is Big Imari's mansion like? And his wife? Tell me, tell me. Did he know who you were?"

"He pretended not to." I looked at my father. "Maybe we're really not related."

"You're talking nonsense. He's a snake in the grass."

"Well, he didn't show any sign of knowing us, although he does have a portrait of Great-grandfather on his wall."

"Did you talk to him about Hizkel?" asked my mother.

"Absolutely not. I didn't have a chance to. He was expecting the Regent and the Pasha for dinner."

"You see? You see?" My mother leaped to her feet. "A word from him and Hizkel could be free!"

"Why do you always hear only what you want to? Didn't you hear Kabi say that he pretended not to know us?"

27.

Even had my father wanted to help, it would have been too late. ARMENIAN HANGED, screamed the huge headline in a special edition of the newspaper *El-Istiklal* the next day. And as though to remove any lingering doubts, three large photographs of the execution accompanied the story. I was badly shaken. All morning I kept picturing the man as I remembered him, waving a shackled hand as though blessing his flock for the last time. Regent Abdullah, whose picture hung on a wall of Hiyawi's shop, had refused to grant clemency or postpone the execution any longer. More than once I had spoken to this picture in my thoughts, pleading with it to help the Jews. Now its silence struck me as sinister.

"The murderers! May God's curse be on them!" exclaimed Hiyawi from the doorway of his shop. Just then Abu Saleh el-Hibaz passed by and signalled me with a wink to follow him. I walked behind him as far as el-Rashid Street. His large, powerful, bull-necked body reminded me of the Armenian's and I shuddered as I imagined him coming to the same end.

I quickened my pace to catch up with him. As we neared el-Rashid Street he slowed down without stopping and whispered: "This afternoon you'll visit Hizkel. See if he's been moved to another cell block. Be careful."

He disappeared down Whores' Alley, and I obeyed an urge to visit the square by the prison and pay my last respects. Although

280

I had seen hanged men before, I had never felt so sick to the stomach: even from afar the body on the scaffold looked very large. The hundreds of people gathered around it were different from the usual crowd. Most were young and wore Western clothes, and they kept eerily silent as if afraid of disturbing the dead man's repose. He must have been executed without advance notice, for the throng that generally attended such spectacles was not there. Those who had come were Communists who had heard the news on the radio or read it in the morning papers.

With no need to restrain a howling mob, the soldiers and police stood by idly. Salim Effendi was there too, flanked by Miss Sylvia and Edouard. I nodded hello and joined them. Salim Effendi stared straight ahead, his lips clenched. There were tears in his eyes. Miss Sylvia's arm, in defiance of local custom, was around his waist. Edouard laid a hand on his shoulder, and all three hugged and wept like a bereaved family. I was moved to tears myself.

Miss Sylvia was the first to recover. "If the police had any brains," she said, turning to go, "they'd arrest this whole crowd and wipe out the Iraqi Communist Party." As we followed her away from the square, I realized I had been foolish to come. I could be in trouble if a plain-clothes policeman recognized me.

Salim Effendi hailed a motor cab to take Miss Sylvia home, and then the three of us boarded a horse-drawn hansom. Despite his disappointment in me and my father, I could see that he was grateful for my presence. Probably he knew that there was nothing we could have done.

By that afternoon the usual curiosity seekers began arriving in the square with their shouts of *Allah akbar*. Although I was afraid to be seen there again, I had my orders from Abu Saleh and had to overcome my qualms. The pimpled jailor seemed pleased to see me and even happier with the bribe I handed over. "Tell them what you saw in the square," he urged me. "None of the prisoners believes it. They've just been given the news."

Indeed, the faces of the prisoners expressed disbelief. Even as they asked me what had happened, their eyes were on the door of the cell block, as if expecting it to swing open for their shackled leader to enter with a blessing and a song. "The bastards!" said Hizkel. "They came for him this morning as if it were just another interrogation. They were afraid we'd riot."

Gradually the realization sank in that they would see the Armenian no more. A few prisoners began hammering with their fists on their cell doors and angrily rattling the bars; soon others joined in, until all were clamouring together, Communists and Zionists, political prisoners and criminals, Moslems and Jews, thieves and murderers, rapists and pimps. I watched Hizkel shake his bars and yell with the others, oblivious of all else. His wounds had healed, and he stood tall again and was his old self. "Down with the government of whores!" he shouted hoarsely, echoed by his cellmates. "Down with the crooks in power!"

"You fucking Jew!" screamed the pimpled jailor. "You want to swing out there with the Armenian? Shut your mouths, you sons of bitches!" He hurried back to his cubby-hole and pressed the alarm button.

"Get out of here fast," Hizkel told me.

"What will they do to you?"

"Nothing. Just get out of here."

Salim Effendi did not come to school the next day.

28.

Crumpled like a foetus, Salim Effendi lay in his dark room. The morning's newspaper had confirmed to him that the famous belly dancer Bahia had left for Egypt with the Egyptian singer Abd el-Muttalib. Two horrendous developments in forty-eight hours were more than he could bear.

His first instinct had been to be alone, and it took him a while to realize that he was sinking into a slough of self-pity in which mourning for a dead father figure and longing for a vanished love were combined. "What kind of revolutionary are you?" he scolded himself, aware of thinking that the Powers That Be had it in for him. The fact was that he deserved his fate for not wooing Bahia harder, for having let the damn Egyptian have her. Though his grief was a double one, he had begun to suspect that each half only dulled the other and kept him from savouring it to the full. Not even the arms of the lovely whore Lutfiya, in which he had often found solace before, offered any hope of consolation.

It was the afternoon when he heard a knock downstairs. The more he tried to ignore it, the more insistent it grew and, starved for human company, he went to open the gate. There stood Miss Sylvia, a bouquet of lilacs in one hand and a shopping basket in the other.

"Sylvia!" He was dumbfounded.

"Great Britain does not abandon her friends," she grinned

mischievously. He tried hiding his unshaven chin with a hand, but his unkempt hair and dirty pyjamas were not concealable.

"Aren't you going to ask me in?" asked Miss Sylvia when he continued to block the entrance.

"Please," he said, cursing himself inwardly. After all he had told her about the hospitality of the Orient so he could hardly turn her away. She followed him up to his filthy, smoky shambles of a room, where he opened the windows, drew the curtains, and tried to tidy up a bit.

"Don't bother," said Miss Sylvia, entering behind him. "Your room looks no worse than my student digs at Huddersfield. And anyway, I like the smell of old pipe tobacco."

Salim Effendi took a clean shirt and pair of trousers from the cupboard and went downstairs to wash and shave. On returning he found Miss Sylvia looking at a book. Feeling that her twinkling eyes had caught him with his pants down, he arranged the papers on his desk as best he could, dusted the cleared space and the desk lamp with a rag, made the bed, and straightened the faded, frayed-edged carpet. Like a naughty pupil facing his teacher, he squirmed and tried to overlook the heaps of dead moths in the corners. "My cleaning woman has been ill," he apologized with a blush. "And I haven't been in the mood for visitors."

"Are you asking me to leave?"

"Oh, no ... no, not at all ... "

"I was worried about you. There have been rumours of Communists being arrested."

"You can see that I'm only under house arrest," he joked.

"Well, that won't bring the Armenian back to life. You should take better care of yourself."

"It's not just that," blurted Salim Effendi. Miss Sylvia waited to hear more, but when nothing was forthcoming she changed the subject and said:

"The Jewish quarter is so noisy and colourful. I like it."

"It's a poor, overcrowded ghetto. Since the war in Palestine, all the Jews feel safer here."

And seeing her blue eyes survey his quarters, he added defensively:

"It's just a one-room flat with a tiny kitchen and a bathroom."

"It reminds me of an artist's studio," she said.

She was a strange one, this English teacher. The worse something smelled, the more fragrant she found it; the uglier it was, the more enchantingly exotic it seemed to her. She was attracted to all that made him want to flee and for preserving all that he wished to see destroyed. And yet though she saw Baghdad through the eyes of a tourist, he felt a great closeness to her. They had the same taste in literature, in art, in music, and agreed about most other things too. Above all, he liked her independence, that sense of being a man's equal that was shared by so few Jewish women in Baghdad, let alone by its veiled, docile Moslem women.

"Who are all those dolled-up ladies sitting outside next door?" she asked.

"Oh, them … " He blushed again. "You might say they are the victims of a sad fate … "

"You mean they're whores."

"Yes and no," laughed Salim Effendi. "Let me tell you about the prettiest of them, Lutfiya. I taught her to read and write. At the time a Moslem artist, a friend of mine who had returned to Baghdad from his studies in Paris, was looking for a model. I brought him to her. He offered to pay her four times as much for a single nude sitting as she made in a day's work – and she turned him down in a huff. When he asked her why, since … well, since she was only a whore anyway, she said: 'What I do with a man behind closed doors is between Allah and me. But you want the whole world to see my tits and ass!'"

"Fabulous," laughed Miss Sylvia, her good humour infecting him.

"They're government-inspected, these places. We call them *karhanas*."

Now it was his turn to laugh at her pronunciation of the word.

"Where's the kitchen?" she asked, rising with her shopping basket. "I've brought you a few things."

"Thank you, don't bother. I'll make us something to eat."

"I think you had better let a woman perform her oriental duties," said Miss Sylvia with an impish wink. They descended together to the little kitchen in the courtyard. In it was an empty ice box, a sooty kerosene burner, and some old utensils.

"Now back upstairs with you and let me work!" she ordered. In his room Salim Effendi put some Brahms on the gramophone, lit his pipe, and stretched out on his bed. Soon Miss Sylvia returned with a tray of little sandwiches filled with imported British sardines and sausage and garnished with sprigs of parsley. Although Salim Effendi would have preferred *kebab* and *amba* in a piece of pitta bread, the meal usually brought to him by Fat'hi, the whorehouse errand boy, the sandwiches were a tasty and welcome change. He went to bring a bottle of whisky from his little pantry, but Miss Sylvia wanted Lebanese arrack.

"I saw in today' s paper that Bahia has left for Egypt with Abd el-Muttalib," said Salim Effendi, trying to make it sound like a casual bit of gossip.

"Oh, dear!" Miss Sylvia pretended to be surprised. Since the night of Bahia's performance in the Semiramis Hotel she had known that Salim Effendi was in love with her. The belly dancer had been all he had talked about afterwards when they strolled along the river, and Sylvia had realized that she would have to bide her time with him. She too had learned that morning from Baghdad's English daily of Bahia's departure, and when Salim Effendi failed to appear in school, she knew it was time to convince him that there were alternatives to his hopeless dream.

Miss Sylvia poured some more arrack, recited an English poem about unrequited love, and gently seized the hand with which Salim Effendi tried hiding his tears. Pulling her towards him, he buried his face in her shoulder-length hair while she patted his back and neck; then she pushed him lightly away and stroked his face with her graceful fingers, brushing the tears from it. Next her hands wandered to his chest and further down, and soon she was underneath him on the bed.

They didn't rise from it for two days and two nights. Fat'hi brought them fresh milk every morning and kebab and *amba* later in the day, and between bouts of love they drank whisky and arrack, listened to Brahms and Mozart, and read English poetry. It was all Miss Sylvia had dreamed of since she had first set sight on him. Even in the heights of passion he was the tender lover that her feminine intuition had told her he would be once she had got over her first exotic impressions of him. She had seen through his façade of masculine bravura and headmasterly authority to the sensitive soul within; and despite the faraway look that still sometimes crept into his eyes, she knew that his convalescence from Bahia would always be remembered by him as the days of his honeymoon with her. She wanted to suggest that they spend the summer break in London, far away from forgotten dangers, but she decided to wait. There would be time for that. There was no need to rush.

29.

The fingertips at the end of Miss Sylvia's bare arms came to rest on her desk, her head bowed with controlled emotion as she read the last lines of Mark Antony's speech:

My heart is in the coffin there with Caesar,
And I must pause till it come back to me.

She held her pose, for she was Mark Antony and we were a silent crowd of Roman citizens admiringly watching the cascade of her blonde hair. Swept along on the splendours of Shakespeare, she had left us far behind, stumbling in the impassable terrain of Elizabethan English while she sped ahead with abandon. Yet we knew that she would double back for us, for she was a born teacher and would elucidate all the details of the text once the actress in her had been given free rein.

And indeed, she now explained the words we did not understand and turned to the subject of mob psychology, which Mark Antony had exploited so well. The more she talked about the ancient forum of Rome, the more we pictured the squares of Baghdad and their crowds pouring out of the mosques, easy prey for every preacher and demagogue.

"One of the great tests of a man's intellect," said Miss Sylvia, "is his ability to stick to his own judgements in the face of an impressionable mob. Let's look at how Mark Antony works such a mob and turns it around. It's a fine example of Shakespeare's dramatic wizardry."

George passed me a note that said: "Dear Editor, My article on the Pasha's party is finished and you are welcome to pick it up at my house after school."

I shook my head. This time my father would not forgive me. "Dear Mr Big Imari Junior Esquire," I wrote back, "I would be most grateful to you if you would bring the material to the library."

"Dear Editor," responded George. "If you are apprehensive about my father, it is my pleasure to inform you that he and his wife are currently holidaying at our summer home in Lebanon. And if it is arriving home late that worries you, and your telephone is still out of order, may I suggest that you send your parents a message with your neighbour, Mr Edouard Sourpuss. Should any other obstacles stand in your way, I would be most happy to remove them."

"Dear Mister Big Imari Junior Esquire," said my next note. "Why must you oblige the editor-in-chief to betake himself to your residence whenever you require his attention?"

"Dear Editor, The reason is obviously that I take pleasure in extending my hospitality to you. Perhaps, too, I wish to solve the conundrum of our consanguinity. Lunch, of course, will be served, and I have requested that a pitcher of your favourite mango juice be put at your disposal."

"Dear Mr Big Imari Junior Esquire, This last detail has favourably disposed me to respond positively to your invitation."

"Will Mr Imari and Mr Imari kindly stop exchanging notes," said Miss Sylvia. "I find it most annoying!" Just then, though, the bell rang. I asked Edouard to tell my parents I was staying late to work on the newspaper.

The Imaris' mansion was deserted except for a few servants

and George's old nanny, whose profession I had previously encountered only in novels. It was she who served us lunch, after which a servant brought us coffee in the sitting room. George asked not to be disturbed unless the Pasha himself was on the phone – well, yes, or his parents calling from Lebanon – sat back in an easy chair, crossed one leg over the other and said: "Let me read it out loud to you. That way I can make corrections as I go along." And without waiting for an answer he began:

"First to arrive were the members of the Jewish ensemble of Baghdad, led by Salim Shibbat, the Pasha's favourite singer and poetry reciter. Taking their place on a low platform by the entrance to the drawing room, they were followed by the electric Salima Pasha, a sumptuous woman with dark hair, coal-black eyes, an enchanting smile, and a chiffony red silk dress worn with a charming nonchalance on her buxom body. From the way she practised a few numbers with the ensemble it was evident that she was a demanding performer who settled for nothing less than perfection. And indeed, as a ring fits a finger, so the musicians responded to her slightest gesture and expression.

"Next arrived the belly dancer Bahia, a bewitching young thing with a purple dress and a flower in her hair, her long-nailed fingers glittering with rings. Watching her rehearse with her drummer and cymbalist, I felt transported to another world. Like the snake that goes on wriggling after its death, may her immortal bottom never cease its gyrations. By God, what an ass! Compared to it, Miss Sylvia's is like a raisin … "

"George, George!" I whooped. "Now I know we're truly cousins. Welcome back to the family fold, you prodigal son! Just tell me, though: is that really in the text?"

"Many thanks, Kabi, both to you and to the splendid ass to which I owe your welcome. But please, Dear Editor, do not interrupt me with your questions. You will be given the manuscript when I finish and you can delete whatever you wish."

"You have, sir, my most respectful attention."

"Well, then. After Bahia, the distinguished guests began to arrive: government ministers, the speakers of the Parliament and the Senate, and several close friends of Nuri Pasha's. There was not a Jew among them – and indeed, my Dear Editor, there are not many Jews important enough to merit being invited by my father to anything. Lastly, arm-in-arm, came Prime Minister Tewfik el-Suweidi and the Pasha. He was – or so at least from my modest eye level he seemed to me – a tall and most handsome man, fair-skinned, full-faced, and thick-browed with a trim moustache, devilishly cunning blue eyes that did not miss a trick, and a mocking smile on his lips.

"I hardly need say that the tables were set for a king. Arrack, whisky, ouzo, vodka, French wines … not being allowed by their religion to touch alcohol, our Moslem leaders drink only the best. In general it is my impression that the decrees and prohibitions of the Koran are meant only for the lower classes, who are taxed by Allah, no less than by their rulers.

"My father served the Pasha an exclusive arrack made for him by a Jew. Then the servants brought a special appetizer, the recipe for which is the Pasha's own – few people know that he is also a skilled chef. All were waiting for Regent Abdullah, and at a signal from a footman that he was outside, my father rose and announced his arrival. The guests leaped to their feet and Salima Pasha sang a quatrain that went:

We welcome the Regent,
'Tis his pleasure to lead,
And now that he's here,
May our evening succeed.

"The Regent stood by the entrance to the drawing room, his right thumb clasped in his left hand, surveying the guests with a faint smile. He had a long, fair, finely-featured face with a high brow and smooth, shiny hair parted in the middle and combed straight back, and if his spine was slightly bent, this was not, God be praised, from the burden of high office but from a surfeit of amusements offered by horses, women, and young boys. I do not know, Dear Editor, what your opinion of him is or whether you have seen him apart from his photographs, except perhaps in his appearances in parades on el-Rashid Street or in newsreels showing him in his royal box at the hippodrome. I myself like him better than all our prime ministers put together, although I cannot for the life of me say why. Perhaps it is because, being Regent, he has a temporary job with no future or security, which makes it a most Jewish occupation. In two years he will step down in favour of his nephew, the current crown prince, who will be crowned King Faisal II upon his eighteenth birthday. One can only imagine what such a man must feel as his days of glory wane before his eyes … While as for Faisal II, you are aware, no doubt, that he is the same age as us. Can you picture yourself being King? Or even me?

"Be that as it may, my illustrious father bowed deeply to the Regent, so deeply indeed that I feared his athletic body was about to scrape the ground. When he straightened up, his eyes gleamed with as precious a light as if he had just been introduced to the Messiah. Leading the Regent to the centre of the room, he seated him between the Pasha and himself. 'Truly, Your Excellency's presence lights the world!' he proclaimed breathlessly, hastening to serve the Regent personally and to wait on him hand and foot. Meanwhile, Salima Pasha began to warble in her throaty voice, painting each word with her lips while swaying rapturously back and forth. The song that burst forth from them flamed like the burning bush. And yet – alas! – the latter was finally consumed, and the end of her first medley found her perspiring and exhausted.

"At that exact moment, Bahia stormed into the room with her seven sheer scarves. One by one she removed them in the course of her dance, the last directly under the smitten eyes of the Regent, on whom her own almond-shaped eyes were fixed hypnotically. Every arabesque, pirouette, ripple of her breasts, and shiver of her thighs enticed him as the fire does the moth. By now he had thawed considerably, although not nearly as much as the Pasha, whose cunning face was the colour of a grilled tomato. Bahia laughed at him flirtatiously, and he flashed back a big smile of warm, toothy passion.

"'What a shame that she's leaving us,' whispered my illustrious father to the Regent. 'This is her last appearance.'

"'Where is she going?' the Regent asked the Pasha.

"'That Egyptian dog, Muhammed Abd el-Muttalib, talked her into it,' said the Pasha to the Regent. 'She's off to Egypt with him.'

"'Shut the borders!' commanded the Regent. 'Ban all departures from the country!'

"'She's only going in order to make a film there,' the Pasha reassured him. 'She'll be back. They all come back in the end. The waters of the Nile, Your Excellency, are less sweet than those of the Tigris.'

"'We'll never see her again if that debauched King Farouk has his way,' fretted the Regent.

"'Then we had better sever diplomatic relations immediately!'

"'With your permission,' cajoled my illustrious father while signalling to Salim Shibbat to begin his act, 'I'll bring her over.' But both the Regent and the Pasha had already forgotten the belly dancer. 'If the Jews had done nothing but give us Salim Shibbat,' whispered the Pasha to my illustrious father, 'it would be a sufficient excuse for their existence.'

"You are no doubt wondering, Dear Editor, how I managed to be positioned in a manner to hear all this. The answer is that I spent most of the evening standing behind its most honoured guests. I am, after all, a mere slip of a lad, and sometimes that is an advantage. I strained to hear every word, especially if it issued from my illustrious father, who deems himself the neck that turns our heads of state. As soon as Bahia finished her dance, he made sure to cleanse their fouled minds with strong liquor, which was followed by a steaming catfish grilled by its anglers in our garden and served on silver trays upon a bed of parsley and pepper-grass. My illustrious father refilled the Regent's glass with his favourite whisky and urged him to eat. Yet the more the Regent sniffed at the fish, the more whisky he gulped from his glass, his inscrutably watery eyes taking on a frightening mien as he thoughtfully tapped his drink with his ring. My illustrious father hovered over him anxiously, fearful he was thinking of his horse, which had come in second that day to our own. The Regent, however, remained silent, as it is the privilege of royalty to do. Perhaps it was his intention to probe my father's nerves for their breaking point.

"'Waiter, some grilled doves, barbecued goose liver, and fried sweetbreads!' ordered my illustrious father. His hands on his knees, he leaned towards the Regent and pleaded like a scolded child: 'Won't Your Excellency at least taste something?'

"The Regent glanced at him, looked the catfish in the eye, and chose a piece of it, tearing a bellyful of flesh that he chewed slowly. My father was as blissful as if he had just given birth to a male child. Success again! And indeed, who knows better than he how to appeal to the animal lusts of the great? Nothing, unless it be the juices lower down, is stronger than those of the digestive tract, which can dissolve even pearls and diamonds … such was the lesson that our great-grandfather, whose portrait peers from the wall of our sitting room, had taught him. You yourself must admit, Dear Editor, that it was the juice of the mango that lured you here today. Won't you have another glass? If you fear denting my father's fortune, let me assure you that this mango juice was a gift to him, sent especially from India.

"But let us return to our tale. The ensemble played throughout the meal, no member of it better than the zitherist, Ibrahim Zion Da'abul. His solos held the guests spellbound and decanted the fine old wine of vintage music into their thick-blooded veins. The Regent bobbed his head and beat time with his gold ring on the table, his face flushed with the glory of the occasion, while the Pasha emerged from his reveries, rose to his feet, and clapped to the rhythm of the zither, the tabor, and the lute, which rewarded his efforts with their own. When they paused to rest, I heard him tell the Regent that the evening reminded him of another long ago, spent partying with a green-eyed Turkish temptress on the banks of the Tigris when he was an officer in the Sultan's army.

"It may surprise you, Dear Editor, but although, as you know, I am no slouch at a Chopin sonata, the musicians moved me to tears: to think that they had to play to all those divine aromas without being offered a bite to eat! I am afraid, indeed, that you too are beginning to salivate, even though you have lunched nicely. If it is any comfort, let me assure you that, despite the roast doves from Mr Edouard Sourpuss's dovecote that I wistfully eyed, I ate nothing that whole evening. I abstained for your sake, wishing to remain entirely open to the impressions, the sensations, the sights, and the conversations all around me. No, please don't interrupt to thank me now!

"When the banquet was over and the waiters brought the fingerbowls, the Regent leaned back in his chair and raised his glass, casting a hush over all. 'Salima,' he ordered, 'sing us that song of yours.'

"'A single song is a poor request for one as rich in gifts as you,' answered Salima with her most enchanting smile. 'Which song is Your Excellency thinking of?'

"'You know the one,' said the Regent with a barely noticeable gesture in the direction of the Pasha.

"Not everyone saw him make it and some thought his tongue was heavy with drink. It was the Pasha himself who came to the rescue by breaking into the first two lines:

O Nuri es-Sa'id's the shoe
And Saleh Jaber is his lace!

"'Hats off to Nuri, the one and only!' cried the Regent, wagging a finger as though conducting the ensemble and the Nightingale of the Tigris. All eyes were on the Pasha singing aloud and making the guests join in a ditty that mocked him, the king of the jungle of Iraqi politics, a man who, whether in or out of office, pulled every string and ruled every corner of the country, hanging and pardoning whom he pleased and imposing his will with the slyness of a fox and the ferocity of a tiger. Salima Pasha had to sing every word of it; but then, making me realize that evening what a clever woman she is, she made up for it with an encore, a medley of the most satirical, black-humoured ballads sung by the street musicians of Baghdad about the other potentates gathered around our table. And I, Dear Editor, wondered at that moment: are all these sons-of-bitches, as Salim Effendi has been known to refer to them, worth a fraction of my illustrious father's kowtowing? For you see, this pampered and arrogant man, who could not tell you where in his own house is the kitchen that prepares his food, had spent the evening so devotedly licking their behinds that a caravan of camels could not have pulled his tongue away from the rear ends it was firmly applied to. Could even his dream of being appointed to the Iraqi Senate have justified such behaviour? You will excuse me, Dear Editor, for speaking in a manner that reveals my feelings of kinship with you. Is it not far better to fly doves or sell watches than be a wealthy man at the mercy of such degenerates?

"I ask you: what would have happened had a little hand grenade rolled into the banquet hall just then and killed all present, clearing the path for a new generation of rulers – Salim Effendi and his cohorts, for example? But permit me to answer that question myself: nothing would have happened at all. You need only read a little history to know that rulers are always the same: if they were any less cunning and cruel, they would lose not only control, they would lose their own heads into the bargain. All the fine words of revolutionaries against tyranny and violence are pure bunk. Let your rebels but get a taste of power and they start guillotining the people for the people's good just like the men they overthrew! And as for the people itself, the immortal bard has shown us in the third act of *Julius Caesar*, so well-played by Salim Effendi's latest lover, what the mob is like. It cheers the Regent and the Pasha today, and the Communists, should they take over, tomorrow.

"But let us return to our banquet, which, far more than paying a call on a cousin whose illustrious father has deprived him of all contact with his family, is what has brought you, my Dear Editor, here today. Since the little hand grenade did not explode, and there was not a drop of poison in the coffee served to the Regent and the Pasha, it was now my turn to perform. Surely you have not forgotten that I had been requested to compose and recite a few obsequious verses of my own in the Regent and the Pasha's honour. Indeed, it may amuse you to be told that, as much as I loathed the task – as much as I thoroughly despised my father for making me his poet laureate – I also enjoyed it. In the silence that greeted me all ears were lent to my creation, giving me a feeling of supreme importance, which I deliberately though by no means unduly prolonged, by taking an extra moment to ready myself.

"I cannot imagine that you expect me, Dear Editor, to recite for you the rot that I wrote – the same lying, grovelling, fawning, hypocritical lies that had already been spoken by my father, although not of course in rhymes like mine. Versifying is not his strong point. I've typed up the poem for you and you can edit it as mercilessly as you wish, as long as you do not tarnish my reputation as a promising young poet …

"When I finished my recital, the soused and surfeited guests turned their pleasure-sodden minds to the voice of Salim Shibbat, and the Regent asked Bahia to dance again. You could see that he had her thighs on his brain like a fishbone in his throat. 'Don't strand yourself in Egypt,' he cautioned her when she was done. 'Iraq is in need of you.'

"'It's just for one little film, Your Excellency,' Bahia said reassuringly. 'Then I'll be back.'

"Another round of coffee was served and the Pasha now turned to my father and asked in an impeccable Jewish dialect: 'Abu George, my friend, how many of your compatriots will leave Iraq if the gates of the kingdom are opened?'

"My illustrious father frowned, cleared his throat, and replied: 'My esteemed Pasha, what can I tell you? Only a jackass would want to leave the Iraqi paradise.'

"'Well then, my dear friend, just how many jackasses are we talking about?'

"'Perhaps two thousand,' said my father. 'Certainly no more than three.'

"'Ten,' corrected Prime Minister Tewfik el-Suweidi.

"'Then why,' asked the Pasha, 'have I been told by the British that the number of jackasses may reach thirty thousand?'

"'When did the British ever guess correctly about the Orient?' replied the prime minister.

"'Well then, my brother,' the Pasha asked my father, 'shall we let them go?'

"'My esteemed Pasha,' said my illustrious father, 'what can I tell you? The Jews must be struck in their pockets. It is the one thing that can influence them.'

"'In that case, my brother, it would be best to let them depart for a place where there is no housing, no work, no fuel, no industry, nothing but refugees from Hitler. It stands to reason that every Jew who leaves for Israel is another nail in its coffin. Wouldn't Your Excellency the Regent agree?'

"The two men burst out laughing and the other guests

laughed too. My illustrious father, the recognized authority on Jewish affairs, made do with an awkward chuckle.

"'We can bring Palestinian refugees in their place,' said the Pasha. 'Let us show King Abdullah, King Farouk, and the Arab League the true nobility of the Iraqi people and the help it extends to the Arab cause! The Palestinians will make good use of what is left behind by the Jews and it won't cost us a single dinar, because the Americans will pay the bill. What do you say to that, Tewfik? You're the prime minister. It can't be done without you.'

"'We'll have to think of how to put it through Parliament,' said the prime minster.

"'The Jews will never leave Iraq,' opined my illustrious father.

"'My dear friend,' said the Pasha, 'the Jewish underground, one of the leaders of which has a name much like your own, is scheming to make every last Jew abandon this country.'

"My father nearly dropped his coffee cup. And you too, Dear Editor, are kindly requested to stay seated despite the allusion to your uncle Yehezkel. I will have to ask you to keep all this to yourself, since otherwise my father's head may not be long for his shoulders. It would be a pity to lose him; he is, after all, the only father that I have. Indeed, my precious sire quickly rallied and said to the Pasha: 'What can I tell Your Excellency? If you can rid us of the subversives, the Communists and the Zionists in one fell swoop, so much the better. Let them be the ruin of each other. It's time to clean the stables.'

"'No one has to live in Iraq against his will,' declared Tewfik el-Suweidi.

"It was then that the Pasha turned to me. 'George, my son,' he inquired, 'tell me by the prophet Moses: does that Jewish state of yours mean anything to you?'

"My illustrious father stared at me with a frozen plea on his face.

"'That state of mine means a great deal to me,' I said and paused. My father turned pale, the Pasha frowned, and Tewfik el-Suweidi's fingers drummed on the table. Only the Regent was too drowsy to react. 'But my homeland,' I went on, 'is here, in the Land of the Two Rivers.' My father clapped his hands like a little boy, raised his glass, and exclaimed: 'There you are, Your Excellency. That's what the young folk all think.'

"'That may be, my brother,' said the Pasha. 'But those sons of dogs keep crossing the borders illegally and getting away with it. They are making a mockery of us with the Shah of Iran, who turns a blind eye and refuses to send them back.'

"'Your Excellency,' said my illustrious father, to whose cheeks the blood had in the meantime returned, 'surely it is not necessary for me to advise you on the proper treatment of border violators.'

"'My friend,' said the Pasha, 'your state may be a small one, a mere speck of fly shit on the map, but it has managed to disrupt our lives and confound the world. Every Jew going to it from Iraq drives a nail not into its coffin but into the infrastructure it is building.' For the first time he sounded angry.

"'Your Excellency exaggerates the importance of the Zionist bandit state,' avowed my illustrious father.

"The Regent shook himself from his slumbers and rose, and all the guests rose with him. When they were gone, my father threw his arms around me and said: 'What an answer! What a brilliant reply! You can have a trip to London or to Paris. Take a friend with you, anyone you want.'

"And so, my Dear Editor," said George, putting down his manuscript, "do either London or Paris appeal to you?"

Before I knew what I was doing I had given him a hug and a kiss on both cheeks. "What a talent!" I exclaimed. "Stad Nawi and Salim Effendi were right. You're a born storyteller. The eye you have, the narrative ability! I wouldn't change a word." I reached for the manuscript.

"Are you crazy? Do you think I'd let you print this?"

"But you promised it to me!"

"What if I did? Would you publish such a piece about your own father?"

"But it's the artistic truth." The words came straight from Stad Nawi's literature class. "We'll weed out anything that might prove harmful."

"You mean you'll take all the life out of it."

"You certainly do hate those people. You don't think any too highly of your own father, either."

"He's the victim of his wealth. He has no choice but to pander to them."

I grinned. "I see that being poor has its advantages."

"You don't know the half of it. Listen, do you think that Salim Effendi would let me join the Communist Party?"

"Are you out of your mind? Do you want to ruin both your father and yourself? And anyway, didn't you just say that revolutionaries are no better than the regimes they overthrow?"

"I did. We're all torn souls. Take Miss Sylvia. One half of her is pro-Communist and the other is for humanism and Western democracy … and like lots of young Europeans who saw the Soviet Union help defeat fascism, she doesn't even notice the contradiction. I suppose I'm like her. And I don't doubt that there's a need for change – anything would be better than the corrupt society and government we have now."

"Then why not join us, the Zionist jackasses?"

We burst out laughing so infectiously that we both ended up rolling on the floor.

"Don't think that doesn't appeal to me," said George, recovering his breath. "But right now, I'd rather look for Paradise elsewhere. And besides, that would be a catastrophe for my family. I'm not about to turn Communist yet either. At the moment I'm just playing with ideas."

We went into the garden and rocked for a long time on the white *jalala*. George seemed exhausted, drained. Suddenly withdrawn, he watched the sun set like a giant peach. Only the distant barking of dogs broke the stillness. I didn't want to leave, although it was time to. I felt a great closeness to him.

When the driver took me home, George came along. This time I wasn't embarrassed. I even took him for a walk through the old Jewish quarter. Like a tourist, he stared wide-eyed at the souk. We parted with an embrace.

30.

When informed by Abu Saleh the baker that no one could be found to take the thousands of dinars that the Movement was ready to pay for Hizkel's release, my father leaned for support on a railing by the bakery oven. "What's happened to the Moslems?" he asked, one hand stroking his chin and the other pressing his amber worry beads to his head. "Don't they even take bribes any more?"

"*Wallah*," murmured the baker, "I don't know what to tell you. Everyone says it's too dangerous."

"It doesn't look good," declared my father, ticking off beads with his fingers.

"Abu Kabi," said the baker in a voice both pleading and firm. "I know it's not easy, but you have to see Big Imari."

"I wish I could trust him. God knows and I know what a scoundrel he is."

"He's still our best chance."

"Where's the Movement? Where's Israel?" my father exclaimed, brushing flour from his coat as if brushing off the baker. "Have they forgotten Hizkel so soon?"

"We have three different escape plans," said Abu Saleh. "But it's too soon for desperate measures."

"It's always too soon until it's too late," my father muttered as he left the bakery.

The next day he returned from work at noon and went down

to the cellar to rest. Then he washed, shaved, put on his blue suit with his pearl tiepin, and told me to dress formally too. Before we set out he straightened my tie and reminded me to keep my shoulders straight.

"There's no choice but to sup with the Devil," he said. "Don't tell anyone, not even your mother. I have no idea what will come of this."

But instead of going straight to Big Imari's office on Bank Street, my father told our cab driver to take us to the river, where he hired a boat that cruised on the quiet summer waters of the Tigris while he crouched in its stern as tensely as if caught in a winter storm. Now and then he shook his head as if driving away a troubling thought, stuck a cigarette that he forgot to light in his mouth, and stared into space while fingering his worry beads or holding them to his nose.

"Baba, what happened between the two of you?" I plucked up the courage to ask. I knew the subject was considered too painful to talk about, but since we were on our way to Big Imari anyway, perhaps I would get an answer this time.

"It's a long story, son. Some other time."

I had often tried putting together the bits of information that I had about their great quarrel. Many of the details were known only to my father, who never talked about them. Most of what I knew came from my mother, and especially from old Hiyawi. The two men, he had told me, were raised together in Imara, where my great-grandfather lived. They belonged to one of the few Jewish families in an area inhabited almost entirely by Moslems, whose homes my father entered and left without fear. He grew up with them, went to school with them, played hide-and-seek with them in the country lanes, and spent long hours in the home of Hadijja, my great-grandfather's maid, whom he sat watching as she made the almost transparently thin local bread, as oblivious of all else as I was later to be with Hairiyya.

My great-grandfather was a rice grower, the biggest and most influential in the region. When Hussein Sam'awi was made provincial governor, rumour had it that the power behind him was my great-grandfather, Salman Imari. Everything belonged to him: the shops, the houses, the large local inn. Hundreds of tenant farmers worked for him, did his bidding, and sought his protection. It was no small privilege to be one of his grandsons, and my father, who was the eldest of them, was the favourite. Showered with love, gifts, and flattery, he had a happy and untroubled childhood.

As boys, he and Big Imari were friends. They studied together and often rambled barefoot through the flooded rice fields, their toes gripping the wet clay soil. Sometimes they had mud fights that turned them both into brown pillars, after which they washed themselves off in my great-grandfather's rose garden. The old man liked to dandle them on his knees and pat their heads.

When Big Imari's father was murdered, my great-grandfather took pity on the boy and welcomed him into his house. Even then, it was said, Big Imari could talk his grandfather into anything. He was a sly, manipulative, backbiting child with a fondness for money and a knack for turning one dinar into two. Once, my father angrily reminisced, when they were both eleven, they were attacked by a band of Moslems from another region as they came home from playing in the rice fields. Although Big Imari, who was not very big then, managed to slip away, he did not bother to call for help and left my father to fend for himself, taunted and beaten by his captors. When they finally let my father go, he was so afraid that he stayed at home for days. Only when his own father promised to send him to high school in Baghdad the next year did he agree to go back to school in Imara.

The two boys stopped being friends. Besides the matter of the inheritance, I had the feeling that my father had never got over this incident, from which his unconquerable fear of Moslems dated. Who knew if his tormenting feelings of guilt for not having gone down to the courtyard on the night of Hizkel's arrest the one time a bribe might have worked – were not also linked to this fear, and thus, to Big Imari?

In any event when, years afterwards, my great-grandfather died without leaving a known will, Big Imari seized control of the estate and dispossessed the other heirs, who were left without a dinar or a hectare of the family fortune. Everything – the rice fields, the modern agricultural equipment, the land in Palestine, all kinds of other property whose worth no one even knew – fell into his hands. He won one court case after another, bribing the judges and lying brazenly while disavowing Hizkel and my father.

Even had my father been able to recover from the immensity of the loss – a wound that Big Imari's very existence constantly rubbed salt in – my mother would not have let him. She could not go long without mentioning Big Imari's treachery and the stories spread by him that all Imaris but himself were charlatans and imposters. Unlike Hizkel, who found consolation in the business he built up, as well as in his writing, his newspaper, the Movement, and Rashel, my father knew no peace. The harder he tried to forget Big Imari, the more he thought of him. Of one thing he had always been sure, that if he ever met the man again he would face him proudly and unflinchingly – and now he was about to break this vow, too, by going to him cap in hand.

As we sailed on the river, he kept taking out his gold pocket watch from his jacket. Although the cruise had been his way of pulling himself together, I could tell how agitated he was by the way he gripped the side of the boat. The fiery wheel of the sun grew larger as it dipped westwards, spraying the water with orange-gold sparks as the day was reeled in by a sky that went from deep blue to dark grey and dull brown. An evening breeze whipped the water, spreading darkness. Our skipper cast anchor in a little bay that smelled unpleasantly.

"Does he know you're coming?" I asked my father as we stood in a dim pool of light by the entrance to Big Imari's office.

"No. But this is the day he receives."

We ascended to the first floor, its black and white tiles resembling a chess board. The furniture – a few faded, brown leather couches and several small tables whose sole function seemed to be to sustain the full ashtrays on top of them – was surprisingly modest, whether to avoid ostentation or, as my mother would no doubt have said, to refrain from provoking the Evil Eye. A flushed, one-armed man who looked ill paced back and forth in a tense silence as though in a doctor's waiting room. A slim, grey-suited receptionist sat in one corner at a desk with a typewriter and a telephone.

"You can say that Salman Moshi Imari is here," my father told him.

"A relative?" The receptionist's Adam's apple bobbed.

"Yes."

"Perhaps it's something I can help you with?"

"No."

The receptionist dipped his pen in an inkwell and jotted something down with a flourish. A bell rang in the office behind him. "Excuse me," he said. "Mr Imari is calling me." He straightened his jacket, threw back his shoulders, paused for a moment outside the brown wooden door, knocked, and entered. When he returned he said to my father: "Please have a seat. Mr Imari will see you."

My father chose to remain standing, breathing unevenly while drumming his fingers on his thigh and staring at the silent fan on the ceiling. Not trusting his elegant suit to convey that he was no ordinary petitioner, he tried his best to look impatient and defiant. The bell rang again and the receptionist rose again and showed us in.

George's father was ensconced in a high armchair behind his desk at the far end of a large room, from which he scrutinized my father carefully without offering him a seat or even saying hello. The two men stared at each other as if waiting to see who blinked first, their glances clashing like swords. Behind the desk hung framed pictures of the Regent and the Pasha with written dedications. To their left was a map of the Imara district, its rice fields clearly marked; to their right was a map of the world dotted with coloured thumbtacks from which lines converged on Baghdad – no doubt the many places where Big Imari did business. He was wearing a light olive-green suit, and the electric light falling from above gave him a yellowish complexion. My father, who was nervously rolling his worry beads, had drops of sweat on his forehead. For a moment both men glanced at me and then my father signalled to me to leave, perhaps because my presence was what was making them so awkward. He pulled up a chair by the desk and took a seat.

"I'm listening," said Big Imari.

"My brother Hizkel, your cousin, is in prison."

"For smuggling arms."

"So you think he's guilty? How do you know it's true?"

"The prime minister told me."

"And the prime minister's word is sacred writ?"

"What is it that you want?"

"For you to get him out."

"And have my name linked to arms smugglers so that I can end up like Shafik Addas?" asked Big Imari.

"You're the only one who can save him," said my father in a choked voice. "Talk to the Pasha."

"Do you suppose the government eats out of my hand? And what makes you think that I owe you anything?"

"Every penny you're worth. You robbed us of our inheritance."

"That's all been settled in court. If that's what brings you here, you may as well leave right now."

"I'm here to ask for my brother's life."

There was a silence. My father and Big Imari lit cigarettes. Big Imari rapped his desk with the large ring on his little finger and said:

"You're doing everything you can to get yourselves expelled from Iraq."

"Are you implying they'll let us leave?" asked my father.

"I'm implying nothing," said Big Imari, as if regretting his words. "But whatever I do for you will be on condition that you leave this country. And that your son keeps away from my son in the meantime."

"Leave our children out of this," said my father. "They've done nothing wrong."

"And one more thing," added Big Imari. "No one is to know that I'm involved in this. Not your wife and not Hizkel's."

"When will I hear from you?"

"When I have news."

"He's rotting away."

"The one cure for a scorpion is to crush it."

"You've never stopped hating us, have you?"

"And why should I love you? One of you is a Zionist, another is a Communist, and you all suck my blood. You can go to hell, all of you!"

"Don't even mention the two of them in the same breath. Salim Effendi is an idiot."

"That he is." It was the first thing they had agreed upon. "But they're both destroying a paradise."

"A paradise? You, whose father was murdered in front of your eyes, call this country a paradise?"

There was no reply.

"His own workers, for whom he had built homes, schools, clinics, stuck their knives in him!"

"That's enough," said Big Imari, shading his eyes with a hand.

"They'll get you in the end too, all those great men you hang out with."

"They're my friends."

"It wasn't me who brought up the subject of Shafik Addas. He also thought he had friends. Don't you remember Grandfather telling us that it's those closest to you who throw the stones? Do you really think you can buy your way out of everything?"

"And do you really think it's safer in Israel? Didn't you see the headline in *El-Zeman* a while ago? 'ISRAEL CELEBRATES FIRST AND LAST BIRTHDAY,' it said."

"Israel will last forever, *inshallah*."

"Who goes to live there? Jews from America? From England? From France? No, no one but refugees, the rejects of all the countries in the world: the survivors of Hitler, the poor of North Africa, the beggars of Yemen, the wretched of Baghdad, girls without dowries, men without jobs, failures here and failures there! Everything is stacked against it: language, economics, geography, strategy, war. I wish I could tell you of the secret reports about Israel that I get from the Pasha and the British ambassador with their terrible predictions. I wish I could tell you of the plans for exterminating Israel being hatched right now in Arab capitals. But I don't need to. You read the newspapers and listen to the radio, don't you? They've declared a holy war on it! Don't you know how many generations an Arab blood-feud lasts? They'll fight until Israel is wiped out. What a man like Hizkel doesn't understand is that a tiny country surrounded by millions of enemies determined to push it into the sea has no future. What chance does it have? Great powers have foundered in the Arab East. The Crusaders were driven out by Saladin, the British and French are gone too, and only the Moslems remain … Yes, we Jews remain too – but only because we've had them as our protectors. And now Hizkel wants to defy history! I ask you, is he a moron or simply an illiterate? I've thought many things about you Imaris, but never until now have I questioned your intelligence. Don't you realize that Israel faces a perpetual state of siege? How long can it hold out? How can such a country survive? It will become such a burden to both the Jews and the world that they'll be happy to see it destroyed! And then what? The wanderer's staff again? Back to Mesopotamia? But the gates will no longer be open.

"Believe me, the Jews in Israel are smarter than you and your brother. *They've* already prepared the escape routes to which they'll run at the first sign of danger: to the United States, to France, to South Africa, to South America. But where will *we* go? Your brother wants to cause a catastrophe and you want me to free him, the new Moses from Taht el-Takya! It took us two thousand four hundred years to get where we are in Iraq, and all he can think of is ruining the situation. And that in an age when King Faisal, the father of this country, declared that we are all Semites and that there is no difference between a Moslem and a Jew!

"We Jews have always been the driving force in Iraq. What more could we want? The first minister of finance after independence was a Jew, the first minister of petroleum, high court judges, members of Parliament, senators, business leaders, merchants, artists, writers, musicians – is that what you now want to end? Is it for that you want me to risk my position, the future of my son George, and the seat waiting for me in the Senate?

"It was Zionists from Palestine who poisoned your brother's mind. I met a few of them, that Italian too, Enzo What's-His-Name. He was a more dangerous false Messiah than Shabbetai Zvi. A pack of wild adventurers, that's all they are, wanting to turn us into cannon fodder and our bridge to the Moslems into a wall! They don't begin to understand the Arabs, and don't understand a single word of Arabic. And now they've got hold of Hizkel and we have to listen to him spouting out their crazy ideas. By what right does he play games with the lives and fates of innocent, hard-pressed Jews? And if he talks them into leaving Baghdad, can he talk them into forgetting it? We are the sons of an Arab land; its culture is our culture. Why the hurry? Why can't we wait a generation, even two or three, and then decide if there's a future for us here? But now? Barely a year after the war in Palestine? We need to take a lesson from the Jews in America, in England, in France. You have to be mad to smuggle arms for use against the Pasha. You have to be mad to endanger us and our children. And *that's* the man you're asking me to save?"

"I thought you wanted us out of Iraq," my father said.

"*You*, yes! I want to be rid of you once and for all. But not of every Jew. Just of those damned Zionists with their Movement that everyone knows is nothing but a travel agency for shipping out the best of our youth and leaving behind the elderly, the women, and the children. And who will foot the bill for it? Irresponsible people, a ruinous movement! But you'll see, Jewish life will go on here. Alongside Jerusalem there was always Babylon."

"Don't you realize that everything has changed?" asked my father. "That the establishment of Israel has killed all hope of living in peace with them?"

"The Pasha has promised me that nothing will happen to those Jews who remain loyal."

"The Jews have always been given such promises before being slaughtered."

"They'll never manage without us. The economy will collapse. Business will be ruined. Where will they get their intellectuals? Their doctors, their lawyers, their pharmacists?"

"They have plenty of young people who will be happy to take our place."

"They don't want us to leave."

"Is that why the Pasha is planning to exchange us for the Palestinian refugees?"

"That's merely for external consumption, to make an impression on the Arab League."

"Fine, stay here if you prefer. It's your business. Just do something to help Hizkel. He's liable to hang."

"I'm not promising you anything."

31.

From Big Imari's we went straight to Abu Ednan's. My father took a seat with a proprietary air, loosened his tie, and stretched himself as if to re-expand after the tight spot he had been in. While sipping a calming glass of arrack he told me, one ear cocked to the voice of Salima Pasha coming from a large gramophone, of his talk with Big Imari. He seemed good-humoured and relaxed, a mood that continued in the days that followed. Having borne his anxiety for his brother in a solitude that nourished little hope, he was relieved to have passed on a part of the responsibility and to be able to think once more of himself and his family, perhaps even to take a decisive action. He had concluded long ago that it was time to leave Iraq, and now he felt that there was not a moment to spare. Nothing would stop him from going to Israel, neither Big Imari's prophecies of doom nor the rumours brought home by my mother from the neighbours, who had received letters from the Jewish state that told of living in hunger, hovels, and the fear of armed attacks from across the border. These letters, my father explained, perhaps most of all to himself, were in fact ironically phrased attempts to get past the Iraqi censor. Men of little faith were to be found throughout Jewish history. How could a believing woman like my mother fail to understand that these were messianic times?

The day after meeting Big Imari he asked Abu Saleh to put

him in touch with the illegal emigration section of the Movement. Abu Saleh warned against rashness. Two young men had recently died in the desert while trying to cross the border; a second group had been robbed and forced to return to Baghdad; and still others had been caught and jailed. The police were stepping up their vigilance and border guides were not eager to run the risk of smuggling a family with small children, not even for a hatful of dinars. The routes they took were meant for good walkers, young men with strong legs and few possessions or, at most, young parents who could carry their children if necessary.

My father resented such aspersions. Since he had never in his life been on a trek or made any great physical effort, he refused to believe that he could not dash across the desert like a Bedouin, especially with Abed to lend a hand. And although Abu Saleh – a powerful man used to toting heavy sacks and walking long distances in the brutal Iraqi sun – knew better, my father failed to understand how his brother's friend and successor was not eager to help him fulfil the prime commandment of Zionism.

Disappointed, he tried finding a border guide on his own but was soon taken to task by the baker. How, chided Abu Saleh, could he behave like such an amateur, putting himself and others in danger? Didn't he know that he was under surveillance and that, even if he made it out of the country, this would provide the CID with new evidence against Hizkel and the Zionist underground? My father stared back as blankly as a rejected lover. He was sure that Hizkel would be convicted unless rescued, and that he himself would be arrested if he remained in Iraq. Returning home that evening, he sat sulkily rocking and smoking on the *jalala*. When served a bowl of *bajili,* his favourite bean dish, he picked at it absent-mindedly.

"What's the matter?" asked my mother.

"The Movement won't smuggle us out of Iraq, that's what's the matter."

"Oh," she said as if the subject did not concern her.

"They say it's too dangerous."

"They're right."

"They are?"

"If one person says you have donkey ears, ignore him. If two people say it, buy a saddle for your back." It was an old proverb.

"Fine, so I'm a donkey." He got down angrily from the *jalala* and paced the yard. "A lot of support I get from you!"

"I've followed you blindly all my life," said my mother, taking out a gold-tipped cigarette from its leather case and lighting it with an aggravated motion. "You should have married that singer of yours."

"What does she have to do with it?" He stalked out of the house, his arms dangling despairingly.

My mother mentioned Salima Pasha on rare occasions, usually when my father had said something implying that his marriage was a mistake. At such times he turned pale and said nothing, and he would soon slip out of the house as if fearing to re-open a closed and mysterious chapter. For the same reason, perhaps, he had adamantly turned down Hiyawi's suggestion that he ask Salima to intervene with the Pasha on Hizkel's behalf.

Who was she? What had happened between them? The one time I had asked my mother, her response was such a hard, blank stare that I didn't dare mention it again.

The next morning I spied Abu Saleh in the doorway of his bakery, gazing at Fat'hiya while crooning:

Thy lap alone can shelter me from death.
But if death comes and plucks me from it too,
May I be buried in a shroud made of your braids,
The sweetness of your mouth my everlasting peace.

He signalled to me to wait for the song's end and then told me that he wanted to see my father.

That evening my father returned, excited and slightly drunk. For the next two weeks his mind seemed far away. Every morning he hurried to buy the newspapers and listened each day to Iraqi radio and the clandestine broadcasts of the Voice of Israel. Baghdad was buzzing with rumours of mysterious Israeli emissaries, secret debates in the Senate and Parliament, even an agreement on the subject of Jewish emigration between the omnipotent Pasha and his prime minister.

I myself was busy with the school paper and not entirely aware of what was happening. I had hardly noticed the arrival of autumn, as usual in Baghdad a brief transition between summer and winter, or of the holiday of Sukkot, the last day of which was my sixteenth birthday. The heady smell of the first showers of the rainy season had barely wafted from the thirsty earth when driving winds slashed the leaves from the trees and brought cold, dry winter weather that froze the water in the pipes and turned our large-roomed, high-ceilinged house, which had been built for hot weather, into a huge icebox in which we huddled by kerosene heaters and charcoal braziers. I hated the winter with its fierce hailstorms and torrential rains that made a quagmire of the lanes and the souk in the Jewish quarter.

My mother was busy too. By now it was almost Purim and she was hard at work preparing gifts of sweets and pastries: a sugared sambusak, a quince-and-peanuts comfit, biscuits with dates and coconut, gingerbread with honey and roses. Only the sugared almonds and the wonderfully sticky "heaven's manna" were bought by her at Abu Shimeil's. She filled china and silver trays with her handiwork, sprinkled the tops with rose leaves, covered them with homemade lace, and sent them to her friends and family. Some two months earlier she had told my father that she was pregnant. He had hugged her happily and said: "I hope it's a son born in Israel."

One night he came home early with his arms full of shopping, looking like a new man. Behind him strode Abed carrying baskets of drinks. My father opened a bottle of wine, melodiously blessed God for having brought us to this day, hugged and kissed my mother, and broke into a funny song-and-dance that I had never seen him perform before.

"What's the occasion, Abu Kabi?" asked my mother gaily.

"For Thou puttest me at the head of all my foes and makest me rejoice," sang my father and we joined in the old hymn.

"Abu Kabi," my mother tried again, "have you won the lottery?"

"Better than that."

"Has Big Imari given you his share of the inheritance?"

"Even better." He took another sip of wine.

"Lord help us! Will you please tell us?"

"Guess," said my father.

"Hizkel's free!" cried my mother, jumping for joy.

"I'm afraid not," replied my father quickly, frowning at the shadow cast over his surprise. "Tewfik el-Suweidi has gone crazy."

"Hush!" my mother rebuked him. "What kind of way is that to talk about the prime minister?"

"I swear to God! They all have. Tewfik, and the Pasha, and Saleh Jaber, and the cabinet, and the Parliament, and the Senate, and everyone!"

He was as excited as a little boy.

"Abu Kabi, the ears have walls!" exclaimed my alarmed mother.

"They've passed a law allowing all Jews who waive their Iraqi citizenship to leave the country. It was on the radio. Soon they'll start taking applications."

"What?"

"*Bukra el-Safr*." My father broke into the words of a popular song of Um Kultoum's. "We're off any day now!"

"What about our house?" wailed my mother. "What about our property?"

"To hell with it!"

"It's you Jews who want to leave who have gone crazy," my mother said, turning pale. "What's sane about giving up your identity papers and all you own?"

"Woman, the ground is burning beneath us!"

"But why leave everything?"

He took the Bible down from its shelf, placed it on the table, and said:

"Here's why!"

It didn't satisfy her. "And your brother ?" she asked, wringing her hands.

My father bit his lip and turned to go to his room.

"How can you take us to a wilderness?" she called after him.

"I'm taking you to the land of milk and honey."

"Do you want Kabi to be a soldier and get killed?" She was shaking all over.

"God forbid! Why do you always think of the worst?"

She sank onto the divan and helplessly grabbed my hand. "Kabi, what will we do?"

"Leave him out of it," my father said angrily. And more conciliatorily he added: "Woman, don't you understand that it's a chance to start a new life?"

"I don't want a new life. I don't want new people. I want my old house in el-Me'azzam."

"That house is dead! Those times are dead!"

"Then go by yourself and leave us here! I'm not coming with you." She turned her back on him.

He went to his room while she walked slowly to the *jalala* and sat on it wearily, her head bowed towards her flowery apron. I sat beside her and put an arm around her. She lit a cigarette and leaned on me like a girl nestling against her mother.

"Why must he do this to me? Who is he running away from?"

"It has nothing to do with you," I said. "It's him."

"But I'm happy here. This is my home. I don't want any other." While my father was marching in step with history, my mother's life had continued to circle in its old orbit. As always she went each day to the souk, where she stopped by the meat stalls, the poultry stalls, the fish and vegetable stalls, choosing and bargaining. Every other week she visited the fabric sellers' lane and came back with lengths of material, out of which she sewed and embroidered the clothes, bedspreads, curtains, and tablecloths that she gave to the friends and acquaintances with whom she shared the knowledge she had acquired in needlework school as a girl and kept adding to. Though it gave her great pleasure to see her embroidery so admired, she had no sense of its artistic worth.

She rarely left the Jewish quarter. She never went away on vacation, took no time off for amusements, and refused to accompany my father to night clubs or other places where women were allowed. The very idea of being entertained when she could be working seemed sinful to her. Her whole life was spent on us and the household, tidying, cleaning, cooking, laundering, ironing, getting out of bed before anyone else in the morning to start the long, hard day yet always giving us the feeling that she enjoyed every minute of it.

Most of all she liked the little garden that she had created on the roof with its flowerpots of roses, lilies, carnations, and different vines that hung down in the inner courtyard. More vines and flowers were trellised on a wooden gazebo that Hizkel had built for her in a corner, overlooking Abu Edouard's dovecote. It was here that she liked to sit when the day's work was done, relaxing barefoot on a divan and smoking a gold-tipped cigarette while listening to the cooing of the doves or an old record of Um Kultoum's. The last of us to turn in for the night, she would go from bed to bed, hugging and fondling her sleeping children, the loves of her life and subjects of her little kingdom whose welfare and reputation she defended tenaciously.

Her only days of rest were Sabbaths and Jewish holidays, when she sat listening to services in the synagogue with a transcendent serenity. Once a year she made the pilgrimage to the grave of the Prophet Ezekiel. She waited a whole year for this journey and spent several days in the prophet's sanctuary, praying, lighting candles, bathing in the holy fountain, and asking for the health and prosperity of her family and the Jewish people. After years of longing for her old home in el-Me'azzam, which she still obsessively spoke of in her quarrels with my father, she had reluctantly made her peace with Taht el-Takya. She hated change and wanted only to remain where she was, rooted like a fruiting tree in the routines of life.

My father was just the opposite. He was always somewhere else, his only home his dreams. Unable to decide between them, I sided with both. For once my father had made up his mind and was determined to press ahead with his plans; but my mother's agonizing doubts and instinctive distrust of all adventures were not easily overcome. Now she gripped my arm on the *jalala* and sat in silence. After a while I noticed she was crying.

"What have I done to him?" she asked at last. "Why doesn't he ever think of me? I never know what goes on in his head. He keeps it all inside himself until he makes up his mind and rams it down my throat. That's how he left his law practice, and then his teaching job to open the watch shop. That's how we left el-Me'azzam. You were too small to remember, but he never even asked me where I wanted to live. He simply hired a truck and loaded the whole house onto it ..."

"It's true that the *Farhood* came soon after, just as he said it would. But he refused to move back even when it was over, and when all the Jews were making money during the war, he thought of everyone but us. He worked for the community, organized the neighbourhood, raised money for the Jews in Israel, argued and gave speeches – he and Hizkel. And now he wants to leave it all! For what? Why won't he ever listen to me?"

She fell silent. It was painful. I won't be like that, I told myself. I'll tell the woman I marry everything, share every decision with her. I kissed my mother on the forehead and went out for a breath of fresh air.

32.

When my grandfather Moshi sent his son Salman from Imara to study in Baghdad, the future Abu Kabi moved in with his mother's brother, his Uncle S'hak. This uncle played the lute and the zither and Salman loved to watch him coax his magic notes from both instruments. Uncle S'hak had recordings of the crooner and movie star Abd el-Wihab, with whom he liked to sing along. Once he came home to find an embarrassed Salman hugging his large lute and plucking its strings with a feather pick while pretending to be Abd el-Wihab. Uncle S'hak smiled, said that his musical talents must have been passed on to his nephew, and offered to give Salman lessons.

And so music became my father's refuge from homesickness. Every day he hurried through his schoolwork in order to have time to practise with Uncle S'hak. These sessions were pure bliss. He became a soloist in the school choir with a great future predicted for him, and at his junior high school graduation he was asked to sing a special number for the guest of honour, King Faisal. The night before the ceremony he dreamed he was on stage, looking down at an empty auditorium with only the King in it, unable to produce a sound from his stricken throat or to revive the dead notes that fell from his lute. He awoke covered with sweat.

His Uncle S'hak and father Moshi, who had come for the occasion from Imara, tried to calm him. That night the school headmaster, Tewfik Thabit, introduced him on stage to the King and his cabinet ministers, the palace officials, and the royal guard in its dashing uniforms, as well as to the assembled parents, teachers, and students. My father trembled with excitement. The only face he made out belonged to Uncle S'hak, with whom he had practised the number many times. There was hearty applause, joined by the King, when he finished. The next day a telephone call came from the palace, asking him to come for an audience with Faisal.

My father's father did not like the idea. Arab kings and their aides, he warned, were infamous pederasts. He only yielded when my father's headmaster agreed to go along. The magnificent royal chamber took my father's breath away, but the King smiled kindly and said that he had known my great-grandfather, and that his son, my grandfather, had been wise to send his own son to study in Baghdad. My father, declared the King, urging him to continue his musical studies, had a splendid voice. Did he have any special request?

Salman Imari was too taken aback to do more than thank His Highness and answer that he lacked for nothing. Later in the day a messenger arrived at Uncle S'hak's with an inlaid Damascene lute and a greeting card from the King.

Salman felt that he was living in a dream. But although he went on playing and singing and was befriended by such Jewish performers as Dahud Akram and Saleh el-Kuwaiti, he enrolled in a teacher training college after finishing school and having been turned down for law school, and his first job was at the el-Wataniyeh Elementary School under the direction of the well-known pedagogue Ezra Haddad. On receiving his first pay, he moved out of Uncle S'hak's home and rented an attic room in which he began to study law on his own.

In honour of his new domicile, his father sent him a bottle of expensive wine. It was a Friday night and my father had to say the Sabbath blessing over the wine by himself. "I was hungry, sad, and lonely," he was to tell me long afterwards, "and I went outside as if looking for something – what, I myself didn't know."

Eventually he found himself in front of the el-Jawahiri Hotel, in which there was a performance that night. He had never been to a hotel show before, but with his newly-earned money he entered, took a seat in a box near the stage, and ordered an arrack. Soon the singer Salima Pasha, the queen of the Baghdad theatre even then, appeared on stage and, with her fiery eyes, she surveyed the audience which was mostly made up of familiar faces. They came to rest on Salman Imari.

My father had heard Salima sing before, because there wasn't a home or a café in which she wasn't listened to on the radio, but she was even more haunting in person. "I had no idea why she was staring at me," he was to say to me. "I thought the arrack might be making me imagine it." At midnight he tore himself away, walked reluctantly back to his room, and fell asleep in his clothes.

The next evening he arrived early for the performance, which he watched from the same box. When Salima Pasha burst stormily on stage, her eyes sought him out again. During the interval a waiter brought him a tray with arrack and snacks. "It's from Salima Pasha," he said.

My father turned up every night and so did the tray. He was too young and inexperienced to know what to do. One night the hotel's pudgy owner, Abu Sa'adun, entered his box, sat down beside him, and said after a few polite remarks:

"You, sir, are a teacher, are you not?"

"How do you know?" asked my father.

"My friend," replied Abu Sa'adun, "we live in a small town. In Baghdad everyone knows everything." He drank to my father's health and said: "I'm looking for a private tutor and I'm willing to pay five times the going rate."

"Why?" asked my father.

Abu Sa'adun grinned and leaned forward to conceal from Salima his finger that pointed at her. "She can't read or write."

"It scared me," my father was to tell me. He asked for time to think it over and consulted Abu Brahim the speech instructor in the teachers' room the next day, "You can't be serious," said Abu Brahim. "There are men who spend their fortunes to be with her. She'll open the gates of Paradise for you. Why don't you recommend me too?"

The next evening my father told Abu Sa'adun that he was agreeable and they set a date for the first lesson. Salman donned his only suit, a white summer suit, chose a red tie, doused himself with eau de Cologne, slicked back his hair, and took a carriage to Bab-el-Shargi. In front of Salima's house a grey-haired man in shabby clothes was walking up and down like a shadow. His eyes seemed to block my father's path as he approached the front gate.

Neighbours, who knew my father and were sitting on the veranda next door, gave him a pitying look as if he were a lamb being led to the slaughter. Singers were thought of as no better than whores, lewd, fallen women. A person might enjoy seeing and hearing them, but no one respectable was caught being with them. And being famous, Salima was considered especially lethal. Dozens of suitors were said to have perished at her feet.

A Muslim maid opened the door and set my father at ease by her friendliness. She brought him to the sitting room, placed a jug of cold water on the table, and said, "Miss Salima will be here in a moment." A minute later, all smiles, she appeared. Sitting down beside my father, she began chatting like an old friend and soon he felt at home. As he discovered to his amazement when they began their first lesson, she really was totally illiterate.

Despite a few small pock marks on her face, Salima was an attractive, charming woman with a lively wit and excellent taste, a pleasure to be with. My father couldn't remember how long the lesson lasted, but soon it was evening and he was invited to accompany Salima Pasha to the hotel.

He declined. More than one sheikh and minister, he knew, was enamoured of her, and his life would not be worth much if he were taken for a rival. Moreover, he was embarrassed. He was a teacher, after all; parents entrusted their children to him, their most precious possessions; he was not expected to be seen in the company of such a woman.

The grey-haired man was still outside when they left the house. "Salima, Salima, I'd give my soul for you," he moaned.

"What am I supposed to do with him?" Salima Pasha asked Salman apologetically as her driver sought to chase the man away.

"I've given up my life for you, my fortune!" the man called after her as she disappeared into her limousine and drove away with a wave.

"Watch out," he hissed to my father, spitting the fire of jealousy in his face. "She'll do the same to you. You're too young to let her ruin your life."

My father fled into the first passing cab and on impulse told the driver to take him to the hotel. Before Salima even appeared on stage she sent him a bottle of French cognac with Turkish cigarettes and other treats. As she sang "Have Mercy On Me, Heart of Stone", he thought of the face of the shadow of the man by her house.

It took him three months to teach her to read, write, do sums, and learn some history. A woman in her prime, she was a quick learner who hungrily sought to cram into her retentive memory all she had missed. Before long she was reciting long poems by heart to please her teacher. When he explained them to her, she sat on her Persian rug and listened.

A few weeks after their lessons began, "We caught fire," were the words my father used. When they weren't studying or making love, they drank and sang together. Her eyes filled with tears when he crooned "I Am Your Slave" to her. He would wrap his arms around her as she told him about her orphaned childhood and failed marriage, which ended with her husband evicting her because her family had reneged on the dowry. It was then that she first began to dance and sing at private parties. Her voice and femininity made her name and she was soon surrounded by artists, actors, sheikhs, wealthy businessmen, and politicians. She even became friendly with the Pasha, Nuri es-Sa'id, in whose house she asked for favours for her acquaintances and fellow Jews. Her fans besieged her wherever she went. She was a star, appearing in Aleppo, in Beirut, in Jerusalem, even in Paris. Authors sang her praises, poets dedicated their verses to her. A clever businesswoman, she saw to it that she was paid well. By now her husband wanted her back, but it was too late. Although she still loved him, her pride did not permit it.

My father was aware that Salima's feelings for him combined a student's crush on her teacher with the need to get away from her admirers, who all wanted the same thing from her. For this reason, he was plagued by doubts as to whether she loved him. Perhaps, too, he did not believe enough in his own powers. They read stories and sad romantic poems together and went to see Greta Garbo films. At a signal from Salima's driver that the lights had gone out, they would slip into the cinema, she in a veil and he in sunglasses. Sometimes they went to the races or sailed on the river, and at midnight, when her show was over, they went out on the town, feeling that all Baghdad was theirs.

But although Salima wanted my father to be with her everywhere, he refused. Even while drawn so inexorably into her orbit that his whole life now revolved around her, he clung to his teaching job, his attic room, and the law studies he excelled in.

Once she invited him to a party at the Pasha's. He did not want to go. It was common knowledge that the Pasha was in love with her and an Arab was an Arab; there was no knowing what poison or knife in the back awaited him there. Salima, however, insisted. She vowed that no harm would befall him and even bought him an elegant grey suit in Uruzdi Beg, along with a light-blue shirt and matching tie. The Pasha's bodyguards bowed low to her when they arrived and ushered the two of them into the huge drawing room, where my father was seated at a table while Salima went to talk to the musicians. Admirers gathered around her and my father poured himself a whisky to feel less awkward. Before he could sip it he caught his breath at the sight of the approaching Pasha.

"Peace be to you, *ya Bek*," said Nuri es-Sa'id.

"And to you, Mr Prime Minister," replied my father, rising from his seat.

"Sit, sit, please," said the Pasha. My father remained standing.

"And what, is your name?" asked the Pasha. My father introduced himself.

"Ah, a cousin from the house of the Imaris!" declared the Pasha in Jewish dialect. "Are you related to Salima too?"

"No," said my father. "I'm only her teacher."

"I didn't know she had anything left to learn," said the Pasha with a mischievous glint.

"I'm helping her polish up her literary Arabic."

"Very interesting," said the Pasha. "Please feel at home." Calling his personal waiter, he whispered something and walked off. My father felt the stares of men known to him from the newspapers and drummed on the chair, trying not to betray his nervousness. The waiter returned with a tray, arranged its contents on the table, and said:

"These dishes are from the Pasha's own kitchen."

They looked superb. But although he had stopped worrying about being poisoned, my father was too tense to eat. Now and then the Pasha glanced at him from his seat near the stage and during the interval Salima came to sit beside him. Everyone stared.

"Why aren't you eating?" she asked. "The Pasha's food is fabulous."

"Can't you see we're being looked at? Who can eat? Besides, I was waiting for you."

"Good," said Salima, patting his hand and attacking the food. A tall general with a chest full of medals strolled over to their table, praised Salima's performance, and asked who her companion was. On hearing the answer he stroked his large moustache and invited them both for a jaunt in his private plane after the party. "I'll give you a good time up in the sky," he said to Salima. "After all, all our nights are dreams because of you."

Salima thanked him profusely but apologized that she was tired and had to rise early in the morning. The general gave Salman a long, disdainful look, bowed, and walked off.

Suddenly my father remembered with a shudder: the man was Muhammed el-Tiyyar, commander of the Iraqi air force and an officer known for his cruelty.

"Watch out for him," said Salima, her gaze wandering after him. He could tell that she was worried.

Back on stage she put on her loveliest smile and launched a comic medley into which she wove the names of many of the guests, her lithe movements holding the audience spellbound and getting them to sing along. Her last number was in honour of the Pasha. The applause was thunderous. A throng of enthusiasts surrounded her when she stepped down from the stage. The Pasha kissed her on both cheeks.

When they left, Muhammed el-Tiyyar was sitting in his limousine by the entrance to the palace. He watched them get into Salima's car and drive off.

They spent three such years together. Salima pampered my father, lent him her car and driver, had a telephone installed in his house, spent lavishly on him, and bought him an even finer Damascan lute than Faisal's, which was smashed by the soldiers on the night of Hizkel's arrest. (Since my mother didn't know its history, he tried to show no emotion over it.) At the end of the third year he accompanied Salima to Lebanon for a quiet holiday in the Land of the Cedars.

When he returned, his Uncle S'hak was waiting for him. So were his father and mother, who had come all the way from Imara. His mother broke down sobbing bitterly. All Imara, she cried, was gossiping. No one wanted to marry his sisters because of his affair. She had even taken to fasting twice a week and making the pilgrimage to the graves of the Prophet Ezekiel and Ezra in the hope of removing the curse.

My father tried explaining that Salima was a good woman

who gave to charity, lit Sabbath candles, fasted on Yom Kippur, and did her best to help her fellow Jews. Uncle S'hak ran about the courtyard like a caged lion until he finally exclaimed: "Is this what I raised you for in my home? I hope they kill you because of her, all those general and bigwigs that the newspapers say run around with her, this one today and that one tomorrow!" My grandfather sat ashen-faced, looking crushed. All he could bring himself to say was:

"When she's had enough of you, she'll leave you."

If they had meant to alarm him, they succeeded; the pressure was too much. He broke off with Salima.

33.

The sandstorms feared by my mother were upon us again. They came suddenly this time, in an apocalyptically hot wind from the desert that drove a red hail before it. It shook the trees wildly, breaking branches, tangling washing-lines, rampaging in blinding, smothering swirls of dust, in a doomsday clash of sand, wind, and fire. In the city that called itself the House of Peace, there was no peace. Frightened inhabitants took refuge in cellars and shelters and remained there for two nights and a day until the wind died down. The whole of the following day Abed was busy sweeping up. We all pitched in, cleaning, mopping, and scrubbing, but there was no end to the sand that hid in every nook and cranny of the house, garden, trees and bushes.

That night there was not a breath of air. Limply I crawled under my white mosquito net on the roof. The moon rose in front of me, wrapped in a hazy caul. I shut my eyes and tried to sleep. The net could not keep out the mosquitos, which were so numerous that they swarmed in through every slight rip in the fabric. It was hopeless trying to ignore their whining and not to scratch their bites. No matter how often I had been told as a child that this only made it worse, I kept sitting up and clawing lustfully at my itchy skin until it bled. Unable to beat back the hateful Lilliputians, I fell asleep from sheer exhaustion in the end, lying insensate until Ismail appeared in a white silk gown and flashed me a radiant smile. We walked hand in hand through a grove of sweet lemon trees and reached the banks of a river where he rowed on the quiet waters. Suddenly we were in rapids. The boat overturned and I thrashed in the water while he struggled to pull me out and shouted: "Get up, Kabi, get up!"

I gave a start and woke to see my father shaking my shoulders.

"What's wrong?"

"We're going to the synagogue."

"Now?"

"Come on, son. Hurry!"

I dressed quickly and went down to the courtyard. My father was standing in the kitchen doorway, the light from the electric bulb glinting on his pomaded hair. Why was he all dressed up so early in the morning and what did it have to do with the synagogue? "What's the rush?" I heard my mother ask. "It's four a.m!"

"I want to be among the first."

"Are you afraid Israel won't last the day?"

"All right, woman. That's enough."

"At least drink something." She put down a tray with glasses of tea.

"Later. Later."

"What about Kabi?"

She seized me and sat me on a stool. My eyes barely open, I burned my tongue on the hot tea while my father looked at me impatiently.

My brother Moshi woke and called for my mother in a frightened voice. She slipped a bag of biscuits into my hand and went back up to the roof. I left the biscuits there in the kitchen and we started down the dark, narrow streets. In the square where Ismail challenged us to belt fights, yellow patches of light from a swaying street lamp flickered on the pavement and the monstrous shadows of djinns danced on the walls. I stuck my hand in my pocket and gripped my knife, ready to fend them off. Unconsciously, I pressed against my father.

"Are you afraid of ghosts?" he asked jokingly, taking my hand like a small boy's.

"Of course not."

"I was too as a child."

"I'm not a child." I let go of his hand as a voice called:

"Halt! Who goes there?"

"Abu Kabi," said my father, halting to be safe.

"What's up?" asked Abu Jassem, the neighbourhood watchman who was always drunk.

"We're on our way to synagogue."

"In the middle of the night?"

"It's for a special prayer," answered my father, placing a coin in Abu Jassem's palm.

"Bless you, Abu Kabi," said Abu Jassem. He walked with us for a while, lighting our path.

"What a dunderhead," said my father when he left us. "If he did his job, there wouldn't be so many thieves around."

"He's probably in thick with them."

"Don't think he isn't."

We reached the main street, where drifts of sand were still visible. A lone car sped by, blinding us with its headlights. There wasn't a carriage in sight. A fresh, pre-dawn breeze made us quicken our stride. Outside the Mas'udah Shemtob Synagogue, which had been chosen as the emigration centre, lit cigarettes glowed like fireflies. My father took out a cigarette too and said:

"Well, we're not the first."

"Too bad." I tried to sound sympathetic.

"That woman! She doesn't let me do anything in time. When I wanted to leave nine years ago, right after the *Farhood*, she didn't let me because she said things would get better. When I wanted to leave two years ago, she didn't let me because there was a war on in Palestine. A year ago she didn't let me because there was a military regime in Iraq. Then I wanted to cross the border into Iran and she wouldn't let me because it was too dangerous." He took a nervous drag of his cigarette. "Have they started taking the applications?" he asked the first man he ran into.

"Not yet. After morning services."

"Then why don't they begin to pray?" he asked curtly, combing the darkness for someone he knew. In the end he remained standing, rolling his worry beads behind his back. Their monotonous click seemed to time the minutes left to our redemption.

"Baba, what is Abu Edouard doing here?"

The bulky silhouette of Edouard's father could be made out in the darkness in a group of waiting men.

We went over to him. "Congratulations," said my father. "So you've become a Zionist at last!"

"God forbid," said Abu Edouard. "I was just curious to see the lunatics who are signing up. Frankly, I don't understand the Moslems either. Because of the Zionists, Jews have been fired, arrested, tortured, hung – and now they're being given a prize for it! What does the government gain in letting them go?"

"What does it gain in making them stay when it can't keep them from crossing the border? It has enough problems with the Sunnis and the Shi'ites and the Communists and the Kurds. Why should it have to worry about the Zionists too?"

"It's probably a trap. Once they have the list of applicants, they can round up all the members of the Movement."

"Then how come you're not afraid to be seen here?" my father taunted.

"Everyone knows what I think," said Abu Edouard. Still, he seemed upset. Without its Jews, the Iraqi paradise would be less paradisical.

"Nuri es-Sa'id may just simply want to get rid of us," said my father, repeating the news dropped by Big Imari as if it were his own thought.

"On the contrary," Abu Edouard countered. "He wants to hold us as hostages."

"Good lord, you *are* talking like a Zionist! I thought this was our home."

"It was, Abu Kabi. You people have ruined it."

I had heard all these arguments a thousand times and was sick of them. Above the horizon the first, groping light began to appear. Minarets slowly pierced the mist and the many necks of the Capital of the Caliphs were bared to the gilded beams of the sun shining through the palm leaves as the city took off its blue tunic of dawn and donned the dazzling robe of day. Streams of Jews poured into the synagogue square, crowding around the entrance to the building, their sense of confidence at being in a crowd mingled with a feeling of fear. Ears half-listened for the tread of spiked army boots. Men talked in hushed tones, their voices dropping even lower at each mention of the name of the country they were bound for.

"Abu Kabi," I heard Abu Edouard say. "Have you thought of how you'll make a living there? What will you and your family do?"

"I'll push a kerosene cart if I have to."

"Why don't you wait a few days longer? What's the rush?"
There was a hint of a plea in his voice. All at once I realized that,
beyond all ideology, Abu Edouard was frightened of losing a
friend.

Perhaps it struck my father too. "You'll come too one day," he
said. "And when we meet in Israel, I'll buy you a drink."

"Fat chance!" Abu Edouard replied. "I'm going back to my
doves. I'll send them to heaven with a special prayer for your
sanity."

Inside the synagogue, the cantor began the morning service.
My father's thoughts were so exclusively on Israel that we had
forgotten to bring our prayer shawls and phylacteries, but no
one seemed to mind, not on a day like this. The congregation's
chant had a different, more poignant tone than usual. The faces
of the worshippers were radiant. The act of prayer dissolved
their tension, restored them to the solid ground of a familiar
reality.

Yet as soon as the service was over, the fear of the unknown
returned. No one knew the answers to all their questions and all
harboured doubts about taking the plunge. Applying for
emigration meant giving up Iraqi citizenship for good. In a
moment, by a single act, seventy generations of life in Iraq
would come to an end.

An awkward silence descended on the synagogue. I looked
at the memorial lamps on the walls with the names of the
dead in gold letters. The bones of my great-grandfather – of his
ancestors, of the multitude of forebears in the great plain of
Babylon – were with us. But what were they saying? To go or to
stay?

Just then Abu Saleh el-Hibaz the baker strode to the front of
the congregation. Like a Samson, he mounted the prayer

podium and read from the Bible he was holding, articulating each word with the same natural dignity that he had shown as a first-year student in Hizkel's night school:

"And the Lord said unto Abram: Get thee out of thy country, and from thy kindred, and from thy father's house unto the land that I will show thee."

Glancing from the book, he read from a note in his hand:

"For the Lord hath chosen Zion; He hath willed it to be His seat."

And he spread his arms and began the old chant:

"My brethren, whence come ye?"

Again there was silence. Then two voices rallied and cried almost together from opposite corners of the synagogue:

"From God's beauteous land!"

A shiver ran through the congregation.

"My brethren, whence come ye?"

This time the whole congregation answered in a mighty voice:

"From God's beauteous land!"

"My brethren, whither go ye?"

"To God's beauteous land!"

"My brethren, what says the Messiah?"

"To God's beauteous land!"

"My brethren, where lies the Redemption?"

"In God's beauteous land!"

His eyes shone. It astonished me how his baritone voice could express such longing for a place he had never seen, plucking the chords of an ancient melody in every heart. It was like a fire racing through dry grass. Everyone had their arms around each other's shoulders and we were all swaying back and forth.

Abu Saleh's young cohorts dispersed through the crowd. At a

signal, one held high his identity card, waited to make sure all had seen it, and marched to the registration table.

"Moshi ben Abraham H'baza is the first!" cried Abu Saleh. "Let him hear our support, you women!" Carried away, he had forgotten that it was a weekday and that the women's gallery was almost empty. Yet as though waiting for just this moment, the handful of women in it broke into a high-pitched ululation.

Abu Saleh was brought a goblet of wine, over which he said the traditional blessing and added: "Blessed art Thou, O Lord our God, King of the Universe, Who hath maintained us, and sustained us, and remained with us to this day."

As though catching a glimpse of the promised land, the men in the synagogue chorused "amen" and formed a snaking line around the podium. More and more of them joined the procession, crowding the aisles and exits, and circling the synagogue in a long column that reminded me of the drawings of the Exodus in the Passover Haggadah.

Abu Saleh put his arms on my father's shoulders. "There's an ember in every Jew," he said, grinning but stirred by his success. "We just have to breathe life into it."

"If only Hizkel could be here to see it," answered my father with moist eyes.

"Today we've lit the kindling. Hizkel will see the bonfire. We'll get him out, I promise you."

"You better get out of here yourself," said my father. "I wouldn't be surprised if there were CID agents around." But Abu Saleh paid no heed and kept circulating through the crowd like a bee pollinating its flowers.

It took the whole morning. The line of applicants moved slowly and the registration turned into tedious paper work. The synagogue was hot, noisy, crowded, full of cigarette smoke. Eyes lost their gleam; the moment no longer seemed sacred. My mouth was dry and the sweat was dripping down me. I wanted to go outside and buy an ice cream, but my father kept me close to him. Apart from the slightly wilted red carnation in his lapel, he looked perfectly fresh. "We'll be done soon, son," he murmured, though it was another hour before we reached the table. We were given forms to fill out and my father was asked for his papers. I saw him hesitate.

It was not the first such case witnessed by the clerk, who merely pointed to several boxes behind him filled with identity cards.

"When can we leave for Israel?" asked my father.

"You'll have to have patience," answered the clerk.

The man behind us was losing his: my father handed in the papers.

It was noon. We parted and he hurried off to his shop, humming the muezzin's call to prayer. *Inna lillah, wa'inna ilayhi raji'un.* "From God we come and to Him we return."

The street vendors had run out of ice cream and cold drinks. A white sun hurled its blinding lances at my eyes. As in a mirage, Ismail danced before them in a long silk gown. "Get out, stranger!" I heard him say. "This isn't your country."

But it was the only country that I knew. I had always felt at home in it. I loved its river, its palm trees, its oleanders lining the roads. I belonged to Taht el-Takya and I wasn't ready to say goodbye to Baghdad. I looked at the little, huddled shops, at the crowded market from which women shoppers were emerging with their arms full, and felt a twinge. In front of Hiyawi's tobacco shop Abu Saleh and Salim Effendi were confronting each other like two fighting cocks. My headmaster reached for some tobacco lying on Hiyawi's work table and filled his pipe with it. "Hey, that's for a hookah," said the old man. Salim Effendi went ahead and lit the pipe, then burst out coughing like a bronchitic.

"I swear, you're like children," laughed Hiyawi, bringing him a jar of cool water. "You don't listen to a word anyone says."

"Sign up for Israel!" Abu Saleh called to those passing in the street. "This is your chance! Do it now, while the registration centre is open!"

"You're leading them to disaster," protested Salim Effendi. "Without their papers they'll be naked, homeless, without rights. They can be harassed, deported, deprived of every bit of property."

"Their home is where I'm sending them," said Abu Saleh.

"What home is that?" taunted the Communist.

"One that even your Stalin has recognized."

"He did it to drive the imperialists out of Palestine. Our home is here. It's where we have our roots, our language, our culture, everything."

"All of which came from the land of Israel," said Abu Saleh. "Go and visit the graves of the victims of the *Farhood* and then tell me that this is our home! O you chosen ones," he cried again, turning back to the street, "your place is in the chosen land! O you Jews, the Messiah is here!"

"What, what?" asked Hiyawi, who had been lost in thought.

"You heard me," said Abu Saleh.

"And the Temple?"

"Zion is our Temple."

"And King David?"

"David Ben-Gurion."

"And the resurrection?"

"Here we are dead. There we will come to life."

"Then where's my wife?" cried Hiyawi. He snapped out of his reverie and went limp with despair. "It's not even the Messiah's donkey!"

"Oh, the Messiah's here all right," laughed Salim Effendi. "He's alive in the Soviet Union. And Hitler was a turd from God's rear."

"You infidel!" cried Hiyawi. "Cover your head with ashes! How dare you talk like that about the Holy One of Israel?"

"It says so in the Bible," chortled Salim Effendi. "'And thou shalt see my rear and not my face.' Those are God's very words to Moses."

"You should wash your mouth out and fast," declared Hiyawi in alarm, reaching for his Book of Psalms.

"Have you registered?" Abu Saleh asked the passing Abu Edouard, detaining him with his protruding belly.

"Let me go," grumbled Abu Edouard. Seeing Salim Effendi he grabbed the Communist's lapel and said:

"Stay away from my son! You're poisoning his mind."

The stain left on his light suit by Abu Edouard's grimy fingers made Salim Effendi grimace. "Edouard is a big boy," he said with a patronizing look at the dove flyer.

"Leave him alone or I'll report you to the CID. I swear I will," snapped Abu Edouard.

"For shame," exclaimed Hiyawi. "It's a sin to inform on a Jew to the police, even if he is an evil-doer. 'And the informers shall have no hope' – it says so in our prayers."

"Right you are," said Abu Saleh, wagging a friendly finger at Abu Edouard.

"I don't need to be defended by Zionists," said Salim Effendi.

"Don't be so sure. One day you might. I only wish I could

quote Scripture like you," teased Abu Saleh wistfully. "What a waste you are! In Israel you could put all that knowledge to use."

Salim Effendi gave Abu Saleh an odd look, as if the same thought had crossed his mind.

34.

Applying for emigration steadied my father's spirits. He had passed the point of no return and now went ahead with the necessary procedures, such as paying his municipal tax debts and obtaining a certificate of good conduct from the police. He bought fabric for Chiflawi the tailor to make him some fancy suits and even purchased a steamer trunk. One day I found him at the desk in his shop, surrounded by books and journals and making notes in a thick ledger in a tiny, dense script.

"What are you doing?" I asked.

He shut the notebook and showed me the single word written on its cover.

"Rice?"

"If I'm going to be Israel's biggest rice grower, I have to bone up on it," he said with a wink, sweeping his arm over the books and journals. They were all, I now saw, about rice and agriculture.

"I'm going to be a farmer."

"You?"

"Yes. Like all the Imaris."

A farmer? This pampered, pressed-and-ironed, tied-and-suited, perfumed-and-hair-oiled, red-carnationed man? Although he had told me about playing as a boy in the rice fields of Imara, childhood games were one thing and farming was another. I tried to picture him looking like the pioneers in the literature of the Movement: sturdy, sun-bronzed, determined young men with high boots, shorts, and hoes on their shoulders, ploughing, sowing, and spreading manure. It was too much for even my fertile imagination.

"I'll grow rice as far as the eye can see," said my father. And as though waking from a dream, he added: "But don't tell anyone, son. I want it to be a surprise. For your mother. For Big Imari. For everyone."

On top of everything, I had a father who suffered from hallucinations!

Actually, he would have been a happy man if not for the long shadow of Hizkel's imprisonment, which gave him no peace. Each day he waited to hear from Big Imari, and once he even boldly sent him a letter requesting permission to tell my mother and Rashel of their meeting. The way the two women treated him, as if accusing him of putting his pride before his brother's life, had become a daily humiliation. Rashel no longer trusted him and rarely talked to him, preferring to deal with her Moslem lawyer. He slept badly and had nightmares. Once his tearful mother appeared to him in a dream and begged him to keep the promise he had made at her deathbed to look after his little brother and pray for him at the grave of the Prophet Ezekiel.

On such nights my father would get out of bed, descend to the dark courtyard, and pace endlessly up and down, chain-smoking until dawn. The straw he clutched at was a remark made by Karim Abd el-Hak that Hizkel would be freed once the Jews could leave Iraq, since no government would imprison Zionists while letting Jews go to Israel. The Pasha, Rashel's lawyer had said, would be glad to get rid of subversive elements.

But the Land of the Two Rivers, my father had learned by now, was not ruled by logic. He was a bundle of tormented

347

expectations, his body in Iraq and his mind in Israel. He no longer had the patience for fixing and selling watches, which he left to Abed, and he would have sold his shop and everything that he owned if not for my mother.

The days came and went and the planes did not arrive from Israel. Hizkel was still in prison and my mother complained all the time. How could my father have let us become stateless? Her carping annoyed him but did not shake his faith. For two thousand years Jews had said, "Next Year in Jerusalem". Did she really expect him to remain in Iraq now that the Messiah's footsteps could be heard? If the flow of applicants for emigration had slowed to a trickle, this was only because Iraq's Jews were like slaves who didn't want to be freed or to comprehend the immensity of the occasion. A new Moses was needed to lead them out, even against their will. Hizkel had been the first to understand that. His favourite words from the Prophets, which he had liked to quote to his comrades in the Movement, were the ones from Ezekiel that went: "As I live, saith the Lord God, I will bring you out from the peoples and gather you out of the countries where you are scattered, with a mighty hand and an outstretched arm, and with wrath poured out."

For the smell of my mother is upon him, sighed my father. If only Hizkel were free, his faith and eloquence might have carried the Jews with him, breathing life into their dry bones. And he also might have lit a fire under whoever in Israel was taking his own sweet time to send the planes!

Each day ran its course of disappointed hopes, by the end of which, exhausted by his anxieties, my father rambled through the neighbourhood, stopping off at Hiyawi's, at Abu Saleh's, and at Abu Ednan's, where he rushed through his old ritual of downing a glass of arrack and taking a few puffs from a hookah before dashing off again without even a quick backgammon game with Abu Edouard. His grim lips when he returned home told us there was no news.

Deep down my mother still hoped that it was all just a passing aberration and that the emigration law would be repealed, our citizenship would be restored, and all would go back to normal as it was after the *Farhood*. She tried to stay calm and, to make up for it when she didn't, she served my father his favourite dishes, which he did no more than nibble at politely.

It was when he stopped eating her saffron rice with fried almonds and raisins that she really began to worry. He had always ceremoniously liked to scoop the rice from its bowl with his fingers, arranging it in balls around the rim of his plate like the numbers on a clock and thumbing them one by one into his mouth while grinning at my attempts to imitate him, as each of my riceballs crumbled against my teeth. Now even this dish ceased giving him pleasure.

"Don't worry so much," my mother would try soothing him after first driving him to distraction. "Everyone's in the same boat."

"Who's worrying?" he would answer so irritably that a new argument became unavoidable.

"You've been taken for a ride again, just like you were by Big Imari. The planes will never come. And if they do, the Moslems won't let you on them."

"Then we'll cross the border illegally. I won't be stopped."

"I'm pregnant. Do you want to risk my life and the baby's?"

"Thousands of Jews have done it safely." My father frowned, thinking of Abu Saleh's warning.

A few days later the police resumed their nightly raids. The scream of sirens kept us awake and full of fear. My father's explanation was that, defeated by the Jews on the battlefield, the Arabs felt the need to get back at them; the greater their humiliation, the greater their thirst for revenge. Hiyawi and Salim Effendi were mistaken if they thought that Iraqis distinguished between Zionists and other Jews; not even the most assimilated Jews, not even those who passed for Moslems, would be spared. A Jew was a Jew – which was to say, a traitor – and would be reckoned with as such. Add to this Iraq's ineptness at stopping the illegal flow across its borders organized by the Movement and it was easy to understand the mass arrests.

Baghdad's Jews now lived with a sense of danger. The fear of a new *Farhood* hung over them. Many moved to Taht el-Takya from mixed neighbourhoods, sending prices in the already overcrowded Jewish quarter skyrocketing. Every last room, each empty courtyard, was snatched by Jews retreating into their stockade. Yet though they felt safer there, there was no way to keep out the police. And there was no sign of the aeroplanes from Israel.

One night the police came for my father.

"Isn't his brother enough for you? Why must you take him too?" screamed my mother, clawing at her face. "Have you no mercy in your hearts?" Although the sergeant tried calming us by explaining that my father was simply being taken for an interrogation, no one believed him.

My father kept silent. Precisely because he had always feared this moment, I had the feeling he was relieved. The nightmares and hopes were behind him. He took the bundle that he had prepared for such an occasion from its hiding place and walked to the waiting jeep. By the front gate, he whispered to me:

"Take good care of them, son. You're the only man left."

My mother wailed as though at a funeral and tried running after the jeep but cursing, spitting, and stamping, she was dragged away from it. Rashel gripped her shoulder and pulled her back inside the house, where she gave her some sugar water and sat with her on the floor. They talked, cried, fell silent, cried again, and ended by staring blankly into space and rocking back and forth as if anaesthetized by the motion. I myself was scared to death, so paralyzed by fright that I could barely talk or even breathe. Suppose my father was not released or was banished to some far place? Who would support us, tell us what to do, keep us going? I had felt sorry for Hizkel, but this was something else, this was my own life. As often as I had imagined myself in such a situation, now that I was, the burden felt too great for my thin shoulders. Every hour that passed without my father felt like an eternity. For the first time in my life he was not someone to be taken for granted.

At least there was Abu Saleh. My father had told me on the night of Hizkel's arrest that I could always go to him in an emergency, and the thought of this eased my tension enough for me to slip into a merciful sleep. In fact, I slept well, perhaps to get away from it all, and was awakened by my mother's glad cries. It was light out. I jumped out of bed and found my parents embracing while Rashel stood sobbing by their side.

"You're free!" I shouted.

"Yes, son," said my father, hugging me. I had a happy lump in my throat.

"You're next, my sister," my mother assured Rashel, hurrying to put an arm around her and walk her back to her house, where she clearly preferred to be.

My father refused to answer any of my questions about his

arrest, saying only that he was asked about Hizkel. "They tried to get me to incriminate him," he told me. "He's facing very serious charges."

After he had eaten and drunk, he said to me: "Kabi, come with me to the bathhouse. I feel dirty and full of lice."

"Now? At this hour of the morning?"

"Yes, boy, I need to wash last night off me."

I could see that he was in high spirits. The neighbours, who had passed the news of his arrest from roof to roof, stepped up to shake his hand. But though he clearly took satisfaction in his new status as a man who had escaped from the lion's jaws, he still clung to his mysterious reserve.

The rusty hinges of the heavy gate of the bathhouse creaked harshly when I gave the gate a push. A drowsing attendant roused himself from a bench by the entrance.

"God bless your morning," he greeted us, adjusting his makeshift loincloth.

"And God bless yours with light," we answered him.

We undressed and entered the labyrinth of vaults and niches.

Stepping into one of the first stalls, I turned on the shower and let the hot water run in a powerful jet that cloaked us in a fog of hot vapour. My father dipped the sponge into a deep bowl of green watermelon soap, lathered himself until he was a single bubbly mass, and rinsed the foam off. It was beyond me how he could stand such hot water. Even after his skin had turned the colour of raw meat and beads of sweat formed on the hairs of his chest, he went on imbibing the sultry, suffocating air. Then, grunting with pleasure, he wrapped himself in a large towel. Red-cheeked, gleaming, his smooth black hair pulled back beneath a black net, he was an impressively handsome man. He had always told me that I would look like him when I grew up, just as he looked like my great-grandfather, but standing next to him, short, thin, and pimply, I could see no signs of this.

A stout, powerful masseur entered our stall, spread a white towel on its marble bench, made my father lie on his stomach, and began kneading the muscles of his neck, shoulders, back, and hips with stubby fingers and slow, circular movements. My father groaned loudly in acknowledgement; when a man took such trouble with your body, anything less would be ungrateful. His groans turned to brief sighs as the half-painful, half-pleasurable massage yielded to a drowsy feeling of pure delight. After a while, he turned over on his back and covered his genitals with a red towel. Soon he was fast asleep, happily exhausted from the bathhouse, the jailhouse, or both.

Meanwhile, the stalls were filling with Arabs. Dirty water gurgled down the open gutters, carrying tufts of hair matted with the white cream they used to shave their pubic hair. There was a terrible din. I looked at my private parts and decided that I liked their black triangle of hair, which seemed very masculine. In fact, I could have wished for more of it. Why would anyone want to shave it? Perhaps they thought a hairless member stood out more. My father shaved there too. Why?

The vapours and heat were too much for me and I decided to go out for some air. "Excuse me, please," I said to some men blocking my way, forgetting to speak in a Moslem dialect. They closed ranks tightly around me, laughing and grinning at each other.

"Are you here by yourself, my little sparrow?" someone asked. I saw the lust in their eyes and stood riveted to the spot, even though I knew that unless I overcame my shame and screamed at the top of my voice they would have me bottom-up and buggered in no time. All my life I had heard stories about such things.

A slim man yanked the towel from my thighs, grabbed my balls, thrust his erect penis at my rear, and began to shuttle back and forth. I jabbed him with both elbows and spun around. As I freed myself, he almost tore my testicles loose.

"Where's your sense of fun, Jewboy?" someone said to a roar of laughter.

I retreated to our stall, naked and without my towel. My father was sleeping soundly. I felt numb. I slumped to the floor, half-crawled to the soap bowl, turned on the tap, and soaped and rinsed myself many times, shivering despite the hot water. Then I wrapped myself in a towel and huddled on the stone bench in a corner, trying to forget the nightmarish memory of the stiff member pressing against me.

I couldn't stop shaking. Tears of fury and humiliation in my eyes, I sobbed quietly so as not to wake my father. I felt that I hated him, perhaps because I knew that I couldn't tell him what had happened, just as I couldn't call to him for help. What could he have done? There had been seven or eight of them, and many more nearby. They could have killed him or at the very least taunted him, and something had told me not to put him to the test. Perhaps I hadn't wanted to discover that he was scared or unwilling to fight against the odds. The less he knew, the better, especially after the night he had been through. This was no time for him to get in trouble with the Law.

The thought of that made me feel a bit better. I rose and went to wash my face.

My father woke and got slowly to his feet. "Your eyes are bloodshot," he said.

"I have soap in them."

We dressed. The lobby of the bathhouse was striped with bright patches of light that fell through the arched, stained glass windows. My father sat on a high chair and beckoned to a shoeshine man, who hurried over with his box. While he worked, another man brought us tea with cardamom. My father put down his empty glass on the brass tray, where it was quickly filled again.

"Don't you want any tea, son?"

"No," I said.

He opened his leather case, offered both men a cigarette, and tipped them. They blessed him with deep bows. As always, he left the bathhouse slowly to adjust to the changing temperature of the air. On the street, he took out his pocket watch which hung by a gold fob attached to a buttonhole of his waistcoat, fingered its lid, released it by pressing a spring, and studied the time.

"Baba, when will we leave this place?"

"Soon," he said. "*Inshallah*, soon."

35.

Despite his bounce on the morning after his arrest, my father returned to his watch shop the next day in low spirits. Even his walk had changed. He seemed to study the ground before each step, looking to the side and over his shoulders to see if he was being followed. The man bit by a snake, says the Arab proverb, fears even the rope. Though he wouldn't talk about his interrogation or the circumstances of his release, he seemed anxious to keep his distance from the Movement. This was also the advice of Abu Saleh, who saw a warning to himself in my father's arrest and suspected that he might be picked up by the CID at any minute. Going right back to work, my father thought, might be taken by the secret service as a sign of turning over a new leaf. He got rid of his rice notebook in which the word "Israel" appeared many times, and tried rebuilding his languishing business, which – having agreed to Abed's leaving illegally for Israel – he would soon have to run by himself. One evening, as he sat relaxing over a glass of tea with fresh basil, he remarked casually to my mother:

"I know someone who would like to rent a room in our house. Lots of Jews have been moving into the neighbourhood to get away from the Moslems."

"That's all I need," snapped my mother. "A lodger."

"I was only asking," he said, cowed.

It was bad enough from my mother's point of view that the

houses of Taht el-Takya stood on top of each other, their roofs looking down on one another's courtyards. She had no privacy as it was. Weren't the children all the witnesses she needed to her unhappiness and quarrels with her husband? Especially since Hizkel's imprisonment, nothing stayed within the four walls of the family.

Once more she felt a pang for her little house in el-Me'azzam, with its Moslem neighbours who asked no questions and stuck, unlike the Jews, to their own business.

My father had loved that house too. It had had something of the seclusion of Imara, which was why my mother failed to fathom at first why he wanted to take in lodgers. It was only when she got the unsuspecting Abed to reveal how poorly the business was doing that she understood that his motives were not selfless. "There's no butter for the man who doesn't milk his cow," she quoted the proverb, urging him to devote more time to his work. She also dismissed our Kurdish laundress and spent every Wednesday, which was wash day, kneeling by heaps of dirty clothing in the courtyard while the kerosene stove sputtered loudly beside her. On Thursdays she filled the iron with hot coals and stood over the ironing board for hours in the hot sun. When my father noticed that the laundress was gone, he asked angrily:

"What makes you think I can't afford her?"

"That's my business," said my mother.

"Um Kabi," he told her, "you're carrying a child. You have to take better care."

But she refused to rehire the laundress. They quarrelled all afternoon until I had had enough and told my father that the five o'clock Arabic news from Israel would soon be on. He stopped arguing in mid-sentence and went up to his room, where he looked at the white grandfather clock smashed by the soldiers on the night of Hizkel's arrest, muttered, "It's time I fixed that," (I had begun to think that he was superstitiously leaving it broken), straightened my great-grandfather's portrait on the wall, and leafed impatiently through a pile of newspapers from Egypt, Syria, and Lebanon before telling me to give them to Abu Saleh. Then he switched on the radio and searched for the station while prodding me to go up to the roof.

"The news will be on in a few minutes," he said.

Listening to the Voice of Israel was illegal. But although my mother kept warning him against it, especially after his arrest, my father stubbornly bought a new Zenith, put up a big aerial, and told anyone who asked that he wanted better reception for the heavenly Um Kultoum, "the voice of the Arab heart", whose all-night programme on the first Friday of each month was loved by everyone. He even invited Abu Edouard, Abu Saleh, and old Hiyawi, who listened while drinking arrack and eating my mother's cooking, blissfully forgetful of their worries until the dawn.

Now, however, the Zenith sounded the theme from "Samson and Delilah", which was my signal to lock the room, warn my mother against opening the front gate, and run to my lookout post on the roof. I remained there for half an hour until the news and commentaries were over and then tapped a code on the roof door and came back down. By then – as if needing his daily ration of hate to keep him going – my father had switched to Damascus and was glued to its military marches and hysterical announcers screaming for the Zionist bandit state to be thrown into the sea. I loathed and feared these broadcasts, which seemed so overpowering that, if I were an Arab, I would run out and start slitting Jewish throats. They made me want to slit a few throats myself until, recalling Miss Sylvia's remarks about mob psychology, I took a deep breath and calmed down.

Although my father claimed that these broadcasts did not affect him, I could see him turn crimson before switching off the radio and taking a sip of my mother's strong tea. Afterwards he would pace thoughtfully in the courtyard, his eyes on the ground and his fingers ticking off the worry beads behind his back.

"Abu Kabi, what did they say on the news today?" my mother would ask.

"Nothing new," he would answer, afraid she might give him away by telling the neighbours something she shouldn't know.

"Still?" she would persist.

"Nothing. That's exactly what worries me." And as though changing the subject, he might add: "There's a steady stream of Palestinians entering Iraq. It looks like the Pasha is serious about a population transfer. But meanwhile the planes aren't coming and we're stuck here." He stopped his pacing. "Kabi, boy, go and see if there's any news at the registration centre."

I dawdled a bit. I liked this hour, which was a break in the day's routine. My mother used it to tell my father the latest neighbourhood gossip – who wanted to marry whom, who had given birth to what, who had sent whom regards – and to extract from him items that she relayed to her friends in the synagogue while swearing them to secrecy. Over a piece of pastry he listened to her, preoccupied, and then went off to tell his cronies the news, which they too passed on until all of Taht el-Takya knew what our Zenith had said. Before long the arguments in the cafés resulted in a thousand different interpretations.

There was nothing new at the registration centre, no lists of

359

passengers or planes for the disappointed group of men who came every day in the hope of hearing good tidings. Although not a single Jew had left for Israel legally, the emigration was already felt in our neighbourhood. Strange Arabs had begun appearing, staring like vultures into houses and courtyards and studying terraces and balconies. According to Hiyawi, they spoke the Arabic of the Palestinians. "They've lost their homes," he said, "and we're the ones who will pay for it. The next refugees will be us."

Indeed, coming home one day I found two of the strangers standing in our courtyard. I circled them and blocked the entrance to the house.

"We're looking to buy," they said in a strange singsong speech, grinning at each other as if dividing up the loot.

"We're not selling," my mother called down from the top balcony.

"Aren't you leaving?"

"No." She spoke quietly, with the special smile she reserved for Arabs. Yet when they were gone she said with a frightening certainty that our house would soon be lived in by strangers who would expunge every trace of our existence.

It would be Ismail's dream come true.

I felt a need to go for a walk like those I had taken with Rashel in the first weeks after Hizkel's imprisonment. When I knocked on her door, though, she wasn't in, so I set out by myself and wandered past the fancy villas of New Baghdad and down the paths of el-Sa'adun Park. Before I knew it, I was in front of my school. Kassem, the one-eyed watchman, peered out surprised from his hut when I told him that I had left something in class.

The schoolyard was deserted. So were the corridors and classrooms, over which hung a deep silence. I entered my classroom, stood on the teacher's platform, and peered down at the desks and my own empty chair, wondering what I must look like from up there.

On the bulletin board outside the locked library was posted my second issue of the newspaper. Nicely coloured and illustrated, it featured my essay on patriotism as its lead. For the hundredth time I stopped to read what I had written. It seemed so lifeless and remote. What a joke if it should win the prize!

Pictures of the school's graduating classes were hanging on the wall by the headmaster's office. I knew that I would never be in one of them. I descended the stairs, stroking the shiny wooden banister that I had shinned down so many times, and roamed the empty schoolyard, already feeling nostalgic. On my way out, old Kassem said to me: "It won't be the same without you." The words stayed with me for a long time.

36.

I opened my eyes and shut them again against the blinding
light, but the hot, orange sun still beat its way past my eyelids.
The Capital of the Caliphs was like a furnace in summer and
sleeping on the roof was unpleasant after sunrise.

I glanced at my watch. I had already missed school. Having no
reason to hurry, I pulled the white sheet over my head and tried
plunging back into sleep and my wet dream of Rashel. In it she
had been mine, all mine.

From the yard came the pounding of a pestle. That meant it
was Thursday and my mother was mashing rice for Friday's
okra *kubba* despite my father's attempts to convince her that
ground, store-bought rice was just as good. The sheet kept out
neither the light nor the noise. It was hopeless. I got up.

With half-shut eyes I groped my way to the slices of cold
watermelon that awaited me every morning on a tray on the
balustrade and stuffed a sliver into my mouth. The sun had
melted its sweet crust and taken the chill out of it. I put my head
beneath the tap but when I turned it on nothing came out. What
a place Baghdad was. A person might think the Tigris had run dry.

Leaning on the balustrade, I watched Abu Edouard's doves
float like little clouds in the blue canopy of the sky. Then I
folded my sheets, careful to hide the telltale stains, gathered the
rest of the bedclothes, my chore ever since I could remember,
and carried them downstairs to the white pile in the yard.

"Kabi, is that you?" asked my mother, stopping her pounding. "May the Evil Eye forget you as I forgot you were on the roof!" She rose from her squatting position, straightened her back, smoothed out her dress, went to the kitchen, and returned with a porcelain kettle on a tray. Wiping the drops from its cracked spout with a dishcloth, she exclaimed: "Damn it! Not even the tinkers come to Taht el-Takya any more."

"Everyone's leaving. Who mends things?"

"Go and wash your face. There's water in the jar. They can all go to hell, them and their damn stoppages!"

I sat beside her on a stool and drank a glass of sweet, strong tea to which I added some homemade fig jam. When I had finished I took the steps to my attic room two at a time and dressed quickly because of the terrible heat there.

"Where are you off to?" asked my mother. "Stay with me for a while."

"I have things to do."

"Just like your father! You Imaris all have ants in your pants. Buy me a reel of white thread."

"All right, mama."

"And of black."

"All right, mama."

"And button your shirt."

"All right, mama. Just give me twenty fils."

"You'll only waste them." She gave me ten.

The street was full of the Moslem traders who swarmed through the neighbourhood looking for bargains. You could rank them by their appearance. The leaders had slick hair and dark suits and ties with white handkerchiefs in their jacket pockets. In the market for houses, Persian rugs, antiques, jewelry, and other valuables, they walked with calm dignity and carried amber worry beads on which they did sums and counted the praises of Allah. At a respectful distance behind them came the pack, dealers looking for cupboards, tables, chests, and old beds, while the rear was brought up by the scavengers, small fry who were the first to arrive, sniffing shyly in the morning, and who returned at nightfall to carry away what was left – old beds, patched clothes, chairs and stools, kitchenware, and other unwanted things.

Common to them all was the desire to buy us out and I hated them, although I had no choice but to walk among them, overhear their conversations, and direct them through the narrow streets. As though driven by a passion to see how we Jews lived, there was nothing they didn't want to peer at or into. No one liked them; no one welcomed them or invited them in. Some people, worried about CID agents, locked their gates when they saw them coming. The women kept chastely away from them. Only the children gaped.

And yet though no one wanted to part with his house or his belongings, many Jews had been laid off work and were in desperate need of money. These were the ones who were now selling off their household goods, though none of them was sure that the planes would ever come. Reluctantly they opened their doors to the dealers, served them coffee, bargained with them, and shook hands on the exchange of their life's possessions for a few dinars.

At this point came the turn of the Kurdish removal men, quiet, muscular and with bare, powerful feet and felt caps on their shaven heads. Shifting beneath their loads, they slowly planted their widely spread legs like heavyweight wrestlers, the soles of their feet, which looked small in the air, splaying out like a camel's on the ground. On their backs were large pads on which they carried the bulky pieces of furniture that seemed about to crush them at any moment. Although I didn't understand their language, something about them intrigued me and I followed their comings and goings. I envied their strength. If we Jews had had anything like it, Ismail and his gang would never have dared invade our neighbourhood.

Actually, Ismail had stopped coming to Taht el-Takya. Perhaps he was busy with his Palestine volunteers. According to Amira, he was active in a secret society that dreamed of overthrowing the monarchy and establishing an Iraqi republic.

Other Moslem boys who made a habit of picking on Jews and strangers now turned up in our neck of the woods and challenged the Kurds as well. "*Kurdi raso be'tizo,*" they taunted them. "A Kurd's brains are in his bottom." It grieved me that the Kurds were so used to such slurs that they never answered back. With fists and muscles like theirs, I would have cracked the skull of the first Moslem to get smart with me, but they put up with it in silence, ordered by their leader, Mullah Mustafa Baban, to turn the other cheek and keep working.

Baban, who was built like a brick wall, could hoist a walk-in wardrobe on his back and carry it by two straps, one in his hand and the other around his head. Although even a giant like him looked small beneath it, he could walk unassisted through the souk and all the way to the waiting trucks and wagons on Razi Street with no more sign of effort than the sweat on his forehead.

The other removal men were nearly as strong. My mother and some of the local women felt sorry for them and gave them hot tea, cold water, and even old clothes and household items.

At noon, when the sun was overhead, Mullah Mustafa Baban would call a lunch break and lead his men to a corner of the souk.

There he stripped off his pads and cap, wiped away the sweat, stuck the spout of a large jug in his mouth, filled his belly with cold water, and strode to the Kurdish food stand where a huge vat of sheep's head stew was bubbling. Lifting the lid, he stuck his head into the steamy vapours, blissfully inhaled the incense of garlic and saffron, and boomed, "In the name of Allah the Merciful and Compassionate," the Moslem blessing over food.

At a satisfied nod from him the cook set to work, first dipping a ladle into the vat and fishing out bits of head, tongue, ears, whole onions, and garlic cloves, and then dousing them with the reddish-yellow broth. Mullah Mustafa reached for a pitta bread, tore it in half, dipped it in his bowl, slurped up the gravy, and sank his teeth into the meat. A yellow layer of fat clung to his moustache, which he licked clean at the end of his meal and twirled back into shape. He then burped loudly, exclaimed "All praise and thanks to Allah the All-Powerful" in a thick Kurdish accent, stretched out on the ground, scratched his private parts lustily, laid his head on his cap, folded his arms on his chest, and dozed off briefly, awakening abruptly to jump to his feet and order his men back to work.

After a long, hard day, the Kurds trooped off to the Moslem market of Souk el-Sharja, by now emptied of its vendors and customers, and pitched camp in the flour sellers' lane. They gathered wood from broken crates, made a bonfire, boiled water in old, empty sugar tins, and brewed tea black as midnight, after which they sprawled around the hot fire, rolled and lit cigarettes of cheap, smelly tobacco, scratched themselves like their leader, and went to sleep. Once, when Mullah Mustafa, who recognized me as the boy who brought his workers tea and water in Taht el-Takya, saw me staring, he invited me with a grand gesture to join them.

I couldn't refuse. After the tea the men broke into sad songs, which were full of yearning and muted suffering. By the fire I couldn't tell if their eyes were gleaming with tears or with the flame of the rebellion then raging in the mountains of the north. Perhaps what moved me most was being reminded of the Armenian's song in prison. Mullah Mustafa, who must have seen my emotion, put his huge hand on my shoulder and said: "We've been through as much as you Jews. But you're luckier than we are, because you have a country and we have nothing."

I knew that for the past several years the army had been battling Kurdish guerrillas, who lured the soldiers into their high, cold mountain strongholds and mauled them there. Sometimes, after our Sabbath strolls in el-Sa'adun Park, my father and I walked a bit further to a nearby army camp, where we saw trucks full of soldiers heading for the front. Once we saw black-draped coffins being unloaded. They must have made my father think of the Iraqi volunteers in Palestine, because he said: "Son, every people that fought the Jews perished in the end."

I felt a kinship with the burly Kurds and imagined them longing for their families in their faraway villages. They were an itinerant crew, Mullah Mustafa told me, sometimes working as porters and sometimes cleaning latrines and sewers, sweeping streets, washing dishes, and doing other poorly-paid work that "Jews and even Arabs would never touch". Once he had saved up some money, Mullah Mustafa said, he would return to the mountains. I felt sure that he would join the guerrilla forces of his legendary namesake Mullah Mustafa Barazani, the very mention of whose name struck fear into the hearts of Iraqi soldiers.

When the last song was sung, his men stretched out on their burlap bags and fell asleep. In the morning they would return to Taht el-Takya to continue carrying away Baghdad's ancient Jewish quarter on behalf of their Arab masters.

One day my father was shown a copy of the newspaper *El-Husun*, in which there was an appeal to Moslems not to buy second-hand Jewish goods and to boycott anyone who did. "When you buy from Jews," said the advertisement, "you undersell Arabs and sabotage the economy." That evening he told my mother that it was time to start selling up. She did not want to hear of it. "I'd rather lock up the house with everything in it," she said.

She had not yet come to terms with leaving, a fate that had seemed avoidable as long as the house was still hers. Why ease the Arabs' conscience by selling them her life's labours for a pittance?

Hiyawi, worriedly watching the Kurds, agreed. "Maybe the government will change its mind and this stupid emigration law will be repealed," he said. Deep down, though, he didn't believe it. "Master of the Universe," he complained, "why have You done this to us? First You made us leave Your holy land as refugees and now You're making us return the same way!"

He mourned for the Jewish quarter, which he could no more save than he could cure the Jews of the madness that had possessed them. "Allah has addled their brains," he muttered. "Since when does a man sell his house or a woman her gold jewelry? Lord, what have You done to Your flock?" Seizing his walking stick, he went off to guard the dead in the cemetery. "They at least will wait for the True Redemption."

37.

Abu Saleh emptied his oven of the last of its pittas, wrapped them still steaming in an old sheet, and sent them with his assistant Sami to the kebab vendor. Lighting a cigarette with floury fingers, he surveyed the passers-by in the souk. For all his renowned physical prowess, he was a cautious man who chose his associates with care, operated under a mantle of secrecy, and never said an unnecessary word about the Movement to anyone. And yet at the same time, he made no bones about being a neighbourhood leader who encouraged Jews to register for emigration. It was as if he were saying to the authorities: "You can see that I don't hide my beliefs, but that's the most that you can accuse me of."

His sense of timing was superb. "He has the instincts of an animal," Hizkel, who relied on him in all things, once said to me. Ever since my uncle's arrest, and especially since my visits to the prison, Abu Saleh had stopped asking me to run the little errands I once performed for him – and so, when told by my father that the baker wished to see me, I assumed it involved another mission to Hizkel and felt the not unpleasant mixture of pride and fear that such an adventure aroused in me.

I waited for Abu Saleh to finish his work. "Take a walk around the block and let me know if you see the police or anyone suspicious," he said when he finally had time for me.

The souk was emptying after a busy day. Shops and stands

were being shut down and scavengers picked at piles of rotting garbage, looking for edible fruit and vegetables. From the fisherman's lane came a suspicious, tapping sound. I hurried to have a look.

A beggar came up the lane on wooden crutches. With astounding rapidity, as if afraid to be caught, he went from stand to stand going through the refuse. Several fish heads swarming with flies stuck out of his tattered straw basket. When he saw me he headed straight towards me, backing me so tightly into a corner that I could feel his breath on my face. His matted hair was dishevelled and his muddy eyes menacing. Slowly he swivelled his wrist until the palm faced up, his dirtily bandaged thumb almost touching my chest. He didn't plead, or whine about his children, as beggars did. He didn't say anything. He just held out his hand.

I took out a coin and dropped it into his palm without touching it. Not even bothering to thank me, he turned and disappeared. I finished my circuit and fled the fish stalls and butcher shops with their odour of death for the life-restoring smell of the bakery.

A fresh batch of fragrant barley pittas was resting on a bamboo tray. I took one and ate it ravenously, its taste like nothing on earth. What an artist Abu Saleh was! He turned off his ovens with an amused look and stood listening with me to the sudden silence, then locked up without a word and nodded to me to follow him. We crossed the back yard, passed through a doorway and a room furnished with a bed and a stool, and came out into a lumber yard. Abu Saleh tugged at a shelf. As if he had said "Open Sesame", a second door opened and we were on a staircase descending to a large cellar.

There was a smell of charred wood in the air. The cellar was dark at its near end and lit at its far one, where a cardboard man was standing with a keffiyeh. A bull's-eye was drawn on his chest, its centre marked by a cross. A young man I didn't know aimed a pistol at it and fired. The report was so loud that it made me jump. It was my first firing range.

"Can't it be heard in the street?" I whispered to Abu Saleh.

"Don't you worry," he said.

The young man fired again and laid the pistol on a table. "I hope there won't be another *Farhood*," Abu Saleh said to me, "but we have to be ready for one. The Moslems are on the warpath. We need to train every youngster who can be trusted." He turned to the marksman and said: "This is Kabi Salman Imari, Hizkel's nephew. Go over the specifications and parts with him, teach him the assembly, loading, firing, and unjamming procedures, put him through some target practice, and show him how to clean and grease the gun. I'll be back in two-and-a-half hours." He left and locked the door behind him.

The young man, whose name I never learned, checked the pistol and put it on a shelf. "You'll clean it when we're finished," he said to me. Taking another gun, he examined it, cocked it, laid it on the table in front of me, and said: "This is a nine millimetre German Parabellum." My pride knew no bounds.

38.

For four days Baghdad sweltered in a desert heat wave that hung over it like a yellow cloud, emptying the streets and driving the river bathers to their cool cellars. Not even the old folk could remember such weather. Like a tyrannical dragon, it stalked the city breathing fire.

And it was then, in the midst of this juggernaut, that the Jewish quarter declared itself. Family by family, the Jews poured onto the streets as if possessed. My father emerged, too, in an elegant white suit and blue tie, a wilted red flower in his lapel. Taking me with him, he hurried to the synagogue. He ran as if fleeing the rioters of the *Farhood,* and though he was not carrying a sack of groceries this time, the ten years that had elapsed – which, needless to say, saw a self-respecting Iraqi like him engage in as little physical activity as possible – had shortened his breath. He was so red and perspiring that I begged him to slow down, but like a stubborn boy he pushed himself on.

From the synagogue came the blast of a ram's horn and joyous singing:

> God of Elijah, God of Elijah,
> For the sake of Elijah
> Bring Thy Messiah!

It was hard to believe. After all the false, contradictory rumours and disappointed hopes, this invincible song! Eyes aglow, my father covered me with embarrassing kisses as if I were a small child.

"We're going, son, we're going, the planes are on their way!" he said, hugging and kissing everyone he met. As on the first day of registration, hundreds of people crowded into the synagogue and many more stood outside it. Bottles of wine appeared and were passed from hand to hand. My father drank with quick gulps, staining his shirt. A group of youngsters, led by Abu Saleh el-Hibaz, began to dance an Israeli hora, drawing my father in with a clumsy jig. After a while he despaired of mastering the youthful steps and moved to the middle of the circle, where he stood swaying and clapping his hands. Abu Saleh capered next to him, waving a keffiyeh.

"God of Elijah, God of Elijah!" The prayer podium rocked. The synagogue shook. The stamps of the hora seemed about to smash the marble floor and lift the ceiling off its columns. "God of Elijah!" Every dream was decanted into the words of that old chant. Abu Saleh tried getting the crowd to sing in unison, then gave up and bellowed along with it.

It went on and on, legs and throats holding out despite the heavy heat and the sweat running down everyone.

In the land that our forefathers tilled.
There where each hope is fulfilled,

sang Abu Saleh's youngsters in Hebrew.

Old Hiyawi stood at the back of the synagogue, watching the celebration wanly.

"Hiyawi, smile for the Messiah!" shouted Abu Saleh.

"It's not even the Messiah's donkey," scoffed Hiyawi. "It's idol worship, Abu Saleh, *ya ibni*, nothing but idol worship. Do you see him, the Messiah? Do you see the resurrection?"

"Don't you care about the Holy Land?"

"It's my dream, son. I go there in all my prayers, whenever I fast, whenever I read a chapter of the Psalms."

"But aren't you curious to see it, smell it, touch it?" asked Abu Saleh.

"My son, the dream and the mystery are worth more. That's something that you won't – that you can't – understand."

Hiyawi fell silent.

Abu Saleh mounted the podium. "Jews, let's have some quiet!" he shouted. When there was silence, he called out: "Let's hear it! 'The Lord hath redeemed His servant Jacob!'"

The great throng repeated the words. My father was invited to the podium. The crowd made way for him. He surveyed the bright faces staring up at him and recited:

"Blessed art Thou, O Lord our God, King of the Universe, Who hath maintained us, and sustained us, and remained with us to this day."

"Amen! Amen!" came the answering cries.

"And may He grant that we see our glorious leader, my brother Hizkel, soon in our midst."

"Amen! Amen!"

Abu Saleh embraced my father. They were brought glasses of wine and both drank. "By the waters of Babylon, there we sat down and wept when we remembered Zion," sang Abu Saleh. The cantor began the afternoon prayer, but the excitement did not die down. Again and again Jews went to look at the list of departing passengers, standing before it without moving. My father congratulated and shook the hands of those chosen to fly first.

"When will it be our turn, Baba?"

"Who knows?" he said. "Once the first plane takes off, the others will soon follow."

On our way home he put his arm around me and hummed gaily. He was a different man from the one I knew at home, who rarely talked, avoided conversations with my mother, and fled from her as soon as he could to his armchair in the sitting room. As soon as we arrived, he told her of the departing planes. She turned her back on him and went to the kitchen, where she shrugged him off like a bug when he ran after her and tried hugging her. Like a scolded child, he followed her back into the courtyard. If only, just once, she would show some excitement when he did!

"You stink of wine," she said stonily.

He hung his head, removed his white jacket, loosened his tie, went down to the cellar, and lay down on a mat. Why must she always spoil his good mood, cast him into a slough of anxiety? She couldn't let him be happy for even one day! Loath to fight with her, I hurried out into the hazy twilight and stopped by Rashel's house.

I hadn't seen Rashel for quite a while. I was still annoyed at the way she had behaved several weeks before when I had accompanied her to Karim Abd el-Hak's. What plans I had had for us then! After a session at the lawyer's we would go to the Casino to dance tangos and I would touch her body, feel her waist beneath my hand, let her head drop on my shoulder, smell the rosewater scent of her. The world would be mine … When we reached the lawyer's, however, she shut the door of his office behind her and left me waiting outside like her valet for such a long time that I nearly got up and walked off. Not even my father's servant Abed was ever treated that way. I sat there like an idiot, boiling mad and full of wild thoughts. Who knew what they were doing in there?

When she came out at last she was purring and smiling as if she had seen God Himself. Without even noticing my anger, she ordered a carriage to take us straight home. And yet though I swore I would have nothing more to do with her, here I was standing in front of her door, its dove-shaped knocker irresistible.

"I've missed you," she said, her eyes glistening. All my anger disappeared at once.

"We're going to Israel."

"When?" Startled, she buttoned her robe. "The planes will be here soon."

"You're all leaving me."

"Come with us. How many times do we have to ask you?"

"The Iraqis would never let me."

"Who told you?"

"Karim."

"Karim, Karim. What is he, a prophet? Of course he doesn't want you to go."

"Just what are you getting at?"

"Nothing," I said. A moment later, though, I blurted out: "Why don't you get a divorce and marry him? Then you could leave Iraq at any time." Then, repentant, I tried to backtrack. "I mean, you could arrange a fictitious marriage to get an exit visa. It's been done before. Hizkel could divorce you from prison."

"You're all leaving me," she repeated, bursting into tears and pulling me towards her. She hugged me hard. The warmth and scent of her made me faint. But even as a wave of desire passed over me, I thought of her wet cheek feeling the pimples on mine. And as if to confirm that I was but a raw adolescent, she released me and stepped back.

"I have to go," I murmured quickly and slipped away.

Great God, I thought. *Why don't You help me?* In the end she really would be left alone, waiting for a man who would never return. The bastards would never free him.

Did I love her? Why else did I keep telling myself that she was hardly older than me? I hadn't taken twenty paces from her door before I longed for her. Why did she want to stay in Iraq with her Moslem lawyer? Was she already his mistress?

I turned around and walked back to her front gate. But what could I say? *What filth you are,* I told myself, thinking of Hizkel. *Your uncle's wife!*

I turned again and wandered through the souk and its lanes. When I reached home I found my father standing in the courtyard like a groom in a blue suit, a white tie fastened to his starched shirt with a shiny pin.

"Kabi, where've you been?" he asked.

"Bumming around."

"Come, let's go out on the town."

"I don't feel like it," I answered.

"Come on, son. This is the day we've been waiting for."

"Why doesn't mother go with you?"

"She doesn't want to. I've asked her a dozen times. Um Kabi," he called, "stop being a spoilsport. Come."

"His brother's rotting in jail and he wants to celebrate," answered my mother from the kitchen.

"And if I stay home, he'll be freed? Come to the Casino."

"Me, go to the Casino? Take Kabi."

"How about it, son? She doesn't want to come." He said it a little too fast, as if relieved.

"Neither do I."

He stepped closer. "If she's not coming," he whispered with a grin and a nod towards the kitchen, "we can go and hear Salima Pasha."

"Do you promise?" I whispered back. I knew enough not to mention her name in front of my mother.

"Certainly. She's giving a performance for those leaving for Israel. Everyone will be there."

39.

"My goodness! Why, it's Abu Kabi. It's been years," exclaimed Abu Sa'adun, the owner of the el-Jawahiri Hotel, in which Salima Pasha was performing that night as she had done on the night my father first set eyes on her. The two men embraced like long-lost brothers.

"Is this Kabi? *Mashallah*, a man already," Abu Sa'adun said, taking my arm with the same warmth he showed my father. We passed down a lit arcade and into a crowded garden. There was a smell of freshly watered earth. The drops of water clinging to the blades of grass and myrtle leaves wet my new shoes and lent a cooling touch to the hot night. Abu Sa'adun steered us to a table of honour in front of the stage. My father hesitated. "Perhaps there are seats further back," he said doubtfully.

"Your place is here," decreed Abu Sa'adun. Summoning a waiter, he informed him: "Abu Kabi is a guest of the house."

The waiter bowed. "*Min eini*, I'll look after him."

"Well, thank you, Abu Sa'adun," said my father. "Thank you very much. Feel free to go about your business."

"*Ya alf marhaba*, a thousand welcomes, Abu Kabi. I'll be back." The garden was overflowing with people, nearly all Jews, eating, drinking, and talking noisily. A young singer came on stage and sang a few numbers, her voice inaudible above the din even when she delivered the great Ismahan's "Nights of Pleasure in Vienna". Everyone was waiting for Salima – who, in a world where women were chattels, had remained a Pasha all these years. For her alone the poets spread their carpets of words; for her alone, the Nightingale of Paradise, all these people had turned out tonight, to hear her for the last time.

The audience rose to its feet with a stormy ovation when Salima stepped briskly on to the stage in a blue, sleeveless dress, a pearl tiara, long earrings, and a gleaming pendant around her neck. She smiled then, the charm of her presence casting its spell as her glance fell on us. The smile froze on her lips and she turned pale, her eyes shifting from me to my father, who smiled wanly while avoiding her piercing gaze. For a long, awkward moment, until she gave the signal to the band, he sat like an animal trapped in the headlights of a car.

> *Ya hala bihbab galbi,*
> All of you whom my heart loves,
> How it revives to see you here.
> The world is full of light!
> O you men who bear the cups,
> Fill them, fill them high!

The audience broke into more applause and raised its glasses at her bidding. Drinking the milky arrack, everyone sighed with pleasure and swayed back and forth with an unearthly rapture. My father filled my glass and I wet my lips with the familiar liquid that I still had not learned to like. He put down his drink, sipped some cold water, and said:

"She hasn't changed. If anything, she's better than ever. Her voice has more depth."

I looked at her, this person who could have been my mother – or rather, who could not have been, because then I would not have been me. Perhaps, making the same mistake, she was thinking that I could have been her son. A slim, proudly borne woman with dark hair, a long face, an upturned nose, and high cheek bones, she inspired warmth and trust. There was a natural grace to her movements, which could calm or excite an audience with a subtle gesture.

During the interval, Abu Sa'adun came over to our table. "Is everything all right, Abu Kabi?"

"*Tislam eydak,* bless you," my father said, toasting him.

"Salima will be waiting for you in her dressing room after the performance," Abu Sa'adun told him. And seeing my father's look, he added: "This time, please don't disappoint her."

Back on stage, Salima began to sing again.

> *Hada mu insaf minnak,*
> It isn't very nice, my dear,
> Your having left me for so long.
> When they ask me where you've gone,
> I don't know what to tell them.

Then she sang some old favourites. Slowly my father brightened and began to move his lips along with hers, his head bobbing and his fingers beating silent time. There was a tenderness in his face, a misty look that made him appear younger and sadder. The band began to play an old, soft tune. Salima's voice was choked. The words she improvised seemed to come from deep within her:

> Who knows the paths that don't come back?
> May the journey be a good one.
> Long is the way to the promised land,

Swift are the planes that leave tomorrow.
Who knows the paths that don't come back?
May the journey be a good one.

It was the song the crowd had been waiting for. At last they had heard from her lips, she who was mother and sister to them, that it was true. As one man all rose prayerfully to their feet, heads nodding ecstatically and silent lips mouthing the refrain. Everyone's desire was in her voice. Everyone's love was offered up to her and to a Baghdad that would be seen no more. She sang in hushed, mournful tones, her eyes glistening wetly.

"God in heaven!" said someone at the next table. "How are we Jews supposed to leave all this?"

The air remained full of music even after the last bravo had been shouted. No one left, though no one knew what he was staying for. A long while passed before the first of the crowd rose to depart.

My father straightened his tie, smoothed his jacket, and ran a pocket comb through his hair. "Wait for me here," he said.

"I want to meet her," I told him.

"No, son," he said, clapping me on the shoulder as if to make sure I stayed put.

And so Salman Moshi Imari, also known as Abu Kabi, went to say goodbye to Salima Pasha before leaving for Israel.

She rose from the table in her dressing room and stood facing him when he entered. For a long while they stared at each other without a word. Then she sat and motioned to him to do the same.

"You haven't changed," he said.

"Eighteen years. Every night I looked for you in the audience."
He kept silent.

"What brought you here tonight?"

"I wanted to hear you one last time. And to say goodbye."

"You're going too?" She took a Turkish cigarette from a gold case and waited. He sat blankly for a while, then understood and lit it for her.

"I couldn't come before," he said, staring at the ground. "Not after I ran away like a sewer rat."

"Like a sewer rat," she repeated with a dreamy melancholy. "You could at least have answered my letters. You could have said something to Abu Sa'adun when I sent him to you."

His head was bowed.

"The family was too much for me. I gave up teaching. I gave up law. I gave up singing. I gave up the lute. I married a rabbi's daughter and opened a watch shop."

For a while neither of them spoke.

"What weren't you getting from me?"

"It wasn't that. I was afraid. I wasn't strong enough to be your man."

"You were ashamed of me. You thought I was a whore."

"My God, no … "

"It's true. Or worse. Maybe you didn't think I was a whore. But you couldn't face those who did."

"I loved you."

"Then why?" she cried. She struggled to compose herself. "It doesn't matter. Was that boy sitting next to you your son?"

"Yes."

"Kabi?"

"Yes."

"That's when I knew you were still mine. I never imagined you would remember my telling you that if we had a son I wanted to name him Kabi. He looks like you."

"The light is blinding me," said my father, rising to turn off the table lamp with a practised movement. His hand, which Salima took as in the old days when he sat down again, had remembered where the switch was. "Why didn't you ever marry?"

"Who would want to marry me? You wanted no part of me. No Jew did. No one did but Moslems. And now that the Jews are leaving, who will I sing for?"

"Come to Israel. This is the time to make a change."

"It's too late." There were wrinkles in the corners of her mouth. "And who would let me go? The Pasha? Don't you remember how he made me bring guarantors that I would return from Lebanon?" The shadow of a smile crossed her face.

"He's still afraid of losing you?"

"More than ever."

"You're a queen. All Iraq bows down to you."

"A queen! Without a people. Without a home. Without an heir." There were tears in her eyes. "None of it's worth a damn. But you never did understand that."

"You're still angry with me."

"Angry with my luck."

His hand stirred in hers. "I have to go."

"You're running away again."

"It's hard for me."

"You never were a man."

He didn't answer. Then it surprised him to hear himself say:

"Who knows? Perhaps all my Zionism and underground work was just my way of trying to make up for it … " He trailed off awkwardly. "Kabi is waiting for me."

"Ask him to come in," she said hoarsely. "I want to meet him."

He pulled his hand away. "No."

He stood for a while outside her door. *You're not a man*, he thought.

40.

It was almost time for the summer holiday and its pleasures, some of which Miss Sylvia had experienced the year before and some of which she had heard about from Salim Effendi, with whom she hoped to enjoy them: the daily swim in the river, the races between islands, the trips to the white city of Mosul, the outings, dances, and parties, the endless days of idleness. Her heart beat faster when she thought that approaching too was the date of her return flight to London at the summer's end. Stad Nawi had told her that although the school board was pleased with her work, her contract could not be renewed because of the school's uncertain future due to the departure of Jews for Israel. It might not even re-open at all. "I don't know if I'll be here myself," he had said, explaining why he couldn't rehire her.

She was still waiting for Salim Effendi to broach the subject of the future. He was the only reason she wasn't returning to England now, and she missed her family, friends, and doctoral work. But although she dreamed of taking him with her, the one time she had mentioned it he had said, rather evasively in her opinion, "I'll have to ask the Party."

In any case, these were her last days in Baghdad and she wished to get all she could from them, to drain the lees of the city's sights and smells, of everything old and new from its most degrading slums to its most fabulous palaces. Perhaps, too, this would be a way of getting closer still to Salim Effendi. She was happiest with him as her guide. Together they went for long drives, looping back and forth through the city while she sat on the edge of her seat, her neck arched forwards as if seeing the world for the first time. Salim Effendi found her insatiable curiosity impressive and enviable. A simple evening's walk with her could become a fascinating excursion into Baghdad's mosaic of Sunni and Shi'ite Moslems, Christians, Jews, Armenians, Kurds, Iranians, and other nationalities. Though he sometimes wished she would not ask so many questions, these spurred him on to know the city better. To his amazement he discovered that, though he thought he was acquainted with every street and public garden, Baghdad still held unknown enchantments for him.

On this particular evening Miss Sylvia was determined to eat pacha at el-Pachachi's, the famous Arab restaurant.

"Wouldn't you prefer a Jewish place?" asked Salim Effendi with one of his Clark Gable smiles. "Oh, no, Arab is better," insisted Miss Sylvia, caressing his scar. For the past few days he had felt the need to be alone, free to lie on his bed with his shoes on and with Miss Sylvia as an unforgettable memory. Could he be getting tired of her? How else to explain that after waiting impatiently for her every evening, he now preferred the company of Brahms and a glass of whisky? Or that she no longer had the power to take his mind off, yes, off *her*. Although several months had passed since her departure for Cairo, he once more found himself thinking of Bahia, even while making love to the Englishwoman.

His request for permission to go to Cairo had been turned down by the Party. Aware of Salim Effendi's new obsession that, far from Baghdad and the lunatic Sheikh Gassem, Bahia might be won over, his friend Tarik, so it seemed, had talked their superiors into vetoing the trip. If only he could get away to some quiet place, even to Imara, where he might go for long walks in the rice fields, listen to the cooing of the doves and the rustling of the grain stalks, and clean his mind of everything, Bahia too ... or, on the contrary, say to hell with everything, including the Party, and follow her to the ends of the earth like a character in a novel! In his present mood either alternative seemed preferable to Miss Sylvia, with whom his affair was so lacklustre that he was disinclined even to take a short trip to London with her.

Her arm on his, she gave his hand a squeeze and hailed a carriage, explaining her destination to the driver partly in a Moslem and partly Jewish dialect, but mostly in English. The driver cast a pleading glance at Salim Effendi, who did not hurry to enlighten him. It amused him when Miss Sylvia played the native. She was indeed a charming woman and not a whit his inferior. In their intellectual needs and attitudes they were eminently compatible. Could his real reason for losing interest in her be his fear of her independence, he who had always told himself that he couldn't live with a submissive Iraqi woman?

Loath to pursue this train of thought, he instructed the driver to take them to the vicinity of the smiths' market. They left the carriage in a nearby Moslem neighbourhood and Miss Sylvia slipped her arm through his. As they were about to cross the street to el-Pachachi's, Salim Effendi saw two men in suits step out of a second carriage behind them. He had seen these secret service men lurking by his house and had known that he was being followed, which was why he had kept his Party activities to a minimum and tried to appear a carefree single man who spent his nights enjoying himself. Why hadn't they arrested him already and put an end to his nightmares?

He was still brooding about this when the two of them were surrounded by ogling Arabs, their eyes fixed on Miss Sylvia's tight trousers and flimsy blouse. More men marched behind her as if she were a drum majorette.

"*Inglizziya*," someone said.

"A film star," suggested another man.

"*Shlon tiz, yiswa addam*," enthused a third man. "What an ass! It's worth hanging for."

"*Ya hmar, hada tiz kulla halwa!* That's not an ass, it's a piece of halvah, you donkey!"

Blushing but enjoying the commotion, Miss Sylvia clung harder to her envied escort. "Enjoy her!" someone shouted. Salim Effendi smiled awkwardly, feigning incomprehension.

"Aren't you ashamed of yourselves?" a fat young man asked the crowd. "A person might think you'd never seen a woman in trousers before."

"Such as your sister?" he was mocked.

"If the bitch thinks she's a man, let's see her take it out and piss!"

There was a gale of laughter. Glancing at the onlookers, Salim Effendi deemed it an inappropriate time for a lecture on women's rights. One had to take local customs into account.

For a revolutionary, this was heresy. Yet might it not be a good thing if the Communists were less dogmatic and in less of a hurry to eliminate time-honoured customs and traditions? If he himself were married to a Jewish woman from Baghdad, would he approve of her walking around in trousers? Intellectually, yes, but emotionally ... well, perhaps at home ... but in the street? And yet in that case, Salim Effendi asked himself, what was the point of all his passionate speeches to Tarik about female equality, which came straight from the mouth of the dead Armenian?

They had reached the door of the restaurant. Had Miss Sylvia been amenable, he would have much preferred taking her to the Hotel Semiramis or some other place where European women were welcomed and accepted. And yet wasn't that abandoning the struggle to change Iraq and liberate it from the dead hand of the past? What change was more imperative than a new attitude towards women?

Speaking English to the waiter, Salim Effendi led Miss Sylvia to a corner table from which she flashed a smile at no one in particular. He felt as if a wall had risen between them.

"How many times must I tell you that smiling like that doesn't mean what you think it does here?"

"And how many times must I tell *you* that you're not going to get me to be a different person?" she replied, laughing so loudly that everyone turned to look. As if in acknowledgement, she shook her long hair. The restaurant smelled of roast lamb, and the noisy fan on the ceiling did little to ease the oppressive heat. Salim Effendi removed his jacket, loosened his tie, and rolled up his shirt sleeves twice. The waiter stared at Miss Sylvia dumbly when she tried ordering in Arabic, his eyes slipping down to her breasts. In the end Salim Effendi ordered for her.

The waiter set Miss Sylvia's place with a knife, fork, and spoon and Salim Effendi's with a spoon only and returned with a reddish tongue-soup, a leg of lamb, and a plate of stuffed tripe. Though tantalized by their aroma of saffron and garlic, Salim Effendi sent him back for another knife and fork, then put these down after the first bite and told Miss Sylvia: "You eat the *pacha* with your hands and the tripe with a spoon, like this." Seizing the leg of lamb, he bit off a piece, put the rest back on its platter, ripped off some bread, fished a piece of tongue with it from the greasy soup, and stuffed both into his mouth.

He ate like an Iraqi, licking and smacking his lips. Miss Sylvia found it a feral spectacle, attractive and repellent at once. Although the local table manners were not easy to adjust to, she too put down her cutlery and ate with her hands to the startled looks of the other diners. She laughed at her long, manicured fingers gripping the lamb's leg while red drops of soup spattered over her blouse. Digging into the tripe with her spoon, Miss Sylvia let grains of rice dribble on her trousers. While her lover gnawed, crunched, and mopped away as if making her a gift of his appetite, she wiped her fingers on her napkin.

Suddenly her shoulders slumped and she shuddered, a sign of the passion that sometimes seized her like cramp. Moving her chair closer to the table, she rubbed Salim Effendi's foot with her own. Though normally this might have excited him, he now drew back in alarm, rebuking her with a nod towards the lascivious looks that were coming her way. Miss Sylvia pretended not to understand and locked her legs around his, eyeing him with hot amusement as he was made to back his chair away and turn sideways. He felt a sudden wave of cruel desire for the shameless woman sitting across from him and reached for the leg bone, sucking its marrow like Turkish Delight.

Were the CID men still outside? What would be his last request before being led to the gallows? A *pacha*! This time, though, he would eat it alone, at the centre table of this very restaurant, chewing and swallowing slowly for the last time. And for dessert he would ask for Bahia. Ah, to fuck her just once! It was indeed worth a hanging.

He studied the Englishwoman. Was Bahia as wild in bed?

Despite Miss Sylvia's many stories, she remained a mysterious figure. He had unzipped everything but her soul. Once she had told him how, during the wartime rationing in London, she had been thrilled to be brought a banana by her father. The abundance of Baghdad enchanted her; she could not stop eating and had already put on weight.

They topped off the meal with a glass of tea for her and a cup of bitter coffee for him, after which he leaned back and lit his pipe.

Outside the restaurant they hailed another carriage. Salim Effendi saw the two men in suits waiting for him. Who were they? If they really were secret service agents, what were they waiting for, damn them? *In the end they'll hang me anyway,* he told himself, deciding to ignore them. "To Taht el-Takya," he told the driver. Back home he would quench the hungry fire kindled by his meal and the Englishwoman. Placing his legs on the footstool, he leaned his head on Miss Sylvia's shoulder and shut his eyes. When he opened them by the entrance to Taht el-Takya, he saw more men in suits. He told the coachman to drive on.

"Are we going to my place?" asked Miss Sylvia, cuddling up to him. She felt equally sleepy and sexy.

"Yes," he said, smiling so as not to worry her. On the King Faisal Bridge he told the driver to turn around and drive past the Jewish souk on Razi Street. There, too, he saw plainclothesmen. He asked to be taken to el-Kark, by the river.

"Have you made up your mind?" Miss Sylvia stroked his back. He rolled back the top of the cab and looked around. Behind them was an open carriage with two men in suits.

"I think we're being followed," said Salim Effendi. His native city had turned into a dark plot against him.

"Oh my! Then come to my place." She held him tight.

"It wouldn't be good for you if I were found there."

"I'm not afraid. I'm a British citizen."

"That would only make it worse for me without helping you."

"Do you think they know about us?"

"Never underestimate them. The first rule of working undercover is to take the enemy seriously."

"But what will we do? Where will you go?"

"Don't worry. An undercover agent has no home but many addresses."

"How will I find you?"

"You don't have to. I'll find you. I'll get in touch when I can."

"We should have gone to London," said Miss Sylvia.

But Salim Effendi was concentrating on Baghdad. "My God!" he exclaimed, so aghast that he struck his own forehead. "There's a Party leaflet in my house."

"Dear me! Why did you take it home with you?"

"To finish editing it. And here I was thinking that I never made mistakes!" He laughed nervously.

"Promise me you won't go home. They'll arrest you."

They shared a cigarette together. Each time one of them turned around warily to look, the carriage was still behind them. "Why haven't they picked you up already?" asked Miss Sylvia. "Is it because of me?"

"No. They want to see where I go, where I take cover. They may be using me as bait for a big round-up. This could go on for days."

He was seeking to reassure himself no less than her.

She put her lips to his. "I love you."

"I don't want to get you into trouble. I'll find a dark place and ditch them."

"Just be careful," she said huskily when he dropped her off near her home, by the statue of the World War I British general Sir Frederick Stanley Maude.

"Don't worry," he said. He told the driver to take him to New Baghdad, settled back in his seat, lit his pipe, and tried to think of his next move. Hiding out with a Party member was out of the question. He reviewed everyone he knew, even briefly considering Big Imari, whose mansion they were passing. But no, his cousin would turn him in at once to prove his loyalty to the Pasha.

"Where now?" asked the driver.

"Drive around these rich sons-of-bitches' mansions. And take your time. We may not own the houses, but the air is free." He offered the driver an expensive cigarette.

"God reward you," said the man, accepting it.

Should he try Abu Kabi? No, he couldn't do that because of Hizkel. His heart sank. What was that music running through his head? He suddenly realized that it was Haydn's Farewell Symphony which, Miss Sylvia had once explained to him, ended with the musicians leaving the stage one by one until there was nothing left but silence. *Great God,* he thought, *here I am in my own city with not a straw to clutch at, more alone than I've ever been in my life. It's a good thing my poor mother isn't here to see me swing above a puddle of piss and shit.* But self-pity was the last thing he could afford to indulge in. *You're a revolutionary,* he thought. *Get a grip on yourself! Keep your mind on your escape.*

"All right, pal, let's go back," he told the driver. He had the man stop in the large square of Bab-el-Sheikh, threw him a hundred fils coin as the carriage tailing them was caught in the traffic, jumped out of the opposite door, sprinted across the

393

street, and disappeared into a parked taxi. "To the King Faisal Bridge, quick," he said.

The taxi sped off. Through the rear window he saw the two detectives trying to stop a passing car, but he was already far away. He changed to another taxi at the bridge, told the driver to make a U-turn on el-Rashid Street, and once sure he was no longer being followed, he asked to be dropped at the far side of Taht el-Takya, near the Jewish souk.

41.

When he knocked the wooden gate swung open to reveal the large figure of Abu Saleh el-Hibaz.

"Well, well," said the baker with a mock bow. "What brings the heretic to the Temple?"

"They're after me," whispered Salim Effendi.

"I always knew you'd turn up here one day," said the baker, looking cautiously up and down the street.

"I've ditched my tail," said Salim Effendi. "I've been standing out here in the dark for two hours, making sure they were gone before I knocked."

Abu Saleh vanished into the yard and came back with a straw basket. Without a word they set out down the dark streets. Near the bakery they flattened themselves against a wall, listening to the silence. When Abu Saleh decided that the coast was clear, he opened a gate and they descended to a small cellar furnished with a bed and a stool. Handing Salim Effendi the basket of food, he asked:

"What more can I do for you?"

"You've done enough," murmured Salim Effendi. "As one orphan to another, thank you. How long can I stay here?"

"The less time the better. I need the bed. The blood goes to my brain if I don't have a woman twice a day."

"You're risking your life for me," said the Communist.

"You're a Jew, aren't you? I'll be back in an hour."

"Make sure they're not outside my house."

When the baker had gone Salim Effendi removed his shoes and walked up and down laughing like a madman. Fuck the Pasha! Fuck the CID! He had screwed them all. From deep down came a prayer he remembered from the studies of his youth: "Blessed art Thou, O Lord our God, King of the Universe, Who doth good even unto sinners." And there being no congregation to respond, he declared: "Amen!"

Now that the tension had eased, he felt hungry. Sitting on the bed, he went through the straw basket and devoured a kebab and *amba* sandwich as if he had never eaten at el-Pachachi's. Thanking the Zionist in his heart, he lit his pipe. The two underground groups, he thought, could accomplish wonders if only they worked together. Now, when the lines were being drawn, was the time for joint action. The secret service considered both movements equally subversive. Indeed, both wished to see the downfall of the regime, and the Pasha was too stupid to tell them apart.

And it was to such a man that Allah had given power! But of course, if Allah really existed the world would be a different place. Salim Effendi lay down on the broad bed, wondering who the baker shared it with. Although he could feel the weariness creeping from his legs into his back, he couldn't sleep. How had they come across his trail? For years he had eluded them, leaving no clues. Could someone have informed on him, just when he was about to be sent to Moscow for a course and be given a high position in the Party? At their last meeting, Tarik, his rival for the job, had argued that Baghdad was a Moslem city and should have a Party led by Moslems. Not that this had surprised him after their midnight cruise with Bahia ... but still ... to think that his best friend was for a Jewish quota!

Instead of waiting for Tarik after the meeting as planned and going to the el-Jawahiri, he had gone straight to Sylvia's. She had cooked him as good a meal as English cuisine permitted, poured him a large quantity of whisky, which was the one thing the English made well, or rather their northern neigbours, and hopped into bed with him while he wondered when the Jews had become second-class citizens in the Communist Party.

Actually, although he had not noticed many new Jews in the Party since the death of the Armenian, this had at first struck him as a consequence of the emigration to Israel. Only now did it occur to him that there might be a secret policy of not accepting Jews.

He recalled the case of the Party member Sa'ad el-Din, arrested with his Jewish girlfriend Miriam Cohen, whose son born while he was in prison, he refused to acknowledge unless she converted to Islam. In a letter smuggled out to the leaders of the Party, she had written:

"It was you who taught me to live without religion and without God. Taking the Moslem confession of faith would now be like spitting in your face. I didn't choose to be a Jew. I was born one, because that's what my ancestors were. Am I now being condemned for belonging to a people older than the age of Muhammed? How could I possibly become a Moslem and still be a good Communist?"

It was about this time that people began to whisper that Jews should be barred from the Party. He himself was told to play his Jewishness down if he wanted to get anywhere. Although he had made a point of it, this infuriated him. Just because the Jews had their Rabbi Bashis and Big Imaris, did that mean they couldn't fight against the regime? Had he again chosen wrongly?

Once, made to kneel and defecate by the roadside with a

sudden attack of cramps as a seven-year-old in Imara, he had been forced to sit in his own excrement by his two older cousins, Big Imari and Salman Imari. To this day he could hear their laughter. Sometimes he felt that he had gone on sitting in shit in Baghdad, where he first attended a Jewish religious school on a scholarship after his destitute parents moved to the city. He had then transferred to a better institution, only to drop out for financial reasons.

Not one of his family's friends or relations had responded when asked for help. "Let him go to work," they had said, or, alluding to Big Imari's fortune, "Charity begins at home." It was then that Salim Effendi came to realize that the Jews were no better than the Moslems; ever since then he had hated all charity givers.

The one person who had cared about him was a Moslem lawyer, Sa'adun Razari, through whose connections he was enrolled in a Moslem school for underprivileged boys, from which he graduated with honours and was accepted by the university despite being a Jew. Indeed, he proved such an outstanding student in languages and literature that, if not for the Party, which took up most of his time, he might have had a successful academic career.

Now, his whole life seemed one big failure. His family had repudiated him. His doctorate would never be finished. He had no money and no wife. Bahia had spurned him. Iraq hadn't changed. And – unkindest blow of all – he suspected his best friend of betraying him to the police.

Still, it wasn't logical. For a Communist to inform on him would be like informing on oneself – unless, of course, that person was a double agent. But in that case, the whole Party leadership would have been rounded up by now. Perhaps it was only his speeches in school that had attracted the attention of the police.

Where was he to go? He couldn't return to his room. Worse still, he had left damaging evidence there – he who had always destroyed every document and lectured new recruits on security. He pictured the police going through his things. They would even find his notebook full of poems, including his latest cycle to Bahia. What a pity he hadn't hidden it in the school library, or given it to Sylvia, although that might have been a bit awkward. It was one thing to teach literature, another to produce it himself.

All his money was in the room too, the 120 dinars that he had purposely kept there for an emergency. He should have bought a white summer suit with it, or the mustardy tweed blazer he had dreamed of. Or even spent it on belly dancers, like the crazy sheikh. Ah, Bahia, Bahia! What wouldn't he give for a night with her? If only he were rich like Big Imari, he would offer to pay her weight in gold for her. What woman could resist such a temptation?

The heretical thought crossed his mind that, had he not been cheated of his inheritance, he might never have become a Communist. "Material circumstances determine consciousness". Why, he had translated this sentence from the Communist Manifesto himself! Lord, what was the point of it? Everything and nothing. *Yea, a man's days are like the grass, like a passing dream.* He would be caught, then hung – then no more Salim Effendi. And he was tired, so tired. Reaching for the bottle of arrack in the basket, he took a burning gulp and chewed on some parsley to soften the sting. *May Allah have mercy on the mother who bore you, Abu Saleh,* he thought. *What a pity we're on different sides.*

The door swung open. Salim jumped from the bed.

It was Abu Saleh. "They're outside your house, all right," he said.

"Are you sure?"

"You forget, my friend, that they're after us too. The great dragnet is on. I can't save all the Communists in Iraq, but I can at least try to save a Jew like you. We're willing to smuggle you to Iran with some of our people. After all, you're our secret agent."

"Your secret agent?"

"Your Party, my dear comrade, is the best possible proof that once a Jew, always a Jew. And your demonstrations have revealed the Pasha's cruelty and made our Jewish fence-sitters realize that they have to jump. For that we owe you our thanks."

"It takes the twisted mind of a Zionist to invent such a dialectic," laughed Salim Effendi. Could Abu Saleh be right? Was that why young Jews were staying away from the Party? "And Iran sounds like a fine idea. There's a strong Party there too."

"You idiot! Do you think I'm saving your life for the Communists? How long must a Jew like you shoulder the world's problems?"

"When I shoulder the world's problems, I shoulder the Jew's too."

"Charity, you ass, begins at home," said the baker.

42.

This time the shouts came from Abu Edouard's house. There was constant shouting in our neighbourhood, in which no one kept his temper for long and everyone, sooner or later, came to loggerheads or blows. Everyone knew who in which family said or did what to whom. Now, though, the sound of screams and smashed dishes was so loud that it brought us all running to our roofs: the source turned out to be Amira. She was throwing plates and jugs while being given the first thrashing of her life by her father.

"I *am* going to Israel!" she shrieked. "You won't tell me what to do!"

There was a whack and Abu Edouard said something indistinct.

"Go on, hit me! Hit me! Hit me like you do mama. You'll have to chain me to this house, because I'm going to Israel. I don't give a damn for this stinking country of yours! You have to be full of shit to stay in it. Shit! Shit! Shit! Shit!"

More dishes shattered, as if an entire shelf had been swept clean of them.

"We're second-class citizens here!" screamed Amira.

"I suppose you thought your father owned Baghdad!" This time Abu Edouard could be heard clearly. "Just what do you expect to find in Israel? War and starvation, that's what!"

"Do you think I got the best marks in Iraq so you could brag about me at Abu Ednan's? Can't you see they're shitting on you too?"

There was silence, punctuated by Amira's sobs.

The real mystery wasn't even Abu Edouard's hitting her, although that too was unprecedented. It was Amira's sudden conversion to Zionism. That evening her mother came to see us.

"So tell me, Um Edouard, doesn't Amira want to go to America any more?" My mother didn't beat around the bush.

"That's just it, that's the whole trouble!" said Amira's mother, clapping her hands in sorrow, "You know, Um Kabi, that her studies were all that poor child ever thought about. Twice she was put up a year in school, and once she set her heart on that scholarship to America she never took her head out of her books. I was sure she'd ruin her eyes. Who wants to marry a girl with glasses?

"Well, she finished school with straight As. She had the best report card in all Iraq, boys included. That's when we went to the ministry of education to fill out the application forms. A fat Moslem with thick, spectacles received us and said that the forms cost five dinars. That's more than Abu Edouard makes in a month, but we agreed to pay and Amira, bless her, started filling out the forms while the Moslem ate her up with his eyes. But it was when he rose to lock the door that I really began to worry. I wasn't afraid for an old thing like myself, but you know I'd give my life for Amira.

"That Moslem kept wanting to say something so badly that his moustache shook. In the end he made us swear by the prophet Moses not to tell on him and showed us a secret order not to give the scholarship to any Jew. It was a waste of five dinars to apply, he said.

"To tell you the truth, Um Kabi, that came as a relief to me. Who knows what would have happened to the child among so many Christians in America? All she wanted was to become an engineer and find a rich husband, and I was scared to death of losing her. And if she didn't marry in America, who in Baghdad would have had her? Who here wants a woman with a university education and a degree in engineering?

"So I thanked that Moslem for saving us the money and I meant it. Not Amira. I'm embarrassed to tell you what a scene she made! She gave the man a dirty look, tore up the forms, threw the pieces in his face, and ran out of there without waiting for me. And don't ask me what I've gone through with her since! For two whole days she shut herself up in the cellar with the bats and did nothing but cry. She wouldn't eat a thing, not even when Abu Edouard begged her to. It was all we could do to get her to drink some water. I tell you, she looked like a wilted flower when she came out of there. *Waweli*, why must it happen to me?

"I suppose that's when she made up her mind to go to Israel, but we only realized it today. Abu Edouard found her studying Hebrew from some book she'd got hold of … and when that child studies, there's no stopping her! A teacher of hers once told me that she has a head like a fisherman's net. Nothing that gets into it gets out again.

"Well, Abu Edouard went and burned that book in the courtyard and Amira had a fit. You heard them both. He actually hit her … I never thought I'd see the day! He wanted to know who gave her the book and said he'd murder him if it was Abu Saleh.

"Um Kabi, you're like a sister to me; I don't have to tell you that that man has beaten me half to death especially on the days he doesn't see his cross-eyed whore. I'm black and blue all over. Did you think I don't know all about it? For all I care, he can run off with her and leave me in peace. He beats poor Edouard too; he makes him pay in blood for every penny that he gives him. But that child … he never touched her. He never said no to her. He'd have given his right arm for her.

"*Waweli* what a mess! At first she cried and cried, but now she just sits and stares … and those eyes of hers, Um Kabi, they frighten me. What didn't she break today? The pitchers, the jugs, the glass panels of the cupboards, everything! I've never in my life seen her this way. She's got her father's hot blood … it comes from the Moslem wet-nurse who suckled him. Allah, what have I done to deserve all this?" She beat her chest like a woman in mourning and wailed.

My mother gave her a quick hug. "Amira needs a husband," she said. "And fast."

"Bless your every word. A woman who's not a wife is a woman without a life. You know who's interested in her? S'hak Attar, the perfume seller's son."

"That good-for-nothing?"

"I'd marry her off to him if it would solve anything," sighed Amira's mother with a resigned look.

"Don't you even think of it! Amira is a flower. She needs to be cherished," said my mother with a glance at me.

"Bless you for saying that, Um Kabi. But what can I do if the young men don't want to get married? They all think some blonde beauty is waiting for them in Israel. And those who are willing to take the plunge have too high an asking price. They've heard there are no dowries in Israel and they want to get all they can while they're here. You'd think they came with solid gold between their legs."

My mother laughed and gestured warningly in my direction.

"Kabi's a grown man," said Um Edouard with an appreciative and not entirely maternal look.

"Don't go knocking on Fate's door, Um Edouard," counselled my mother. "What's written on the forehead will be seen by the eye."

"The poor child! As pretty as Queen Esther and without a beau," said Um Edouard.

"Don't you worry. Every pot has its lid. You know what they say. If a girl's looks don't find her a husband, leave it to her parents, and if her parents don't find her one, leave it to their money."

"And if there's no money? I'd go to Israel with her like everyone else, but how can I convince Abu Edouard?"

Amira's mother rose to go. My mother walked her to the front gate and returned looking thoughtful. "Do you realize what she came for?" she asked me.

"To get it off her chest."

"No, Kabi. She came for you."

"For me?"

"Yes, son. If it weren't for Amira's father, I'd marry you off to her."

That threw me for a moment. Although I wasn't exactly an adult, I expected to be asked first! Not that it seemed such a bad idea. But ideas at my age were cheap. I would have gladly married Rashel too.

"What's wrong with her father?"

"A thorn bush that grew a rose!"

"Why blame Amira for that?"

"People should stick to their own."

"A person might think that father was Big Imari and you were God's daughter," I mocked.

"That's true, Kabi," my mother said proudly. "We're Imaris."

"Mama, Amira's not even sixteen and yet she has finished high school with the highest grades in Iraq. Isn't that good enough even for the Imaris?"

She gave me a startled look, as if the thought had never occurred to her. Although she had barely learned to read and write, her father, Rabbi Moshi, had passed on to her a true respect for learning and the learned.

"Then what do you think?" she asked, the light of revelation in her eyes. "I've been told that married men don't have to go to the army in Israel."

"But I want to go to the army there."

"*Waweli*, do you want to kill me?"

I went out for a walk and stopped by the shop of the *zingula* vendor. I liked watching him work. Using a large funnel with a curved spout, he drew circular figures of dough in a pan of bubbling oil. One looked like a dog chasing a cat. He waited for the dough to turn brown and puff up, then scooped it out nimbly, dipped it in a bowl of honey and rosewater, and cried at the top of his lungs:

"Jews, come and get it! *Zingula* and honey, I don't take any money!"

I was licking the honey from my fingers when I felt a thump on my back. I spun around, ready to fight, and found myself staring at Amira's grin. Gallantly I whipped out my purse and bought her a helping, handing the change magnanimously to a crippled beggar.

"Well, has your mother agreed?" she asked.

"To what?"

"As if you didn't know that I'm up for sale to the highest bidder!"

"I don't know what you're talking about."

"Liar!"

I had to laugh. She finished her *zingula*, washed her sticky fingers inside the shop, and took my hand as if I were a little brother in need of minding. I had never held a girl's hand before and was afraid to show my embarrassment. Of course, if she didn't mind what anyone said, why should I? Yet I kept my head down as I walked beside her.

There was a large crowd on both sides of el-Rashid street, which was devoid of traffic. Helmeted policemen kept the onlookers on the pavements. Others on horseback held back vehicles entering from the side streets. Drums beat a military tattoo in the distance.

"What's happening?" I asked.

"It's the annual Scouts Parade," a woman answered.

"That's an anti-Semitic organization," I whispered to Amira. "Its leaders are Nazis who studied in Germany."

But she wanted to see the parade. There was a holiday atmosphere and a colourful crowd lined the streets. Near us stood a group of women in black cloaks and veils. The spectators jostled each other and stood on tiptoe, craning their necks though the procession was not in sight. Amira was wearing her school uniform, a blue and white striped dress with a round white collar. With her dark complexion, her tresses of coal-black hair, and her deep brown eyes flecked with light, she looked like a Moslem and could afford to stand as confidently as she did.

I glanced at her breasts. This was something I did at the bakery, coming home from school, and at every other opportunity, and I had seen them in all their fruiting stages: the size of apricots, of pears, of apples, of pomegranates, and now, of wonderful plump melons. With someone so gorgeous at my side, I had good reason to stand proud myself.

The drum rolls grew closer. For a while, before I caught myself, I tapped out their rhythm with my feet. The men in the coffeehouses took their chairs to the pavement and stood on them, clapping their hands to the beat. Women ululated and threw flowers and sweets as though it were a bar mitzvah in a synagogue. Boisterous Arabs surrounded us on all sides.

I felt out of place, a stranger. A wave of humanity swept us off the pavement, and when the police shoved us back, I was pinned against an electric pole. A woman had climbed up its ladder-like base and was shrieking: "Down with the Communists! Down with the Zionists!"

Her huge behind in its broad dress was right above me. I fought my way back to Amira.

"Look," she said, pointing to the Scout leaders in the front row of khaki marchers. Behind them came two columns of sturdy young flag bearers. Amira stood on tiptoe. Then, still unable to get a good view, she pulled me after her to the front of the crowd.

"Where's Ismail?" she asked anxiously.

So that was it! All the bitch wanted was to see her big strong Moslem, whom she rooted for in our belt fights! If I were the man her mother had said I was, I would walk out on her here and now ... except that no man would leave a Jewish girl on a street packed with Moslems.

"Here they come!" she cried, gripping my hand and jumping with excitement. Her breast grazed my arm. The more I tried moving away from it the more she pressed its soft but firm flesh against me.

Was she just pretending to be so absorbed in the parade?

"Ismail, Ismail!" she cried, waving her free hand while holding me more tightly with the other. Although she seemed to have spotted someone in the distance, I still couldn't make him out.

She smelled of soap and watermelon. A delicious shiver ran down me. Was Amira's mother right? My grandfather, I knew from my father, had married my grandmother when he was fifteen and she was thirteen.

Just then I spied Ismail. Tall and handsome, he was on the right flank of the first row of the Youth Corps. He wore a brown neckerchief and swung his arms forcefully, chest out, chin up, and eyes front as if the world belonged to him alone. And he didn't have pimples.

"Ismail! Ismail!" Amira's thigh rubbed against mine, but as her hero was about to pass us, she sprang away and ran into the street. "*Nahnu ibna'a el-watn, nasunuhu tul el-zeman,*" she sang full-throatedly with the marchers, "We are the sons of the fatherland, always on guard to defend it." Her eyes met Ismail's and he smiled at her while I cursed him in my thoughts. A regular Romeo and Juliet!

A marshal stepped up to lead Amira away and Ismail signalled to him to be gentle while striding on like a prince. When she rejoined me, she seized my hand again and pulled me after her like a pet dog.

"Where to now?"

"To the ceremony."

"What for?"

She gave me an icy stare. "Are you going to leave me here?"

I trailed reluctantly after her, engulfed by the mob bringing up the rear. The magic of escorting her was beginning to pall.

"I thought you wanted to go to Israel, you jerk!" I whispered to her furiously.

"Kabi, what's the matter with you? Why don't you sing?"

I refused to.

For a moment I did not even see the parade. In my thoughts I was back in front of the defence ministry; in the large square with its scaffold ... Then my eyes re-focused on the Scouts, who had formed a half-circle on a stage festooned with flags. At a signal, the drummers and buglers fell still.

"The national anthem!" called an announcer.

There was a hush and "Peace be to the King" burst from the throats of thousands of Arabs. Although it was the same song that we sang every Thursday at our school assembly, the words sounded different now: they were no longer those I knew, they were theirs.

Amira was singing with all her might. She might have lost her scholarship to America, but her years in a Moslem school had made her one of them. Or was it just an act? "It's a Jew's job to pretend," Hiyawi had told me more than once.

But this was one time I didn't feel like it. Although I stood to attention like everyone else, I didn't join in the anthem. The setting sun streaked the sky with blood. Then darkness descended, lit by the fiery words of the speakers.

"Death to the Communists! Death to the Zionists!" screamed the crowd. How was this different from a hanging? Both ended with the cry *Allah akbar* and a mob thirsty for the blood of the Jews, who were to blame for everything and were the cause of every frustration and punctured dream. While fear seized me by the throat I thought of the *Farhood*, picturing Jews quickly rolling down their shutters and fleeing for the safety of their homes. The hysterical shouts grew louder, like the cries of an ancient ritual passed down through the ages. After a while the announcer called for silence and introduced a young Scout speaker. It was Ismail. In a fierce, proud voice he began:

"Brothers and sisters! We, the sons of the Moslem nation ... we, the children of the glorious Iraqi people ... pledge allegiance to our flag. We swear to usher Iraq into a new age! We swear to combat her enemies, to cleanse the rot from her midst, and to expel the aliens who endanger her ... the blood-sucking lackeys of the English and the treacherous toadies of the Russians, the Jewish Communists and Zionists! No enemy is more vicious or dangerous to Islam. We are the generation of the future, sent to restore the glory of the past to the Land of the Caliphs. Once more Iraq will lead the Moslem world and be the pride of all the Arabs!"

There was thunderous applause. "Death to the Communists! Death to the Zionists!" yelled the crowd.

Amira gazed at Ismail radiantly. "He speaks so beautifully."

"You *are* dumb," I whispered. "Didn't you hear what he said?"

"You know the Moslems. It's just talk."

"Let's get out of here," I said. "Things are heating up. Soon they'll start looking for Jews."

She nodded and threw a last glance at Ismail, who had returned to his phalanx. Slowly, so as not to attract attention, we made our way through the excited throng and back towards el-Rashid Street. Amira took my hand again. I could feel her desire for closeness, perhaps even for me. In the first sidestreet, I steered her into a dark corner and stood before her breathing heavily, my blood throbbing to the tempo of the shrilling crickets. Her eyes shone in the darkness and we fell into each other's arms. My lips brushed her face, feeling her warm breath and searching for her mouth. Then they settled on it and sucked greedily. I slipped my tongue into it, where it flicked against hers that tasted of quince jam and salt. It was my first kiss, and even while still in the throes of its delights I wondered how it compared with Gary Cooper and Ingrid Bergman's in *For Whom The Bell Tolls*.

I kept drinking from Amira's lips. My hand spooned her behind, my stiff member poking her belly. She had to have felt it. Her fingers clawed my neck. Then, pushing me away, she cried:

"Stop, stop. I can't!" We parted for a second and she flung herself at me again like a wildcat, running her fingers through my hair and kissing my lips, my face, my forehead, with a desperate thirst. And just as suddenly she stopped again, dropping her arms with tears in her eyes.

"What's the matter?"

"I can't. You wouldn't understand."

I held her hands and we stood there, the tears running down her cheeks. A dim cluster of people appeared up the street.

"Arabs!" she cried, letting go of me. She slipped out of her clogs and began to run. So did I. We ran until she was out of breath, slowing down only when we reached the river. Amira threw herself on the soft ground and I sprawled beside her. We lay on our backs, watching the moon spread its silver tent. Then we turned on our sides and faced each other. I stroked her cheek gently and watched the calm return. She put an arm around me and held me so tight that I felt the dampness on her cheek. I propped myself on an elbow.

"Are you in love with him?" She didn't answer.

"He's a Moslem who hates Jews."

"I know. It was only a dream. I went to say goodbye to him today. Thank you for coming."

All was forgiven.

"Abu Saleh wants to marry you," I said.

"He's better off without me. We could never be happy together. He's a simple soul with a heart of gold and I'm not only educated, I'm also ambitious and wild. I'm going to be an engineer. I'd only make him suffer."

That startled me. Although I was older than her, I suddenly felt ten years younger. She had already thought of everything. And she knew what she wanted.

"He knows what I think. He proposed to me."

"Abu Saleh? When?"

"A while ago. I told him to forget about me."

"You'll end up marrying the spice seller's son."

"Not me. No one's marrying me to anyone. I'll marry for love."

She rose and stood looking at the silvery glimmer of the river and the golden brushstrokes of the street lamps. "It's hard to leave all this," she said, embracing the water and the star-strewn sky with a sweep of her arm. "We'd better go home. It's late."

We walked by the river bank, dogs barking forlornly at our backs.

"And you?" she asked.

"Me?"

"Would you marry me?"

I knew it was just girlish curiosity. "First come to Israel," I said. "Then we can talk about it."

We both burst out laughing. It was a glorious moment of friendship and intimacy. We crossed el-Rashid Street and, holding hands, walked down the sidestreets.

Edouard was waiting by the entrance to the neighbourhood. In one motion, like a boxer, he slapped Amira's cheek and cuffed her head.

"Stop that, you idiot!" I yelled.

"She's my sister, shitface. Where have you been?"

"It's none of your business," said Amira quietly. "And don't you ever raise your hand to me again."

"You whore!" he screamed. "Just where do you think you're gallivanting at night?"

"God damn it," I said. "Don't talk to her like that."

"It's all right, Kabi, go home," said Amira. "There won't be much more of this. Thanks for everything."

43.

"The fucking whore!" yelled Abu Edouard.

"*Waweli*, help! He's got a knife!" screamed Amira's mother. Beneath my sheet, I shook off the last strands of sleep in the morning light. My heart was in my throat. He was going to kill Amira because of me. Edouard must have told him.

"I'll murder you, I swear to God! I'm dishonoured! I have no more daughter!"

"Kabi!" my mother shouted. "Go and get your father. He'll really kill her!"

I was already out of bed and running in my underpants to where she stood by the balcony of our roof. In the next courtyard Abu Edouard was gripping his wife's hair while holding a knife to her throat.

"The fucking whore!" he shouted again. "It's you who gave birth to that slut! Why didn't you keep an eye on her? Tell me who smuggled her out of Iraq or I'll slit your throat right now!"

"I don't know," wailed Um Edouard, gasping with fear. "Maybe it was the Movement. Maybe it was Abu Saleh."

I felt an indescribable relief. So it was only Um Edouard he was about to kill, not Amira! He threw down the knife and shoved her hard, then yanked off his shoe and beat her with it on the head and face, knocking her to the ground and spitting on her. Then, still unpurged, he ran around the courtyard like a man possessed before halting by a column and banging his head against it while braying rhythmically: "No more daugh-ter! No more ho-nour! No more daugh-ter!"

After a while he stopped and stood stiff as a tree. "Abu Saleh," he muttered in a quietly menacing tone, as if the name had just penetrated. Picking up the knife, he rushed from the courtyard and nearly collided with Edouard, who was innocently returning from the baker's with a stack of fresh pittas. Edouard hurried to his mother's side.

"Kabi, quick," my mother called. "Go and warn Abu Saleh!"

I didn't have to be told. I threw on my clothes and sandals and sprinted down the stairs while buttoning my trousers. A night, a day, and another night had passed since that enchanted evening with Amira and I could still taste her kisses, smell her scent, feel her embrace. The whole of the next day I had longed for her and hoped to see her. Did she feel the same way about me? Even if I was not the man of her dreams, perhaps the evening had changed her. How would she look at me when we met?

All day I had hung around her house, making frequent trips to our roof. There had been no sign of her. And now I understood why.

She had known Abu Saleh would get her out of Iraq when she had said to me "There won't be much more of this." Perhaps they had already set a time. It could have been decided on the day she turned down his proposal. Or else he had mustered the courage to propose after being told by her that she had to leave home. He had known her father would never agree to such a marriage.

Despite my anguish at losing her, this made me feel less guilty. What had happened between us was unthinkable in Baghdad and certainly to my mother, whom I wouldn't have dreamed of telling about it; and though her moral standards were not mine, they were too much a part of me to ignore them. A decent young lady let no one touch her before her wedding and a decent young man respected her for it, abetted by a special class of women named whores; and despite my wonderful evening with Amira, the insidious poison of my education made me wonder whether she might not be a bit of a whore herself. True, I was old enough to realize that such an unconventional person threatened the male egotism catered to by local custom, and I had been exposed to enough books, films, and discussions with my teachers to know that she was worth all the slave girls of Baghdad. Still, there was enough of Baghdad still inside me to make me feel ashamed and frightened.

Not that I was thinking so logically as I tried outrunning Abu Edouard to the bakery, nor would I for a long time to come. I was little more than a confused jumble of feelings that were not very different from Edouard's, except that I was at least asking the right questions.

I caught up with Abu Edouard outside the bakery.

"How would you like to marry my daughter?" he asked Abu Saleh from the doorway, breathing heavily.

"Would I ever!" The baker jumped up delighted. "So you finally agree?"

It was only an act. He knew that Amira was no longer in Iraq and that she didn't want him for a husband.

"When you're dead and I dance on your grave!" declared Abu Edouard, whipping out the knife. With his other hand he gave the burlap tablecloth a quick tug, sending the hot pittas flying.

"What's the matter with you?" asked the baker.

"You're asking *me*, you son of a whore?"

"Leave my mother out of this. She's dead and buried."

"Just like you'll be," snarled Abu Edouard, brandishing the knife.

Street vendors and passers-by began gathering outside. "Have you two Jews gone crazy?" asked the sambusak man. "Cut it out!"

"First you screw her, then you screw me, is that the deal?" shouted Amira's father, an insane glint in his eyes.

"You're out of your mind. How can you talk about your daughter like that?" asked the baker.

Abu Edouard crouched for the spring. He tried turning over the heavy table, then sought to circle it to the left and to the right, but Abu Saleh, who was younger and quicker, kept it between them until the older man was exhausted.

"Why did you do it? You think she'll marry you there?"

"Would I smuggle a little girl to Israel?"

"Then who the hell did?"

"How do you know that's where she is?"

"Read!" Abu Edouard tossed him a crumpled piece of paper. The baker didn't even look at it. In an injured voice Abu Edouard read:

"Baba, I've gone to Israel. I'll see you some time, Amira."

"So what do you want from me?" asked Abu Saleh.

"I'll turn you in to the police, *wihyat Allah!*"

"You'll pay for it if you do."

"She'll never be yours! Not as long as I live, I'll see you in hell first!" He hurled the baker's tongs at him.

"That's enough, Abu Edouard. I'm warning you."

"How could you do it to me? I'll drink your blood! Who asked you for your fucking Movement? You've ruined our daughters. You've poisoned them."

The dove flyer darted one way and then the other, slashing the air with his knife.

418

"Call the police," someone yelled.

"Are you crazy?" said the sambusak man. "They'll jail them both."

"All right, that's enough," ordered old Hiyawi, appearing as if out of nowhere. "Abu Edouard, give me that knife. The police are on their way and you have other children at home to bring up." He put his arm around the dove flyer, took the knife from him, and threw it into the flaming oven. Then he manoeuvred Abu Edouard into his tobacco shop.

There was something touching and pathetic in the sight of the frail old man leading his burly neighbour like a donkey. Inside the shop he sat Abu Edouard on a stool and poured a jug of cold water over his head. Abu Edouard sat with the water running down him, wiping the eternal sniffle from his nose.

"There were times when men listened to their betters and Rabbi Bashi's word was law," sighed old Hiyawi. "A son obeyed his father and no daughter talked back to her mother. That's all gone now. Parents don't even know where their children are any more."

Abu Edouard sat staring into space. His fleshy face hung limply on its bones. After a while he stirred, staggered out, and went home.

For three whole days Abu Edouard went from tavern to tavern, drinking himself into such a stupor that he could not have told you where or when he ate and slept. Through it all he kept seeing the daughter he loved.

When the three days were over, he went down to the river bank with a straw basket filled with bottles of arrack and garlic cloves. There he clawed at the soft earth as if to bury his pain and lay down to wallow by the water. The sun rose and set and rose and set again, and Abu Edouard remained where he was.

He spent the days in the water with a bottle and the nights on the shore with a bottle. Giddy with arrack fumes and belching garlic, he saw a strange sight. Suitcases. Dozens, hundreds, thousands of suitcases, a whole river of them. Blue suitcases. Green suitcases. Grey suitcases. Brown suitcases. Metal suitcases. Wooden suitcases. Leather suitcases. Canvas suitcases. All floating past him down the Tigris. And in every one of them, if only he could open it, was Amira. Yes, he need only open them all and the world would be full of gorgeous, Princess Amiras.

When Abu Edouard opened his eyes the suitcases were gone. There was nothing but water lapping at the stones of a nearby bridge. And in that brief moment of lucidity, Abu Edouard glimpsed the great idea that he had been searching for all his life. He would sell suitcases to the sons-of-bitches going to the goddamn Jewish state! Their misfortune would be his profit and with the money he made he would crush Abu Saleh. First he would buy out his bakery. Then he would kill him, drink his blood, roast his flesh, burn his bones, and scatter the ashes in the river.

As soon as he was sober Abu Edouard went to Iwa the swimming instructor's shack, borrowed clean clothes, threw his dirty clothes in the river, jumped in after them to clean himself, and emerged like a week-long mourner ready to start a new life. First he rented a large wooden rubbish cart, trundled it to his shop, and emptied a lifetime's accumulation of junk into it, including his British army surplus uniform. Then he painted the place a bright blue and asked little Salumi the sign-printer to make a big sign on which a white dove with golden stripes carried a suitcase with its legs. With his gifted brush Salumi covered the walls with doves too: brown ones, white ones, grey ones, black ones, even one red one, the largest and prettiest of them all, which hopped by itself over the entrance.

Next, Abu Edouard bought an English safari suit and filled his shop with suitcases. These he sold at a discount, throwing in a free lock and home delivery, which he paid Edouard to do. Business boomed. In no time the market had been cornered. Long lines of customers waited outside the store. Never had the proverb proved truer that when Allah takes, he also gives.

Abu Edouard was now too busy to deliver any more orations about the imminent doom of the Jewish state and the folly of settling in it. On the contrary, he joined his bitter enemy Abu Saleh in urging Jews to apply for emigration. "It will weed out the chaff," he told himself, convinced that with the traitors gone the Moslems would take more kindly to patriots like himself who held out against the Zionist mirage. Let the Abu Salehs and the riffraff clear out and life would go back to its old pleasant course, as it had done after the *Farhood* and every other calamity!

Abu Edouard kept his store open until late at night and remained after closing time to count the daily takings, sniffing the piles of dinars as if they were jasmine flowers. Thinking of his daughter Amira, he would moan and murmur through his tears:

"What wouldn't I have done for you? I would have showered you with gold, sent you to America. Why did you leave me? Allah, for forty years You let me live like a beggar, and when I finally strike it rich, You have taken my daughter from me first! What kind of cockeyed way is that to run a world?"

44.

When Abu Saleh told my father how he had hidden Salim Effendi, the two men grinned at each other. Within an hour they came up with a plan.

That evening my father went to see Big Imari in his office. "I thought I told you not to come here," said Big Imari, rising from behind his desk. "It won't do your brother any good."

"Have you spoken to the Pasha?"

"No. And your disregarding my instructions isn't helping. There's no need to call attention to the connection between us."

"I'm glad to hear you acknowledge that there is a connection. But I have news for you. The CID is also looking for one Rahamim Imari, alias Salim Effendi. If I'm not mistaken you're connected to him too."

"What's it to me if I am?"

"Nothing at all except that both your cousins happen to know a few things about you."

"They don't know anything about me!"

"Salim Effendi has told the Movement that you've sent large sums of money to Israel."

"Is that some kind of a joke? What does that filthy Communist have to do with the Movement?"

"You'll have to take my word for it."

"Birds of different feathers don't flock together," said Big Imari.

"They do if they're Jewish birds."

"If I get what you're driving at, you're barking up the wrong tree. That madman has no evidence."

"Since when does evidence matter in this country?"

"All that matters is who is believed."

"Precisely," said my father as if talking to himself. "And also what is believed. Your sending money to Israel is too absurd a charge for anyone to invent. Shafik Addas never thought that the accusations against him would be believed either. 'Selling arms to the Zionist entity' ... it sounded like a joke to him. A military band played by his scaffold and all his property was confiscated after his execution. Five million dinars, they say. That's a very tempting sum, don't you think?"

"You're trying to blackmail me!"

"I am? Perish the thought! But your esteemed cousin, your son's tutor, claims to have some unfinished business with you."

Big Imari sat down and mopped the sweat from his pale face.

"What does he want?"

"To get to Iran," said my father serenely.

"What?"

"Naturally, the Movement expects you to arrange for Hizkel to travel with him."

"You're all out of your minds!"

"There's no need to get excited. You should take better care of your health. Salim Effendi says that your heart isn't what it used to be."

"It's all George's fault. I warned him to stay away from that Communist!"

"When will you talk to the Pasha?"

"I'm flying to London tomorrow," said Big Imari after a moment's silence. "I'll do it when I get back."

"You'll do it before you leave. A man's life is at stake."

"I can't. This isn't a pleasure jaunt. I'm going for my heart," said Big Imari, suddenly meek. As my father turned to go, he added: "How do I know that madman won't tell his crazy stories in Iran too?"

"Leave that to us," said my father, who knew Salim Effendi was already on his way to Iran and would never dream of framing his cousin.

Long afterwards I learned from George that Big Imari, after spending the flight to London debating what to do, decided not to go to the Pasha. It was wisest not to trouble him with such a matter. And besides, if he refused, where else could one turn?

On returning from London with new medicine, George's father threw a party for the minister of the interior. After the guests had left and the two men were left alone, he presented the minister with twelve silk ties and a case of "Red arrack", as the latter called his favourite Russian vodka. Going out to the veranda, the two men rocked for a while in the white *jalala* while Big Imari regaled his guest with stories about the escapades of certain of their acquaintances with the fair sex of Great Britain. When the vodka had gone sufficiently to the minister's head, he said to him:

"There's a small favour I'd like to ask of you."

"Ask, my friend. The keys to the kingdom are yours."

"I'd like expelled from Iraq two young men whose parents were owed a debt of gratitude by my parents. They're troublemakers."

"A small request from a great man," said the minister. "Write their names for me."

When he looked at the piece of paper that was handed to him however, he sobered up at once. "You call them just troublemakers? One is not in my hands at the moment. The other is a big catch and a big trial is planned for him."

"Catch and grill another fish instead," suggested Big Imari.

"I swear by your son George and my son Jamal, it's more than I can do. You'll have to talk to the Pasha. Both men happen to be related to you, don't they?"

"Distantly," murmured Big Imari, beads of perspiration forming on his forehead.

He walked his friend to the gate. When they reached it, the minister put his hand on Big Imari's shoulder and said: "By the way, your son is heading for a bit of trouble. I'd keep an eye on him."

"My son?" Big Imari turned pale.

"Why not send him to Eton? It's one of the finest English schools. My own son is a student there."

Big Imari stumbled back to the garden and downed a glass of vodka against his doctors' advice. Then he sat for a while on the *jalala*. A talk with the Pasha was unavoidable.

George's mother brought him two pills, one white and one yellow.

"Woman," said Big Imari, "pack George's things."
"Why?"
"I've decided to send him to school in England."

45.

His clothes stained with flour, Salim Effendi climbed down from the truck after a long, exhausting trip. He had sat scrunched up between the sacks for so many hours that he could barely straighten himself out.

He was in the northern city of Kirkuk where, as Abu Saleh had predicted, he was met by a strapping young man called Baruch who took him home and put him up in a bare room with a low wooden bed. In his worst dreams he had never imagined leaving Iraq like a thief in the night, a man without papers, without even a name, with nothing but the bundle of clothes under his arm.

Baruch showed him where to wash, served him a sour Kurdish *kubba* soup and some strong, sweet tea, and said he would have to wait a few days for the rest of the group. That was all Salim Effendi could get out of him. Even when the two of them sat playing backgammon, Baruch volunteered no further information.

It took ten days for the group to form, after which they set out at night with two mules and walked in single file until dawn, when they took cover in a cave. Their guide, a man with a stammer and a quick temper, gave them two sooty cans, one for coffee and one for tea, gathered some wood that was still wet with dew, helped them to light a fire, and disappeared. He returned a little later with some pittas and hard-boiled eggs in a straw basket and vanished again until dusk.

Salim Effendi felt fear steal into his heart. Five Jews, a member of the group had told him, had already been killed along the route they were taking. What a place to die in! And his family would die with him. He was the only one left. He should have married long ago and had children to name after his dead parents.

And yet what did it matter? Why should someone who wanted to change the world and redeem its millions care about having a son or a daughter?

Why be a revolutionary if this was only an alibi for his failure to be a husband and a father? And then again, if it was marriage that he wanted, why his obsession with Bahia, who could never be his wife, when he had his Englishwoman with her British passport? He could ask her to come to Israel with him, or lead a life of luxury with her in London.

Alas, he did not even have the money to get there. In his pocket was the grand total of ten dinars, loaned him by Abu Saleh in return for a promise to repay the Movement when he could.

What had it been about the rough-and-ready baker that seemed so likeable and inspired such confidence? Now he had no one to talk to. The others in the group, who were already friends despite having just met, were young enough to be his pupils. There were twenty of them in total, all Zionist activists wanted by the CID, and it was hard to keep up with their pace. He was thankful for Abed, Abu Kabi's Kurdish helper and the natural leader of the group, who brought up the rear and helped the others through difficult spots. Who would have thought that this meek servant from the watch shop would be able to take charge so competently?

For a fatiguing week they climbed densely thicketed hills by night, their fate in the hands of their nameless guide. One morning, as the first light was dawning, the man pointed to a police station flying the Iranian flag, collected three more dinars from each of them, showed them where to wait, and vanished for the last time.

They did not sit there long, for a bus soon appeared out of nowhere. A young man with a crewcut welcomed them in Hebrew and Arabic, handed out chicken sandwiches and lemon-flavoured drinks, and explained the last leg of their route, which ended with their driving through a large gate near the Jewish cemetery of Teheran and arriving in a fenced compound of tents and brick huts. There they were given camp vouchers and shown to their quarters in a large hut crammed with bunk beds.

Salim Effendi lay on one of them for a long time in his sticky underwear, his legs and back aching. Far from being relieved by the knowledge that he was safe, he felt crushed and stripped of all illusions. He, old Imari's grandson, running for his life from his own country!

Outside the tent the Zionists had built a bonfire, around which they were hugging and kissing and singing and dancing and shouting for joy. He had no desire to watch them. Perhaps he was too worn out from the grinding tension of the march, though they, who had been through it too, were jumping up and down like young goats. Well, their future was before them. Where was his?

The next morning he awoke and went to wash at the outdoor sink. A tall girl in a white track suit was leading the group in calisthenics; he smiled at her invitation to join them. After an insipid breakfast, he obtained special permission to leave the camp for a few hours.

Having committed his address to memory, he went off to find his friend Mas'ud, the Iranian Communist Party's liaison in Teheran. Mas'ud was startled to see him and invited him out for a meal. It was good to eat real food at last, a superb kebab with buttered rice and cold yoghurt, washed down by beer drunk while munching pistachio nuts. But Mas'ud explained that there was no hope of finding Salim Effendi work with the Party in Teheran. If the police arrested him he would be extradited to Iraq. The sooner he left for Israel the better, especially since the Communist party operated legally there and was even represented in parliament.

On his way back to the camp, Salim Effendi entered a bathhouse and scrubbed himself feverishly, as if seeking to cleanse himself of the trip and Mas'ud's bad news. All roads led to Israel, then! It was a revolutionary's luck never to know what reversals awaited him in life. Perhaps from Israel he could get to Moscow. Or perhaps he would enter Party life, unafraid this time of the hangman's noose. A democracy, Mas'ud had called it. A bourgeois one, of course, but the Jews were a soft-hearted people, or at least were reputed to be. Who knew how they would behave once they had the whip hand?

Yes, we Jews, thought Salim Effendi, surprised by the word "we", are the only people in the world that has never slaughtered or oppressed anyone, but that's only because we never had the chance. Now that we have, will we be any better than the others?

True, Israel was at least a country where being Jewish would not count against him. But there would be, he mused, thinking of the youngsters dancing around the bonfire, a different problem there: how could the Communist revolution possibly compete with the Zionist one?

He had never understood the secret of the Zionists' success.

Why did they always seem able to make things work for them? And why had they taken such risks in stockpiling arms in Iraq when all they wanted was to get the Jews out of the country? Glorified travel agents, that was all they really were! They had no universal idea, no basis in history, nothing but simple, ordinary answers. To make the Jews just another people: that was their great dream! He would have to seek his future home elsewhere.

It was night when he returned to the camp. An Iranian Jew in a bunk next to his had died and the corpse had been left to lie there until morning; the Jews from Iran, who were in transit to Israel too, had all kinds of infectious diseases. Cats yowled outside, as if demanding the dead body. Salim Effendi was stricken with fear. He missed Sylvia. He waited impatiently for the next day when he had an appointment with an Israeli official.

The Israeli was an impressive-looking man in his forties, elegantly dressed in a suit and tie. He looked nothing like the pioneers in khaki shorts that Salim Effendi had seen in Zionist publications.

"Are you related to Hizkel Imari?" the man asked.

"I'm his cousin. But I'm a Communist."

"Good."

"I was in charge of the Communist Party's youth and agitprop sections in Baghdad."

"Good."

"I could have gone all the way to the top."

"Good," said the Israeli.

"I want to go to Moscow. Or to Prague."

"Good. Do you have a passport?"

"No. But ... "

"Do you have any papers?"

"No. But perhaps … " Salim Effendi fell silent.

"Good," said the Israeli, putting down a list he had been looking at. "When would you like to leave?"

"For where?"

"For Israel."

"But I just told you I'm a Communist."

"A Jewish one?"

"Y … yes."

"Good," said the Israeli, handing Salim Effendi some documents. "The bus to the airport will depart from the front gate of the camp at three o'clock on Wednesday afternoon. I'll see you in Israel."

46.

The first Jews to board the first plane for Israel, which left on 10 May 1950, were S'haik the shoemaker with his twin boys and Mas'udah, a woman abandoned by her husband. Abu Saleh el-Hibaz did a little dance around them, singing, "And I will carry ye on eagles' wings and bring ye unto Me." My father was thrilled and wanted to share the moment with his brother, and it was with a heavy heart that he pressed notes into my hand and forced himself to ask me to go to the prison once more and tell Hizkel the news.

"We've won," said Hizkel when I told him, tears shining in his eyes. He wanted to know about the mood in the Jewish quarter, how many had signed up to leave, and whether the pace was quickening. Abu Saleh, he said, should strike while the iron was hot. It was time for Operation If I Forget Thee, Jerusalem.

That was all Abu Saleh needed to hear. That night the baker assembled the Movement's cell leaders, gave them Hizkel's orders, and sent them to the synagogues, the schools, the coffee houses, the marketplaces, and the homes of Baghdad's Jews. "Plead with them," he said. "Threaten them. Tell them that the Moslems can't tell a Zionist from any other Jew. Tell them the Pasha has it in for them."

Abu Saleh was in a fighting mood. Emigration was still a thin trickle. The Jews asked for redemption every day in their prayers but clung to exile in their lives. If not for his promise to

Hizkel to remain in Iraq until the last Jew had departed, he himself would have left by now. In his thoughts he was already in Israel. Only Fat'hiya the *kemar* seller calmed his anger at the lack of faith around him.

Ever since Amira turned down his proposal, he had sought to forget her in the arms of the beautiful Bedouin. As never before, he was entirely hers.

He had first met Fat'hiya, a new arrival in Baghdad, three years previously. Thirteen years of married life had failed to produce a child, and her husband's two other wives, who were more fruitful, had talked him into divorcing her. Rather than return at the age of twenty-seven to her parents, who were none too happy to have her back, she left her village and set out for Baghdad.

One day she walked into Abu Saleh's bakery and asked permission to sell her wares in the corner. A few weeks later she gave herself to him. A ripe, sensual woman, she washed his clothes, hand-fed him *kemar* topped with quince honey, whispered sweet Bedouin nothings into his ear, amused him with her stories and proverbs, and loved him to distraction in place of the son she never had.

His love for Amira, Abu Saleh realized, had been nourished by his hopes, and now that these were buried, the princess, as he called her, faded so quickly from his mind that he could hardly remember what she looked like. And at the same time, his worry for Fat'hiya increased from day to day. What would happen to her when he left? He told my father that he thought of taking her to Israel or even sending her illegally ahead of him; perhaps she would convert and he would marry her there, or else she could help his Jewish wife with the children and the housework. It may only have been a fantasy, but he genuinely cared for her.

Abu Saleh told Fat'hiya nothing of his plans, nor did she begin to understand what was happening. Zionism was beyond her ken. Who, if Abu Saleh left, would be her man, she who had grown accustomed to a sensitive lover who never beat her, an oversight that in her village would have cast grave doubt on his masculinity? Who would pamper her, buy her jewelry, sing her Bedouin love songs, jest with her, the warmth of his voice enough to make her laugh at jokes she didn't understand? Even though she was a divorcee, her family might slit her throat if it found out about the two of them. There was no knowing what such people were capable of. As far as they were concerned, you didn't have to be a virgin to shame your family and deserve to die.

It was partly to escape such thoughts that Abu Saleh threw himself more than ever into the work of getting Jews to Israel by fair means or foul. All of his operatives were now functioning at fever pitch too.

One day I found old Hiyawi sitting stiffly in his shop, grunting and sweating with a jaundiced look. His lips muttered words I couldn't make out. I wet his face with cold water from the jug, dried it, propped his head against a pillow, and cooled him with his bamboo fan. "Where is she going at a time like this?" I heard him say.

"Who?" I asked.

Just then I turned and saw Rashel passing in the street. "Why don't you drop by sometime?" she asked and was gone before I could answer.

I hadn't seen her for a while. I hadn't even told her about my last visit to Hizkel. I was still in an electric glow of longing after my magical evening with Amira. A kind of order had crept into my indiscriminate lust for every woman, and I had begun to understand that not every throb of my loins was a palpitation of my heart. Days now went by without my thinking of Rashel, and no sooner had I turned back to Hiyawi than her casually uttered words, which had revived my old desire, were forgotten.

Hiyawi really didn't look good. "I'm going for Dr Mrad," I told him.

"You don't have to," he murmured, clutching me with his sinewy hand. "It's a waste of good money."

I took no notice and Dr. Mrad came with me straight away. He had a look at the old man, and assured us both that it was "just a spell of old folk's weakness". He gave Hiyawi some pills and ordered him to rest. I took the old man home, put him to bed, and went to the kitchen to make tea.

There was a smell of smoke in the kitchen. Ever since his young wife's death long ago, the kerosene burner was kept lit day and night like a kind of memorial lamp. Although Hiyawi made sure to trim its wick now and then, tentacles of black soot had spread across the walls and ceiling and the kettle was encrusted with black grease. By the time I returned to his room with the tea, he was fast asleep.

I sat beside him and drank the tea myself. Hiyawi's snores were comforting. At least his lungs were still strong! Leaving the light on, I went home.

When I arrived my brother Nuri hugged me joyously and told me that the synagogue had been bombed and that my parents, who were afraid I might have been there, were frantic.

I ran to the bakery. It was closed ... a bad sign. I raced to the synagogue. A large throng filled the square outside. Groups of people were talking in low tones.

"Who threw the bombs?" I asked someone.

"The damned Moslems."

"Don't be so gullible," said a bearded Jew. "The Movement did it."

He was shaking.

"You mean Jews tried killing Jews?"

"Why would Moslems throw bombs when we're leaving anyway?"

"That's just it! To kill us while we're still here. Who will they take it out on when we're gone?"

"Was anyone hurt?" I asked.

"Lots of people. One's dead."

I shinned up a drainpipe and looked down on the hundreds of heads. My mother was there, her hand over her mouth as if stifling a cry. I tried calling to her but my voice was lost in the din. "Kabi, Kabi," she cried, throwing her arms around me when I climbed down and made my way to her. She was faint with relief.

"Where's Baba?" I asked.

"Helping Abu Saleh with the wounded."

"Who threw the bombs?"

"Abu Saleh and his men," she answered. "That's what everyone's saying."

"Watch what men you blame. Baba is one of them."

"Your father would never do such a thing. He's too much of a coward. But some people are ready to see Jews die in order to scare them into leaving. Where were you, Kabi? I've been looking for you everywhere. I was crazy with worry."

I told her about Hiyawi.

"Bless you. It was your good deed that saved you. May Allah give you and the old man a long life."

The next morning she rose early to make Hiyawi a rice porridge and told me to take it to him but he wasn't home.

I went to the synagogue and found him there, his old, irascible self. It was good to see him that way, although not to listen to him.

"Those Zionists!" he growled. "Nothing is holy for them. They've split the community, they've smuggled the best of our young people abroad, and now they're trying to create a stampede with the rest of us. There's nothing they'll stop at, not even murder. They've tormented Rabbi Bashi and made a mockery of our leaders. It's they who threw the bombs! They'll do anything to have their way. They want to destroy the oldest Jewish community on earth. They're worse than the Communists."

"I don't believe it," I said.

"You're young and innocent, son. My God, what have we come to? Woe to the eyes that have seen Jews bombing a Jewish synagogue! Lord, put out the light in them and take back this soul from my body!"

His eyes were bloodshot and frightening. He looked as if he wanted to die.

47

The argument over who threw the bombs would go on for
years, but one thing was clear: the emigration centre had come
to life again. New faces appeared there: the families of
youngsters who had already left for Israel illegally, prosperous
businessmen and shopkeepers, residents of well-to-do
neighbourhoods such as Karadeh, Bab-el-Shargi, Ilwi, and New
Baghdad, even those who until now had avoided the Movement
like poison.

The lines grew longer by the day. Diehards like Abu Edouard
continued to carp, but even they, it seemed, now realized that
the tide could not be stemmed. An entire tribe was heading for
what my father called "the final destination", and Abu Edouard,
"just another stop on the road."

Taht el-Takya was emptying of its Jews. Even the widow
Farha, who once had hoped that Abu Edouard would marry
her, signed up for emigration. Every day someone else was
missing from school. Classrooms were deserted. Lessons were
cancelled. Teachers disappeared. There were rumours that
Moslems would be hired to take their place, and even that the
school itself would stop being a Jewish one. Kassem, the one-
eyed Moslem watchman, was in a funereal mood.

The shops in the Jewish market now sold mostly clothing.
Abu Edouard's luggage shop was doing extraordinary business.
He had, my father told me, heard from Amira. She was living in

a kibbutz called Kiryat Oranim and Abu Edouard joked that he would buy the whole place for her with the money he was making. Giving my father his hand, he swore half in earnest and half in jest that Amira and I would get married in Israel and that he would send us a big dowry via London.

"The young couple," said my father, humouring him, "will expect your personal attendance at its wedding in Jerusalem."

Men with bright cloaks and banded keffiyehs began appearing in Taht el-Takya. At first they took over shops and stands in the Jewish market. Then they started moving into houses, filling every empty room. It happened so quickly that the neighbourhood became mixed before anyone realized.

With the Moslems came a wave of Palestinian refugees. They were hard-working and thirsting for revenge, and I liked listening to their singsong Arabic, so different from the stiff, wooden speech of Iraq. If they had been less full of hate, they would have been more deserving of pity. Here and there a Jew tried to help them. In the beginning they sought to hide their malice, though it oozed from every pore. They strode about Taht el-Takya like its rightful heirs, impatient for it to pass into their hands.

The neighbourhood no longer teemed with agents and dealers. Prices had plunged and Jews selling their valuables for a song could not find buyers. Why spend money on what would soon be yours anyway? Furniture, utensils, books, and other things that the law forbade taking to Israel were thrown into the street. It was heartbreaking. The only permissible items were clothes and personal possessions.

Hungry and penniless, the Palestinians swooped down on these piles of discarded goods and carried them off. Old Hiyawi watched them through slit eyes and muttered: "They leap upon the city, they run upon the walls; they climb up into the houses, they enter through the windows like a thief."

"What are you mumbling, Hiyawi?" I asked.

He opened the Book of Joel and showed me the verse. "They're like locusts, son."

"Then come with us. Why stay behind?"

"An old tree can't be replanted."

"But it can be eaten by locusts."

"Not if it's dead. And I'll die where I was born."

There should be, I thought, a clause allowing one to waive Iraqi citizenship for an old man too irresponsible to do it for himself.

"And anyway," Hiyawi added, "Israel doesn't want us either." It was hard to argue with that. Although the residents of Taht el-Takya had sold their homes or given up their leases and were now roofless as well as jobless – they went from house to house with their suitcases and stayed with friends and relatives or slept in the synagogue and other communal buildings – the planes from Israel still came in dribs and drabs. There was at most one a day, and Baghdad's Jews, dressed in their new clothes like bridegrooms at a wedding to which the bride had not come, felt the world collapsing around them.

An epidemic of rumours sapped their strength. Each day they clutched at new straws and argued who was at fault, Israel for not sending the planes or Iraq for not letting them land. The debate was still in progress when another rumour reached us that the government was planning to confiscate all Jewish property. This was, it was said, part of the Pasha's plot to turn the Jews into refugees like the Palestinians, stateless ghosts held hostage by the Moslems.

Baghdad, the City of Roses, had become the city of thorns.

And as if we were not already hanging by a thread, more Jews now descended on us, whole caravans from Arbil, from Mosul, from Zaku, many of them stocky, colourfully dressed men with swords and turbans, as flinty as the mountains of the Kurdish revolt that they hailed from. They came with nothing, having had to fight their way past brigands and highwaymen, and were put up in already crowded hostels. Illness broke out, children took sick, old people died. My father and Abu Saleh organized a relief society, for which they levied a tax on the Jewish shopkeepers. We young people pitched in.

The Kurdish Jews were funnily dressed and odd to look at, but they inspired pride. There was something strong and free-spirited about them. They sat around campfires, baked a thin, crisp bread, and talked loudly in a language no one understood. Apart from that, they were like us: their past was gone, their present was in their bundles, and their future was anyone's guess.

The Jewish quarter had turned into a huge transit camp crowded with local Jews, Kurds, poor Moslems, and Palestinian refugees, all unemployed and living from hand to mouth. The children played among piles of rubbish with no homes or schools to go to.

The relief work quickly bored me. I would have stopped it altogether if I hadn't felt guilty about my parents, who worked around the clock and had even learned to speak a few sentences of Kurdish. I couldn't wait for the plane that would take us from this nightmare to the country of our dreams, where all Jews were as good and wise as the angels of Paradise and my father would plant vast fields of rice in the dazzling light.

48.

In his deepening melancholy Abu Edouard began to suffer from delusions of persecution. It was no accident, he was convinced, that the home of his neighbour S'haik had been acquired by an Arab who was a dove flyer too. The man had moved in next door on purpose and built a large dovecote for nefarious ends.

At first Abu Edouard had tried being nice to the newcomer, Abdel Majid Abu Hamid, a large, moustachioed Moslem with a slight limp, two wives, and thirteen children who rushed to do his bidding. Effusively he explained to him that Jews and Zionists were different species and that he himself had no intention of abandoning his Iraqi dovecote to migrate to Palestine. But Abu Hamid was not interested in explanations. A Jew was a Jew and everyone knew that Jews who were not Zionists were a figment of the imagination.

At first Abu Hamid simply smiled and showed his gold teeth while his wives and children cooked on the roof, kindling fires with dried bird droppings whose stench filled our house. Abu Edouard actually thought he was lucky to have a neighbour who raised doves and could share his hobby with him in place of Abu Kabi.

True, Abu Hamid's dovecote was much larger than his own and a source of some anxiety, but why not hope for the best?

Before long, however, it transpired that Abu Hamid flew his doves at the exact same times of day as Abu Edouard, and the

Jewish birds joined their more numerous Moslem counterparts. As his flock began to dwindle Abu Edouard tried changing its schedule, but the Moslem changed his too and kept luring more deserters. In the end Abu Edouard threw up his hands and with a mournful smile resigned himself to his fate. He thought of the days when, bestriding the doorway of his junk shop or seated at Abu Ednan's, he had told his neighbours with a grin of his own flock's conquests. Old Hiyawi had told him that this was theft, which was why Rabbi Bashi had disqualified dove flyers as witnesses in rabbinical courts, since they were all gamblers and cheats. "Just wait and see," the old man had said. "One day you'll be given a taste of your own medicine."

Although that had been more than Abu Edouard could imagine, it was now happening before his eyes. Each flight of his doves brought less pleasure and more worry than the one before. No longer did he picture himself as a second Tarik ibn Ziyad, the fabled Andalusian general, commanding his airborne troops.

So great became his hate of the Moslem, who rubbed his hands with pleasure each time he brought his flock down with a great whistle, that Abu Edouard even began to detest his neighbours' doves. He no longer had a single carefree moment. Only his booming luggage business kept him from drowning his sorrows in arrack at Abu Ednan's. His old self-confidence gone, he grew so silent and timid that he seemed to have become inches shorter. "Even the sky has turned against me," he told his son Edouard as his flock continued to decline.

Edouard now tended to the doves while his nervous wreck of a father stood below in the courtyard, biting his thumb while watching the last of his dwindling flock wheel drunkenly as though flying in its sleep. Edouard did not like the work or consider it an art like his father. His mind was on his activity in the Party, which had recently given him his first official assignment, and on his Christian girlfriend Gloria. In recent months he had become even taller and more manly. Preoccupied with the mass arrests of Communists, especially since the disappearance of Salim Effendi, he cared for the doves fitfully. The flock that had been the pride of Taht el-Takya was down to its last few birds. The Jews were being driven from the heavens no less than from the earth.

My father, saddened by his friend's depression, did not like our new neighbour either. Unable to listen to the Arabic news from Israel because of him, he was like a man deprived of oxygen; worse still, loath to dismantle our antenna, the biggest in the Jewish quarter, he was forced to invite Abu Hamid to his Um Kultoum parties.

The Moslem sat in our courtyard as if he owned it, twirling his moustache like a sheikh while his eyes devoured Rashel, who helped my mother serve refreshments. His appetite for what seemed to him easy prey grew even greater when he found out that her husband was in prison. "It's an insult to Allah for such a woman to be alone," he was heard to say. Not even the fact that Rashel was my father's sister-in-law cooled his passion.

One such evening Abu Hamid was lavishly praising Rashel's beauty while she served tea and coffee from a tray and thanked him for his compliments, politely nodding even when he proposed marriage. If only she would agree to be his number one wife, all her problems would be solved! I couldn't believe my ears. She needed to be removed from his clutches. Before I could decide what to do Edouard went over to her and said: "Um Kabi needs you in the kitchen." She made a beeline for the door.

"That was quick thinking," I said to Edouard.

"I hope you're planning to leave her behind for me," he joked.

"Some chance!" My laughter was too loud. Once again I felt drawn to Rashel like a moth to a flame.

"Seriously," said Edouard. "You have to take her with you. You can't leave her alone in a neighbourhood without Jews."

"Try telling that to her. She's as stubborn as a mule."

"By the way, do you have any idea what happened to Salim Effendi?"

"The Zionists got him out of the country," I whispered.

"Unbelievable!" he whistled. To my surprise, he seemed on the verge of tears.

So did Miss Sylvia when I told her in carefully rehearsed English on instructions from Abu Saleh, who must have been asked by Salim Effendi to let her know: "I have been requested to inform you that Stad Salem has been taken to Israel. That is all I can say."

She threw me a startled look, put her hand on my shoulder, gave it a squeeze, and said: "Thank you, Kabi."

It was the first and last time she ever called me that. Usually, I was "Mr Kabi Imari".

Edouard punched my arm and said:

"I'll miss you. If you run into Amira there tell her I miss her too. And that I'm sorry for everything."

Now it was me who nearly burst out crying. I gave him a friendly punch back and walked away.

I left the guests listening to Um Kultoum and went to the kitchen. Rashel was sobbing.

"Just look at who you're leaving me with," she said, her shoulders heaving.

"Then come with us. How are you helping Hizkel by staying? You're not even allowed to visit him."

"I can't leave him here! What kind of wife would I be? I'll never abandon him like your father has."

"If you have accounts to settle with my father, do so with him," I told her.

"Where has the Movement been? Where has Israel been? They've thrown Hizkel to the dogs." She began to cry again.

"Abu Saleh has plans to free him. He's doing all he can."

"Don't mention Abu Saleh to me. A big hero! I could fill the Tigris with his promises. He's glad to have Hizkel out of the way so that he can run the Movement. Since the arrest he's avoided me. He's so afraid of me that he doesn't even come to your Um Kultoum parties."

"He has to be careful.

"Why hasn't your father been to see Big Imari?"

"Who says he hasn't?"

The words were out of my mouth before I knew it. My father should have broken his damned promise to Big Imari and told her! It was her right to know.

"Then why hasn't he said so? Don't I matter to him? Oh, I know what he thinks. I'm just a woman who can't keep a secret. What's Big Imari going to do?" She rose to go. "It's time for bed. I didn't sleep a wink last night. I really don't know what I'm doing here. These parties aren't for me."

I followed her to the gate. "You needn't come with me," she said, giving my arm a squeeze. "I want to be alone."

49.

My father was not in his shop, nor at Hiyawi's, nor at the baker's, nor at Abu Ednan's. I ran home.

"Mama, where's Baba?"

"Hush. He's taking a nap in the cellar."

"We're on the departure list!"

"So?"

Why couldn't she show some sign of happiness? All at once the wind went out of my sails. I had been overjoyed when I saw the name Salman Moshi Imari on the bulletin board but now everything seemed up in the air again. I couldn't stand being in the middle of their tug-of-war.

"Let him sleep," my mother said. "He's exhausted."

I roamed the courtyard restlessly and went down to the dusky cellar as soon as she returned to the kitchen. My father lay in his underwear, stretched out on a mat. I looked at him. Even in sleep he looked tense. Little ripples ran beneath the skin on his face, which had grown lined, especially on the forehead and in the corners of the eyes. Now and then his body twitched as if from a bad dream. His breathing was laboured and jerky.

Neither my mother nor Rashel had been making life easy for him. Both complained constantly and accused him of deserting his brother. Neither wanted to go to Israel, a subject about which my mother was becoming more outspoken. It showed itself in small things: a casually uttered word, a raised eyebrow, a dismissive motion of her hand. My father was not used to such rebelliousness. There had been arguments between the two of them before, but these had been fought openly and ended with her deferring to him, the natural master of the household. Now, however, not only her looks and remarks but also her silences denied that he was the ultimate authority and implied that some things were not worth quarrelling about because she would decide for herself. My father felt it and didn't like it, though outwardly he maintained the affable exterior on which his position and dignity depended.

He tossed again on the mat, groaned, fell still for a moment, and opened his eyes as though sensing my presence. At the sight of me, he raised his head and propped it on one elbow. "What is it, boy?" he asked. "What's happened?"

"We're on the departure list."

"What?" He rubbed his sleepy eyes. "Are you sure?"

"Yes."

He rose, put an arm around me, pressed his cheek to mine, and swayed wordlessly back and forth with me. Then, tears in his eyes, he took my hand and led me up the stairs to the courtyard.

"Um Kabi, did you hear?" He reached out to embrace my mother. "We're on our way!"

She faced him defiantly, mouth pursed, chin down, arms folded on her chest. "Just look at yourself," she scolded.

"Woman," he said, "the bad times are over." His hands described a circle in the air.

"They're just beginning," said my mother.

My father's arms dropped. He turned and went to the shower.

When he returned to the courtyard he was freshly shaved, smelling nicely of cologne, his brilliantined hair combed straight back, and he was nattily dressed in a white suit and blue tie. "We'll celebrate tonight," he said, rubbing his hands while walking dreamily about the courtyard.

I helped to bring up from the cellar a case of Lebanese arrack that had been kept for special occasions and then went to invite the neighbours and to tell them to spread the word. Now that Arabs had moved into the neighbourhood, it was no longer possible to shout invitations from the rooftop. No one wanted them gate-crashing their party, especially not Abu Hamid, who had ceased to be welcome in our house after the incident of his proposing to Rashel. When I called on her, her answer was that she wasn't coming. Although I didn't try to argue, I was disappointed and went home.

My mother had done her hair and was wearing a white dress with a gold brooch. Whatever her feelings about Israel, she would perform her duties as a hostess. Open insubordination was one thing she did not wish to be accused of. Proud and tall in her already visible pregnancy, she presided over the preparations. Edouard's mother and some other neighbours came to help, setting the tables and bringing dishes they had made. Even cross-eyed Farha joined in, working side by side with Um Edouard as if all were forgiven and forgotten.

My father hired a band. "Abu Saleh is busy tonight," he told me, explaining why the baker couldn't come. Even though I knew this meant underground work, I suspected it was an excuse, because Abu Saleh had kept away from our house since Hizkel's arrest. And while Rashel may have been right that she was the reason, that certainly was not the whole of it.

Our courtyard filled with guests. My parents were besieged by people bearing notes and letters, or even a few words of regards, for relatives in Israel. "There's a thorough search at the airport," my father told them, explaining why he wouldn't take written messages. He circulated through the crowd, greeting people, shaking hands, hugging, kissing, laughing nervously.

Abu Edouard wore a fancy suit I had not seen before and drank lots of arrack. "Are you sure they'll let you out?" he asked, putting his arm around my father.

"Never trust a goy," my father joked back.

Night fell, wrapping the sky in a pearly gauze all the way to the horizon. A light breeze blew. The band arrived and struck up songs of parting, their words composed long ago by wandering poets. The air grew thick with melody as Allah spread a deep blue, mysterious sky over His world.

There was a farewell party in Baghdad nearly every night now and the same songs were played at each, but every night they were sung with the same longing as the night before. My father stared at the guests as if seeing them in a vision. If he had had any doubts that his trials were over, the mood of the evening set them to rest.

And yet his happiness was not complete. He went to the *jalala*, lit one of Hiyawi's Zabana cigarettes from the butt of another, and sat in hunched solitude, looking so sad and lonely that I had to go over to him. "Son," he said, "you may think that I'm crazy, but I'm still waiting for a last-minute miracle to save Hizkel."

It was the last straw. I wanted to forget Hizkel. My father's need to treat me as a grown-up was too much for me. *Baba*, I wanted to shout, *enough, I'm only a boy!* I hated his fears and hesitations and I was worried that they might keep us from leaving. His face was as wrinkled as a crust of dry milk. He must have drunk too much. When I brought him a bowl of cold yoghurt, he pushed it away and said:

"Go and see why Hiyawi hasn't come."

I stepped out into the street. In the shafts of light falling from the windows of the houses I could see that the old man's gate was ajar. He was sitting just inside, slumped on a chair.

"Why are you out here at this hour of the night?" I asked.

"For a handful of beans," he replied.

The line came from the old story of the bean seller who killed his young assistant for sleeping with his wife, though the merchants in the market, who knew nothing of the affair, thought it was for stealing a handful of beans. The yellow light from the sooty street lamp shone through the gate and brought out the deep furrows in Hiyawi's face.

"Come to our party," I said.

"What would I do at your party?" he asked, wiping his brow with a dirty handkerchief. "Pull up a chair and sit down."

I had a feeling there was something he wanted to show me. Perhaps his dead wife in a séance. The thought made me curious and afraid.

I pulled up a chair. For a while neither of us spoke.

My father's guests began departing. The street lamp flickered and went out. The street was deserted. And yet though I kept yawning and wanting to sleep, I could not bring myself to leave.

A shadow approached from the top of the street and turned into the shape of a confidently striding man. I recognized him at once and half-rose to ask if he was bringing good news, but Hiyawi's palsied hand on my shoulder restrained me.

"Was he at our party?"

Hiyawi's other hand gagged me. Karim Abd el-Hak rounded a bend and disappeared in the direction of el-Rashid Street. The old man stared until he was gone. His voice rasped frightfully as he said:

"The Moslems are giving it to Hizkel and he's giving it to Hizkel's wife."

"Maybe he had something urgent to tell her."

"He's been coming every night for weeks. How many urgent messages can he have?"

My ears felt seared by a branding iron. "How can he?" I asked, simply to say something. My head was spinning.

Hiyawi spat. "They have lust in their hearts, not God. And where there's no fear of God, there's no fear of God's creatures."

"But how can she?" I nearly shouted.

"How? Don't you know that a man needs many things but a woman needs only one?"

I jumped up and ran to the empty street leading to the souk. I was no longer afraid of djinns because I now had one in my own heart.

I raced through Taht el-Takya but stopped short when I reached el-Rashid Street. What did I think I was doing, chasing after this man who had just left Rashel's sheets? What would I say to him if I caught up with him? I turned around and headed sheepishly back until I reached the gate to her house.

The whore! Death was too good for her. The Moslems were right. A woman cheating on her husband deserved to die. So that was why she had asked me not to walk her home on that evening of the Um Kultoum party!

I raised a hand to pound on her gate and then lowered it. Although our courtyard was dark, my mother was still doing the dishes in the kitchen. I went to the roof and looked down at Rashel's yard. She wasn't there. Of course not: she was asleep in her dark bedroom. Had I really thought that she did it with the Moslem in the open air and fell asleep there?

My father was snoring loudly on the roof. The lousy

drunkard! I climbed into bed and shut my eyes, but I was too upset to fall asleep. I could smell the rosewater scent of Rashel as if she were lying next to me. Her and her goddamn smells! I wished I had never known her. Filth, that's all she was … and I had been afraid to start anything with her. Why, I should have raped her. Yes, raped her, without giving a damn what anyone said. Each time I had thought of sleeping with her I had pictured my mother dressed in black. And meanwhile the Moslem came and took her. The Moslems acted as if everything was theirs.

But would I be thinking that Rashel deserved an adulterer's death if I had lost my virginity in her arms? I knew that I wouldn't. *Admit it, you ass,* I told myself. *You're just jealous.* And there was nothing worse than jealousy. It was like the scorpion that bit me when I was seven. First there had been a light prick and then, right afterwards, red-hot needles spreading from my thumb to my fingers and up my arm to my shoulder and into my whole body, as if my veins flowed with venom.

I lay awake until almost dawn, imagining the Moslem doing it with Rashel in every way and position which I had pictured myself. Not even the climax with which my fantasies ended could bring me to the haven of slumber. My member had a life of its own and perked up again as soon as I wretchedly thought of them making love.

In the end I must have fallen asleep, because it was already light when I awoke with a splitting headache and an old eye infection that I had thought I was rid of. The face staring at me from the mirror in the shower was pulpy and full of pimples. The birthmark beneath my left eye, which my mother said was a sign of good luck, looked uglier than ever. I went to the kitchen to make tea to soak my eye with.

Afterwards I walked to the river and strolled along its banks. The water smiled quietly. Could I have imagined it all? Was it just a bad dream, the delusion of a crazy old man who thought his drowned wife had been born again in Rashel? Could this be his revenge for her refusal to accept his money and his help?

But no, she herself had once told me that ever since her parents were killed in the *Farhood* she had been like an orphan, ready to clutch at the first hand. I had wanted that hand to be mine, but now, though we had done all we could for her and Hizkel, it was Karim's.

And yet how close I had felt to her! One memory followed another. I remembered her looking joyful in front of the el-Rafidain Bank; bewildered on the leather maker's stool; full of hope at the fortune teller's in Bab-el-Sheikh; determined on her way to the prison; horrified in the hangman's square; tearful as she begged to see Hizkel; mute on the carriage ride home; giddy as she danced in her courtyard; mysterious in the café; merry in the park's myrtle fields. She could be fresh as the morning, languid as the afternoon, elusive as the dusk, alluring as the night. No sooner did I think that I had her in focus than her image blurred and changed.

The Tigris lapped at its banks, the pale morning sun reflected in its waters. I was standing on the very same spot where I had stood that evening with Amira. Had my legs led me to it without my knowing? What was wrong with me that I felt so confused? In books and films, everything was so simple: boy loved girl, girl loved boy, cut. Why couldn't I make up my mind? Perhaps what I thought was love was only sex and I should go to some whore and have done with it. There would be no misunderstandings; no false hopes; no disappointments; no envy. Except, of course, that a romantic like me could fall in love even with a whore!

I inhaled the river air, feeling better. In my imagination I saw Hizkel, his jaw twisted and his face swollen from blows as on the night of his arrest. Was it really for him she insisted on staying? Would she go back to him if he were freed? Oddly, I judged she would. Yet how could she? And how could I look him in the eye then, much less be honest with him? Sometimes, falling asleep at night, I saw his body hanging in the square ...

I was ashamed of myself and my thoughts. Karim Abd el-Hak was a stranger, but I was Hizkel's nephew – and if *I* dreamed of such things, who was I to complain about Karim? I had no choice but to live with the secret. It was what Hiyawi had done and expected me to do too. Some things were too painful to talk about, like the time I was molested in the bathhouse the day after my father's arrest. Thinking of it still filled me with a helpless, murderous rage. Now my young soul had something else to bury.

50.

Taht el-Takya was in shock. Abu Saleh el-Hibaz the baker had been hung in Army Square.

The previous day the police had raided the neighbourhood, sealing it off on all sides. A task force stormed the bakery and another made straight for the firing range in the cellar. Shopkeepers and passers-by stood boggle-eyed at the sight of the weapons carried out and loaded onto a waiting truck. There were dozens of pistols – Berettas, Brownings, Parabellums; Sten guns, tommy-guns, and Schmeisser submachine guns; English rifles and Canadian carbines; a Bren machine gun; several crates of hand grenades; and various boxes of ammunition.

Abu Saleh stood by his oven with his powerful arms on his chest and watched without a word, the light gone from his eyes. The policemen were silent too, so mild-mannered that it seemed for a moment that they simply meant to take the guns and go away. Only when the cache was empty did they handcuff him and lead him off.

My father, who watched from Hiyawi's tobacco shop, was frozen with fear. Taht el-Takya was stunned. Many shops were closed early and their owners went home. Those who remained made no attempt to do business. Like sleepwalkers they drifted through the streets of the souk, speculating in whispers.

It was hard to grasp that the high-spirited baker who crooned love songs and synagogue hymns while he worked, had kept an

456

arsenal in the middle of the souk. And it was just as hard to credit that this local hero and scourge of every evildoer had been marched off to prison, a bound titan. No one knew what to do. It seemed just a matter of time before the next blow descended. Had the police and army razed the quarter to the ground, nobody would have been surprised.

Soon after Abu Saleh's arrest, I saw Stad Nawi in the company of several young men and wondered what he was doing in Taht el-Takya. Only years afterwards did I discover to my amazement that this slender man, who looked like an accountant though he was a famous author and the rector of a school renowned for its Iraqi patriotism, was an underground leader in the Movement, a man responsible for many of its activities when he was not at some literary soirée. It was among the Movement's best-kept secrets, one never revealed to my father even by Hizkel, who was himself recruited by Stad Nawi's Italian friend Enzo Sereni.

It was Abu Saleh's arrest that brought Stad Nawi to Taht el-Takya to reorganize the Movement, strengthen morale, and keep emigration from faltering. After receiving a coded telephone message that the arms had been seized, he sent out an underground press release, accompanied by photographs of anti-Jewish atrocities during the *Farhood,* in which it was stated that the weapons were strictly for self-defence and not for use against the regime.

This was the same line that Abu Saleh was instructed to take, and the authorities, evidently convinced by it, chose to appease both the clamour for Jewish blood at home and pro-Jewish public opinion abroad by administering swift justice to the lone figure of the baker, who was tried that same night for stockpiling arms and bombing the Mas'udah Shemtob Synagogue.

Following the precedent of the Shafik Addas trial, the judge made do with the testimony of a single informer, a frightened young Jew, broken by interrogation, who testified against Abu Saleh with tears of shame in his eyes. No defence witnesses were called and the defence lawyer's drowsy summation was spoken into his moustache. At midnight Abu Saleh was taken to the condemned cell and in the morning he was hung.

I didn't go to the square. I could not bring myself to see my idol hanging from a rope. By noon his body was taken down from the gallows. It was over before the journalists could get there or any effort be made to save him.

Hiyawi told the undertakers to bury Abu Saleh next to the mass grave of the *Farhood* victims. This was a request that the baker had once made during an argument. At the time it had seemed a sarcastic remark to remind the old tobacconist that such would be the fate of all Jews staying in Iraq, but Hiyawi now believed – perhaps rightly so – that it was in fact a last wish.

The whole neighbourhood came to the funeral. Not even Baghdad's oldest Jews could remember such a turn-out. Although the presence of secret servicemen ruled out eulogies, there wasn't a dry eye when Hiyawi chanted the memorial prayer in a cracked voice and asked God to have mercy on the martyr David ben-Yosef, also known as Abu Saleh el-Hibaz. "May the King of Kings show compassion and mercifully hide him in His wings and bring him to life at the End of Days and give him to drink of the Waters of Paradise and bind his soul in the Bond of Life and honour his eternal rest, for the Lord is his inheritance … "

For the seven days of mourning, Abu Saleh's family sat in the bakery, to which all of Taht el-Takya and the souk came to pay their condolences. The market was shut down. All classes were cancelled in the schools. Hiyawi, who had held many a bitter debate with the baker, grieved as for a son and led the prayers and the Psalms. Abu Edouard joined them every day, standing mortified in a corner, from which he begged the baker for forgiveness. My mother and the other women of the neighbourhood brought bread rings for the blessing over bread; dates, almonds, raisins, and apples for the blessing over fruit; peeled cucumbers for the blessing over greens; and tea and coffee for the blessing over sundries.

Only Rashel did not put in an appearance. According to my mother, she stayed in bed weeping as if what had happened were her punishment from God.

Before the week was out, tens of thousands of new Jews had signed up for emigration. Many went straight from the bakery to the registration centre. Abu Saleh sent more immigrants to Israel in his death than in his life.

Fat'hiya sat with her pots in a corner of the bakery, skimming her slices of curdled milk for her customers with her long mattress-maker's needle, crying silently. She came before dawn and left after dusk, refusing to believe that a man so full of life could be dead. From time to time she turned to stare at the cold oven, as if straining to hear one of Abu Saleh's medleys of sacred music and bawdy song.

On the seventh day the mourners rose and the bakery stood empty. Dusk fell. The wails of the *kemar* seller could be heard throughout the neighbourhood.

51.

Though it was the middle of the night, Taht el-Takya was wide awake. Groups of men, women, and children made final preparations for the talons of the great eagle that was soon to tear them up by the root and transport them to a distant land. The lights were on in the shops of the souk, where artisans rushed to fill last-minute orders as if it were the day before a holiday.

Only the bakery was shut. From it came no smell of bread, no sound of song, no laughing bustle of customers. It was hard for me to pass its metal shutter. I looked the other way and walked faster, my sorrow clawing at me.

But Ezra the shoemaker was in his usual spot, plucking nails from his mouth and banging them in quickly with his hammer as if he feared they might run away. I took the two pairs of shiny new shoes my father had ordered for me, tied them together by the laces, and slung them over my shoulder, breathing in the good smell of the leather.

Next I went to Chiflawi, the old tailor. "It's about time!" he said with a looping motion of his needle. I stood facing him while he gently straightened my shoulders and tried a half-finished tweed jacket on me. Telling me to stand taller, he pressed and pulled at it, stuck in a few needles, chalked a line across the chest, took two steps backwards, uttered a pleased exclamation, stepped back up to me, and stuck his hands in my armpits, which tickled me and made me laugh.

"God willing, I'll make your wedding suit too," said Chiflawi. "I made your father's."

"Are you coming to Israel too?" I asked.

"As soon as every Jew has a new jacket."

Hiyawi's tobacco shop was also open around the clock, more because of insomnia than extra business. Hiyawi had been acting strangely since Abu Saleh's death and had begun to show signs of senility. Taking out his thick diary, in which he was in the habit of jotting down his thoughts in the Aramaic of the Talmud, he would sit staring at its dense writing, fiddle with his pencil, and shut the volume without adding a line. His old voice cracked when he recited the Psalms and he often trailed off in the middle as if he had lost his place. He had all but stopped eating, too, and had even refused the strips of salty goat's cheese soaked with an onion in hot water with which he liked to fill the soft pittas that I used to bring him from Abu Saleh. Instead of looking for another bakery he now smoked incessantly and each fit of his clogged lungs sounded like his last.

Death was consuming his gaunt body. His step was a totter, his face was long and haggard, his lips were sunken, and his paper-thin, liver-spotted skin hung limply on his jowls. The once half-impish, half-zealous gleam was gone from his eyes, which looked like two dark holes.

One Sabbath he failed to appear in synagogue. Halfway through the prayer, which my mother had insisted we attend every week during our last days in Iraq, I told my father that I was going to check on him and slipped out. I found him in bed, his face the colour of parchment.

"What's the matter?" I asked.

"I'm dying."

"Don't scare me, Hiyawi," I cried. "That's crazy."

"Kabi, boy, my time has come to go the way of all flesh. I can't see, I can't hear, I can't chew, I can't smell, I can hardly go to the bathroom. I'm childless and the chain stops with me. What is there to live for? I have only death to look forward to while you still have a long life. But you should know, son, that death is part of life. Life wouldn't be life without it. I know now how wrong I was."

"You were?"

"Yes, son. Life is like a cigarette – a spark of light, a few good puffs, and ashes – and death is waiting at the end of it. That's why we mustn't dwell on it, because in the end it will have its fill of us. And that was my mistake, because I fell in love with it after my poor wife died. It was all I thought about. I stayed true to a dead woman instead of having children with another, and today I'm a lonely old man who lived his life with ghosts. I spent nights sitting up and waiting for the Moslem to visit that she-devil, but in my heart I kept hoping against hope ... and it was only when we buried Abu Saleh that I understood that life is for the living and death is for the dead and never the twain shall meet! My poor wife is gone, and that she-devil is a she-devil, and there's no connection between them."

It was his final reckoning.

"Hiyawi," I said, a lump in my throat.

"Don't you cry, Kabi, my boy. At least you've seen me one last time with all my wits about me. You said that I was crazy, and for a long time I was, but I've never been more clear-minded than I am now."

"You mustn't talk like that Hiyawi," I said, the tears running down my cheeks.

"I've always gone around with my wedding ring. Today I threw it in the gutter."

"I don't believe you," I cried and grabbed his hand. The sunken band of skin at the base of his ring finger told me he was telling the truth.

"There's no point in crying, Kabi, boy. Since the *Farhood* I've been burying the dead. I took care of them and of every Jewish funeral. I should have taken better care of the living. That's something they understood."

"Who?"

"The Zionists. Hizkel. Abu Saleh. Kabi, my boy, now that he's dead and buried I can see that our Abu Saleh was life itself. He was right. I was wrong. I chose the path of death."

"Then come with us to Israel," I cried desperately.

"It's too late for that, son. I'm ... I'm ... " In a twinkling he had become a forgetful old man again. He took a Zabana from his pocket, stuck it in his mouth, and fumbled mechanically for a box of matches.

"Hiyawi, it's the Sabbath!" I shouted in horror.

His hand halted and he threw the match away like a frightened child that does not know why it is being scolded. His dull eyes were unseeing.

I ran back towards the synagogue and met my parents on their way home. "Babba," I said half-incoherently, "Hiyawi's dying. He wanted to smoke."

My father sat by Hiyawi's side for the rest of the day. He could barely get him to swallow a bit of soup sent by my mother. Dr Mrad was called for and explained to us the little that there was for us to do.

Hiyawi's mind kept clearing and clouding over. Later in the day he dozed off and slept peacefully, and when he awoke he conversed with my father quite lucidly. Only afterwards did I learn that two weeks previously he had asked my father

463

and Baruch the *kubba* vendor to witness the signing of his will.

In it he left nearly nine hundred dinars. His shop had done well over the years and his expenses had been few. (It later turned out that he had given away many more thousands of dinars to charity in his lifetime, especially to widows and orphans who had survived the *Farhood*.) Half of this sum was bequeathed to me, "Ya'akub Kabi Sa'id Salman Imari, who is like my grandson," and the other half to my father and Baruch with instructions to donate it to the Movement. He had actually wanted to give the Movement the money before he died, but my father, concerned that he might end up sick and indigent, talked him out of it.

Soon he lost consciousness and began to wheeze, and at one in the morning he passed away.

I was deeply moved by being remembered in his will, but my father reminded me that fifty dinars a person was all we could take from Iraq and suggested that I give the rest to the Movement's legal defence fund. Although loath to relinquish the small fortune that had come my way, I knew I had no choice.

Hiyawi had sold his house to an estate agent on the condition that he be allowed to stay in it for as long as he lived. After his corpse was taken by the burial society, we emptied the place of its valuables. Its two rooms had the musty smell of old age and were piled high with worn clothes and old shoes, dusty turbans, and dozens of boxes used for storing and preparing tobacco. A grandfather clock, repaired more than once by my father, was still ticking behind its broken glass frame.

One of the items we took was Hiyawi's wedding picture, a photograph of himself in a Turkish officer's uniform beside his poor dead wife in a white bridal gown and bridal veil. He had been very proud of it. In vain I searched for a resemblance between her and the "she-devil". I also took his thick diary and his tattered old book of Psalms.

The funeral was quiet. Not many people followed the bier and there were no professional mourners or women to beat their breasts and scratch their faces. The only damp eyes were mine.

A carriage drew up in front of the grave Hiyawi had chosen and a man with a long beard stepped out of it and came over to join us. At first we failed to recognize him without his vestments and turban. Only when he came closer did we see it was Rabbi Bashi. His beard had grown greyer and his face more lined. An awed hush fell over us, synagogue elders and Zionists alike. As the rabbi led the prayer and delivered a brief eulogy for a man who "never lost his faith in Providence and knew that the End of Days would come in the fullness of time", my father and I exchanged glances. In spite of it all, I thought it would have made Hiyawi happy to know that Rabbi Bashi, Haham Bashi, had presided at his funeral.

Years later, when my oldest daughter was born in Israel, I had Hiyawi's tattered Book of Psalms rebound. At my request the binder added several blank pages on which I wrote our family tree, ending with my firstborn child. Since then I have entered the names of more of my children, and I hope that one day still more pages will be added for the names of their children and children's children.

I recorded all my ancestors as far back as I could remember, writing the name of Shmuel Yosef Yoel Avraham Hiyawi next to that of my grandparents along with the date of his death. No one knew when he was born. And so, though he died alone and childless, he was given a family in the end.

52.

Big Imari did not look forward to his talk with the Pasha. He would have preferred avoiding it, because he knew that things would never be the same again afterwards. Many years had gone by since the two of them had first met on one of the Pasha's visits to the family rice fields. My great-grandfather, who was then a very old man, had told his son that the visitor was a cousin of King Faisal's and a man well worth knowing.

Later, when Big Imari moved to Baghdad and became active in its Jewish community, Rabbi Bashi hatched a plan to assign a wealthy Jew to every high Iraqi politician, whom it would be his job to cultivate and keep in contact with. Sasson Abed was given the Shi'ite leader Saleh Jaber; Hizkel Shemtob, the Sunni politician Tewfik el-Suweidi; and Big Imari, the Pasha. All three Iraqi leaders eventually served as prime minister, just as Rabbi Bashi had foreseen.

In time, Big Imari's ties with the Pasha grew to include various business partnerships, some of which were public knowledge and some of which were not. He saw to it that the Pasha was financially secure and advised him on economic and even political issues, particularly those involving Jews. The Pasha came to count on him, and when the Pasha's only son Sabah was born, Big Imari looked after him too.

The two became good friends, as did their wives Na'ima and Flora. Big Imari was a frequent guest at the Pasha's gatherings, headed communal delegations to him, visited him with Rabbi Bashi, and intervened privately with him for Jewish interests. In turn, well aware that he lived on Moslem sufferance, he never turned down a request from the Pasha, who generally responded in kind, nor troubled him with minor matters, with which he turned to the Pasha's assistants or to other ministers whose confidence he enjoyed.

Although he was suspicious by nature, Big Imari could not help liking the Pasha, who had great personal charm, an excellent education, many talents, and no little cunning. A clever statesman and behind-the-scenes manipulator with a sure instinct for politics, the Pasha was intensely loyal to his benefactor King Faisal and a great admirer of the British, without whom, as he liked to put it, "We would still be stuck in the same old mud." At social gatherings, family affairs, and the parties at which Salima Pasha sang and Salim Shibbat recited poetry, Big Imari was almost obsequiously deferential to him. When they were alone, however, the Pasha spoke candidly to his Jewish friend about everything, even his problems with Sabah – a subject close to Big Imari's heart, since he too had an only son. Unlike his public persona, which was dignified if often wry, the private Pasha was emotional, quick-tempered, and unpredictable. Big Imari had to learn to keep his poise with him and to divine which parts of their conversation were strictly confidential.

And yet despite his long acquaintance with the Pasha, the man remained a mystery. He was both magnanimous and cruel, decisive and devious, with a bold ambition that knew no bounds. After all these years, Big Imari still did not know what the Pasha really thought of the Jews. Was he as well-disposed towards them as he pretended, or was he – as many younger

467

Jews believed – an Arab nationalist determined to rid Iraq of its minorities? In either case, he was a puzzle, and when Big Imari phoned his office and was told that he was out and had no time for appointments, it seemed an inauspicious sign. An hour later, however, the Pasha's secretary called back to announce that the Pasha would be glad to receive his friend at home at four o'clock that afternoon.

Dressed in a house robe and slippers, the Pasha was waiting in his favourite armchair in the large guest room, vigorously fingering his amber worry beads. He was hoarse and pale-looking and had lost weight. "Ah, Abu-George," he said after a servant had brought mint tea, giving Big Imari a blue-eyed stare as if he had not seen him in ages, "you're turning grey!"

"So would you if you were a Jew for twenty-four hours," said Big Imari.

"What's wrong with being a Jew? You're better off than the Moslems. When a Moslem gets out of line, I hang him. When I try hanging a Jew, the whole world is up in arms."

"It didn't keep you from hanging that baker."

"There was no way I could avoid it after all the weapons that were found. It was better to get it over with quickly. Personally, I believed the Zionists that the arms were for self-defence. It would be absurd to think they were aimed at the government. But that's exactly what many people did think."

"And it didn't keep you from hanging Shafik Addas either despite my pleas to spare him."

"His case wasn't simple. The British had it in for him. Listen to something I've never told you before. When Rommel was at el-Alamein, the Germans, or so the British say, counterfeited millions of pounds sterling and put them into circulation throughout the Middle East with the help of a Turkish agent and of Addas, who was given a ten per cent cut. Don't ask me if it's true or not, because I never looked into it and can't get a clear story from the CID. Addas himself denied it and claimed he never knew that the money was forged or came from the Germans; the whole transaction, he said, was presented to him as a secret part of the Allied war effort, a way of channelling British funds to people who weren't supposed to know where they came from.

"It's hard to know where the truth lay. The British, at any rate, were out to get Addas, perhaps because he knew too much. That's why they first involved him with army surplus equipment that allegedly turned up in Jewish hands in Palestine and then leaked it to the press. Even if he had paid the journalist who broke the story the thousand-dinar bribe he was asked for, his fate was sealed. I can assure you that the article would have appeared anyway and that the dinars would have ended up in someone's pocket.

"Once the mob took to the streets and called for the Jew Addas's blood, things got out of hand. Not even the Regent could have saved him then, although you may recall that he put off signing the execution order for three days. He even convened the cabinet and said, 'Our war is with the Zionists in Palestine, not with innocent Jews in Iraq.' Do you know what he was told? 'Either you hang the Jew or this government will fall and take you with it.'

"There's never any bad without some good, though. Poor Addas was the reason there was not another *Farhood* when all those Iraqi coffins began coming back from your Jewish state. You know I was minister of defence at the time. Although I could have kept casualties down by committing regular army units to the war and accepting King Farouk's proposal for a joint command, I yielded to the mob and sent a pack of inexperienced, overzealous volunteers who quite frankly I was glad to get rid of. They thought fighting the Jews would be a picnic from which each of them would return with a blonde slave-girl. When they came back in coffins, there was no stopping the rabble and the press from howling for Jewish heads to roll. Everyone was shouting *Allah akbar,* humiliated by having been defeated by a pack of Jews. How could a slave-people have beaten seven Arab countries and established a state in the middle of the Moslem world?

"It was too much and Addas was the scapegoat. You must admit, Abu George, that he was the only Jew touched.

"I saw you wince when I said 'your Jewish state'. Just between the two of us, though, what Jew doesn't identify with it? Why, that would be unnatural, even inhuman! I won't test you by asking how you would feel if the Arabs destroyed Israel … no, don't even try to answer. It's pointless.

"Shall I tell you when I first realized that Iraq was not your real homeland? It was at the time of the Portsmouth Treaty with Great Britain. I was told by Bahjat Attiya, the head of the CID, that Rabbi Bashi and several other prominent Jews – you, thank God, were not among them – had joined an anti-British protest aimed at me and Saleh Jaber. At first I didn't believe it, but I checked and found it was true. Well, well, I thought: if that's how it stands even with Rabbi Bashi and his close associates, it's time you Jews went to Palestine.

"You know better than anyone that I've always supported the Jews; supported Rabbi Bashi too. Didn't I go to him in the middle of the night, back in 1931, to warn him of the rabbinical rebellion against him? I suggested that he resign for his own good, even if he was in the right; I knew from experience that sometimes you have to bend with the wind. As soon as it blew over, I promised him, he would be reinstated. I saw to it that he was, too … and now here he was demonstrating against me! One would have thought that a man of his intelligence, which would have made him deserving of the highest office if only he were a Moslem, would have understood that we were lost without the English! The Russians were making noises, the Iranians were threatening to foment a Shi'ite revolt, the Communists were gaining strength, the Kurds had risen in the North – and now I had these crazy Jews on my hands too! It did not take much knowledge of diplomacy to grasp that in a world divided into East and West we had to take sides. Did Rabbi Bashi really imagine that we could go our independent way without England, relying on our glorious army whose prowess we all saw in Palestine?"

"Abu Sabah," said Big Imari, finally getting a word in, "you know how loyal Rabbi Bashi has been and how much he has put up with for your sake, especially from the younger generation. He has a public to deal with just as you have. And suppose he erred. Do all the Jews have to suffer for it? Must those of us who have been faithful to the Iraqi crown all these years now flee to Palestine too?"

Though his voice was calm, the words sounded like a cry.

"Everything has changed," said the Pasha. "I don't know what the future holds in store. The Iraqis are putty in the hands of their leaders – they can be made to do anything, good or bad. That's why I think you would be wise to leave. All of you. Listen, Abu George. Bahjat Attiya sent me a report a while ago on a rally held by a pro-fascist youth movement here in Baghdad. One of its leaders, a butcher's son named Ismail, if I'm not mistaken, delivered a tirade against everyone – the British, the

Jews, the regime, the whole world. The mob cheered wildly. I'm told he dreams of being a new Haroun el-Rashid, the leader of all the Arabs. Who is to say that some such fanatic won't assassinate the Regent and me one day and assume power?"

"God forbid," said Big Imari. "The man does not exist who would think of murdering you."

"I once thought that myself. But the devil is loose in the streets and I'm not so sure any more. Just look at what happened when the British left Palestine and the French left Syria, where there's now a new coup d'état every month. And that degenerate drunkard Farouk is about to topple in Egypt. (By the way, did Bahia ever return? ... No? ... Ah, well, too bad!) What makes you think that, with the British out of Iraq, we're more immune? Anything can happen. The Ismails are stirring up the mob, the Communists are on the rise, and the storm clouds are gathering. I don't know if I and the royal house will survive. And who is to blame? Your little state, which is the size of a speck of fly shit on the map! It's changed the Middle East, turned the world upside down."

The Pasha fell into a meditative silence. Big Imari made no attempt to speak. "Is there anything I can do for you?" asked the Pasha at last.

"I just came to pay a call, Abu Sabah. I didn't know you weren't feeling well. May God give you health and long days. But as long as I'm here, permit me to put in a word for those Jews who have stayed, myself included. If not for your new emigration law, they would have been a big majority."

"You're wrong, Abu George. Eighty out of one hundred and thirty thousand Iraqi Jews have asked to go to Israel already and I'm told that the number keeps climbing."

"What do you expect people to do when they're fired from

their jobs, expelled from the universities, harassed by the police, arrested for no good reason, vilified in public?"

"And not wanted by Israel! That's the only explanation for its not sending enough planes. Yes, I know: the country is overflowing with immigrants. It can't absorb you all, it would rather you came more gradually. Your minister of finance over there, I'm told, can't find enough work and homes for you. But the ground is burning beneath your feet and who has time to wait? Just recently I sent a secret emissary there to see if things can't be speeded up for the poor unfortunates who are stranded here without papers, without jobs, without a roof over their heads. He carried a message from me that the planes will be allowed to fly straight to Israel, rather than via Cyprus as they have been required to do until now. So far there has been no response.

"I've been to Jordan, too. I spoke to the prime minister and asked for safe conduct to the Israeli border for five thousand Iraqi Jews. I told him that my son Sabah, who is a pilot, would have them flown to Irbid, from where they could cross the Jordan River into Israel. He declined though I offered him twenty thousand tons of wheat, twenty dinars for each Jew in transit, and another two dinars for each entry visa.

"I met Kirkbride, the British ambassador to Amman, and got nowhere with him either. In fact, I lost my temper so badly that we nearly came to blows. He refused to guarantee the safety of any Jews and said that the Palestinian refugees in Jordan would kill them all. When I offered to have the Iraqi army escort them, he yelled at me that I was crazy. He accused me of being ready to start a war between the Moslems for the sake of the Jews.

"I've turned to the Americans, too, and asked them to put pressure on Israel. There's still nothing definite, but perhaps the planes will start coming faster. An Iraqi-born friend of mine with American Jewish connections told me yesterday on the telephone that Ben-Gurion is rumoured to have ordered you all brought to Israel immediately, after which he'll figure out what to do with you. A great man, Ben-Gurion! I'd like to meet him some day, though I suspect he'd find our dinner parties a waste of time. But if the rumour proves false and the Americans don't help, I'll have to put all our stateless Jews in detention camps."

The Pasha spoke these last words grimly.

"Abu Sabah," said Big Imari bitterly, "I trust that my friendship and loyalty to you will answer for me, and I beg a thousand pardons if I'm about to say something that I shouldn't, but your whole attitude towards us has changed. You're kicking us all out, indiscriminately."

"I'm trying to help poor Jews who have lost everything, both *de jure* and *de facto*. Are you telling me that's wrong? That it means I'm against you? I believe that Iraq has become a dangerous place for you. Do you want to be permanent hostages in the hands of the mob and its Ismails? And if *I* can't promise you there'll be no more *Farhoods*, there's certainly no one else who can. Don't you see, Abu George, that the hatred between Arabs and Jews has reached monstrous proportions? Can't you understand that the old war between Judaism and Islam has flared up again? God only knows when it will end, *if* it will end. Does that make me a Jew-hater? One day, when we are both dead and buried, there will be a monument to me in Tel Aviv. I'll be a hero who saved Jews, the same as Mordecai on your holiday of Purim."

"May you live for many more years, Abu Sabah! But if you ask me, history will hand down a different verdict. It will remember you as the man who drove the Jews from Iraq after thousands of years of living here."

"It will remember Faisal, rest his soul, and my late brother-in-law Ja'afar el-Askari, and Regent Abdullah, and Tewfik el-Suweidi, and even the Shi'ite Saleh Jaber and myself as friends and allies of the Jews who returned them to their land when we could no longer protect them in ours. The day will come when you'll tell that to your son George. He's a fine poet and perhaps he'll make an epic out of it … Tell me, Abu George, how many Jews have lost their lives in Iraq up to this day? You can even count the *Farhood*, though it took place during the reign of Rashid Ali and the Mufti when the Regent and I were in exile. Getting the numbers right is your profession." The Pasha was speaking angrily now. "Compare the figures with those for Christian Europe, even before Hitler came along."

"Since you mention the *Farhood*, my dear Abu Sabah, permit me to ask you a question that the Zionists raise all the time. The Regent, it so happens, returned from exile in June 1941 while the rioting was still in progress. Why didn't he order the pogromists shot on the spot? Why did he do nothing at all?"

"Abu George, my good man, you yourself observe that he had just returned to Iraq. The reins of power were not yet in his hands. You know as well as I do that shortly afterwards, when I was re-appointed prime minister, I demanded the extradition from Iran of that scoundrel Yunis Sab'awi, who was one of the *Farhood's* instigators. You know I had him hung."

"And God bless you for it! It's a pity that such men generally die too late. Which brings me to speak again of the Regent, if I may. The day after his return, on the second of June, he delivered a coronation address in which he did not so much as refer to what had happened. Jews were still being slaughtered in the streets and with him it was business as usual. Of course, I must admit that those killed were ordinary people, not tycoons like Shafik Addas, for whom it was worth his while to try to do something … "

"Those are harsh words, Abu George," the Pasha interrupted severely.

"Believe me, my dear Pasha, I'm speaking from the heart. What am I supposed to tell our young people, who complain that your government is infested with Jew-hatred? How am I supposed to answer them when they say that the older generation has failed to protect them and must make room for new leadership? If we hadn't been stabbed in the back in the *Farhood,* there would never have been a Zionist movement here in the first place!"

"You accuse me of stabbing you in the back, while the Arab leaders accuse me of betraying them to Israel and being a Zionist stooge! Don't you understand that my attacks on the Zionists are against Israel, not Jews? Is that also forbidden to me? When you Jews left Egypt, Pharaoh drove you into the sea, and here am I rolling out a red carpet for you to leave Iraq on! Who would have believed that this country, which hasn't even signed a ceasefire with Israel, would be sending it so many potential soldiers who the Israelis will put to better use than we would … Why don't you answer me? You do know that Tewfik el-Suweidi and I are being called traitors, don't you? The word is out that we're making a profit from it, that we're expelling the Jews to lay hands on their money."

"And to replace us with Palestinians, so I've heard."

"You too, Abu George? I swear, I miss Rabbi Bashi – there was a wise man for you! I wish he would come out of retirement. As if I wanted Palestinian refugees here! Why, they're nothing but trouble wherever they go, a cunning, dangerous, treacherous lot of manipulative ingrates! Don't you think I have enough problems without them? Don't you think I learned my lesson from the Mufti and his men? He almost turned us into a Nazi puppet-state. And I assure you that he knew very well that Hitler's racial theories could be turned against us Arabs too. Weren't we Semites like you, monkeys in human clothing who only understood the whip and existed to serve our Aryan masters? I assure you, the Mufti would have treated me no differently than he wanted to treat the Jews of Palestine!

"The Palestinians will stir up every Arab country, the whole world, against you; they'll hound you everywhere. They'll fight you with guns, with knives, with sticks, with stones, with their fingernails, with their teeth. They'll drown you in the spittle of their curses. And *I* need them here? Have I not enough madmen as it is?"

The Pasha said these last words in Hebrew and added: "Don't look so surprised. It's an expression I learned from Rabbi Bashi. He translated it and told me about the king in the Bible who used it, and I liked it so much that I memorized it and even taught it to my son. A most practical turn of phrase … Do you know, by the way, how many Arab leaders have suggested that I keep you Jews as hostages? I could do it, you know. I could use you to blackmail both the Americans and the Israelis on a regular basis. But the trouble is that you're quite right: we are cousins, after all. You've lived as our loyal subjects for hundreds of years and deserve better. That's why I want to end this long chapter of history amicably. The Lord will reward me for it."

"My dear Pasha," said Big Imari, "I'm sorry to have to vex you, but it's not every day that you're available for so cordial a conversation. I was just wondering about a new law that I've heard you're about to pass, one confiscating the money and goods of all the emigrants."

"That's because every day I'm besieged by army officers and senators – and by the way, I'll soon arrange your election to the Senate and we'll have a party to celebrate – who blame me for letting the Jews abscond with all the silver and gold they've made at our expense. It's more than I can cope with. I've discussed the matter with Tewfik el-Suweidi and he's proposed that for a period of a year, until March 1951, the property of Jews who have waived their citizenship will continue to belong to them. I said I was willing to go along with that. You Jews have a head for business. Do I have to tell you what to do? If any of you is too dim-witted to liquidate his holdings within a year, confiscation is too good a punishment! And don't forget that Israel has expropriated the property of all the Palestinian refugees or, as I believe they're called there, of all absentee owners."

"Abu Sabah, my dear friend, I can see I haven't picked a good day. I'll ascribe your mood and all you've said to your poor health. The one thing I wish to ask is that you free my cousin Hizkel Imari and let him get to Iran with another moron in my family, the Communist Salim Effendi. My relatives keep pestering me."

"If I hadn't been aware that Hizkel Imari was your cousin, he wouldn't be alive today. Speaking perfectly frankly, however, the person to thank for it is Salima Pasha. You know I have a weakness for that wonderful Jewess, whom you've kindly invited to every party that you've given me. When she heard about Hizkel, she came to me and begged for his life. It all goes back to his brother, Salman Imari, with whom she once had an affair. It's beyond me what she saw in that watchmaker when so many real men were desperate to have her, but I gave up trying to understand women long ago ... and especially a woman like her. In any case, she made me swear to tell Salman Imari nothing, and I'll thank you to help me keep that promise.

"I'm working with Bahjat Attiya on the matter. It's he who has kept your cousin out of court and who ordered his brother Salman to be treated with kid gloves and freed the morning after his arrest. I would gladly pardon Hizkel if it were only a matter of his Zionist activities, but his smuggling arms right under our noses rather complicates things. It's been all I could do to keep him from being strung up.

"I don't want to create any illusions. I'm not sure I'll be able to help, though I'm glad to see that it's not only us wicked goyim who care more for rich Jews than ordinary ones. Perhaps it will prove possible to lay the blame on the baker and clear your cousin, who can be deported when things blow over, but I wouldn't hope for too much. The most Bahjat could do for now was improve his conditions in prison.

"As for your Communist, I would gladly tear him limb from limb. You know how I feel about Communists. They're worse than idol worshippers. They want to change human nature, to rebel against the world that God made. Fortunately, however, he isn't in our hands, as the minister of the interior has already informed you. That should enable us to remain friends."

The Pasha pronounced these last words ironically.

"My dear Abu Sabah," said Big Imari, "I don't want to tire you. You need to rest and take good care of yourself. I can only wish you health and many more years of leading the nation. You have made Iraq a good place to live in. A man like me has no other home. Allah watch over you! If your illness weren't such a secret, I would have public prayers held on your behalf."

"We are all at the mercy of Allah," said the Pasha with a

479

finality that conveyed his awareness that Big Imari had guessed his condition.

Big Imari's brow was covered with sweat when he left the Pasha's house and he felt sharp pains in his chest. *That damned minister of the interior,* he thought. *The man tells me that I have to speak to the Pasha and then runs to tell him himself. Never trust a goy!*

He asked his chauffeur to drive slowly along the Tigris and opened the window to let in some fresh air. And yet he felt shrouded in darkness. He now knew that he would never fulfil his dream of being a senator in a country that not even the Pasha felt safe in any more. Perhaps he should move to London, where he would be closer to his son. And to the very best physicians.

53.

The passengers took a few steps from the aeroplane, knelt, stretched out on the tarmac staining their new clothes, and kissed the ground. Then, with an upward glance, they murmured their thanks to the Almighty for bringing them back to the Holy Land. The roar of planes taking off drowned out their prayers.

My father moved away from the crowd, hungrily absorbing the new landscape. "Blessed art Thou, O Lord our God, King of the Universe, Who hath maintained us, and sustained us, and remained with us to this day," he proclaimed loudly. He stood youthfully tall and his eyes shone at the sight of the greyish trees surrounding the airport. *Here in our forefathers' land*, as the words of the old song promised, *all will come true as planned.* Here he would build his castle, plant the paddies of the Imari-Israel Agricultural Corporation, and become a bigger rice grower than his cousin.

He danced as he walked, singing verses of the Psalms like a prisoner freed from his cell. And as though he were their cantor and they his congregation, the Jews descending from the plane responded. Men and boys in summery, pinstripe suits, women and girls in flowery dresses, children in bright shirts – all joined arms beneath the protective wings of the plane, singing and dancing. They did not even notice when two canvas-topped trucks drove up, honking and racing their engines.

At last they made way for the trucks. Blue-overalled workers scrambled out to unload the luggage from the plane's fuselage and pile it on a vehicle. Meanwhile, a team of mechanics prepared the plane for its return flight to Baghdad.

"Are those Jews?" an old woman asked.

"Everyone here is a Jew," she was told.

To make sure, she waddled off to two policemen standing beside their motorcycles. "*Intum yahud?*" she asked in Arabic.

Used to such queries, one of them nodded with a smile. The old woman seized both men with bony hands and tried pulling them back to the dancing throng as if they were her children. The policemen grinned and carefully extricated themselves.

"Long live the State of Israel!" shouted someone.

"The Messiah has come, the Messiah!" cried someone else.

"Where are they taking our luggage?" a man called out as the trucks drove slowly off towards a group of huts.

"To that office over there," one of the workmen told him in Arabic. "Don't worry."

By the office stood some young officials. They looked handsome and rugged in their open-necked khaki shirts, like the Israelis we were familiar with from the photographs we had seen in Iraq. One of them told us to line up with our papers.

"Shalom!" my father greeted him with a big smile.

The official returned an expressionless stare and replied:

"Shalom. Please get back into line."

My father's outstretched hand remained dangling in midair. A second official in a brimmed, khaki cap climbed on a truck, checked the luggage, and told the driver to drive off.

"To Jerusalem!" cried the old woman. "To Jerusalem!"

"Abu Kabi," exclaimed my mother, "do something! Don't you see they're driving off with our suitcases?"

"It's all right," answered my father knowingly. "There are no thieves in Israel."

"But it's all we own in the world," my mother protested.

"Go and keep an eye on the suitcases, Kabi," my father said to placate her. He opened the back flap of the truck and helped me into the dark interior. I held my breath when the driver came to retie the canvas. He didn't notice me.

The truck set off with a lurch, sending the suitcases sliding from side to side. I held on tightly to the metal bars of the frame to keep from being crushed. I was still in my suit and tight-fitting cap, and I was drenched with sweat. The canvas had a hot, unpleasant smell and flapped wildly, swelling and cracking with the wind as if we were about to take to the air. Where was I heading? Suppose the others were going somewhere else? Through the cracks in the canvas, I saw yellow earth speeding by, bare and desolate. We drove on and on with no sign of the big homes with their gardens and lawns that had appeared in Zionist literature in Baghdad. I did not even see any of the little, square, tombstone-like houses that we had glimpsed from the air.

The sky was overcast. Damn it all, why must my first journey in Israel be as a stowaway? We passed a long building with a high wall and watchtowers that resembled Baghdad's central prison. Were there criminals in the Holy Land too? Or was this where the British had imprisoned the Zionists?

The journey seemed endless. I sat on a suitcase and gripped the back of the truck, only realizing that I must have dozed and dreamed of Baghdad when waking from a vision of flowering oleander bushes. I widened the crack in the canvas and peered through it. There was an unidentifiable smell in the air, a heavy, sticky, salty odour. Beyond the golden sand lining the roadside something glittered off into infinity, an enormous blue river, bigger than the Tigris and the Euphrates together. The Jordan, I told myself.

A minute later I realized what an ass I was. I must have been still half-asleep. Why, it was the sea, the Mediterranean! The sight was enchanting and a little scary for someone who had only ever seen so much water in films. I would have enjoyed the white curls of the lapping waves more if I hadn't needed to pee so badly.

Soon the truck turned to the right, slowed, and stopped. Unsure if we had reached our destination, I was debating whether to clamber down when the driver undid the back flap and discovered me – suit, hat, and all in the broiling heat. I grinned at him awkwardly, baffled by the laughter of the crew that came to unload.

He helped me down and said something in a Hebrew that sounded nothing like the language I knew from the prayer book and school. I should never have stopped my Hebrew lessons in the Movement after Hizkel's arrest. How did you say, "I have to pee"? Surely it must have occurred to someone that this was one of the first sentences a beginner needed to learn? Not that I could say it in English either. No one ever performed such an act in *Hamlet, Julius Caesar,* or any of Miss Sylvia's other favourite plays.

In the end I had to ask for a toilet in Arabic. The laughter yielded to a sense of male solidarity and I was shown a narrow tin shack near a perimeter fence, to which I went while the men unloaded the suitcases and stacked them in an already crowded warehouse. Celebrating my minor salvation, I turned to contemplate the site of our major one.

I was in a huge tent city full of people, an exotic motley crowd

484

wearing every conceivable shape and colour of shirts, trousers, and hats. Some were dressed like Israelis in boots, brimmed hats, and shorts. I asked someone where I was and received an answer in an incomprehensible tongue that sounded like another question. Suppose the old woman by the plane was right and my parents were on their way to Jerusalem? I had better not stray too far from the truck and get lost.

Cursing my father for thinking that I knew my way around here as if it were Baghdad, I returned to the warehouse to find the doors were now locked. There was an open area in front, barbed wire further back, and sand and water beyond that. The sea!

I wanted to run to it. Could one swim in it? That was too frightening to think of. This wasn't the Tigris with a far shore you could cross to.

In the other direction, far away and growing higher as they receded, were bluish peaks covered with green woods. The tallest of them seemed to jab the sky. It took me a minute to realize what they were. Mountains, right in front of me. Perhaps one was Mount Gezirim or Mount Moriah, which I had learned about in Bible class.

Allah! Even on our class outing to Nineveh, the capital of the kingdom of Sancherib, there hadn't been anything like them.

I needed to find out where I was. Someone here had to know Arabic. Where were all the Jews from Iraq? On the beach beyond the fence a boy and girl of my age walked with their arms around each other. I couldn't take my eyes off them. Was this what the Holy Land was like? The girl was bright against the water. It would have been enough to have made an instant Zionist out of Edouard. Why do with his Christian girlfriend in secret what he could do in Israel with a Jewish girl in broad daylight?

I wondered if Amira's family had heard from her. I would tell her to write to them via George in London. She was on a kibbutz called Kiryat Oranim, but where was it? I would find it and visit her.

I wandered back among the tents. All around me people spoke a babble of tongues, so full of strange chirps and whistles that I might have been listening to a band of crickets. I had never felt more of an outsider. By a smelly, barrel-roofed building, black bins overflowed with rubbish and giant flies that were feeding on white, maggot-like noodles. Nauseated, I headed back for the sea, which was edged by a scarlet horizon crowned by the largest sun I had ever seen.

Three trucks swung through the gate of the camp and halted in front of the warehouse.

"Kabi!" called my brother Nuri, who was the first to jump out. I hugged him as if I hadn't seen him for years. Leaning on my father, my pregnant mother rose from the floor of the truck with difficulty and eased herself down.

"Where have you brought me?" she asked, glancing wearily at her surroundings.

"Woman," said my father, "we've just arrived. Give a man a chance."

"Where's the house you promised me?"

"Woman, that's enough!"

"There goes my life," said my mother with a sharp clap of her palms. "I knew it the minute I saw the colour of the tea at the airport. Just look at this hole that they've dumped us in."

The more she grumbled, the less angry at my father I became.

A throng of Iraqis appeared magically around us, looking for family and friends. Men and women hugged, kissed, and mingled.

"Abu Kabi! Abu Kabi!"

It was Abed, my father's Kurdish servant. The two men embraced. Although this was something that Abed would never have dared do in Baghdad, my mother's eyes lit up for the first time since we landed. She shook Abed's hand while he hugged each one of us and lifted Moshi in the air as once he used to lift me. "So you've made it!" he said, surveying us. "Well, take a minute to catch your breath and then go and change into some work clothes and roll up your sleeves. It's not easy here."

"Did you hear that?" my mother asked triumphantly.

"All right, all right," my father almost pleaded. "I'm exhausted."

"What is this place called?" inquired my mother.

"Sha'ar Ha-Aliyah. That means the Gate of Immigration in Hebrew."

"Where are all the houses and gardens?"

"Don't you see them?" asked Abed, extending his arm towards the forest of tents. "Just look at the villas, the grand parks."

"This is your Israeli paradise?"

"What there is of it."

"We were told that this is only a transit camp," said my father, turning to gaze at the sea.

"Abu Kabi," commanded Abed, "the sea won't run away. Let's find you a place to lay your heads down. You need a tent to sleep in."

"Go and find one with him, Kabi," my father told me.

"You go," objected my mother. "Can't you see the poor boy's exhausted?"

Abed, though, preferred me. My father blinked nervously.

"Don't forget the suitcases," my mother said. "There are things in them that I need."

"They'll be brought to you soon," Abed told her. "And stay near them. This place is full of thieves."

"*Waweli*, we're done for!" wailed my mother. "Thieves in the Holy Land!"

"Take off that silly hat," Abed ordered. "And that jacket, too."

I did as I was told.

It was hard to keep up with him. On our way he said that he no longer lived in the camp, having moved to a nearby town called Pardes Hanna. He had seen our names on a list of new arrivals, taken two days off work, and come to help us get settled.

When we reached "Iraqitown", as he called it, Abed stuck his head into tent after tent until he found an empty one. "Okay, Kabi," he said. "Here's your new home."

"All of us in one tent?"

"This isn't Baghdad." Was he thinking of our big house in Taht el-Takya, in which I had my own attic room? "You should see the other tents. You're lucky there are only five of you. Let's hope you don't have to share this with another family."

I followed him to a big, crowded tent that served as a storeroom. He chose five folding cots and five dirty mattresses, and piled everything on a cot. I helped him lift the pile but could barely get my end off the ground.

"You'll get used to it," he said.

We removed two cots and mattresses and left them by the side of the path. When we came back for them they were gone.

"Damn!" said Abed. "You can't leave a pin unguarded here."

"I see that Iraqitown has its thieves too."

He burst out laughing and said: "Come on, your family is waiting."

We fetched two more cots and mattresses from the store and

took them to the tent. Abed tied the flap well to keep out unwelcome visitors.

We found my mother sitting on a suitcase near the warehouse with Moshi asleep on another suitcase, his head in her lap. Nuri looked wan and withdrawn. I was thirsty and hungry. Since eating a sandwich on the plane, I hadn't had a bite to eat. My father smoked and continued to gaze at the sea, in which a setting sun struggled not to drown. Quickly, the watery depths dragged it down.

"*Yallah,* we're off to the Imaris' castle," announced Abed. "Keep an eye on your things. Even your cigarettes," he barked at my father. "Forget about being generous. This isn't the place for it. Let's go."

My mother clapped her palms again and balked, refusing to rise from her suitcase.

"Couldn't we call for a porter?" asked my father.

"A porter?" laughed Abed. "The only porter available is your two arms."

He swung a suitcase onto his shoulder while my father wrestled with a second one and Nuri and I lifted a third. Moshi woke up and started to cry. His sobs spurred us on, but halfway to the tent we had to rest.

"You're in Israel now," Abed said. "You'll have to toughen up. There are no Moslems or Kurds here to do your work for you."

My father lost his patience. "I think I've had enough for one lesson!"

"Fine. Someone else will grab the tent. Do you want to sleep outside tonight?"

Moshi stopped crying and looked at the darkening hills. "Abed," he asked, "are there lions out there?"

"And leopards and wolves," said Abed scarily.

489

"That will do, Abed," my father rebuked his old servant.

"We should have stayed in Baghdad," groaned my mother, who could barely keep up with us.

As we reached the tent with the last of our strength, a voice thundered at us from the sky. My mother looked frantically around for its source, spitting against the Evil Eye.

"That's the voice of God from Mount Sinai," explained Abed. "You'll hear it morning, afternoon, and night." He pointed to some loudspeakers in the tall trees. "The Lord makes His will known in ten different languages here."

A middle-aged woman passing by stopped when she heard us speaking Arabic. In the dialect of Mosul she said:

"Welcome. Have you just arrived?"

"Thank you," said my mother. "Have you been here long?"

"A week. They've already taken our oldest boy to the army. I don't know what kind of Jews these are. They have no heart."

"*Waweli*, what have we done?" said my mother. She whispered something in the woman's ear.

"Come, sister, I'll show you." She led my mother off to the women's bathroom.

"*Yallah*, Abu Kabi," said Abed. "Let's get cracking. Kabi, Nuri, you too. It's time for some food. Shish kebab, grilled fish, stuffed doves on rice!"

"We'll go to the restaurant as soon as Um Kabi comes back," my father agreed.

Abed nearly doubled over with laughter. "Restaurant? You first have to queue up for ration tickets and then stand in a line like the one in front of Noah's Ark."

"I don't get it. Do you mean we get free food here?"

"You bet!" chortled Abed. "Whole legs of lamb, just like el-Pachachi's."

"I'm hungry," howled Moshi, stamping his foot.

"You sit tight and watch the tent till your mother comes," said Abed harshly.

To our surprise Moshi fell silent, perhaps because he sensed at last that there was someone in charge.

Darkness fell. A bleary glow of kerosene lamps flickered from the tents. Abed hummed to himself all the way to the queue that stretched past the camp's offices. There he grew grave-looking, said "Excuse me", in a firm Hebrew, and dragged my father like a blind man to the front. Whether it was because he looked like he knew what he was doing, or because of his khaki clothes that resembled an official's, people made way.

Abed told my father to sign some papers handed to him through a small window and we walked away, the proud owners of mess kits, some grey winter blankets smelling of mothballs, a kerosene lamp, a bucket, and a broom.

"Shame on you, jumping the queue!" a man said seizing my father, whose arms were too full to defend himself.

"He's an Imari. He's from the Movement. He has privileges," jeered another man.

"I'm terribly sorry," my father apologized. "I didn't realize. We're new here. Please don't do that again," he said to Abed.

"We would have been stuck there all night," Abed replied without contrition. "Leave Nuri and the mess kits with me and go back to the tent."

We waited there a long while. When the two of them arrived with the food, Nuri removed a tray from his shoulder and displayed its contents. "Look, worms!" he said, pointing in disgust to the same noodles I had seen in the rubbish. I felt sick.

My mother and Abed filled plates and passed them out.

"I want *bajili* and *ful*," cried Moshi, starting to weep again.

"Just where am I supposed to get *bajili?*" asked my mother, who had made my little brother his favourite bean dish every day in Baghdad.

Moshi dumped his plate on the ground and ran from the tent. "Abed," my mother screamed, "go and get him!"

"Relax, Um Kabi. This is a closed camp. There's barbed wire all around. He won't get far. And I promise you that in two days' time he'll eat what's on his plate. Let him go hungry. It's good for him."

I went to look for him anyway. He was standing in the dark near the tent, sobbing his heart out. It took all my cajoling to make him return to the tent, where he sprawled out on a cot and fell asleep in his clothes. Nuri soon collapsed and dozed off too.

"Kabi, have some chocolate cake from el-Afrah's bakery," said Abed, handing me half a round rye loaf from the tray. "This is Zionist bread. Don't expect any pittas."

I cut myself a slice. It tasted strange and stuck to my gums and teeth when I tried chewing it.

Abed left for the night. My father leaned against the tentpole, smoking his Craven As from Baghdad with their good smell. My mother, bone-weary, lay drowsing on a cot. No one bothered to make the beds or put on their new pyjamas. It was as though we had merely stopped at one more place along the way.

54.

As tired as I was, I couldn't sleep. I stepped out of the tent and took a deep breath of the fresh sea breeze, which made my body tingle languidly. The sea boomed, its serried waves piling on to the shore as if about to overrun the camp. Could that happen? I remembered a time when the Tigris overflowed and my father volunteered to carry sandbags for the dykes built to keep the clay-red water from inundating Baghdad. But the sea, I told myself, was not a river.

Others emerged from their tents in the moonlight flooding the camp. On the far horizon the stars ran into the dark mass of wooded mountains that I had gazed at during the day. Their silhouette, now domed, now spired, made me think of a city of mosques. What was beyond them? Were there djinns there? It was said there were no demons in the Holy Land. Did a revolutionary like Salim Effendi really not believe in them? Although I too thought they were superstition, a part of me was still scared of them. Where was Salim Effendi now? Perhaps he was even in our camp.

I returned to our tent. The kerosene lamp was sputtering sootily with a foul smell. Moshi murmured something in his sleep and turned over. I covered him with a blanket and he threw it on the sandy floor. Despite all the water, there were almost no mosquitoes. I started to drag my cot into the fresh air, then changed my mind and left it half in the tent. I still hadn't slept a wink.

The sky was bluer and deeper here. I searched for the Plough and the Pole Star. What would Edouard be doing tomorrow? An hour's time difference was all there was between us and yet there was no going back. I would never see Baghdad again, not even on a short visit. I was a citizen of an enemy state. I, the enemy of my native land and of the city I loved!

A cat screeched on the tent with what sounded like a wail of longing. Who was swinging in my cracked old *jalala* now? When the time had come to pack, I couldn't decide what to take. Spread out on my bed were gifts I had received, books I had loved, compositions I had written, one of them my prize-winning essay on patriotism. "Kabi," smiled my mother, looking at the huge pile, "we're only allowed to take three suitcases." I left everything on the bed and sought refuge as always on the swing that I had saved from Ismail when we moved on the eve of the *Farhood*.

Picturing Abu Hamid's children fighting over it, I had tears of self-pity in my eyes. And how was Rashel? On the day of Abu Saleh's execution, all my jealousy had disappeared as if by magic, taken over by real worries … Now, lying in a tent in Israel far from our little street in Baghdad, I actually prayed for Karim Abd el-Hak to rescue Rashel from the Abu Hamids. Stubborn to the last, she had refused to waive her citizenship even when the Movement offered to put her on our flight at the last minute.

I woke from a deep sleep to a chill dawn. I rose, wrapped myself in my grey blanket as in a prayer shawl, and stood watching the turquoise strands of the first light. Pearly drops of dew had collected on top of the tent and dripped in a dark line on the sand. A gleam beyond the mountains heralded the sun striving to rise on a new day. Children stepped out into the narrow passageways between the tents and went to defecate by the fence, covering their excrement with sand like a cat.

The camp was waking up. Men fetched water from stand-pipes in buckets and pots and long lines began to form everywhere. My mother, uncombed and wrinkled-looking, peered out from the tent flaps at a queue in front of the toilet and muttered:

"For this we left our house in Baghdad?"

Dozens of men were waiting for the men's toilet, some holding kettles in their hands. A young man in pyjamas clutched at his stomach and spun around like a top. When he came to a halt he looked up and said: "Allah, what have we done to deserve having to queue even to shit?"

"Fuck the Movement," said a man. "They fucked us when they brought us here."

"O Baghdad," exclaimed a dandyish-looking fellow who was still wearing his good clothes, "what wouldn't we give to see you now!"

"Just look at you longing for the fleshpots of Egypt as soon as you've left them!" rejoined an old man with a kettle.

"Is that a Hebrew newspaper? Can I have a look at it?" someone asked the person in front of him. "It's the first I've seen."

"It's for wiping your arse, not for reading," said the owner of the newspaper to the newcomer.

"With a *newspaper?*"

"It's the Zionist way, pal."

"Here, have a page of mine," offered someone else.

Forewarned by Abed, I was equipped with part of a paper he had left with us.

"You mustn't do that with the Holy Tongue," protested the man with the kettle.

"Shit!" said the dandy. "Shit! Shit! Shit! Shit! Shit!"

The whole line took up the refrain.

My turn came at last. The toilet was a raised concrete platform divided into open stalls, each with a round hole in the floor. A fresh deposit of badly aimed, still steaming excrement lay next to the hole I squatted over. I looked down at the chasm beneath me. If I lost my footing I was done for. *Waweli*, what a way to die!

For children, it was a really dangerous place. Far better for them to go by the fence, even if everyone could see them.

"*Yallah*, let's get a move on!" yelled the next man in line. "This isn't a picnic."

Brackish water, topped by dirty foam laced with stubble, ran down concrete channels in the washroom. The place was as crowded as the bathhouse in Baghdad. I elbowed my way to a tap, washed my hands, wet my face, and fled outside.

Women and boys were shaking out blankets, beating mattresses, and hanging laundry on the guy ropes. In front of our tent stood Abed, washed, shaven, and neatly combed. My father stood beside him, smoking his morning cigarette. Tired and lined, he had a day's growth of beard. "What's the nearest city?" he asked hesitantly.

"Haifa," said Abed.

"Why don't we take a trip there?"

"It isn't worth missing breakfast. There's eggs, cocoa, rye bread, jam, and margarine."

"What's margarine?" Nuri wanted to know.

"*Kemar*."

"*Kemar*?" asked Moshi eagerly.

"*Kemar* that doesn't taste like *kemar* because it's made of grass. Did you ever hear of such a thing?"

"*Ya Allah!* Did you hear that, Um Kabi?" enthused my father. "They make *kemar* out of grass here."

My mother did not dignify him with a reply.

When we returned with the breakfast trays, she was washed and wearing her blue dress, her hair pulled back and fastened with a brown comb. She sliced the rye bread and dished out the food, careful we all got the same amount. My father didn't touch his. He drank a cup of tea and smoked another cigarette. "Um Kabi," he finally asked, "would you like to go to Haifa?"

"What's in Haifa? And who'll watch our things if I go? I'd rather learn the ropes of this dump that you've brought me to."

"It won't run away," Abed said.

"Neither will Haifa," retorted my mother.

Before setting out, my father and Abed had a long argument. My father wanted to leave by the front gate. Abed said that we had to sneak through the fence. "Don't you realize that you're in quarantine? You're carrying diseases, infections, fleas, lice, the ten plagues of Egypt … "

"I don't want to hear this!" shouted my father. "Even in Baghdad I tried never to break the law. Where's your sense of shame?"

"Shame? There is none here," said Abed. "*Yallah,* are you coming or not? I don't need to go to Haifa, I've been there."

Nuri and Moshi pushed and pulled my father to the fence. Abed headed for a place that was torn and knelt to lift the strands of wire for us to crawl under. My father remained on the other side.

"Come on, be a free man," said Abed. "Isn't that what you came to Israel for? Don't worry about your clothes. There's nothing like a suit and tie for crawling under a fence in."

"Now you're telling me how to dress," complained my father

bitterly. "What makes you think you're such a conquering hero just because you got here three months before us?"

"To the sea!" whooped Nuri and Moshi, racing to the water's edge.

Between the gold and the blue was a wide stretch of white foam. There was no far shore and the one we stood on was hammered by the waves like a tray by a Baghdad coppersmith. The water, flecked with green, was nothing like the light brown Tigris. My father scooped the bright sand in his hands and capered like a boy. He took off his shoes, rolled up his trousers, and ran into the water with a shout of joy.

"Just look at him," said Abed. "He's like a baby."

"Don't you talk like that about my father!" yelled Nuri, punching Abed's belly with his little fist.

A large, crested wave was bearing down on us.

"Baba, Baba, you'll drown," screamed Moshi, hypnotized by the onrushing water.

"Don't you know I can swim?" asked my father.

He looked happy and young in the bright sunlight. Soon he would leave the camp, plant his rice fields, and build his castle. He had dreamed of it so often that he knew exactly what it would look like; he couldn't wait for my mother, who had humiliated him in front of his old servant, to see it with her own eyes ... What neither she, nor Abed, nor any of the complainers and grumblers understood was that our tent city was like the camps pitched by the Israelites in the desert, a cheap and mobile if uncomfortable way to start anew, a stroke of Zionist genius!

It took the exhaustion of all Nuri and Moshi's patience (and of mine too, although I tried not to show it) to persuade my father to finish his water games and return to dry land.

From the windows of the bus we saw Haifa with its hanging gardens like Hammurabi's climbing up Mount Carmel, its houses that clung to the mountainside, its grand, gold-domed Bahai temple, its port full of ships. And – alas – its Arabs in keffiyehs when we disembarked at the central station.

"Why do they have to be everywhere?" whispered Moshi, clutching my father's hand.

"Don't be afraid," my father told him, reaching for his worry beads. "These are our Arabs." And seeing that Moshi was still unconvinced, he called out to them: "*Marhaba ya ihwan!*"

"*Ahlan wa-sahlan,*" they answered in an Arabic different from ours.

My father halted by a newspaper stand and read the Hebrew letters of the headlines out loud like a child. One of the papers had a familiar face on its front page. I had walked another twenty paces before I decided to turn back for another look. When I did, I cried out in amazement:

"Hey, come and look! It's Salim Effendi."

My old teacher was staring out at me from an Arabic newspaper called *Al-Ittihad*. My father, as incredulous as I was, took a dinar from his wallet to pay for it.

"What are you doing?" asked Abed, handing over a coin. "That's Iraqi money."

"Isn't it any good here?" marvelled my father.

"It's too good. That's why the banks will exchange it for Israeli pounds at half its value."

"I don't believe you."

"You don't know them. You can give your dinars to me. I know some honest people who will give you their full worth."

I was too curious about Salim Effendi to realize that the "honest people" were black marketeers. After the argument over the fence, Abed did not want to suggest anything else illegal. My father read out loud:

"Comrade Rahamim Imari, known as Salim Effendi, has joined the ranks of the Israeli Communist Party after a courageous escape from the Iraqi secret service and a roundabout journey to Israel. We are proud to announce his appointment to our editorial staff. He will also play a senior role in the Party's campaign against the Israeli military government in the Galilee … "

"What kind of military government?" wondered my father. "Isn't Israel a democracy?"

"Not for the Arabs. As long as we're at war with them, we have to keep them from getting uppity," said Abed with a patriotic fervour that contrasted oddly with his previous cynicism. "They need to know who's boss. Better still, we should kick them all out of here … "

"But that would be treating them the way the Moslems treated us," my father objected.

"No sooner does that Communist of yours from Baghdad get here than he's already sucking up to the Arabs," Abed went on angrily. "That's a left-wing paper. It should be shut down. We should jail every one of them."

"No, we shouldn't. When I was studying law, I had an English tutor who explained that the test of a democracy is a man's willingness to fight for the freedom of speech of his enemies. Not that I don't think that Salim Effendi has a lot of nerve. He wouldn't be here if it weren't for the Movement and Abu Saleh."

"You're telling me? I was with him all the way from Iraq. Abu Saleh asked me to keep an eye on him and to give him a hand if he needed it. It was beneath him to have anything to do with us. A real big shot! And here in Israel he got a cushy job right away.

He had been in the immigrants' camp no more then two days when the Communists whisked him out of it. The bastard knows how to land on his feet!"

"Baba, I'm hungry," whined Moshi.

Abed took us to a little restaurant that had three tables and some folding chairs. A single photograph hung on its bare wall. My father saluted it and fingered its glass frame. "Boys, take a good look," he said. "This is Ben-Gurion, David King of Israel!"

"Are there kings here too?" Moshi asked.

"*Yallah,* what will you have to eat, boys?" Abed prodded us.

"Kebab," we all piped in unison.

"Ten spits of kebabs," my father told the waitress. "Make it lamb."

The waitress smiled and shook her head.

Abed smiled too. "There's no meat here, Abu Kabi," he said.

"Then let's go to another restaurant."

"There won't be any there either. Meat is rationed."

"Then we'll eat chicken. Or fish."

"There is no chicken. There is no fish."

"Then what did we come to a restaurant for?"

"To eat what there is." Abed exchanged a few words in Hebrew with the waitress and said: "There's vegetable soup, salad … "

"We don't want any," cried Nuri and Moshi.

Abed spoke to the waitress again in low tones and announced: "If you behave yourselves, you'll get a special fish."

"Like in Baghdad," whooped Moshi, clapping his hands. After a while the waitress came back with some slices of cod fillet in fried batter. Nuri looked at them suspiciously, tasted a piece, and admitted grudgingly: "It's all right."

Abed and my father took the rolls they were served, sliced

them lengthwise, filled them with a piece of fish and some salad, and ate ravenously. Moshi and I looked on silently.

"Have something to drink," said my father.

"Coca-Cola," Moshi said.

Abed laughed. "There isn't any."

"Then what *is* there here?" sobbed Moshi.

The waitress brought some soda water with raspberry and lemon syrup. Even Moshi agreed it wasn't bad. At least it was cold and sweet.

As we were leaving, Abed asked the waitress for the leftovers.

"How could you take home leftovers from a restaurant?" scolded my father.

"Why waste money?" said Abed. "Just look at what these spoiled kids of yours left on their plates. My Romanian girlfriend will kiss me for it. The Ashkenazim know better than to throw food away. They spent too many years going hungry in Europe. All that food that you see in the rubbish bins in the camp was dumped there by Iraqis and Moroccans."

My father was mortified. "That's true," he murmured. "We forget what happened over there. It's beyond our comprehension … "

I saw he had tears in his eyes and turned away.

The sound of an oud was coming from an Arab café. My father followed the rhythm inside and ordered two hookahs. Abed sent Nuri and Moshi off for some ice cream to keep them from getting bored. He and my father sucked hungrily on the water pipes and listened to the oud with their eyes shut.

"Who's your Romanian girlfriend?" asked my father. It was a question I hadn't dared raise.

"I met her in the camp. She shared a tent with some other girls from Romania, Hungary, and Poland. They had all lost their families in the war and were orphans. The first night I helped them carry their cots and mattresses. It was dark and cold, with no moon or even any stars. You couldn't see yourself pee. The men cursed and the women and children cried. It beats me why they don't hook the place up to some electricity.

"Anyway, I helped them settle in. The next day she came to my tent to thank me. I could see she had her eye on me. Some of them like darkies like me. The funny part of it was that we couldn't talk until we started going to Hebrew classes together, because Nadia knew only Romanian and Yiddish and I spoke only Arabic. After two weeks, I decided to look for a construction job. Building workers are in demand here and twenty-seven is too old for the army. All I'll have to do is a month of reserve duty every year.

"What can I tell you, Abu Kabi? If I have to get up every morning, at least I now have someone to do it for. I'm happy with her. I worry about her and help her. It's different from being someone's servant. It's made me feel more of a man. Some day I'd like to be a construction foreman, or even a contractor. Nadia is willing to have me as I am, but I'll build her a castle, I swear."

I looked at my father's ex-servant. I didn't doubt he would build his castle before my father.

"At night we slept together on the beach, beyond the fence. We took our blankets and had a good time."

"But ... " My father glanced at me, decided I was old enough, and asked: "Didn't people in the camp gossip?"

"Abu Kabi, it's a different world here. It's not Baghdad. Who is going to tell me what to do? After two weeks we moved to Pardes Hanna, where we found a little shack to live in. When we find a better place, *inshallah*, we'll get married."

My father was sombre and thoughtful all the way home. Back in the camp we found the tent cleaned, the beds made, the suitcases arranged neatly in a corner, and the kerosene lamp polished until it gleamed. My mother had been hard at work.

We went to the camp offices where long lines of men waited. My father, in a blue suit, a starched, blue shirt, and a white tie with blue polka dots, took his place in one of the queues. His hair was slicked back as if he were about to see Salima Pasha. When our turn came, we entered the office of a man wearing khaki and in his shirtsleeves. Next to him sat a translator, dressed in khaki too.

"I'm Salman Moshi Imari, the brother of Hizkel Imari, one of the Movement's leaders in Baghdad who is now in prison there," my father introduced himself.

"Welcome," said the official. "What can I do for you?"

"I want to grow rice," my father told him.

"Rice? In Israel?"

"Yes."

"I thought rice grew in China," said the man with a smile.

"And in Iraq. And in Asia and in Africa and in Brazil. It can be grown in Israel too."

"I see you know something about it. But … "

"The biggest rice fields in Iraq belonged to my family. We used the most modern equipment. We had tractors, combines … " My father talked quickly, trying to get it all in. Seeing the official open his mouth to speak, he hurried even more.

"I need land, water, and credit. All I want is your help to get started."

"We don't have the water."

"What about the Jordan?"

The man burst out laughing. "That's a river for praying, not for rice growing."

"I see that I amuse you," said my father, his brow covered with sweat.

"Not at all, comrade. We really don't have enough water in this country for rice cultivation."

"Perhaps a small farm in an agricultural village," said Abed, trying to be more practical. Not that he believed that my father was suited to that either.

The official looked at my father's papers and said in Hebrew: "He's too old."

"You're not young enough," the translator told my father.

"Old?" muttered my father. "Me?"

"I said not young enough."

The official laid his pen on his desk and said: "Let me think it over for a few days."

"What's there to think about?" asked my father, blinking his eyes.

"You need more patience," said the official. "Patience is what you need here. Everything will turn out fine."

Outside the office, Abed took his leave of us. He had to get back to his job in Pardes Hanna. We thanked him for his help and walked him to the bus. On our way to the tent my father kept clearing his throat. No words came.

55.

For three weeks he went daily to the camp offices in his fancy suits and shirts pressed with a coal-heated iron that my mother borrowed from a neighbour. One might have thought he was going to see the Pasha. All that was missing was a flower in his lapel, but there were no flowers in the immigrants' camp.

He couldn't get over the sloppy appearance of the Israeli officials with their khaki trousers held up by broad-buckled belts, their short-sleeved, open-necked shirts, their sandals or dusty boots. At first he took it as a personal slight; then, when he saw that they dressed the same for everyone, he decided that it was themselves they had no respect for. In Baghdad every government clerk wore a suit and tie. Did Israeli diplomats abroad go about like this too?

He was now waiting for a promised meeting with the director general of the immigration department. The days were so filled with anticipation that there was no time to do anything for his brother Hizkel. Although in Baghdad he had vowed to move heaven and earth for Hizkel, he had yet to speak to anyone about him. His greatest fear was of missing his meeting if he should go to Tel Aviv on Hizkel's behalf on the very day the director general was free to see him. And maybe the director general could do something for Hizkel too.

Israel was no different from Iraq in this respect: you had to get to the higher-ups, because the lower-downs had no power.

When Grandfather Imari had wanted a licence to import agricultural machinery, he had been obliged to invite the minister of trade to a party in his villa, to wine and dine him, and to ply him with flattery and bribes. The trick was to get to the wazirs of Israel.

Of course, my father never suspected for a moment that high officials in Israel took bribes, nor would he have offered them any even if he had. Men who wore nothing but khaki – indeed, maybe this was why they wore it – seemed to him incorruptible. In a Jewish country you had to work differently.

And so, having pestered the director general's underlings into getting him an appointment, he set out to learn more about the man. It was a disappointment, almost an insult, to find out that the man knew no English. How could anyone hold a high position without it? He saw that he would have to learn Hebrew fast, because an interpreter was a poor substitute for direct communication.

Hizkel had been right. He should have begun his Hebrew studies in Iraq. Well, he would devote himself to them now. Not just yet, though. He would wait until he was better able to concentrate. But he would learn. His quick tongue was all he had going for him. Although Abed kept telling him that in Israel you had to pull strings, he had no idea where to look for them. He could only talk, demand, explain, wheedle, cajole, and be patient. Patience was everything, a strong but bitter medicine to be taken daily.

And yet every conversation with an official exhausted him, left him baffled and speechless. What, after all, was he begging for? Some earth, some water, and a bit of bank credit, that was all. And to do even this much he had to abandon his sense of shame and honour, the last two possessions he had.

507

There was something cruel about how decisions were made here. Perhaps it had to do with their being so out in the open. Everyone knew what one man had been granted and what another had been refused. It was like belonging to one big family that did not act like a family. Sometimes he felt so weary that he was tempted to chuck in the whole business. Let there be no new life – let there be no dream fulfilled – let there just be a job and a steady income! He would become a teacher again. He would start in an Arab village, and later, after learning Hebrew, he would teach in a Jewish school.

But was this what he had come here for? Something had gone wrong. He had been sure that Israel was waiting for him with open arms, that everyone knew about him and his brother and the arms cache and Abu Saleh and the time and money they had put into the Movement – and now it turned out that the facts had been left behind in Baghdad and that every other immigrant from there pretended to have been active in the Movement. Who could tell who was telling the truth and who was not? The very name of Imari, known to every Iraqi, was more than most Israelis could pronounce. One official called him Amuri, another Emori, another Amrani. If only Hizkel were here with his Hebrew, his connections, and his powers of persuasion, it would have been possible to hang on to his coat-tails. Hizkel could have been a leader in Israel too. He could have been one anywhere.

True, not even Hizkel had shown much enthusiasm for my father's dream of growing rice. "In Israel," he had said, "we should do something different, something that will turn over a new page." Had this been Hizkel's way of telling his brother that his latest plans were just one more pretext for continuing the lost battle for his grandfather's inheritance? And yet he had dreamed of rice since he was a boy. In the end he would show them who his grandfather's true grandson was! Indeed, Grandfather Imari had once bought land in Palestine that might be good for rice. Who might know something about it?

O my brother with the smell of my mother upon thee, what made me leave you there, he asked in a frightening moment of doubt. He felt so alone in this country. Until now there had always been Hizkel, Abu Saleh, his friends in the Movement, even Abu Edouard. There was nothing like friendship to put mettle in a man.

He wondered if he had perhaps not begun to depend too much on his own son Kabi. No, there was no need to overstate it. He was still a capable father and it was his children who needed him. He was just so isolated, little better than a deaf man in his ignorance of the language. Kabi didn't yet know enough Hebrew to be of any help, and besides, what was needed here was something else, something indefinable, a different posture towards the world. As much as he hated to admit it, it was precisely this that Abed had.

Abed had been trying to convince my father to move to Pardes Hanna. "I can help you more there," he had said. But my father wanted to prove that he could manage on his own.

To Abed everything seemed simple. Whatever happened to him in Israel would be an improvement on his old life. He and his Romanian girlfriend Nadia, who was actually quite nice, lived in a shack and took a bus every day to Hadera, where he worked on a construction site and she had a job in a restaurant kitchen. Between the leftovers that Nadia took home and the extra rationing cards that he received for doing hard physical labour, there was enough food to pass on to Um Kabi. He found ways to get what he wanted, and it was easy to see that he and

Nadia were happy. They even had the energy to attend Hebrew classes three nights a week, and on a fourth they visited the immigrants' camp and tried convincing my father to move to Pardes Hanna.

I liked Nadia, though I couldn't decide whether or not she was pretty because I had never seen types like her in Baghdad. She had a long face, very straight hair that sometimes fell over it, and a lot of dimples when she smiled. At first my mother was cool towards her. She couldn't understand how two unmarried people could live together, or why Abed had picked a Romanian instead of an Iraqi, or what made him so sure she wasn't just some tart.

Abed took it well; he knew that my mother cared about him and he listened to her patiently, explaining that customs in Israel were different and that it was a good thing that they were. How, he asked diplomatically, could Israelis become one people if they not only came from a thousand different places but clung to a thousand different customs? He knew he couldn't talk to my mother as bluntly as he did to my father, whom he straightforwardly told that the morals of Iraq were outdated.

Gradually, my mother saw Nadia's good points and the love and respect she showed Abed. Once she was convinced that they had honourable intentions towards each other, she relaxed, or pretended to relax her standards and greeted them happily when they came.

My father, who kept insisting that "our next stop is the rice fields", knew that my mother hoped that Abed and Nadia would rescue us from the camp, which she loathed. He spent his days roaming the camp with his suit and worry beads, preparing for his talk with the director general and rehearsing the one Hebrew sentence that he knew, "Zionism is pioneering."

Perhaps he would try it out first on the camp's officials, whose Hebrew he now understood perfectly when they joked: "Here comes the farmer in the blue suit." As if khaki were the only colour in which you could get anything done!

My father loved the Hebrew word *halutz*, pioneer, and even considered changing our family name to it. Abed, with his usual alacrity, had accepted his Hebrew teacher's proposal that he call himself Oved, which was the name of David's grandfather in the Bible. A week later, encouraged by my father to make inquiries, he returned with the teacher's suggestion that Salman Imari be changed to Shlomo Amir. The word *amir*, explained Abed's teacher, meant a sheaf of grain stalks – perfect for a rice grower. In the end, though, my father was reluctant to abandon the name Imari. How could he surrender anything so time-honoured?

On the long-awaited day of his meeting with the director general he rose early, dressed meticulously, even putting on his silver cuff links, and left the tent without any breakfast, walking stiffly on the sand as if practising standing erect. The director general arrived late and was besieged by a throng of immigrants, and my father chain-smoked and paced nervously while awaiting his turn. After an hour a secretary came out and said: "I'm very sorry. The director general will not be able to see anyone else today. There's a problem with a ship load of immigrants in Haifa and he's needed there urgently."

There were grumbles and curses. Salman Imari clasped his locked fingers and remained in front of the closed door until everyone had left, then turned and wandered aimlessly through the camp. I saw him muttering and gesturing as if lodging a formal complaint. When he returned to the tent, abject and out of breath, my mother did not even say hello.

She hated the place and its inhabitants. Even the lapping of the surf, which lulled us children pleasantly to sleep at night, kept her angrily awake. She worried that we would sneak through the fence to the sea like other children, one of whom had drowned the week before. She was sick and tired of the transiency; of the belongings scattered about and the suitcases that were our only cupboards; of the repulsive food; of the lack of privacy, which bared her most intimate moments to the world; of "this whole damn railway station", as she called the camp. "All you can do with a tent," she said, "is walk into it and back out of it."

Even Maa'uda, the woman from Mosul, had departed by now, leaving my mother behind with my crazy father. She wanted a home, a place to call her own, and a school for her children, who did nothing all day. Before long she would lose all control over them.

The immigration officials had offered my father a dwelling in Cheriya, in Zakkiya, in Pardes Katz, in ... well, somewhere up north near the mountains, she couldn't remember the name. And he had turned each one down while she trudged the camp with her swelling stomach, asking, inquiring, listening to the gossip in the synagogue, informing him of the best places to live in, which he refused even to consider. In the few weeks since our arrival the whole population had moved on except for us.

Although many of the women had found employment in the area or even in the camp kitchen, my mother was too pregnant for such drudgery. "Kabi," she said, "we'll have to think of a way to make some money. Maybe you should look for work." She even sent me to inquire about a job on a road gang and told my father that she was about to give birth any minute in the hope of making him get a job. "I'm worried about the baby," she threatened. "You're murdering your own offspring."

In the end she managed to frighten him. He had been waiting longingly for this child, "conceived in exile and born in redemption", as he put it, and had even decided to call his new son David in honour of Abu Saleh and Ben-Gurion. My mother was praying for a daughter.

In his distress my father asked me to accompany him to a hilltop town called Zichron Ya'akov near which, he had heard, there was land for sale for which perhaps, he could get a government loan.

By now we were able to exit via the front gate, whose guardians would have been happy had he walked through and never returned. When we got off the bus, my father headed straight for the fields between the town and the sea. We spent hours walking there. He surveyed the area, measured the fields, and looked for sources of water. Flocks of white egrets wheeled above our heads and he gazed at them with a smile. "Birds are close to Allah," he told me. "They know a lot. There are always egrets near rice fields."

But he did not find any water, not even when he came back a second and a third time. No one could make him out, this strange man in a suit who wandered back and forth across the fields, scooping up handfuls of dirt while consulting a thick notebook densely written in Arabic and English. (I myself had by now exchanged my uncomfortable clothes for shorts and walking shoes, a development my father had chosen to overlook. Perhaps he was loath to acknowledge the beginnings of a revolt, although he was feeling so vulnerable that I did my best to defer to him.) At night he returned to our tent, silent and empty-handed.

My mother's aggravation turned into depression. Or perhaps it was just an act. One way or another, she took to her bed and lay staring wordlessly at the tent flap. The dirt went uncleaned, flies settled on the leftover food, and everything lay about in disorder.

Always a model housekeeper, she seemed not to notice. Not even Abed and Nadia, with whom she was frankest about her problems, could get her to talk.

My father was so alarmed that he went to the office and demanded to see the camp director. To his amazement, he was received at once in the friendliest fashion. The director circled his desk, sat beside my father, took his hand, gave it a pat, and said:

"I've found an excellent solution for you, Comrade Amiri."

"Imari, Imari! How many times do I have to tell you?"

"Forgive me. I'll bet you can't pronounce my name either. It's Zalman Szczechowilski."

"Salman Stash … Stu … "

My father laughed in spite of himself and was joined by the interpreter.

"You see? Well then, Comrade Am … Imari, I want to send you to a very nice place, an immigrants' hostel in Pardes Hanna. Perhaps I can arrange a canvas-top for you. I can't promise, but I'll do what I can."

"What's a canvas-top?"

"It's a little house with a canvas roof."

"Do you mean another tent?" asked my father despairingly, taking his worry beads from his pocket. "Did you hear that, Kabi? He makes it sound like Big Imari's mansion. It's out of the question. I want to meet the director general."

"Everyone who came on your flight has gone from here. They all listened to me and are glad that they did. You're the only one

514

left. Your wife is about to give birth. This is no place for her. There's not even a hospital nearby. Where will she deliver? Suppose somthing happens to the baby? You know all the diseases that the refugees from Europe bring to this camp. Tuberculosis, polio, dysentery, and even worse … "

"I'm glad to see that you're concerned about my wife. How do you think I feel?"

"Comrade Imari, in Pardes Hanna you'll have a better chance of meeting the director general. He's frequently there on business."

My father's resistance crumbled. "Is there a school there?" he asked, looking for an honourable way out.

"Of course," said the director, as if given a new lease of life. "Of course."

Only later did I discover that he, Abed, and my mother had conspired behind my father's back. The truth was that the director general, as Comrade Szczechowilski told Abed, had refused to see my father and declared that he had no time for lunatics. Nor did my father have any way of knowing that thousands of immigrants were already stranded in Pardes Hanna with nowhere to go from there.

On the day we moved, Abed again took time off work. I saw him grin at my mother as she suddenly came to life. He sat her in the driver's cabin of the pick-up truck, told us to climb into the back, and scrambled in next to us. "Don't forget that you've got a pregnant woman there," called my father to the driver before turning to look out at the view with his cheek cradled in his palm like a general contemplating a campaign. The sight of so much sandy, rocky, empty land must have oppressed him. After a wearisome drive we turned off onto a side road. A forest of tents, stretching to the horizon, met our eyes.

"At least there's a road here," said Nuri, pointing at a bumpy strip of asphalt running through the tent forest.

We were driven to Camp 3, where Abed had obtained a canvas-top for us. The camp management was apparently in on the conspiracy too.

"There's not even any sea here," said Moshi, on the verge of tears. Although my mother tried pretending that we had arrived at the tent of her dreams, she could barely suppress the shudder that ran through her. It would take her months to recover completely from the filth, the neglect, the thousands of idle immigrants living in a pall of noise and hopelessness.

And yet the next morning, as if prearranged, she rose determinedly, went with Abed and the rest of us to Hadera, and bought a bucket, a broom, a bowl, a kerosene stove, and a baking dish with the Israeli money that Abed had obtained for my father's dinars. She also bought Nuri and Moshi khaki clothes.

My father and I walked along the main street, looking at its shops that were so different from Baghdad's. I bought myself a *kova tembel*, the Israeli hat that looked like a dunce's cap. As I replaced my felt cap with the *kova tembel*, I caught my father's eye; he looked away as if he hadn't seen me. He bought some locally made cigarettes, nearly choked on the first puff, and said that Hiyawi, may he rest in peace, would have thrown such tobacco in the rubbish bin.

We also stopped by a watch shop, where my father examined a window display composed of cheaper ware than he had sold in Baghdad. The owner, a plump man with glasses, was standing in the doorway and invited us in with a smile. My father tried talking English, while the watchmaker, a Polish Jew, sought to answer in Yiddish and French; finally, aided by my own feeble efforts, they compromised on broken Hebrew. The man, it turned out, had been in Israel for three years and was happy to meet a colleague from Baghdad. He showed my father his stock, went over the prices with him, handed him a watch, and said: "I can't seem to fix this one. It's made by a firm that I never heard of back in Warsaw."

My father took the watch and sat down with it at the work table. Screwing a watchmaker's lens to his eye, he did something with tiny pliers, turned a screw, brushed and reset the mechanism, and handed the ticking timepiece back with a grin.

The watchmaker took five piastres from his pocket. Still grinning, my father raised his hand in a gesture of refusal.

"If you're looking for work," said the man, "I can give you some."

"I'm going to grow rice," said my father.

"Forget about rice. Come and work for me."

My father's face darkened imperceptibly. No one else would have noticed, but I knew every shade of his complexion. He rose and took his leave icily, leaving the watchmaker unaware that he had insulted him.

The next morning my mother said to him:

"All the men are going out to work on the road. Why don't you join them?"

"Should *I* work on a road gang?"

"Why not? Didn't you tell me in Baghdad that in Israel you would sell kerosene from a wagon if you had to?"

"He was offered a job by a watchmaker in Hadera," I said before I could catch myself. My father looked as if he were ready to murder me.

"You turned it down?" said my mother. "You could start there and open a store of your own within a year."

"I come from a long line of farmers. I have a farmer's soul."

"Abu Kabi, don't you see what's happening? You're being laughed at behind your back. There's no water in this country. Half the time the taps run dry. And you're still dreaming of rice paddies?"

"Let them laugh," my father said, ticking off his worry beads.

"How long can you go on like this? Soon we'll use up the last of our money. Is this the new life you promised me? It's time you stopped dreaming and thought of making a living. Or do you expect me to do so?" Her voice grew hard. "I'll send Kabi and Nuri to work."

"You will not. They're going to grow rice with me."

"And I'll find a job too."

"Doing what?"

"Cleaning houses, taking in sewing, picking fruit, mopping floors – whatever there is. I'd be doing it already if I weren't pregnant. All the women work in this country."

"Not in our family," said my father. He seemed stunned. "I'm not going to be supported by a woman."

"Listen to him! Big Imari won't let his wife support him. It's beneath the tycoon's dignity." My mother was beside herself. "As if you didn't sponge off that singer of yours for three whole years! Don't tell me that you could have kept that expensive whore on your miserable salary as a teacher. I'm going to work. I'm going to learn a trade. I'm going to make money and if you find that shameful, you can stop dreaming about rice and go and find a job like other men. What's there to be ashamed about anyway? This isn't Baghdad where you can tell me what to do. You'll have to live with it. I haven't had a happy moment since the day we arrived here. What a fool I was to come with you!"

She sat on the bed, buried her face in her hands, and burst into tears, as astonished by her outburst as the rest of us. It was clear to us all that nothing in our family would be the same again.

"Do you know who'll make something of himself here?" she went on sobbing. "Whoever will work at anything. Abed."

"Abed!" shouted my father, still in shock. "All I hear throughout the day is Abed, Abed, Abed. Why must you drag him into everything?"

"For you to learn the meaning of responsibility," my mother screamed back.

My father stalked out of the tent, sat down on an empty vegetable crate, and stuck a cigarette that he forgot to light in his mouth. I could feel the self-pity welling up in him. He had been grievously wronged, and bitterly he kicked an old tin can like a boy. He was still sitting there disconsolately when night came.

The next morning he rose early and announced that he was taking a trip and might not come home that night. We all hoped it was a good sign. I myself took advantage of the opportunity to sign up for the road gang. When he returned it would be a fait accompli.

The work was hard, worse than I had imagined. If I hadn't been ashamed to face Abed or let down my mother, I would never have stuck it out. She was waiting for me when I came home exhausted, my clothes full of dust and stained with tar and oil. She stroked my cheek and said, her eyes flooded with tears: "In Baghdad it would have been a disgrace to work like a Moslem or a Kurd. But here? You should feel proud of yourself. Anyone can be knocked down, but it takes a man to get up again."

Abed looked at my blisters and told her that in a few days I would have calluses. "Soon he can help Nadia and me renovate the old Arab house that we're hoping to buy in Jaffa," he told my mother. For the first time since we had arrived in Israel, I saw her smile.

She had been busy that day in the tent, cooking and arranging things. She had pinned some of Moshi's drawings to the tent flaps, made a cupboard out of some old crates, and – with the help of my two brothers, whom she infected with her enthusiasm – built a little fence around the tent and planted vegetables and parsley. She had also hung an awning for shade, made flowerpots from some old cans, and strung a trellis for a climbing plant. "It's not my greenhouse in Baghdad," she said, "but it's better than nothing."

From Jaffa, where they had been looking at abandoned houses, Nadia and Abed brought her a bag of leftover fabric that she had asked for, and she began to stitch it with the fine embroidery that she had learned as a child. Abed took her work to a store that catered to tourists in Haifa, where it did so well that the owner inquired if my mother would be willing to train a few girls for a small production line.

My mother laughed and said, "First let my baby be born." But Abed was already planning a tourist shop of our own in Jaffa. Meanwhile, Nadia had enrolled in a cookery school. According to Abed, her years of going hungry in Europe made her want to be around food all the time.

Despite their limited Hebrew, my mother and Nadia became good friends. Each filled a need in the other. Nadia was looking for a mother figure, while my mother, with her desire to give, found in Nadia what she hadn't found in Rashel. It amazed me how quickly she accepted Nadia's relationship with Abed. Perhaps she even welcomed the new morality of the polyglot hodgepodge of Israel, for it gave her independence from the man who had forced her to be part of it.

The change in her struck me one evening when two girl soldiers approached us as we were sitting in front of our tent. They were the first native-born Israelis my mother had met and I think it was love at first sight.

One of the soldiers, Lieutenant Naomi Ozeri, was a slim, dark, stunning Yemenite with a bright smile and a quiet, confident air. The other, Sergeant Noa Weingarten, (Vangarter, –Ventagren – it wasn't easy to learn how to pronounce it), was a fiery redhead with a freckled face and a maddening body. In my dreams at night I had a hard time choosing between them until I decided to compromise on both.

"Good for you, Mrs Imari," said the lieutenant. "Look how nicely you've arranged your tent and the ground around it."

It was the beginning of a long friendship between the two of them and our family. Lieutenant Ozeri, it turned out, was a welfare officer on a visit to our transit camp, while Sergeant Weingarten had come "to lure you, Mrs Imari, to evening classes for busy mothers given in Hebrew twice a week. I'll be your teacher."

"I don't have to be lured," said my mother, her face lighting up at my translation. "I'll be glad to come."

The two soldiers applauded and we joined them. After they left, my mother patted her round belly, smiled to the child she was carrying, and said: "I'm going to have a little Israeli of my own."

It didn't take long for me to realize that road work wasn't for me. It felt good to give my mother my earnings, which I hoped might ease her demands on my father, but I knew I had to look for something else. My Hebrew wasn't good enough to go back to school, or at least not good enough to do well there, and I had no energy for evening classes after a hard day's work. The one temptation was the thought of all the Polish and Romanian girls I might meet there, who made my seventeen-year-old's juices run.

It was a good thing that the road work took some of that juice out of me. What an idiot I had been not to go to a whorehouse in Iraq, where such things were at least government inspected! Was Abed any the worse for having spent a few years rolling in the hay with Fauzia? Whatever he had learned from her must have come in handy with Nadia.

For a while I thought of joining a kibbutz. It was time to visit Amira. I had received a lovely answer to the letter I had sent her, full of love and longing for my family. Perhaps she was thinking of her own family when she wrote it. There was no mention of her old dream of studying in America.

I also considered applying for early induction into the army. After all, I would have to serve in it anyway.

First, though, I had to help my father get settled. I was worried about him. The three days he was away did not seem to have changed him for the better. He had gone to Tel Aviv on behalf of Hizkel and met there with some people who took notes, asked questions, and promised to do what they could. He seemed tired and vague when he returned, and my mother hovered over him, not knowing what to say. He made no comment when I came home from the road gang.

The next morning, however, he surprised us by announcing that he was joining me. He put on a grey shirt and a pair of striped suit trousers, took a canvas bag from my mother with some hastily made jam sandwiches, and walked with me to the Binyamina-Pardes Hanna road where we were working. Some of the gang knew him, including my old drawing teacher Stad Anwar, who soon afterwards had to be hospitalized with a nervous breakdown. I chose not to work in the same crew as him in order to spare him the embarrassment of my presence. The shingle undersurface had been spread and tamped and now the dump trucks deposited piles of gravel, which we poured from baskets over hot asphalt, raking it evenly under the eyes of the foreman before the roller went over it.

Now and then I glanced at my father. His clothes were smeared with black tar. He wore a handkerchief, knotted at the corners, on his head and shuffled clumsily in his fancy-toed shoes along the edges of the wet asphalt, not knowing what to do with his rake. Now and then he paused to look at his watch and wipe the sweat from his face, after which he engaged in a spurt of aimless activity as if to make up for lost time. The foreman kept looking at him but said nothing. It broke my heart to see him. When we stopped for lunch he sat mindlessly with his crew in the shade of a truck, barely able to swallow his sandwich. After the lunch break he moved even more sluggishly.

At the end of a day that seemed to last forever we headed back, the last stragglers in the column. My father was dead on his feet, too weary to say a word. He stumbled slowly along, straightening up at times to take a deep breath while trying to flex his bent body that I supported. His face was burned to a crisp and his large hands were black with grease. Now and then he looked at the dirty fingernails that he had always groomed so carefully. I didn't want to hurt him by telling him to lean harder on me.

My mother was aghast to see him. He didn't touch the food she served. She made him a cup of strong tea and said:

"Abu Kabi, why don't you take a few days off and think things over? Don't go back to the road gang. It's not for you. You have to take care of yourself. You're all I have."

A tear rolled down her cheek. My father shut his eyes and patted her hand as she stroked his shoulder. He spent the next two days in bed, getting over his aches and pains, and then resumed his travels. But each time he returned to our transit camp he seemed to sink back into himself. Sometimes he went for walks in the eucalyptus grove beyond the tents, near which ran a smelly sewer, roaming for hours among the dry brambles and heaps of rubbish swarming with flies and pocked with rusty cans. He didn't even mind the smoke from the fires in the dump. Perhaps he had come to the conclusion that nothing could harm him any more, and perhaps he enjoyed courting danger.

Looking at him, I thought of the tall, handsome man I had known in Baghdad. I remembered one Sabbath when the stroll we took brought us to a wealthy villa under construction. My father liked to see such houses going up. Many of the workers who built them were barefoot, brown-skinned Arab boys who sweated in the brutal sun from dawn to dusk, trudging through sand and sludge to make a few pennies. It was them Salim Effendi had in mind when he spoke of the class struggle. One really couldn't argue with him.

We had passed a vast array of oleander bushes. A breeze ruffled their pink and white flowers, carrying their strong, sweet smell. Birds chirped and jumped in their branches which bobbed in a kind of dance.

An acrobat was performing by the entrance to el-Sa'adun Park. Vendors had set out their stands with sweets, rolls and bread rings, toffee apples, nuts and seeds, egg sandwiches, black-eyed beans, slices of pickled mango and tomato, and fruits of the season. On Saturdays, when they emerged from the synagogues and came looking for a shady refuge beneath the trees and flowery parasols, the park belonged to the Jews, and hundreds of them were there, admiring the mansions of the rich and dreaming of the day they could move here themselves from the run-down Jewish Quarter. Oblivious of the scoldings of the Arab sanitation workers, they littered the park with peel and nutshells while flocking to the food stands, whose wares they bought with money that they were not supposed to carry on the Sabbath.

My father stepped up to a stand that was selling limes, lifted one of them to his flared nostrils, and took a deep breath. Then, his bright eyes ranging over the green lashes of the grass in the pink-and-white tapestry waving in the wind, he replaced the lime on its stand, inhaled again, threw back his shoulders, and said:

"What a paradise of smells there will be there!"

"Where?" I asked, startled.

"In the land of Israel," he said knowingly. "A paradise of smells."

What a beacon of happiness he had been! Now, as he shuffled unkempt past the stinking piles of rubbish, I could see him mumbling to himself, dull eyes on the ground, face wan, shoulders slumped, arms dangling limply by his sides. I tried to stay out of his sight.

Sometimes, returning from work at night, I took his hand and tried to interest him in what was happening in the country. I let him know that there were free evening classes in Hebrew and that I would attend them with him. "My head's not on my shoulders now, son," was his answer. Though he smiled, his eyes were frozen with despair. One night he thought about it and said: "Soon, Kabi. After my meeting with the director general."

56.

In the end the director general came. He was a big, heavyset man with glasses, thin, greying hair, and a jovial face. He received my father cordially and asked him to take a seat, rising to shake hands with him across the desk. He shook my hand too and said:

"My name is Giora." And through an interpreter he asked: "What can I do for you, Mr Imari?"

My father, who had learned that officials in Israel expected him to talk quickly, spoke in staccato sentences about himself, the Movement, and Hizkel, demanding to know why his brother had not been freed. Giora listened to him patiently and even nodded in encouragement. He made a few appreciative remarks about Hizkel, apologized that the matter was not in his hands, and referred my father to an address in Tel Aviv that he had already been to.

"And now, what would you like for yourself?" he asked.

"To grow rice," said my father.

"Ah," said Giora. *So this is the rice maniac,* he must have been thinking. He said nothing for a while and then declared: "I'll be frank with you, Mr Imari. It's out of the question."

"But why?" asked my father, turning pale.

"This country lacks the proper conditions. There's no water."

"There's the Hula Marsh," said my father. "Look." He handed the director general an English book that he must have bought on one of his travels. "It says here that rice was once grown in the Hula, an Italian strain called Ballila. But the Japanese Nuri would do better. It's the perfect variety. Believe me, I'm an expert … "

"I have the greatest respect for your expertise, Mr Imari. It's a pity that we can't make use of it. And you should know that the Hula Marsh is going to be drained. Work is scheduled to begin on it next spring."

It took a good many explanations via the interpreter before my father understood.

"Drained?" His eyes blinked rapidly. "What for?"

"It's a worthless, mosquito-ridden swamp, a breeding place for malaria and all kinds of diseases like any body of standing water. We'll dry it out, settle people, pave roads, and make it bloom."

"Mr Director General, the place is a paradise. It has water buffalo, fish, fowl, a rich plant life … "

"We'll leave a small nature reserve."

"But there must be someone I can talk to … " murmured my father. "Someone to whom I can explain that … that the Hula mustn't be drained … "

"The person to talk to is Ben-Gurion. I'm afraid I can't be of any help. In my opinion, though, you'd be wasting your time. The government has made the decision and preliminary work is underway."

Outside the office my father had an odd attack of sneezing. His chest heaved and he grew short of breath. I held his hand apprehensively. Many Iraqis had developed asthma in Israel. I urged him to rest and he sat down on the stairs to the office.

"Do you think I'm crazy too?" he asked, opening the English book. "Look, son, look!"

"Baba, you heard what he said. There's been a government decision."

"So what? Does that make the government God? Government decisions can be changed. Your great-grandfather did it all the time. He went right to the ministers, to the King even. I'll go to Ben-Gurion. You have to be crazy to drain the Hula. It could be a huge rice bowl. And I'll grow the best rice in the world there. I'll tell you where we'll live, too. In Rosh Pina. I've looked at the map and I know exactly which mountain we'll build our castle on. It will be like Big Imari's, but even grander because of the view: a golden sun, turquoise skies, towering mountains, green trees, the marsh below us, rice paddies as far as the eye can see. Allah, nothing but rice! One day Big Imari will come to visit from Baghdad or London, and I'll give him a royal reception. Oh, won't he turn green with envy … "

This harangue was heard by several people standing nearby. One of them, who seemed to know my father, said hoarsely: "This country will make lunatics of us all."

That evening my father went to Abu Samir's makeshift café and took his usual side table. No one joined him. From an old radio came the voice of Salima Pasha singing:

O sing to my brother a lullaby,
For the smell of my mother is upon him,
O gladden my brother with song,
For the smell of my mother is upon him,
O wish my brother long years,
For the smell of my mother is upon him,

He asked for a glass of arrack. Since coming to Israel he had avoided strong drink, perhaps because he was embarrassed to spend money on it. "Pay me when you can afford to, Abu Kabi," Abu Samir, who knew him from Baghdad, would say, but he would order only coffee. Now, though, he downed the arrack in one gulp, asked for more, and swallowed that too. Then he shut his eyes, propped his chin on his hands, and let the smell of the Tigris and its oleander bushes waft his way.

There wasn't a day that he didn't go back to something in Baghdad. This time it was to the oily taste of winter lettuce, the smell of limes, the fresh dates that had melted in his mouth, all buffed to a crystalline clarity by Salima Pasha's velvet voice. He thought of el-Me'azzam and Hairiyya. What peaceful times those had been. He could hear the sounds of the celebratory dinners on the nights Kabi and Ismail were born. It was all dead now, nothing left but the rags of memory.

But what kept drawing the heart back to it? What, indeed, when he had no home here, no income, no connections, nothing that ever worked out! Allah, why had he come? Why had he given it all up and left his brother? Ah, Baghdad, Baghdad! All he had wanted after the *Farhood* was to flee from her, to banish her from his thoughts, from his dreams ... and she, the goddamn slut, the Great Whore of Babylon, pursued him everywhere, haunted his daydreams and his night-time dreams, made him pay for his desertion like a woman scorned. Who was it who once told him that a native land was not a home to be razed, or a rotten tooth to be pulled out? As if you could extract the earth, the river, the palm trees, the graveyards, from a man's heart ... Ah, yes: it was Salim Effendi, at a dinner party in their house, during an argument with Hizkel. And now the son-of-a-bitch was here, living off the Party and the fat of the land!

"Ah, great Allah," sighed my father, draining a third glass. If

Zionism was right, what had gone wrong? Why didn't he feel in a Jewish state the freedom, the independence, he had yearned for in Iraq? In Baghdad he could not have said whatever he wanted, but whatever he said was listened to; here, in this democracy on the other hand, he could talk until he was blue in the face without being listened to by a single person. And whoever did hear him said he was mad. They had a treasure in the Hula and they were letting it seep into the ground! Whoever heard of wasting water? And that made *him* mad and *them* sane?

Even the nonentities he was surrounded by laughed at him. Even his own family. Even Kabi thought he was deranged. Not that he said so, but it was obvious. And his own wife had grown distant. He couldn't take her barbs any more, even if she tried making up for them afterwards. He hadn't touched her since coming to Israel. He couldn't have, of course, in the tent with all the children, but he hadn't even wanted to. Something had died in him.

Perhaps he should have married Salima Pasha. They could have gone on living in an endless dream of drink and song, wallowing in dinars. He could have forgotten about growing rice, forgotten about Big Imari, dropped out of a hopeless competition.

"Abu Kabi, are you feeling all right?" whispered Abu Samir, bringing him a glass of water.

"Yes," said my father, staring at the ground.

He had to save his honour with Kabi. Perhaps he should take him to see the Hula. Let him see for himself what the mad dream could have become if only it had been allowed to …

*

The next morning he woke me before dawn. "What's up?"

"We're going to the Hula."

"I'll lose a day's work," I mumbled. But I got up.

The bus was packed. My father shut his eyes and opened them only in Haifa, where we changed buses. It was my first time up north. There were magnificent mountains, the broadest valleys I had ever seen, towns, villages, construction and activity everywhere.

"Baba, look," I kept saying.

He would turn his head slightly and smile at me weakly without even glancing out of the window. The landscape made no impression on him. He was elsewhere, back in the Zion of Baghdad with its paradise of smells, its lawns and flowers so different from these mountains. I didn't know whether to feel furious at the self-absorbed drone of his thoughts, or to be full of pity for the exile torn out by the roots. In the end I escaped into sleep.

"Who asked for the Hula?" the driver called out.

"I did." My father came to life, a visionary look on his face. We got off. My first instinct was to stand still and look at all the water. There was a feeling of things happening. Surveyors and tractors were at work, preparing for the drainage project that would start in the spring. My father hurried ahead.

"Where are you going, Baba?" I called after him. But he strode on as though he hadn't heard me, paying no attention to the angry shouts of a surveyor.

"Baba, where are you going?"

He walked until he reached the water's edge. Bending down, he scooped some wet earth and squeezed it between his fingers. Then he raised it to his mouth and nose, sniffing it like the hair of a woman. He was back in the paddies of Imara with their fluted stalks of green, yellow, and purple grain, between whose rows he had played hide-and-seek with Big Imari.

Troubled by the tractors which they sensed had come to drive them from their habitat, the marsh birds wheeled above him in a panoply of feathered hues, screeching curses at his greying hair. Paying no heed, he stepped into the water and sat down.

Two hefty drivers in vests turned off the engines of their tractors and ran to help me pull him out of the swamp. He neither resisted nor responded to their questions. I felt too helpless to say anything. They dragged him to a water pipe, attached a rubber hose to a tap, and washed him like a tractor at the end of a day's work. The mud ran down his best summer suit. He looked old and forlorn.

"He'll dry out in half an hour," said one of the drivers. "Then take him home. What got into him?"

I didn't answer. Had I known enough Hebrew, I might have told them that a dove had fallen by the wayside. Let them think I was crazy too. Or that my father wished to perish with his dream of rice paddies. Or nothing at all.

My father remained silent and let me do what I wanted with him.

On the long ride back I didn't look out of the window either. My father slept most of the way, grunting and wheezing in his sleep, which was interrupted by a rasping cough. It was night when we reached the transit camp and passed through the cloud of dust thrown up by the bus.

Abed stepped out of the darkness as we walked to our tent. "Congratulations, Abu Kabi," he said. "You have a new son."

I looked at my father and thought I saw a gleam in his eyes.